THE CROWN OF EDEN

THE CROWN OF EDEN

A Novel

THOMAS WILLIAMS

WORD PUBLISHING

NASHVILLE

A Thomas Nelson Company

Library of Congress Cataloging-in-Publication Data

Williams, T. M. (Thomas Myron), 1941–
    The crown of Eden : a novel / Thomas Williams.
     p. cm.
    ISBN 0-8499-1610-0
    I. Title.
  PS3573.I45562C76   1999
  813'.54—dc21

                                        99-33562
                                            CIP

Printed in the United States of America

00 01 02 03 04 QPV 9 8 7 6 5 4 3 2

CONTENTS

To John and Sherrinda Ketchersid

THE SEVEN KINGDOMS

Macrennon

Blackmore Forest

GRAYSTONE MOUNTAINS

Valthorne

VALOMAR

Widdcroft

LOCHLAUND

Ridgedale

Stenholm

RHONDILAR

Sunderlon

Surinfax

Maldor Castle

Garvane

ORANTH

DRAGONTOOTH MOUNTAINS

Corenham

MERIDAN

Braegan Wood

Ironwood Estate

Lenshaw

Northmere

Evenshire

Hallifax

Kallenstone

Kemstead

Farandale

Llewenham

Leverton

Rokestrand

Sothemer

Parandor

Newfrith

Kerrigorn

Mithrach

SORENDALE

VENSAUR

Ensovandor

PROLOGUE

ong ago in a time the world has forgotten, there was a kingdom known as Meridan. The largest of the Seven Kingdoms of King Perivale's fallen empire, Meridan was a rugged, austere land of towering mountains and deep forests. The trees of the fabled Braegan Wood often measured five arm spans or more in girth. The Dragontooth Mountains, stony and sharp, bordered the western edge of the kingdom and boasted peaks that often penetrated the cloudy canopy of heaven.

The giant scale and upward thrust of woods and mountains gave the land a persistent vertical theme, as if all aspirations were heavenward and man was too small, too bound to the earth, to be of significance. Yet the land was not hostile to its human inhabitants. Between the mountains and dense tracts of forest lay patchworks of fertile fields and green pastures.

Meridan was once a mighty kingdom of great renown. Seven broad highways had linked more than twoscore towns and villages to Corenham, the city King Perivale had made his shining capital, and ranged far into the six adjacent kingdoms, binding well over three hundred willing cities and shires to the benevolent rule of the great warrior-king. Perivale had united Meridan and the six surrounding kingdoms into a single empire, known widely as the Seven Kingdoms, through a decisive war with the terrible, ancient Morgultha. In that same war, Perivale also gained the legendary Crown of Eden.

In those days the halls of Morningstone Castle and the streets of Corenham rang with the brogues of an endless procession of ambassadors from distant lands, merchants, and knights on quest. Meridan's shop owners and innkeepers prospered, and the farmers and shepherds marketed all they could produce, at fair prices willingly paid.

It even seemed that the earth was more fertile in those days. The fields appeared eager to fill the hand that tilled them; it was said that crops would spring up at the very heels of the planter. Even wayward arrows felled hare and stag in the edges of Braegan Wood, and the crystal streams shimmered with trout waiting for the hook. It was a time of dancing in springtime and feasting at harvest.

But in the twelfth year of Perivale's reign, Meridan's glory ended. The great conqueror rode out to battle and disappeared. Though the corpses of his men were found, his body was not among them. Perivale the Conqueror and his glorious Crown of Eden had vanished from the realm.

Soon afterward a strange and ancient man, white-bearded and robed in forest colors, came before the peers of the kingdom and proclaimed that Perivale had been struck down for daring to commit a dire offense against heaven. As a result his empire would crumble and Meridan would sink back into obscurity. He concluded by chanting the rhyming verses of a prophecy, the words of which lingered and loomed, cryptic and obscure, as the cadence of the prophet's voice halted. But the wise men and scholars who studied the mysterious stranger's prophecy later found within it a nugget of hope. All agreed that it predicted the Crown would in time be found and come to rest on the head of a distant son of Perivale, greater and more worthy than he, who would ascend the throne and restore the empire in all its glory.

After Perivale's disappearance, his son Rondale became king. But Rondale lacked his father's strength and could not hold Meridan's alliances intact. As the prophet predicted, the borders of the empire shrank as one by one cities and kingdoms fell from Rondale's weak grasp. Soon wilderness reclaimed most of the roads linking the Seven Kingdoms, and those that remained in use became mere trails, infested with marauding fugitives and rogues. Travelers became few, and many of Corenham's shops and inns closed their doors for good. The land still yielded to the plow but more grudgingly. Hunters in search of quarry found it necessary to venture ever deeper into Braegan Wood, which they did with increasing dread for the forest was beginning to spawn ominous tales of hauntings by foul, unearthly creatures.

Thus shadows engulfed the great Perivale's kingdom, and Meridan's former glory survived only in verse and song, a memory lamented and a dream cherished by the faithful few who believed in the prophecy they could not fully understand. The rest went about their business hoping to find a little joy, a little comfort, or a little pleasure in the everyday struggle to keep body and soul intact. Most hoped for little else.

PART I

THE PRINCESS

CHAPTER ONE

The Midwife

King Alfron's huntsman Rolstag had just finished a hearty supper of roast venison, bread, and ale and now sat snug by his crackling hearth, listening to the wind moaning through the tall oaks that sheltered his cottage. It was early spring, but the cold of winter still lingered. After a long day out in that weather, it was good to be inside, and he savored the mug of steaming mead that warmed the roughened hands in which he cupped it. He gazed fondly at his wife, Gensel, who sat opposite him, firelight bathing her face and breast as she nursed their infant son and hummed a soft lullaby. Little Talmon was their only child.

Rolstag's rest was well earned tonight. Not two hours ago he had delivered to Morningstone Castle the last of the five stags Alfron required for the banquet he was planning to celebrate his son's impending birth. *His son indeed,* Rolstag mused. The king was cocksure the child would be a boy. After delivering the stag to the castle slaughterhouse, Rolstag had reported his success to the king, who had clapped his huntsman heartily on the back with his great hand and said, "In a few years, when my boy can handle a bow, we'll join you in the woods and bring back a dozen such stags."

Rolstag's shoulder still smarted from the blow, but he understood the king's good spirits. Alfron was Meridan's fifth king in the hundred years since the great Perivale, and although he had been married for almost a decade, he had begotten no child. The people had begun to talk. It was little wonder that Alfron had given a great banquet when it became certain that the queen had conceived and less a wonder that he now planned an even greater one to celebrate the child's imminent birth. For Alfron's sake, Rolstag hoped the king would get a boy, but after the babe was born, it would matter little. A child of either sex would banish the ache from the good king's heart. This Rolstag knew from experience.

Rolstag and Gensel had wed a dozen years ago with dreams of a cottage full of children, but those dreams had faded as the years slipped away. Rolstag had borne the disappointment, but he had been greatly concerned about his wife. Such things were more painful to women.

He soon found he need not have worried. Although Gensel's crib was empty, she was determined that her life would not be. As hope of the little girl for which she longed flickered and died, the barren woman had become a midwife. Another in her shoes might have found only bitterness and envy in a calling that reminded her so continually of thwarted dreams, but Gensel caught in her own heart a share of the joy that flowed from each birth she attended. She borrowed the happiness she was denied and in return gave each mother and newborn a full measure of care drawn from her vast store of love for the child that had never come.

Then little Talmon was born. The ecstatic Gensel forgot that she had ever wanted a girl and lived joyously in the light the little duplicate of her beloved husband brought to their home. Gensel abandoned midwifery to devote herself wholly to her new son.

But when the swelling belly of Alfron's queen made it apparent that the king had sired a royal heir, the queen's ladies-in-waiting insisted that no midwife but Gensel would do. Gensel could not refuse her queen and was now expecting the summons to Morningstone Castle at any moment. As she listened to the moaning of the wind outside, she hoped it would not come tonight.

When Talmon's gentle sucking ceased and Gensel felt the soft breath of his sleep on her breast, she laid the precious bundle in his crib and tucked the doeskin coverlet about his shoulders. She poured her own mug of steaming mead and had just settled into her chair when a sharp knock sounded at the cottage door. Rolstag, cautious at such an hour, kept his hand on his knife as he went to the door, opened it a few inches, and peered into the darkness outside.

A lone courier stood at the door. He was wrapped in a gray woolen cloak with a hood drawn over his head. "I'm lookin' for Gensel the midwife," said the man.

"Who summons her?" Rolstag asked.

"King Alfron bids her to come to the castle at once," he said. "The queen nears her time." Rolstag opened the door for the man to enter, and a blast of chill air invaded the cottage, rustling the curtains and angering the fire. But the man merely stood unmoving in the wind. "The queen will thank ye to make haste, midwife," he said.

"I've been ready for a week," Gensel replied as she retrieved her bag of supplies from the cupboard, "though she could have picked a better night." She checked the covering on the sleeping baby before moving on toward the door. As her husband wrapped her shoulders in a warm cloak, she said, "Rolstag, if I've not returned by morning, you'd best take Talmon to your sister. Her majesty may think the royal heir is about to break through the gate, but there's little reason to expect him to hurry now. After all, he's dawdled enough getting here." She picked up her bag and followed the courier to the waiting coach, hunching her shoulders against the pitiless wind.

Had Gensel possessed a less trusting nature, she would have thought it strange that King Alfron's coach did not bear his coat of arms. But if she noticed this at all, she gave it little thought because she was often rushed to birthings in the handiest transportation available—carts and carriages of all sorts and in various conditions. Yet soon after the coach swung into the road, swaying and creaking to the buffeting of the wind, she began to sense that things were not as they should be. She looked up at the cold, pale moon, dimming and flashing as shroudlike clouds brushed across its face. Beside her the courier sat staring straight ahead, eyes and mouth set like stone, and unlike most of the amiable servants of Alfron, silent as a tomb. And the coach was moving much too fast. Gensel knew there was no need for such speed to cover the scant two miles to Corenham, yet the coachman was driving the horses hard, cracking his whip across their backs, and urging them to an even faster pace. She had never known a servant of Alfron to mistreat an animal.

Her growing apprehension became genuine alarm when the coachman suddenly veered to the left from the main road and, without slowing his pace, struck off down a narrow, weedy trail between two fields. She gripped the top of the door to keep from being bounced from her seat and wondered if the coach would hold together. "Where are you taking me?" she shouted, her voice a broken staccato as they lurched and careened on the stony path.

"A shorter route," the courier answered. "One that few outside the king's service know."

"This cannot be a shorter route to Morningstone. We're going around the city instead of through it. Where are you taking me?"

The courier gave no sign that he had heard but looked impassively ahead as the coach continued at breakneck speed.

Thus they rode for another mile. Then the coach turned sharply left again, this time onto an even rockier path that led straight away from Corenham and toward Braegan Wood. Gensel knew that further questions would be useless, so she sat silent, her terror growing as she saw ahead the looming mass of the fabled forest, lying gray on the horizon like some decaying dead thing.

Now her fear became a cold hand clutching at her heart. She did not want to enter that forest. All her life she had feared Braegan Wood. She remembered her father and uncles sitting about the winter fire telling horrid tales of loathsome creatures said to haunt the forest—remnants of Morgultha's vanquished army—patched, misshapen monsters contrived from the products of exhumed graves and slaughtered animals and animated by dark necromancy. And now as she stared in terror toward the approaching forest, these tales seemed all too plausible. She shuddered, a chill creeping up her spine and her brain churning with visions of stalking corpses and disembodied spirits.

The road they traveled shone pale and mottled in the rancid moonlight. Just ahead of them it disappeared into a gaping blackness between the gnarled trees at the edge of the forest, looking like a leprous tongue emerging from a rotting mouth. Gensel suppressed a scream as that gaping maw swallowed them and the world went black. She flinched and cringed in the blind darkness as clawlike branches pulled at her cloak and weblike hangings raked her face.

Gradually her eyes adjusted to the darkness, but what she could see brought her no relief. They swept past the dim, twisted forms of tree boles looking like diseased and malformed monsters, hideous with swollen knots and tumorlike fungi, their dry, twisted limbs reaching for her like the brittle fingers of dead hands. Massive boulders, gray and scaly with a canker of lichen, jutted from the earth like tombstones. The acrid odor of rotting leaves sickened her like the smell of death. Suddenly the unearthly howl of some forest creature pierced the darkness, and Gensel screamed, now overcome by utter terror.

"Quiet! D'ya want to wake up the forest? There be creatures here that would not take kindly to havin' their sleep disturbed." Gensel had no doubt that he was right and bit her lip to stifle any further sound.

Moments later she could barely make out an eerie glow reflecting dimly off the edges of the dead trees ahead. With each passing moment the glow grew stronger. As the coach rounded a wide curve and came to a stop in a small clearing, she saw the cause of it: in the midst of the clearing burned a fire, contained in a circle of stones the diameter of a wagon wheel. Its flames shown gaseous green, and putrid gray smoke writhed upward from them like a tortured spirit. In front of the fire sat a very tall figure, draped in black and straight and still as a gravestone. The wind had ceased to blow, yet Gensel could hear it in the distance, a heartbreaking moan like that of a mother lamenting a lost child.

"Get out," the courier said.

"But why? What am I to do here?" Gensel asked.

"Ye're a midwife, are ye not? Yer services are needed by the lady yonder, and I'd advise ye not to keep her waiting."

Gensel's fingers trembled as she opened the door and stepped down from the coach. With uncertain steps she waded through the brittle weeds toward the rigid figure at the fire. She stopped abruptly, ten paces short, when she saw the face. It was the face of a woman, and in terms of form and line, a beautiful face, but Gensel shuddered as she looked at it. It was pale and cold and hard, as if carved from slate, and the creature's eyes, which stared unblinking into the fire, were heavy-lidded and pale, almost to the point of being colorless.

Suddenly the head turned, the eyes fixing upon Gensel. The mouth opened, and a whisper issued from deep in the throat. "Come here, Gensel."

Gensel forced her trembling knees to obey. "W—who are you? Why have you brought me here?" she stammered.

"Who I am need not concern you now, my dear Gensel. I have brought you here because you are a midwife, one in a position to perform a valuable service for me."

With effort Gensel tore her eyes from the compelling stare and looked at the creature's body, clearly long and thin even within the voluminous robes. "But you do not appear to be with child."

"I am not now with child for my son was born two hours ago."

"Then why—" began Gensel.

"Because you are to be a player on my stage." The black-robed figure stood, towering nearly a full head over Gensel. The midwife stepped back involuntarily. "I have written the script, and tonight you make your entrance. You are expecting a summons to Morningstone to attend delivery of the royal heir, are you not? When you perform your duty at the castle, you will make a delivery for me." With her left hand the creature held toward Gensel a small bundle wrapped in black cloth. The folds of her robe hid the fact that her right hand was missing. "Take this," she commanded, "and look inside."

Gensel took the bundle and parted the black cloth to reveal a naked newborn child, a boy.

The black-robed figure leaned forward until her face was inches above Gensel's. "Now you listen, and listen well. When you go to the queen, you will take with you my son, this child you now hold in your arms. I have given him a potion that will cause him to sleep for several hours. You may hide him in your bag without fear that his cry will betray you." Then she withdrew from the folds of her robe a small vial of greenish liquid. "When the royal heir is born and you hear his first cry, place two drops of this same potion on a linen cloth and press it to the babe's nostrils. He will pass into a deep, quiet sleep.

Send the queen's attendant after a blanket or some such thing, and while she is gone, lay my son on the breast of the queen. Hide her child in your bag and carry it home. When the king's carriage returns you to your cottage, place the new little prince or princess in the hollow of the split oak at your gate. I will see that the child is gone before the next dawn."

Gensel was aghast. "I will never do such a thing!" she cried.

"Oh, but I think you will." The face smiled—or at least its lips stretched open and exposed its long, white teeth. "Even as we talk, your dear little Talmon sleeps nestled in his crib. My servants who wander in the shadows of the night need never disturb his happy little dreams, but they are charged to carry off a child from your home. If they fail to find the one at the gate, they will certainly find the one in the crib."

"But why do you want the queen's child?"

"You waste time, Gensel. What I do with King Alfron's heir is my own concern. Your concern had best be what happens to your Talmon."

"But this is your own child. How can you give him up so easily? And what of your husband? Hasn't he any say in the matter?"

The creature threw back her head and shrieked with hideous laughter. Gensel started violently.

"My husband!" she cried as her laughter subsided. "My husband indeed! Ah, my dear, innocent Gensel, I have no husband. But if you knew who is the father of this child, you would understand why he cares not a whit either for your son or the king's, or even his own." Her voice seemed to quaver slightly, and for a moment her face was darkened by a look that Gensel thought must be fear. But the shadow passed. "His only interest is his own devices and how they can best be served. You, Gensel, are merely a player on his stage, to be written out of the script when his ends are achieved. So beware, midwife, and hearken well. If you would save your son, you will play your part precisely as I have instructed. Now begone!"

Gensel stood immobilized by the impossible dilemma. To do what the dark creature demanded was unthinkable. But to refuse and risk the life of her son was equally unthinkable. Frantically she searched her mind for some way out—for some alternative without such appalling consequences.

"You waste time, midwife. Now go!"

Without a word the anguished Gensel turned and stumbled back to the waiting carriage, clutching the black-wrapped bundle in her arms. Tears began to stream down her face as she climbed into her seat. The driver cracked his whip, and the carriage lurched into the blackness of the forest.

The tall, black-robed creature gave no heed but stood still as stone and stared without seeing into the writhing fire.

CHAPTER TWO

ThE prophEcy
anD ThE plEDgE

It was an hour before midnight, and all the guests had at last left the great banquet hall at Morningstone Castle. Now, candles having been snuffed and tables cleared, the only light was from the dwindling flames in the wide, stone hearth. The only sounds were the slow crackling of the fire and a faint chatter of voices coming through the pantry and buttery from the kitchen, where servants were cleaning up after the evening's festivities.

The two men lounging in their heavily carved chairs, legs stretched toward the fire, were kings, but nothing in their demeanor bespoke their royalty now. They had shed their regal bearing, courtly manners, and heavily embroidered tunics the instant the last guest left the hall, and for the moment crowns, armies, and affairs of state were thrust aside. Now they were just men—two friends enjoying the sort of relaxed fellowship a king can never find among his subjects once the weight of the crown rests upon his brow.

King Tallis of Valomar stretched and loosened the belt around his trim waist another inch or two. "Ah, dear Alfron," he said, "if the citizens of Meridan often dine half as well as we did tonight, I'll gladly trade my crown for a cottage in the shadow of Morningstone."

King Alfron's tall, athletic frame seemed large even in his ample chair, which was adorned, like the dressed stone walls around them, with antlers and pelts from his own kills. Running his large, strong hands through his blond mane, he grinned at his friend. "Keep your crown, Tallis," he replied, "unless you would sell it to replenish my treasury. I could have fed your army and mine for the price of this banquet. Indeed, I almost think I may have done just that. Next time I will have a closer look at the queen's invitation list."

"But surely the occasion merits the cost," said Tallis. "After all, how often do two kings of allied countries have children born on the same day? Though it happened ten days ago, I wonder at it yet—that your son and my daughter were born within the same hour."

"It is an amazing coincidence," said Alfron.

King Tallis turned to his friend, his aristocratic face now strangely serious. "Is it really coincidence, Alfron? I sometimes wonder if the word has real meaning. I am beginning to suspect that what we call chance and coincidence are actually events that have been deliberately set in order for some definite purpose."

"Ah, Tallis, Tallis. You were always the mystic, with your nose in your books and your eyes on the stars, peering behind the curtains of the universe hoping to discover its gears and pulleys. But surely you push the idea of order too far. Of course there is order in the large movements of nature—in the cycle of the seasons and the movements of the planets—but beneath all these lofty operations, chance and chaos tumble us around like pebbles in a springtime river. Disease, accidents, disasters, and untimely deaths strike at random, wreaking havoc in our lives. The great cycles of the universe maintain a general order because their wheels are so huge and ponderous that they can roll unaffected over the pebbles of chance. But we don't live among the planets—at least, most of us don't," he added, grinning at his friend. "We live among the pebbles, where many things just happen with no plan or purpose."

"I am suggesting that the same hand that drives the wheels of order also moves the pebbles," Tallis replied, "and always moves them toward some definite purpose."

Alfron's brow furrowed. "You are suggesting that chance does not exist at all. But surely you don't really believe it. You know from experience that the most carefully planned battle can be lost because a spear breaks or a horse stumbles. Or the most invincible army can be routed by a thunderstorm. Remember how your own Sir Thringal was saved from six highwaymen because his attackers accidentally knocked down a beehive?"

"My point is," replied Tallis, "that the beehives, thunderstorms, broken spears, and stumbling horses are as much a part of the order of things as the sunrise or a peach blossom. We call them chance because we cannot anticipate them. We call them coincidence when they happen in conjunction with related events. I believe the same weaver works them all into one great tapestry. They only seem to be unplanned because we cannot see the design they are part of. Or we assume that what little of the pattern we see must be all the pattern there is."

"So you really believe, then, that this birthday that our new offspring share is a significant thread in some planned pattern," said Alfron, still skeptical.

"Perhaps a very significant thread," Tallis replied. "I am convinced that they are destined to share much more than a birthday. Tell me, Alfron, do you believe the prophecy that was spoken after the disappearance of your great ancestor, Perivale?"

"I believe what I understand of it," Alfron answered. "But you know the prophecy remains an unraveled mystery. Every scholar and mystic since Perivale has squeezed it like a thirsty milkmaid but with nary a drop in the pail to show for it."

"But you do know the prophecy."

"As does everyone in Meridan and most of the Seven Kingdoms," affirmed Alfron. "My father made me memorize it as a boy:

> *Beyond the fateful fall that followed pride,*
> *A hundred times shall ring the fount of light,*
> *When glow of golden prince and silver bride,*
> *Are heaven born to 'lume the ebon night.*
>
> *Then times shall ring the light a score and one,*
> *Ere Eden's hues from darkness shall emerge,*
> *To coronate the Perivalian son,*
> *As golden star and silver bride converge.*

Then shall the king his cherished princess wed,
As gold and silver blend in unison,
To glorify the throne inherited,
And bind his father's seven into one."

"The prophecy is a hard one," said Tallis, "but I think I discovered the key to it six days ago, when the messenger brought news of your son's birth."

"So the moment you got that message you rushed here to tell me that you have succeeded where every wise man since Perivale has failed," laughed Alfron.

"Laugh if you will, but not too loudly to listen. As you know, most scholars agree that the first line of the prophecy speaks of Perivale's strange disappearance at the battle of Maldor. However, that second line—'a hundred times shall ring the fount of light'—has baffled wise men for generations, but I'm now convinced that the true meaning is very simple. How many years have passed since the prophet appeared after Perivale's disappearance and uttered the prophecy?"

"Let's see, it must have been about a hundred years ago—almost exactly a hundred years ago, now that I think of it."

"In fact, it was exactly one hundred years from the day of that prophecy to the day of the births of our two children," said Tallis.

"Well, bless my bones!" exclaimed Alfron.

"The prophecy is not as cryptic or obscure as we have made it out to be. 'A hundred times shall ring the fount of light' simply means a hundred years will pass. 'Times' is a longstanding prophetic term for years. The 'fount of light' is the sun. 'Ring' means to circle. The sun—the fount of light—has circled the earth in its seasonal journey one hundred times since the prophecy was uttered. That means its fulfillment is beginning now."

"It is a possibility," Alfron said, "but it could be mere coincidence even so."

"Could it be?" asked Tallis. "Let's look a bit deeper. What is meant by the lines, 'When glow of golden prince and silver bride,/Are heaven born to 'lume the ebon night'?"

"I have no idea," admitted Alfron.

"Come with me to the window," said Tallis. The two kings walked along the tapestried wall to the slender western window, their footsteps echoing in the vast, empty hall. Tallis opened the shutter to the bracing night. He pointed to a star low on the horizon, brilliant and golden with a trailing stream of light that disappeared behind a distant hill. "Do you see that star?"

"Yes, it's the new comet. Our astronomers recorded its first appearance a few nights ago."

"It was exactly ten nights ago," said Tallis. "While you were strutting like a rooster over the hatching of your first chick, this regal star with its trailing cape made its first appearance in the skies of the Seven Kingdoms." Then Tallis pointed again to a dazzling silver star high above the comet. "Did your astronomers also notice that new star?"

"Of course. How could they have missed a gem like that?"

"Do you see anything significant about the colors of these two new stars? Notice that the comet has a golden hue like the field of your family crest, and the higher star is bright silver like the field of my family crest. Do you really think it mere coincidence that these stars in these particular colors appeared on the same night that your son and my daughter were born?"

"What sort of significance do you suggest they have?"

"All that wine you poured down your gullet tonight must have bloated your brain. Can't you see that these stars herald the births of our children? They are the 'golden prince and silver bride' predicted by the prophecy. The gold comet announces your son and the silver star my daughter. These two heavenly bodies are the prophetic sign we have been awaiting. They tell us that the births of our two children are very significant to the fulfillment of the prophecy."

"You make a fair case, but I still say it's all too vague for certainty. It could be chance even yet," Alfron replied. "If the silver star announces the birth of your daughter, why does the prophecy call it a 'silver bride' instead of, say, a silver babe?"

Tallis didn't answer directly but asked, "Did your astronomers plot the path of the golden comet?"

"I don't think so," Alfron responded, a puzzled look on his face. "What is your point?"

"The astronomers of our Camerton College studied it for three nights. They found that it is moving directly toward the new silver star. They calculated that the two will meet in precisely twenty-one years. This is exactly what the next lines of the prophecy predict:

> *Then times shall ring the light a score and one, . . .*
> *As golden star and silver bride converge.*
> *Then shall the king his cherished princess wed, . . ."*

Tallis paused, looking intently at Alfron. "That is why the prophecy calls the star a silver bride. Our two children, born under the sign of the two new stars, will marry as their heavenly counterparts blend. My daughter is destined to be the bride of your son."

"So, the whole point of this ancient, celebrated prophecy is to find mates for our children?" laughed Alfron. "You had me almost believing you for a moment, Tallis, but you go too far. Of course you can make the prophecy mean whatever you want by picking out some lines and ignoring others. You completely skipped over what some think is the most baffling line of all, 'Ere Eden's hues from darkness shall emerge.'"

"I was coming back to that," replied Tallis. "In fact, that line is one of the most astounding of the entire prophecy. It predicts that the lost Crown of Eden will be found. The term 'Eden's hues' tells us this line speaks of the Crown. It refers to the legend that the stone set in that crown emits colors not seen on earth since the fall of Adam.

"'To coronate the Perivalian son' tells us that the Crown will rest upon the head of the descendant of Perivale born under the sign of the golden star. 'And bind his father's seven into one' means he will reunite the Seven Kingdoms under one rule, to be once again as they were in the day of his forefather Perivale. Don't you see?" A note of urgency came into Tallis's voice. "Your son is the king foretold by the prophecy—the king who will bring about the rebirth of Perivale's empire—and my daughter is to be his bride."

King Alfron stared long at the two stars as if they were hostile invaders. He believed in order and predictability, but he also believed in chance. And to him chance meant freedom. The existence of chance meant that the Master of the Universe had left zones in creation untouched by his controlling hand. It was in these zones that a man's own actions had meaning, where his deeds and decisions could make a difference. But if there were no room in the universe for chance, there would be no room for freedom either. Freedom would be an illusion, with all under the control of a master puppeteer.

Without a word, Alfron closed the shutters and returned to his seat by the fire. For long moments he just stared into the flames. Finally he asked quietly, "Are we not free? Are we mere pawns, simply moved about by divine will to accomplish what has been engraved on the foundation of the universe since the beginning of time? Do our own efforts count for nothing?"

"Certainly we are free," Tallis replied. "But nothing we do can destroy the order and beauty of the master tapestry. Each of us is given a thread and a pattern for its weaving. We are utterly free to weave our thread either by the pattern or in defiance of it. But regardless of how we weave it, we will always find that our thread has been anticipated. You may even choose to leave your thread unwoven, but if you do, there will be no gap in the fabric. You will find that another has already been laid down to take its place and the resulting design will be the one originally planned. It is inevitable."

Alfron sighed. "Assuming that the prophecy is showing us such a pattern and that you have interpreted it correctly, what steps would you propose we take?"

Tallis stood with his hands on the back of his chair and leaned toward Alfron. "The prophecy tells us that your son and my daughter will wed in twenty-one years, after the golden comet meets the silver star and after the coronation of your son with the Crown of Eden. Therefore—" Tallis poured their empty cups full again and handed one to Alfron. "I propose that you and I affirm our belief in the prophecy by pledging our newborn children to each other in marriage."

"Before I answer, I have just two more questions," replied Alfron, holding the cup unsipped in his hands. "First, do you not see that this marriage you propose may well mean the end of Valomar as an independent kingdom? You have no sons, and your two older daughters are pledged in marriage already. When your new-hatched daughter marries my son, the throne of Valomar will be left empty. As I see it, Valomar would likely be ruled from Morningstone as a province of Meridan."

"Quite likely, quite likely," agreed Tallis. "But there is little reason for a nation to desire independence unless she is under the heel of a tyrant. Valomar has been ruled from Morningstone before. In Perivale's empire Valomar shared Meridan's glory and prosperity. When Perivale's empire broke apart, Valomar left Meridan's dominion with regret and by agreement, not as malcontents or rebels. The prophecy shows us that Meridan's new golden age will begin in twenty-one years. Valomar could wish no better fate than to become one again with Meridan and share the rebirth of her glory."

"You are a strange king, to have so little esteem for your nation's freedom. Surely your citizens will not part with that treasure as easily as their monarch."

"I did not propose to deal away my nation's freedom, merely its independence," Tallis replied. "Freedom is precious indeed, and every citizen is right to desire it. But individual freedom and national independence are not the same things. When Meridan ruled Valomar, its citizens were still free."

"That, I fear, is a fine point that would be lost on some of the ambitious noblemen of Valomar. I could name more than a handful here in Meridan who would find it unthinkable to submit to the throne of another kingdom."

King Tallis sighed. "Yes, I know that to be true. We desire independence because our pride resists authority, and this sort of national chauvinism certainly exists in Valomar. But I cannot let the pride of a few undermine the good of the entire country. I will deal with the dissenters when the time comes."

"My second question is this," said Alfron, "if you are convinced that the prophecy is certain, why should we pledge anything at all? If the course of events is inevitable, why not simply stand aside and let the tapestry weave itself?"

Tallis replied, "It would be perilous indeed to ignore a prophecy that has you enmeshed in it so deeply. You are in Perivale's line, our two

kingdoms are pa[...]
stars, and the core o[...]
ter. With so many threa[...]
and leave them unwoven? Yes[...]
Yes, even if you refuse your respo[...]
your refusal will have been foreseen[...]
replace you. But you would be pronoun[...]
would stand outside the loom, your unwoven [...]
only to be swept into the trash heap. The inevitabl[...]
comes to pass by our own hands freely accepting the ta[...]
inevitable. Your son will marry my daughter whether or no[...]
them. Yet it may be our pledge that brings the event about."

"You talk in circles till my head spins," said Alfron, "yet I ag[...]
to your proposal. In fact, old friend, you need not have dragged in all
this prophecy business to persuade me. There is no other family from
which I would rather choose my future daughter-in-law."

The two men drained their cups and embraced heartily. King
Alfron called for a scribe, and thus it was written for the annals of
Meridan and the chronicles of Valomar:

Be it known to all
that Tallis, King of Valomar,
does hereby pledge his thirdborn daughter,
yet unchristened,
to wed the firstborn son of Alfron, King of Meridan,
yet unchristened,
on the day following the coronation
of Alfron's said firstborn son as King of Meridan
with the Crown of Eden
by this agreement signed by our own hands,
Alfron, King of Meridan
Tallis, King of Valomar
on the tenth day following the births of their
pledged children.

rts of his old empire, we have witnessed the predicted
the prophecy centers on your son and my daugh-
s in your hand, would you dare stand aside
fulfillment of the prophecy is inevitable,
nsibility, the result will be the same;
and there will be a thread to
cing your own doom. You
thread worthless and fit
is inevitable, but it
sk of making it
we pledge
ee

...ounds of chat-
...shop window
...oot on his last,
...eather sole with
their nat, ... ped his hands on
his leather apron, and p... hurriedly put his
tools away. It was early yet to be clos... ...hop, the sun only
halfway down to the horizon, but he had good reason. It was the time
of year most of Valomar put aside all its duties for one week and
thronged to the great Harvest Fair. Even now the street was teeming
with merry pedestrians—men, women, children, peasants, merchants, tradesmen, and even noblemen—all spilling through the
streets toward the fairgrounds on the eastern edge of town.

In spite of his haste to close up, Halcom paused as he caught
sight of two young women, laughing and chatting in happy animation as they came near, moving with the crowd. They were clad as
simple peasants, skirts and bodices of homespun in earthy browns
and grays, knitted shawls draped around their shoulders in readiness
for the evening chill. But the plainness of their garb did not matter.
What drew Halcom's eye was the beauty of the pair as they hurried
down the street, their forms outlined in a glowing rim of gold created by the sunlight at their backs. Indeed, as Halcom stared at the
taller of the two, he was sure he had never seen a face more perfect

or a form more splendid. Head held high, she moved with utter grace. Dark hair, almost black but for the glow of burnished gold at the sunlit edges, fell in soft waves down her back. Her smooth skin carried a soft blush from the joy of the day, and her wide, blue eyes danced as she talked with her friend. Halcom sighed. "Eve 'erself, shaped by the very fingers of the Master could not 'ave looked lovelier." He gazed in rapt attention until the two disappeared in the moving crowd. Then he remembered his haste to close his shop and join the march.

While the peasant dress the young woman wore could not hide her beauty, it did hide her identity. She was no peasant; indeed she was the Princess Volanna, thirdborn daughter of King Tallis of Valomar. The girl at her side was her maidservant, Kalley.

No one who saw this winsome pair or overheard them speak would guess that there was any difference in their rank for Kalley was more than a maidservant to the young princess. She was in reality Volanna's one true friend. Volanna certainly knew others of rank closer to her own—daughters of the earls, counts, and knights in her father's court—but of these friends, if such they could be called, there was none to whom her soul was bonded as it was with Kalley. There were those who thought it unfitting that the daughter of the king would choose as her closest friend a mere servant, but Volanna was not like other princesses.

Indeed, in some ways she had hardly been raised like a princess at all. King Tallis and his queen, Ravella, had seen too much of overindulged children among the nobility. They were determined that their three daughters would grow up as free as possible from the arrogance and superior attitudes that so often accompany wealth and position. Thus from early childhood on, Volanna had enjoyed very few of the special privileges common to royalty. From the time she was able, she was made to do her own chores. She was expected to keep her own chamber clean and orderly and to care for her own wardrobe. She even took her turn with the scullery servants, with whom she rotated between kitchen duty, cleaning, and caring for some of the smaller domestic animals in the castle pens. King Tallis was teaching her "the inversion principle," as he called it—that she, as a member of the royal family, was a servant to her people, not the other way around.

Today Volanna and Kalley wore the garb of peasant girls not with any intent toward mischief but because it was the only way for the princess to enjoy the fair as a fair should be enjoyed. By their plain dress the girls could avoid the circle of respect that so insulated royalty from reality and be free to plunge wholeheartedly into the community festivities.

"Hurry, Kalley," urged Volanna. "We don't want to miss any of the performances."

"Don't try to fool me," replied Kalley. "There's no performance that could get you as goggle-eyed and breathless as you are now."

"Brendal said he would be at the dance at sundown, and I don't want to keep him waiting. You know how he gets when he has to wait."

"Yes, I know. If you ask me, you should deliberately make him wait more often. He could use a lesson in patience."

"And you could use a lesson in haste. Come on, let's hurry." Volanna grabbed Kalley's hand and quickened their pace.

As houses and shops began to give way to countryside, the young women could hear the brays, barks, bleatings, and squeals of animals mingled with the merry chatter and laughter of the celebrating crowd. Soon they could see the red banners waving atop brightly colored pavilions, competing with the autumn foliage for the championship of color.

The two girls reached the fair and plunged delightedly into its labyrinth of aisles and paths. The pungent but not altogether unpleasant country smell of hay and cattle dung assailed their nostrils as they passed through row after row of pens and stalls filled with prize livestock. Some of the animals were contentedly munching their fodder, oblivious to all passersby; others paced nervously in their stalls. The girls gave wide berth to an enormous black bull with hoofs wide as dinner plates and sides like walls, oiled and curried till he shone like ebony. A stallion with shoulders higher than their heads nickered as they passed, causing Kalley to squeal and jump aside.

Soon livestock pens gave way to vendors' stands. Sellers of fish, fowl, pumpkins, baskets, nuts, pastries, and a hundred other crafts and edibles lined their way, proprietors waving their wares in the air and barking out the virtues of their offerings, hoping to entice the eyes, ears, or nostrils of everyone who passed by. Volanna flinched as a plucked chicken carcass was thrust in her face. "A fine, fat hen to fill your pot, young mistress," grinned the apple-cheeked farmer through his thick, red beard. Volanna smiled a polite refusal and the girls went giggling on.

Among the food and craft stands were many games as well. Winners could take prizes of small crafts and foodstuffs by pitching a horseshoe, tossing pebbles into an earthen jar, guessing a number, or trying some similar feat of minimal skill or chance.

"Step over here, young lassies," cried the barker at the ringtoss. "If your luck matches your beauty you should never miss."

"Let's try it," urged Kalley, and Volanna consented.

They paid their coins, and each tossed three rings at stakes four paces away, but the rings all bounced and tumbled to the ground. The vendor smiled and cut two wedges from a hanging cylinder of golden cheese. He handed the slices to the girls, bowing deeply as he said, "Such beauty as yours merits its own reward." The girls giggled and reddened, but they took the cheese with a thank-you, dropped graceful curtsies, and moved on.

"Now all we need is a little bread and something to drink," said Volanna as they jostled their way through the crowd. Soon the aromas of spitted pork, roasting corn, and baking bread told them they were heading in the right direction. In moments they came to a large open space ringed with vendors of food and drink. Perched on every available box, stump, and stone, fairgoers sat eating cheeses, honeycakes, sweetbreads, and baked fowl. Jugglers, puppeteers, acrobats, minstrels, and mimes had staked out their own spots throughout the area and now performed, hats upturned on the ground to be filled with coins from appreciative spectators.

"There's a breadseller over there," said Kalley, pointing.

The girls bought a small loaf and found an unoccupied, hay-covered spot where they could sit untrampled. Making themselves comfortable, they split the loaf of bread and began to eat while watching the various entertainers. To their left a contortionist was gathering a small crowd as he twisted, curled, and tucked his body until he was standing on his hands with his head thrust between his legs. To their right they saw tumbling balls of fire passing back and forth through the air as a pair of jugglers kept eight fiery torches flying between them. The hats of these entertainers were soon filled, for ale, cheap and abundant, lubricated the flow of commerce by turning many a frugal farmer into a profligate spender.

Soon the girls noticed a rising stir of noise and excitement as a crowd began to cluster on the far side of the circle. Kalley stood on a nearby stone, just vacated by another fairgoer, to see the cause of the commotion.

"It's an old magician," she said. "And he's about to begin his show. Let's go watch."

"But we're late for the dance. Brendal may be there already."

"Oh, let him wait. This won't take long, and the dance will go on till morning's light. Come on." Volanna gave in, and they joined the crowd around a raised platform where the white-haired magician was beginning his show.

At first she paid little attention. Her mind was already on the dance and Brendal. She was in no mood to watch the same, tired trickery she had seen performed time after time by traveling magicians at the royal court. But as this magician began his performance, Volanna soon realized these were not ordinary feats of magic. Many were similar to standard tricks she had often seen before, but this time each ended with an unexpected turn. She had seen butterflies emerge from empty silk scarves, but never had she seen them turn into flowers midflight and rain petals over the crowd. She had seen magicians pull rabbits from empty hats—even her father's jester could do that—but never had she seen one pull a dozen rabbits from a single hat. Each feat the magician performed was more spectacular than the last, and after a dozen or more he paused and addressed his now sizable audience.

"For my next performance, I shall need an assistant."

The crowd was in awe of what they had seen and a little fearful of the old man's powers. Everyone shrank back or tried to hide his face behind the head in front. The magician scanned the crowd, absently tapping a finger on his bearded chin, until his gaze rested on Volanna.

"Ah, you—the young woman with the wide blue eyes and raven hair; you'll do just fine," he called.

Volanna started to protest, but the crowd pushed her forward until someone lifted her to the stage. She hastily pulled up her shawl and wrapped it around her head, holding it close lest someone recognize her. As the magician took Volanna's hand and led her to the center of the platform, she looked on him with wonder. He was not old at all. Or was he? There was a look about him that suggested a vast accumulation of ancient wisdom and peace, like that acquired only with great age. But his smooth face, clear eyes, and the glowing, supple skin were like those of a youth little older than she was. And the white hair of his head and beard had not the lank, often yellowed, dullness of old age, but the prismatic whiteness of pure light. She thought she could almost see hints of rainbow-like colors shimmering softly at the edges.

"What is your name, my fair queen?" asked the magician.

"Vo—uh—Dovey," stammered Volanna, almost slipping but quickly substituting the nickname her father had given her in childhood and often used even yet.

"Dovey," the magician repeated. "It sounds very much like a pet name a doting father would give an innocent, soft-eyed girl." Volanna smiled at the magician, and the only sign of the slight shock she felt at the uncanny accuracy of his guess was a blush she hoped he would ignore.

"Very well, Dovey," he said. "With your assistance I shall perform a feat of magic suggested by your gentle name. If you will be so kind as to hold this, we shall proceed." From a table he picked up a delicate but tightly knit bird's nest and placed it in her cupped hands. Then he plucked from the air a tiny, speckled egg, which he carefully placed in the nest.

"Now watch," he exhorted the crowd needlessly. For perhaps ten seconds, nothing happened. Then Volanna felt a slight quivering of the nest as the little egg began to stir and jerk. After a moment she heard a soft, cracking sound as it split open and a gangly baby dove unfolded itself. The tiny creature sat for a moment cupped in the opened shell, then stretched its nubby wings and began to grow visibly larger. In seconds a downy coating sprouted over it. The body lengthened and rounded. Elegant, silky feathers fanned out from tail and wings, and in less time than it takes to lace a shoe, a fully-grown female sat on the edge of the nest, silvery white and sleek, the most beautiful bird Volanna had ever seen. The dove stood and stretched her wings, then settled comfortably into the nest, cooing softly.

Suddenly a blur of beating wings and feathers swooped down from the sky, and with much flutter and commotion, a large, gray dove—a male—perched beside the silver one, almost knocking the nest from Volanna's hands. The gray turned his full attention on the silver, cooing, bobbing, billing, and caressing her elegant neck with his beak. Soon he began to fly off the nest and then quickly return, over and over, obviously tempting the silver dove to follow. And she was clearly tempted. Each time the gray dove returned, she responded to him more eagerly, first standing, then fluttering her wings and stretching her neck toward her suitor.

"Be wise, little dove," said the magician. "Close your eyes and stop your ears. You think the gray one calls you away to a flight of bliss, but mark my words, his gray is but an imitation of your silver. You are created for the golden one that awaits you beyond the horizon, and you will never find joy heeding the siren call of this impatient imitator. Stay and await your destiny."

The magician's words burned into Volanna's mind and caused her face to flush. She glanced up from the drama being played in her hands and found that as he spoke, the magician was looking directly at her. She quickly dropped her eyes to the nest, unable to bear the intensity of his gaze. But before she had time to wonder at the meaning of his words, the silver dove suddenly bolted and flew after the gray, knocking the nest from her hands and scattering it in frayed pieces across the planking.

The silver dove joined the gray one overhead, and together they flew in ecstatic, wheeling loops, higher and higher into the evening sky. Suddenly the spectators gasped in horror. As the silver dove circled toward the gray in an airborne dance of joy, his feathers darkened, his beak grew into a horny hook, and his wingspan doubled. He took on the shape of a deadly hawk, swift and black, and gave chase to the betrayed dove. With a cry of terror, she dived and circled and darted in a valiant attempt to lose her pursuer. But the hawk followed like a shadow and with ever increasing speed. The frantic dove swooped toward the nearby grove of trees, now silhouetted against the setting sun. But before she reached it the hawk closed the gap. A shrill cry pierced the air as the hawk's talons clutched her body and the two birds vanished altogether, leaving nothing but a shower of silver feathers tumbling earthward to tell the crowd that the drama had ended.

Volanna stood as if frozen, her mouth agape, her eyes staring at the feathers flashing like fireflies as they spun downward in the fading sunlight. The rest of the audience was shocked as well but not for long. The ale soon reasserted its influence, and they cheered and applauded, tossing showers of coins into the magician's pail before dispersing to find other wonders. But for the moment Volanna had wonder enough right where she stood. She had little doubt that the flight of the hapless dove was conjured as a parable for her own benefit. But what could it mean? Was the gray dove meant as a warning about Brendal? Was he unfit to be her consort? Surely not. He was the most promising young knight in her father's court. As to his being a threat or a menace, the idea was unthinkable. She glanced again at the magician and found his eyes still locked on hers as if to say, *Heed my warning well.*

"Volanna, we can go now." Kalley took her arm and led her down the steps and away from the magician's stage. Volanna moved like a wooden puppet, oblivious to the new wonders they passed in every aisle as she pondered the magician's disturbing parable.

The dancing was already underway when they arrived. The sun had set, and the darkness was growing deeper, so torches fixed to tall poles surrounding the dancing ground had already been lit. A small but lusty band of lutes, pipes, and tambourines was playing a lively jig, and couples of all ages—gangly youths and budding lasses, starry-eyed courting pairs, married couples, and even balding and graying grandparents—bobbed and whirled in churning circles. For the moment all were youths and maidens again. The squeal of laughter from the whirling matron being nuzzled by her amorous husband could not be distinguished from that of the blushing milkmaid spinning in the arms of the grinning stableboy.

Volanna and Kalley scanned the field but found no sign of Brendal, so they joined the bystanders to watch while they waited. Kalley immediately caught the spirit of things and began tapping her toe and clapping her hands to the vigorous rhythms of the band. Volanna, however, was yet bewildered by the vivid parable of the dove and stared unheeding into the swirl of color and laughter before her. Was it possible that Brendal was not the person he seemed to be? Was it possible that he was a hawk in dove's feathers, as the avian parable seemed to suggest? Was it possible that Brendal's courtly manner and gentle touch hid a heart bent on some dark purpose? She could not bring herself to think it. She knew Brendal too well. Yet the magician had apparently singled her out and contrived an incredible feat of magic explicitly to warn her of just such a danger. What was she to make of it all?

"What a lovely dress her highness wears tonight," said a masculine voice at her ear. Volanna started from her reverie and turned toward the speaker. At the sight of the two chestnut-colored eyes before her, glowing in the torchlight and sparkling with humor, all her sprouting doubts withered.

"Brendal!" she said, "Keep your voice down; people will hear you."

"Why are you dressed like a peasant?" he asked in lowered tones. "Are you sneaking out against your father's wishes?"

"Of course not!" Volanna replied. "You know I would never do that. I am simply trying to avoid attracting attention."

"Then you should have worn a veil. A face as beautiful as yours is as sure to attract stares as a buttercup attracts bees."

Had Volanna been more experienced with men, such easily spoken flattery would have rolled off like a dewdrop from a rose petal. But Brendal was the only suitor she had known, and the compliment kindled a warm blush.

"Besides," Brendal continued, "why shouldn't you want to attract attention? Attention is one of the privileges of royalty."

"It is one of its curses," Volanna rejoined. "If I were to come here decked out in royal finery lined with gold and jewels, the fowler wouldn't dangle his chicken carcass in my face, the purse maker wouldn't haggle with me, and the barker at the ring game would not even try to get me to look his way. I couldn't really enjoy the fair while being held at a distance by everyone's respect. In fact, I would never even know what a fair is really about."

"You mean you want stinking chicken carcasses shoved in your face?"

"Of course!" she laughed. "I want to enjoy the fair like everyone else, and I want the people to enjoy it. When royalty comes strutting in, fun goes slinking out."

"What a terribly unprincesslike attitude."

"Thank you," replied Volanna as she took his arm and began pulling him toward the dancing. "Come. Let's see if your feet are as agile as your jaw."

But Brendal held back. "First I want to talk. I have been doing much thinking, and I have something I need to say."

He took her hand and led her toward the nearby grove. The moon had now risen and was shining orange and full above the eastern horizon. When they were well beyond the glare of the torches and bathed only in the soft glow of moonlight, Brendal stopped. Before Volanna could protest, his arms encircled her slender waist and he drew her to him and kissed her forehead. She caught her breath. Her pulse quickened at his embrace, and her brow burned at the touch of his lips. Although they had often met and talked and she had allowed him to hold her hand, he had never held her close until now. The gentle firmness of his arms and chest gave her melting sensations of warmth and bliss beyond anything she had imagined—and she had imagined much. His lips brushed downward over her cheeks and toward her mouth, leaving a lingering trail of exquisite fire. Before his lips reached hers, however, uneasiness at entering uncharted territory fought against her desire, and she turned her face aside. But she closed her eyes and sighed happily as she rested her head upon his shoulder.

When she did open her eyes again, she was met by the sight of the frowning black hawk of his family crest blazoned on the shoulder of his tailored, gray tunic. With a sudden wave of alarm, she remembered the magician's deadly black hawk and the tragic shower of silver feathers falling from the heavens like the wings of Icarus, shattered remnants of unholy desire.

"No, Brendal," she murmured, trying to push herself away. "This is not right."

"Not right?" he whispered hoarsely. "I have come to realize that I love you, Volanna. That is what I wanted to tell you tonight. What could be more right?"

"I . . . I love you too, Brendal," she replied. "But we are going about this the wrong way. You know the law in Valomar as well as I do: no offspring of the king may initiate or accept courtship until his or her twentieth birthday—and then only by permission of the king."

"Of course I know the law," he said. "'Perivale's Prevention' they call it. But we both know that this particular law has often been bent to fit the inclinations of royal desire."

"It has been bent but not broken, at least not by members of my father's house. But if you and I step beyond where we are at this moment, my father would surely think I had ignored the law and its intent."

"Be serious, Volanna. Almost everyone ignores his father's will when it comes to matters of love. Such things have their own laws. I want to marry you, and that is law enough for me."

She pulled herself from his grasp but held his hands in hers and smiled at him. "But we don't have to ignore the law or my father. Ask him for my hand. Surely there is no reason for him to refuse." Indeed, Volanna felt sure the king would agree to the match. Suitable consorts for princesses were not abundant, and where would her father find a consort more suitable than Brendal—at twenty-five already a knight in the king's court, current jousting champion of Valomar, and son of a high-ranking nobleman? Her father was certain to consent, and with his consent she would not be an escaping dove. Yes, that must have been the meaning of the magician's parable: don't violate the law; don't defy legal and traditional restraints in the heat of passion; manage the process. Dot the i's and cross the t's, and do the thing up right. Don't let a rash flight of passion tear apart her family nest of love and authority; be escorted from it with the protection of parental blessing. She breathed easier as her inner alarm subsided and vanished.

"But we'll have to wait until your twentieth birthday," Brendal complained.

"It's only five months away," laughed Volanna. "I'm beginning to think rumors of your impatience are not exaggerated."

"But five months! It may as well be five years."

"Would that be so terrible? Remember the ancient patriarch Jacob? He served his father-in-law seven years for the hand of his bride, and because he loved her so much it seemed to him but a few days."

"That does not ring true. When one loves so much, waiting even one day seems like forever."

"Brendal, Brendal, true love is patient. I'm beginning to think the flower of patience has withered in your garden of virtues."

"Very well, I'll wait," he sighed. "I will be at your presentation ball on the night of your birthday. And after the dinner and all the tedious speeches and other silly formalities, I will get your father off to the side and ask him for your hand. You can count on it."

"I will count on it," she said, still holding his hands and gazing happily into his eyes. "Now, can we dance?"

Brendal and Volanna returned hand in hand to the dancing ground and entered the dance as the musicians played a sweeping waltz. Volanna had never been happier. Her heart was light as a bird in its first flight, and she floated through each dance as if on wing. She was blissfully aware of the touch of Brendal's firm hand on her waist and of the play of the powerful muscles in his shoulder under her own hand. Looking into his eyes was a pleasure almost beyond bearing, yet she could not bear to look away. After what seemed only minutes but was in reality more than two hours, she felt a tap on her shoulder and Kalley's voice calling her down from her flight into paradise.

"It is time to go, Volanna. The carriage is here."

Reluctantly Volanna withdrew her hand from Brendal's and bade him farewell. She and Kalley walked to the carriage waiting behind the grove and returned to the castle.

CHAPTER FOUR

ThE BARTERED BRIDE

rendal and Volanna both experienced the same period of five months between their meeting at the Harvest Fair and Volanna's presentation ceremony. But to Brendal the day approached at the pace of a crawling tortoise. Each day was a barrier to the time when he would achieve his desire. To Volanna the same time seemed to last but a moment. To her the joy of anticipation was itself a pleasure that gave each day its own completeness.

For both, however, the night of the presentation ceremony and the banquet that would follow finally came, and over sevenscore guests filled the great hall of Oakendale, Valomar's royal castle. As was the custom of King Tallis, the list included not only members of the nobility but the king's most valued common folk as well—his tailor, his huntsman, his daughter's tutor, and some of the village mayors. This very unkingly practice was firmly disapproved by some of Valomar's noblemen—most notably Sir Borethane, an ambitious knight who often vocalized his dissatisfaction with King Tallis's non-progressive reign—but the king ignored their outrage and calmly continued his custom. Others, at first shocked by his unorthodox invitation lists, came around to his view and even came to enjoy the rough-hewn wisdom and goodwill of the ordinary citizens with whom they shared table.

Tonight both gentry and commoners were united on at least one point: all eagerly awaited the grand entrance of Princess Volanna. As custom dictated, the guests mingled in informal clusters about the room, chatting and sipping from goblets of mead until a short fanfare reverberated off the stone walls of the hall, blown by six liveried trumpeters all holding their long, straight horns up in perfect alignment. An expectant silence followed and, as one, all heads turned toward the grand stairway. A herald in royal colors stepped forward and announced in resonant tones, "The Princess Volanna, daughter of His Majesty, King Tallis and heir to the throne of Valomar!"

A consort of musicians began to play a stately march, and a hundred breaths were suddenly drawn as Volanna appeared at the top of the stairway, standing tall and stately, gowned in silver and cerulean. She paused as the guests burst into applause and then gracefully descended into the hall like an angel coming down to brighten the existence of mortals with beauty from heaven.

As men gazed on Volanna descending, their breaths came deeper and their spirits quickened with the inexplicable exhilaration rare beauty brings. The exquisite flow of line and contour, the effortless grace of movement, the radiant warmth of the rose-tinted, ivory face, the lustrous cascade of sable hair, the paradoxical sense of sufficiency and vulnerability, all seemed the outward emanations of a reality within.

No man was abashed by the openness of his gaze at the young princess because for the moment he was not aware of himself at all. Many found themselves moved for the first time, not by mere female attractiveness and the animal pleasure it often incites, but by the deeper, richer, more elemental beauty of the feminine which is to the female as a rose is to its shadow. Without shame they were basking, breathing, bathing, existing in the entrancing glow of that mysterious power.

Volanna descended and took the seat of honor at the table between her father and mother. The hallful of adoring subjects found their own seats and the banquet began.

The hospitality of King Tallis was legendary, and the occasion of presenting his daughter to the kingdom as a functioning member of the royal family was not one on which to risk that reputation. In addition to the endless fountain of wine and mead, there was beef and fowl and cheeses and nuts in abundance. The servants did not suffer the plate or cup of any guest to remain empty but circulated among the tables to ensure that no appetite could outstrip King Tallis's hospitality.

Volanna looked around the hall until she found Brendal sitting at a table opposite and to the right of hers. Her heart beat faster and her breath came deeper at the sight of him. When she caught him glancing up at her, she smiled broadly and then blushed as he furtively returned the smile and quickly looked away.

"Are you ill, Volanna?" asked her mother. "Your face is red as a cherry."

"Oh, no, not at all. I think it's just the hot peppers Comelda used to spice the soup. I feel very well, Mother, very well indeed."

"You will feel even better after we have finished our plates and your father announces his gift to you. You simply will not believe it."

"Tell me what it is."

"I'm sorry, I can't do that, but you will know soon enough."

When King Tallis saw that most of the guests had had their fill, he rose from his chair and signaled the chamberlain to rap the hall to attention. When the crowd was silent, he began his speech.

"My beloved citizens of Valomar. Tonight we rejoice in the coming of age of my daughter, and your princess, Volanna. I am grateful to each of you for joining us in celebration of this event. It is now my duty, as well as my privilege, to officially proclaim that the Princess Volanna, having today completed her twentieth year, is hereby authorized to take her position as a fully functioning member of the royal family of Valomar." King Tallis paused, and stepping behind her chair, he placed a silver necklace bearing the royal seal of Valomar around Volanna's neck. Then returning to his place, he continued his speech. "As such she is endowed with all the rights and duties accompanying that position herewith laid upon her." He turned toward his daughter and smiled. "In other words, my dear Volanna, you've finally grown up." Volanna returned the smile as the guests cheered and applauded.

The king motioned with his hands to quiet the crowd, then continued. "Under normal circumstances, I would also announce to you at this time that since I have no sons and my two older daughters are married to husbands with other responsibilities, Volanna should be designated as my successor." Here the king paused, looked in the direction of Sir Borethane, then continued with added gravity. "However, I am not able to do that." A low murmur of surprise rippled through the crowd. The king now had the full attention of every person in the hall.

"As every citizen of Valomar knows," he continued, "our country has not always been independent. One hundred twenty years ago, it was part of the great Seven Kingdoms empire ruled by Perivale the Strong of Meridan. It reverted to an independent kingdom only out of necessity, when Perivale's disappearance left the empire in danger of anarchy and its constituent peoples vulnerable to opportunistic plunderers.

"But national independence was never a thing Valomar desired for itself. The prosperity and peace we experienced under Perivale's benevolent rule has not since been equaled, and every honest student of history knows it." King Tallis's voice rose and took on uncharacteristic sternness as he glared into the scowling face of Sir Borethane. "In contradiction to the general assumption of mankind," the King continued, "independence is not the highest good for man or kingdom. Standing alone and unbowed is not better than standing true. Being one's own master is not better than serving a rightful master. We must not insist, to the detriment of our nation's well-being, that the banner of Valomar fly alone on the mast." By now Sir Borethane was sitting bolt upright, arms crossed, face livid, and eyes glaring beneath his heavy brow.

"There is not a man, maid, or matron in Valomar who is unfamiliar with the prophecy uttered after the fall of Perivale and who does not understand that whatever its mysteries and difficulties, it does indeed predict the rebirth of the empire. I have good reason to believe that this prophecy is soon to be fulfilled. We are on the eve of the rebirth of the empire, and the new emperor is alive even as we speak. He is Prince Lomar of Meridan. And I am convinced that his brow will soon bear the ancient Crown of Eden, which will be found before the golden comet that lights our eastern sky reaches its destination—conjunction with the silver star in about one year from now.

"As most of you know, my daughter Volanna and Meridan's Crown Prince Lomar were born twenty years ago on this very day. In fact, they were born within the same hour. Meridan's late King Alfron and I agreed that these simultaneous births signaled a common destiny for the two royal babes, a destiny that has much to do with the rebirth of Perivale's empire."

Volanna had been only half attending her father's speech. Her thoughts were drawn forward to the approaching moment when Brendal would speak with him and secure their future together. But as King Tallis continued, she began to realize that he was setting the stage for a major announcement. She began to feel a rising sense of uneasiness at the direction that his speech was taking.

"Twenty years ago, only days after the births of our two children, King Alfron and I made a pact. We agreed that on the day following the coronation of Alfron's son as King of Meridan, my daughter would become his bride. Citizens of Valomar, your Princess Volanna is to become the queen of the second empire." Here the king turned back to his daughter. "My dear Volanna, for the traditional gift on the occasion of your coming of age, I give you not a prince, nor even a king, but an emperor."

Most of the crowd cheered and shouted their approval. Poor Volanna sat bolt upright, pale as parchment, tears flooding her eyes. Her mother was crying as well but with tears of pride and joy that blinded her to the shock on her daughter's face.

"Oh, Volanna," she said, squeezing the princess's leaden shoulders, "what a match your father has made for you!"

Brendal sat utterly still for a moment, absorbing the stunning news. Then he rose abruptly, prepared to stalk from the room. "Don't be a fool, son." Sir Borethane put a firm hand on the young knight's shoulder and pressed him back into his seat. "Stay and be the man. A rash act now will ruin any chance you may have later."

"What chance?" growled Brendal through clenched teeth. "The king has spoken." He sat stiffly upright, his eyes glaring and his jaw muscles working rhythmically.

"The princess is not being wed tonight and will not be for a year hence. The future is yet in the inkwell, and it may not be Tallis's pen that writes it. Be patient and wait."

"Patience is for vultures. Remember that we bear the mark of the hawk. Hawks don't sit and wait for their prey to die; they take what they want."

"Yes, but not now. The first thing we must take is time. We will work out a new plan, then act."

King Tallis again raised his hands to quiet the crowd. "Dear citizens of Valomar, I know you have heard enough of my words and that now you are ready to dance. As the custom is on these occasions, the princess will begin the dancing by choosing her escort for the evening. So all you young, unwed men, please stand at your places, and we shall await Princess Volanna's decision."

The stricken Volanna remembered that she was a princess and at the moment the focus of everyone in the hall. She would lay aside her grief and play her part. She pushed back her tears, gave a convincing imitation of a smile, and rose from her chair. The musicians began to play as she stepped down from the dais to walk among the rows of tables.

Almost a score of young men were standing, each hoping the ravishing young princess would tie her scarf to his arm. Commonly on such occasions as this, the honoree would tease the young hopefuls by pretending to scrutinize each as she passed his chair, sometimes making as if to reach for his arm, then pulling back and moving on past. But tonight Volanna had no heart for the game. She walked slowly but directly to Sir Brendal, tied her scarf to his upper arm, and led him to the open area of the hall. The musicians struck the opening chords of an elegant round dance, and the devastated couple began to move through the intricate steps, Volanna smiling gamely and Brendal looking as though he had been struck by a mace. Other young couples quickly followed them into the dance, and the rest of the guests reassembled to discuss vigorously what the king had announced.

Volanna and Brendal danced silently for several rounds, but as soon as they thought they could escape without notice, they danced their way out of the crowded room and into a presently deserted corridor. Brendal grasped Volanna by the shoulders and faced her angrily.

"Why didn't you tell me?" he demanded.

"I did not know until tonight. Do you think I would have encouraged you if I had known of my father's plans?"

"Do you mean to say that your father would force a husband on you, sight unseen, without consulting you?"

"He would not think of it that way. It would never occur to him that I would be anything but grateful for a match such as he announced tonight. And it would never occur to him that I would ignore the edict and fall in love before my presentation. He has no idea that he has just made me the most miserable—" Her voice began to quiver and she choked on the words as wrenching sobs overtook her.

"I will not let this happen," said Brendal.

"And what will you do, violate the royal edict?"

"Why not? We can elope."

"No, Brendal. Even if we did manage to escape, where could we hide? All Valomar would be alerted to watch for us. And besides, I could never disobey my father in such a matter as this, even if he were not the king."

"But this is not right, Volanna, and you know it as well as I do. To send you away forever to wed a prince you don't even know is outrageous. We must do something."

"I will talk with father. He doesn't know about you and me. Perhaps he could work out some way to undo the pact. I will talk with him this very night."

"And I will work out some kind of plan in case your talking does no good, which I am convinced will be the case."

Volanna started to reply, but Brendal drew her to him and stifled her words with an ardent kiss. She stiffened but then yielded to the bittersweet ecstasy of this first true kiss before finding the will to push away. "We must get back to the ball," she said after she caught her breath. "If they miss us, there will be an awful scandal."

"Tonight," Brendal said, holding her fast as she tried to turn away. "You will talk to your father tonight, then send me his reply in the morning."

"Yes, Brendal, I will," she promised. He released her, and they returned to the ball to endure two more hours of masking their shattered hopes with feigned happiness.

CHAPTER FIVE

The Chessboard Queen

King Tallis was tired but happy. The ball had been a huge success. He had long anticipated this night, and as he left the hall, empty but for the servants busily mopping and moving tables, he smiled with satisfaction. Events seemed to be progressing smoothly toward the destiny predicted by the prophecy.

Tallis climbed the stairway, entered his private apartment, and headed directly for his bedchamber, where he removed his crown and carefully placed it in its casket, then slipped out of his heavy outer robe. Queen Ravella was not yet in the room. *Probably giving unnecessary instructions to the kitchen servants,* he thought. He stretched luxuriously, then sat down beside the fire with a comfortable sigh.

Before him next to the hearth was a low table bearing his chessboard. He gazed at the elaborately carved and delicately painted pieces arranged on it. The set had been a gift from his old friend Alfron. He picked up the oaken king and turned it in his fingers, admiring the detail in the folds of the robe, the glitter of actual jewels embedded in the gilded crown, the realistic texture of the blond beard—a detail which gave the figure an uncanny resemblance to his late friend. He felt a pang of regret that Alfron was not alive to see this day. He remembered exactly where he was and what he had been doing the moment the messenger brought him the news nineteen years ago that both Alfron and his queen had died. The cause was food poisoning, the man had said, but Tallis wondered even yet.

With a shake of his head, he replaced the chess piece and settled into his chair.

Just as he began to rise, intending to finish changing for bed, there was a knock on the door. "Come in," he called.

The door opened slowly as Volanna stepped halfway into the room and stopped. "Father, I . . . I need to talk with you," she said. There was a quiver in her voice and a look of despair in her reddened eyes.

"What is wrong, Dovey?" Tallis asked, quickly going to her and drawing her into the room.

At the sound of the childhood nickname, Volanna's composure broke. "Father, please don't make me do it," she wailed as she fell into his arms and buried her face in his robe.

"Make you do what?"

"Don't force me to marry Prince Lomar," she sobbed.

"Why in heaven's name not? No girl could hope for a better match than the crown prince of Meridan."

"But I don't love him."

"Of course not," he chuckled. "You haven't even seen him, at least not since both of you were very small children. You will learn to love him just as other royal brides learn to love their husbands. But you understand all this. There must be some other reason that you are so upset."

"I . . . I'm in love with someone else."

Tallis held his daughter away and looked intensely into her face. "With whom?" he asked sternly.

Unable to meet her father's gaze, Volanna dropped her eyes. "Sir Brendal. He and I—"

"Sir Brendal!" Tallis exploded. "I should have guessed. Let me tell you, Volanna, that even if there were no pact with Alfron and no Prince Lomar, I would still absolutely forbid you to marry Sir Brendal."

"But why?" she asked, stunned by the uncharacteristic passion that gripped her father.

"Because he is the son of a man who is doing everything he can to undermine the welfare of our country—a man who may even be a traitor."

"Oh, Father, surely not! You are taking a mere political difference too seriously—as if it were a personal affront."

"You forget, my daughter, that I am the king. Political differences are not merely abstractions to me. Farmers chatting in Market Square can differ politically without consequence, but in my position a political confrontation can jeopardize the fate of the entire country. No, I would not have you marry a man who I am convinced would lead our nation into ruin if given the power, all in the name of independence.

"Let me explain something to you. From time to time I have ventured to mention to the Hall of Knights the thing I explained tonight—that Valomar might do well to relinquish her independence voluntarily to the new Meridanic empire. I often lay some matter I am pondering before the hall to get the thing viewed from all sides and solicit frank discussion. From the beginning, Borethane's opposition to Valomar's confederation with Meridan has been vocal and bitter. But about four or five months ago, suddenly and without explanation, he ceased his defiance to the idea and became most courteous to me. Now, I have known Sir Borethane too long to think he would simply drop such strongly held views overnight. No, he has hatched another plan to thwart me, and my goodwill is apparently necessary for that plan to work."

"Father, none of this has anything to do with Brendal."

"Yes, I fear it does," said Tallis. "Borethane is now fighting me through his son. He was hoping Brendal would win your hand. Then, with you and his son wed, Borethane would have gained a solid foothold from which to affect the politics of Valomar—or worse. Brendal does not love you, Volanna. He is using you to advance his father's ambitions."

"Surely you are judging Brendal unfairly. I hate to disagree with you, but you are building a case without evidence and making accusations you cannot prove. It is not Brendal who has opposed you but Brendal's father. Brendal is not like his father, and he would never use me that way!"

"My dear child, all men are like their fathers more than they know and more than they can help," said Tallis with a sigh. "And that is another reason I promised you to Alfron's son. Alfron was a man of unwavering honor who loved his family and his kingdom beyond measure. As to judging without evidence, if I could catalog the political machinations of Borethane for the past few years, I think you would be well convinced that he is not a friend of Valomar. The look on his face tonight when I announced your marriage was almost enough to convict him with no other evidence at all. He was not a happy man."

"His anger still does not prove your case. Perhaps he was angry because he wants his son to have the bride of his choice. I know that Brendal would never do anything to hurt you or me or Valomar. He loves me, Father. I know he does."

"How do you know?"

"Well, he . . . he's courteous, thoughtful, uh, and kind. He sends me gifts, he . . ."

"Volanna," interrupted Tallis gently, "suitors often put on manners for the same reason thieves put on masks. They hide their true natures in order to take what they want. You cannot really love Brendal. You cannot even know him yet. All you see of him is what he chooses to reveal to you—a mask of manners, fashioned in a false likeness of love, which you are mistaking for the true Brendal. Let me assure you that the face behind Brendal's mask is Sir Borethane. He is an ambitious father using his handsome son as bait to snare the crown of Valomar."

"If only you knew Brendal, Father, you would know this cannot be true," cried Volanna, feeling herself sinking into an abyss of despair.

With a growing ache in his heart, Tallis took a deep breath and addressed his daughter gravely. "Volanna, as painful as this is for you, I must forbid you to see Brendal again. It is your duty as Princess of Valomar to fulfill the pact with King Alfron and become the queen of Meridan."

"That is unfair!" Volanna cried. "Why must the accident of my royal birth consign me to a future of misery in a loveless political marriage? I did not ask to be a princess, and I do not want to continue as one. I want simply to be a woman and to be cherished by a man who loves me as a woman, not as a means of building an empire or in homage to a prophecy. Please, Father, let me renounce my royalty and simply be a woman."

"And how much of a woman will you be if you run from your duty?"

"At least I would be woman enough to make my own choices. Our royalty deprives us of humanity and forces us to be posed figures—showpieces like these stiff, painted pieces on your chessboard, whose every move is limited by arbitrary rules."

"Do you really think that breaking free of the rules that prescribe royal behavior will make you a whole person? Oh, Volanna, Volanna! I thought I taught you better. The fullness of your personhood depends on your freely accepting the duties and obligations laid on you. What will your life be worth if you refuse the light you were born to bear? No, Volanna. Renounce your duty as a princess for some supposed freer vision of womanhood, and you will find that you made a bad bargain. You are destined to be a princess. For you, to be less than a princess is to be less than a woman. Turn away from the obligations heaven has assigned and you sacrifice the only means you have of validating your integrity as a person."

"But I will be miserable the rest of my days. Surely, if you have any concern for my happiness, you won't make me go through with this."

Tallis gazed on Volanna with sadness in his eyes. "Only one thing in life means more to me than your happiness, and that is performing my duty before the Master of the Universe. I have made a vow before him, and you know what he expects from those who make vows. Yet (may he forgive me) I fear I would break that vow if I truly thought that doing so would ensure your happiness. But it would not, Volanna. You will never find happiness by turning your back on duty and chasing the butterfly of desire. Performing your duty will not make you miserable for the rest of your days. You will learn to love the prince, and time will dissolve the ache you now feel at the loss of your young knight. There is nothing more to be said. Now go and get some rest. Tomorrow we begin to prepare for your departure to Meridan."

Volanna started. "My departure to Meridan? What do you mean?"

"You are to become the queen of Meridan, yet you know nothing of that country—its customs, its people, its laws, or even its prince. It is important that you become accustomed to your new home in the year before the wedding. You will leave in thirty days."

For the second time that evening, Volanna was too stunned for words. Thirty days! The thin hope she had clung to had drawn its life from the expectation that she would not leave for Meridan until the wedding drew near one year hence. Now she felt even that hope wilting within her.

For a long moment she stared without seeing at her father. The anger she had kept contained behind the wall of her overtaxed composure seeped into the great void of her despair. Tears filled her eyes, her lips quivered, and her hands clenched into tight fists. She looked at the queen on her father's chessboard, held upright but immobile for eternity by the rigid, oaken folds of her regal robe. The placid face of the painted carving seemed to mock her as if to say, "We are no different, you and I." With great effort Volanna resisted the impulse to seize the offending figure and dash it to splinters against the floor. Instead she turned and without another word left her father's chamber.

Volanna stalked numbly down the corridor toward the stairway that led to her room. Unfamiliar and alarming emotions burrowed and surfaced like moles, stirring her mind into a chaotic jumble. In a single evening she had lost the one she loved, found herself promised to an unmet prince in a distant land, become the queen-to-be of an unformed empire, and learned she was being shuffled forever out of her lifelong home. It was too much for her to bear. The thought of losing Brendal filled her with sinking despair. The contract that forced her to wed an unknown prince filled her with outrage. The very thought of being uprooted from her childhood home sent waves of homesickness surging through her.

She felt uncustomary anger and resentment toward her father. He had wronged her greatly. How could he sell his own daughter (for that is how she thought of it) to someone she did not even know? How could he so callously arrange her marriage without even wondering how she would feel about the match? Did he think her emotions would lie dormant, waiting to be quickened at his bidding? Did it not occur to him that she might already have begun to make her own plans for her life?

"Oh, Brendal, Brendal," she sobbed bitterly as she made her way

down the corridor, hot tears blurring the hallway torches into dancing splashes of liquid light. She climbed the stairway to her tower
room, stumbled in, and fell facedown upon her bed. Her entire inner
body was one great ache.

A soft knock sounded at the door.

"Who is it?" Volanna demanded.

"It's Mother," responded a gentle voice.

"Come in." Volanna wiped away her tears but did not rise from
her bed as Queen Ravella slipped into the room and quietly closed
the door behind her.

"I just saw your father. He said little but enough for me to know
that you had a difficult meeting." Ravella sat down on the edge of
the bed and reached out tenderly to push dampened strands of hair
out of Volanna's face. "I could see at the ball that something was
amiss tonight. You tried to hide it, and you probably succeeded with
most of the guests, but I know you too well. Then when I returned
to our rooms and saw your father sitting and staring so grimly into
the fire . . ."

For a long moment Volanna said nothing. Then she began,
slowly, haltingly, to unfold the entire story of Brendal and herself,
from their first meeting to the night of the fair when they formed
their intentions to wed. As she reached the end of her tale, Volanna's
tears poured once more. She sat up and threw herself into the queen's
arms.

"Mother, I will never see him again," she cried. "What am I to do?"

Queen Ravella held her daughter to her breast as great sobs
wracked the girl's body. "You will learn to love the prince," she said.

Volanna pulled away. "That is not really the point," she protested.
"Why am I not allowed to make my own decisions and plot my own
future?"

"There are matters here that are more important than your personal wants. You and the prince of Meridan are destined to establish
a dynasty that will rule the reformed empire for generations to come.
You are a spoke in the wheel of history."

"A spoke in the wheel of history, am I?" Volanna's voice rose, her
eyes flashing. "I am so many things for so many purposes, I can but

wonder what use I'll be put to next. First I am a chattel, currency that can be bartered to fulfill my father's grand visions. Then I am a puppet of destiny, expected to sacrifice my own happiness to unite a political empire. Then I am a brood mare, a concubine for some obscure prophecy to breed on, a field for the new king to plow to raise his crop of princes. I am everything for everyone except a woman for a man who cherishes me. Why, Mother, why? Why must we women give up our dreams and be bartered and bedded by the men? Why must they be the choosers and we the chosen? Who made the rules that say we belong to them and not they to us?"

"You don't belong to your father, nor will you belong to Prince Lomar," replied the queen. "It's just that your father is responsible for you before marriage and—"

"And my husband is responsible for me after marriage," interrupted Volanna. "Why must they assume responsibility for us? Why shouldn't we just as readily be the ones responsible for them: You were promised and given to father. Didn't it make you angry that just as your life was about to begin you were placed under the dominion of an unknown man?"

"No, I knew from childhood that my father would arrange my marriage. I never expected anything different. And I knew my father would not pick a man who would make me unhappy. I was not angry—only a little scared."

"But you did not already love someone else."

"No, and you should not have done so either. You knew the protocol about royalty and courtship. That problem you brought upon yourself."

"I could not help it. There was something between us from the moment we met. Oh, Mother, how can I make you understand? When he looks at me or when I watch him at the tournaments, I get this quivering in my stomach and the whole world seems to get warmer and softer. And when he touches me, my breath comes deeper and my heart beats faster. His voice sends shivers up my spine. I could just sit and look at him all day and never want to do anything else."

"Are you sure it's love?" asked the queen with a faint smile. "It sounds to me more like winter fever."

"I knew you wouldn't understand," Volanna sighed. "How could you? You were bartered yourself and have never truly been in love."

"You know so much about me, then?"

"No, I don't suppose I really do. I can't imagine how it must feel to be married to someone you first met on the day of the wedding."

"Then let me tell you how it feels. When he looks at me, I get this quivering in my stomach. When he touches me, my breath comes deeper and my heart beats faster. And his voice sends shivers up my spine."

"Mother, you are mocking me. I know that you and Father have lived a harmonious life together, but surely you can't fall deeply in love with someone who is picked for you like a farmer picks a yearling."

"Volanna," said her mother, "I quickly came to love your father as deeply and as magically as you, uh, love Sir Brendal—palpitations, tingles, and all. But in time we found our love growing far beyond these quivering ecstasies of touch and look. Now our very souls have knit together so closely that neither of us can hardly draw a breath without sensing the presence of the other. The magic of our bodies delighting in each other never left us, but it became an expression of the deeper unity we found growing within."

Volanna was rather shocked at this glimpse into her mother's intimate life. It had never occurred to her that her parents could experience the kind of youthful magic she felt with Brendal. Especially not at their age. "Do you think Father feels the same toward you?"

"Of course he does," said Queen Ravella. "He doesn't wear his crown to bed, you know. In fact—I'll tell you this in confidence— often when he thinks no one is about he will come up behind me, grab me and kiss me on the neck, or pinch me like one of the idlers on the streets, or pat me on the—uh—well, never mind where he pats me." The queen blushed royally.

"Father did that?" Volanna's eyes widened.

"Your father *does* that," asserted the queen. "This king who is known in distant lands to have the wisdom of Solomon is, in some wonderful ways, still a boy of twenty. And may the Master of the Universe grant that he never completely grows up."

Volanna was quiet for a moment, then sighed. "All this really changes nothing, Mother. I still love Brendal, and I cannot bear the thought of losing him and being forced to marry a prince I have never met."

"Volanna, if you will accept your responsibility and do this thing you dread so much, I assure you that a great blessing will follow. On the other hand, if you fail, a curse will follow just as certainly."

"Surely you and Father would not wish me cursed!"

"Of course we do not wish it," replied the queen, "but the law of natural consequences will ultimately reward loyalty and punish rebellion. It has nothing to do with our wishes; it is simply according to the nature of things."

As Volanna listened to her mother, it seemed that the room got warmer and the air heavier. The walls seemed to be moving in on her. She felt that she would soon be stifled in a coffin-sized closet without doors or windows, so close and confining that she could not even bend her arms to wipe the tear that glistened on her cheek. She quieted the rising urge to run screaming from the room, and suddenly felt very tired.

"I must go to bed now, Mother," Volanna said finally. Ravella embraced her, gently stroking her head for just a moment, as she had done so often over twenty years. Then she rose and quietly left the room, and Volanna disrobed and slipped beneath the coverlet.

Sleep escaped her, however. For what seemed like hours, she tossed and turned, her mind searching for some way to prevent this unendurable loss—or to survive its agony. When at last she did sleep, it was fitfully, with alternating dreams of bliss and grief. For a moment she was in Brendal's arms. He kissed her, and when their lips blended, she closed her eyes and gave in to the ecstasy she had held at bay the evening of the fair. She opened her eyes to find him not in her arms but some six feet distant. She reached for him and found that he was not merely six feet away but ten, receding farther with each step she took toward him, until finally, she began to run and call his name. But the more she ran, the farther he receded until he disappeared, leaving her facing an empty horizon. "Oh, Brendal, Brendal," she sobbed as hot, bitter tears soaked her pillow.

CHAPTER SIX

escape from destiny

The morning sun was well above the rolling, oak-covered hills that formed the horizon outside Volanna's window when a knock came at her bedchamber door. The knock sounded a third time before it penetrated the fog that dulled her mind. She opened her eyes, which seemed heavy as stones, momentarily forgetting the tragedy of the previous evening. But when she saw her blue- and silver-gown crumpled on the floor like the ruined armor of a defeated champion, it all came back. With a leaden sinking in the pit of her stomach, she remembered that she was forever cut off from her beloved Brendal and promised to an unknown prince in a distant kingdom.

"Who is it?" she called.

"It's Kalley. Let me in, Volanna. I have something for you."

Sluggishly Volanna got up, slipped on her robe, and opened the door, then turned back to the bed without looking at her friend. She loved Kalley like a sister, but on this particular morning she was not sure she could endure the girl's tendency toward cheerful chatter even when she had nothing to say.

"Well, good morning to you too," said Kalley with mock sarcasm. But sensing the misery of her mistress, she dropped her cheery facade and took Volanna's listless hand in her own. "Oh, Volanna, I am sorry," she said. "I would not have awakened you this morning, but I have a message for you that may be important." Kalley handed

Volanna a small parchment scroll tied with a blue ribbon. "I was on my way to the shop of Halcom the cobbler—you asked me to pay him for your slippers the first thing this morning—when a street urchin slipped this into my hand and said it was for the Princess Volanna."

Listlessly Volanna took the scroll Kalley held out, slipped off the ribbon, unrolled the note, and stared at it.

"Are you going to read it, or do I have to read it for you?" chided Kalley.

Volanna began to read:

Dear Volanna:

Things cannot end this way. We must talk. Dress as you did at the fair and meet me at the farmer's market at midafternoon today. I will be dressed as a stable hand and will wait for you at the north end of the square where the horses are stabled. Please do not fail me. We must talk.

—Brendal

"You are not going, are you?" Kalley asked.

"Why should I not? He simply wants to talk. There can be no harm in that."

"That is probably what Eve said when Adam asked what that snake was doing in their garden. Don't go, Volanna. No good can come of it. I know you are hurting, but the thing is done, and there is nothing you can do about it. Going to him now, even to talk, will be like deliberately smelling the baking bread you cannot have. It will only make you more miserable."

"He only wants to say good-bye. I owe him that at least," responded Volanna.

"I wish I could believe that. But if I know Brendal, he wants more than a tender parting." Kalley's red curls bounced with the emphatic shake of her head. "I'll wager he has hatched up some scheme to get around your father's command. I tell you that no good can come from such a meeting. Begin now to do what you must do eventually: forget Brendal. Set him on a shelf in your memory as your first taste of love and point your heart toward the future. You don't have to see him; write a letter. I will deliver it myself. Your wound will be probed no further, and you can begin to heal."

For the first time that morning Volanna stirred from her listlessness, and fire flashed from her eyes. "Do you realize that I, the daughter of a king—who lives in a majestic castle and wears the finest clothes in the land, who dines daily on cornfed beef, pheasant, blueberries, smoked cheese, and wine, who is entertained almost nightly by minstrels, dancers, musicians, puppeteers, and mimes—am actually a slave? You have often told me that I am the envy of every milkmaid and chargirl in the kingdom. If they only knew! Where is the scullery girl who is forbidden to leave her front door without a preplanned itinerary and military escort? Where is the barmaid whose every hour is planned and managed by the demands of royal protocol? Is there a girl in the kingdom for whom any contact with an eligible suitor is banned by royal decree, who has no say in so important a decision as whom she will wed?"

"But, Volanna," Kalley said, "most fathers arrange the matches for their daughters. Especially among the nobility."

"But not without their daughter's consent," corrected Volanna. "Can you think of any girl in Valomar who was forced to marry against her will? Remember the Earl of Fenstar's daughter, Narova? Her father had pledged her to some count in Oranth, but when Narova revealed that she was already in love with Sir Pentamon's son, the Earl dissolved the contract. But do you think such consideration could be given to me, the king's daughter? No! The king's daughter is not really a woman; she is a commodity, a bartering medium to be exchanged for the kingdom's political advantage. Her feelings don't matter; her wishes can be disregarded; her happiness is unimportant."

"I know how you must feel, Volanna, but your greater privileges do carry greater responsibilities. It's the price of being a princess."

"It is too high a price," retorted Volanna. "I don't want to be a princess; I just want to be loved and cherished. I don't care if I have to dress in rags and live in a thatch-roofed mud cottage. But it doesn't matter what I want, does it? As you said, the thing is done. My father made a vow, and he will never relent. I will go see Brendal for the last time. Then I will learn to live with my future."

When the sun was midway between its zenith and the western horizon, the two girls dressed in the plain clothes they had used for the fair. They then slipped out of the castle, closely following a laden tinker's cart across the drawbridge, and made their way through the city streets to the farmers' market square.

True to his promise, Brendal was there, leaning against the stall of a large plow horse, idly chewing on a piece of straw. Volanna left Kalley to examine the fruits and flowers of a nearby produce stand. Then alone she wound her way through the labyrinth of stalls, Brendal following at a discreet distance, until she could slip behind a wall of crates stacked just over the height of a man's head.

"Volanna," Brendal whispered, moving to her with open arms.

"No, Brendal," she warned as she pushed him away. "We can't. It will only make things worse to stir up feelings we can't fulfill."

"But we can fulfill them. And we will."

"No, we cannot. We are not married, and we can never be."

"Yes, we can," he whispered, "in just a few nights. Now listen carefully. I have everything arranged—no, don't say anything, just listen— I have everything arranged for us to escape tomorrow night. We can make it through Blackmore Forest and reach the border of Lochlaund before the next morning. Here is what you need to do—"

"Brendal, don't be a fool! We cannot do this. We would surely be caught. I would be locked up in a tower forever, and you would be punished in a way that would make you useless as a husband."

"We will not be caught," said Brendal emphatically.

"But think about it, Brendal. What kind of life would we have? Banished from our homeland, estranged from our families, raising children cut off from their heritage—"

"But we would have each other," he said as he caught her up in his arms. "Nothing else matters." He pressed burning kisses to her forehead and cheeks as he muttered, "They can't do this to you. You have a right to your own happiness. You should be free to live your own life and pursue your own dreams. Besides, your estrangement from your family would not last. In time your father would forgive you and we could come home again."

Volanna's resistance dissolved as she melted into his embrace. A lifetime of obedience had conditioned her to accept her father's will reflexively as her own rule of behavior. Despite the wrenching despair she felt at her thwarted betrothal to Brendal, she had not entertained a serious doubt that she would obey her father. But now, encircled by the white-hot touch of Brendal's arms, she saw her father's will as a cold, dark shadow that would eclipse forever the dancing sunlight of Brendal's love, and she could not bear it.

As her body relaxed, so did her resistance to Brendal's appeal. She thrilled at the vibrant warmth of his throaty whisper and the throbbing pressure of his firm, broad chest. Duty to her father and kingdom were driven to the edges of her consciousness. Before long she had agreed to leave with Brendal the following midnight and ride to neighboring Lochlaund, where they would secretly wed and reside.

Volanna listened carefully as Brendal explained her part of the escape, then at his insistence, repeated back to him the details as he corrected and affirmed. When he was satisfied that she understood the plan thoroughly, they left their hiding place separately and in opposite directions.

For the rest of that day and the next, Volanna busied herself with preparations for their escape. She could not bring herself to tell Kalley of her plan. She sent the poor girl into town with a list containing every reasonable errand or purchase she could think of, more to keep her away than to fill any real need. Indeed, she found that since her meeting with Brendal, she could hardly bear to have Kalley around, and the girl's tendency to prattle had little to do with it. Deceit and duplicity were utterly foreign to Volanna's nature, and she was fearful that Kalley would detect her guilty secret in her failure to meet her friend's eyes, her artificial cheeriness, her blushing deflection of all conversation about her meeting with Brendal, or even by the pounding of her heart, which she was sure could be heard across the room.

She even found herself agitated and suspicious at the most innocent of Kalley's questions: "Do you want your red robe mended for Sunday's banquet?" "Shall I tell the Duchess of Elvay that you will meet with her on Tuesday next to plan the Maypole Festival?" At best Volanna wondered impatiently, *Why can't she handle such things her-*

self? And at worst, *She suspects something and is trying to trick me into revealing that I won't be here when these things happen.*

A thousand times Volanna thought of bringing Kalley in on the secret, but she could not do it. She told herself that this was for Kalley's own good; the less she knew, the less she would have to answer for when Volanna was found to be missing. But in reality it was because she knew Kalley would not approve. Kalley would be solidly on the side of the king and queen, parroting their obsession with duty, subservience, and abdication of self, and agreeing with their distrust of Brendal.

Everyone was against her. Everyone had an agenda for her life. No one cared what she wanted. Very well, then. They would all be sorry when they found that their lack of interest in her happiness had driven her away.

This angry resentment and sense of violated selfhood festered in Volanna's mind as she selected the few things she could take with her. They would have only three horses between them: one for each to ride and a packhorse to carry everything they would own in their new life. She remembered Brendal's instructions: *Select only the most practical and nondescript clothing. We don't want anyone in Lochlaund reporting that royalty has settled among them. The most valuable thing you can bring is gold. Draw all you can of your allotment from the treasury. With that we can purchase our needs in our new home.* Volanna complied as best she could.

When Amram the bookseller called on Tuesday afternoon, Volanna looked through several volumes of poetry, a romance of Galleson the Troubadour, and a history of the wars of Perivale before she selected a curious volume of folk cures for common ailments, including colds, warts, colic, barrenness, aching joints, and toothaches. Before she paid the bookseller, she asked if he would be so kind as to convey two parcels of hers back to his shop.

"It would save my servant a trip into the city," she explained. "I will pay you fifteen pence and will send someone to pick up the parcels later this afternoon."

The bookseller readily agreed, and with the help of a palace porter, carried two large bundles containing Volanna's makeshift trousseau to his cart. Later that afternoon Brendal's squire picked them up at Amram's shop and loaded them, along with Brendal's gear, onto the packhorse.

That evening Volanna attended dinner with her parents, who were entertaining an official emissary from Sorendale. King Tallis was suffering from a pounding headache, but he managed to listen with an earnest expression of apparent interest as his guest gave a detailed account of the great castle King Morgamund was constructing in his homeland. Unwell though he was, Tallis could not resist offering a word of advice to his neighbor. He explained how he had installed angled chutes in his kitchen to empty waste into the moat on the downstream side of the castle, thus keeping the water in his moat, which was fed by the River Tynor, pure and fresh. The enlightened Tallis had long suspected a connection between filth and disease and was very protective of the rivers and streams in his land. As a result the people of Valomar (and Meridan which, under the rule of the late King Alfron, had adopted King Tallis's program) were known to be the most disease free of any people in that part of the continent.

Rather than finding herself bored beyond endurance, Volanna was grateful for the two men's verbosity; it removed the need for her to engage in much conversation. When she did speak, she was terrified that any misspoken word, any false inflection, any tremor in her voice would expose her guilty secret.

"Volanna, are you feeling well?" asked Queen Ravella.

"Oh, yes, quite well, Mother," answered Volanna. "I . . . I'm just a little tired tonight."

"It's no wonder you're tired," said the queen. "You haven't eaten enough to keep a titmouse alive."

Volanna suddenly realized it might be many hours before she could eat again and began a determined attack on her plate. When she had completed her meal, she excused herself, claiming a need for rest, and returned to her room. She dismissed Kalley with instructions not to disturb her in the morning, explaining that she wanted to sleep late.

After Kalley left, Volanna stripped off her dinner gown and donned the dark gray breeches and tunic of a peasant boy. She tied up her hair and stuffed it into a dark-colored sheepskin hat. She looked at herself in the mirror. The disguise would not fool anyone up close. Her delicate features could never be mistaken for a boy's, nor could the womanly contours of her form asserting themselves against the sacklike cut of the tunic. But seen from a distance or at a casual glance, she thought most observers would not suspect she was a girl.

With all preparations completed, Volanna curled up in her chair and tried to sleep, but she was too much on edge. Her ability to find serene pleasure in anticipation had vanished, and impatience filled the vacuum, causing time to move at the pace of a growing tree. She tried to read from her new book but found herself staring at the pages with unfocused eyes as her mind drifted to thoughts of Brendal. Was his part of the plan going well? Would he meet her at the agreed time and place? What if he were detained—or caught?

She laid aside her book and rechecked her clothing. She thought through Brendal's instructions several times, checking her preparations item by item. She paced. She looked out her tower window. She counted the stones in her chamber wall as she listened to the voice of the town crier drifting toward her window, calling the ninth hour, the tenth, the eleventh. She was beginning to think the man must have fallen asleep as she waited for what seemed half the remaining night before he finally called the midnight hour.

Volanna slowly opened her door and peered into the antechamber where Kalley slept. She waited until she could hear the girl's soft, regular breathing, then she tiptoed past the bed and reached the door to the stairway. She drew the bolt with great care and holding her breath, eased the door open. To her horror the great hinges protested their awakening with a low but dissonant growl and Kalley stirred in her covers. Volanna froze where she stood. She held the door still and listened, but Kalley made no more sound.

Volanna looked through the opening into the spiral stairway, lit by a single torch set in the stone wall above the door. She slipped through the door, closed it gently behind her, and slowly began to descend the stairway. She took great care not to let her feet scrape on the steps for the narrow stairwell amplified each sound like a trumpet.

When she reached the second floor, she kept to the shadows behind a pillar and looked into the hallway. She was thirty feet away from the main stairway to the ground floor, and to reach it she would have to pass the door to her parents' bedchamber.

Volanna left the shadows and tiptoed into the hallway. She had passed a few steps beyond the bedchamber door when to her horror she heard it creak open. Quickly she slid into the black shadow behind a pillar and flattened herself against the stone wall. She heard the door close and a rustling of skirts as footsteps approached her hiding place. She drew further back into the narrow space, not daring to breathe, as a serving maid carrying an empty tray bustled past her so closely that she felt the maid's skirts brush her ankle. No doubt her father had required a poultice or a potion for his head-ache, thought Volanna.

She dared not move until she heard the serving maid's footsteps descending the stairway and echoing in the cavernous great hall below. Then with her heart thumping like a drum, she slipped from her hiding place and tiptoed to the stairs. With panic pushing against caution, she descended like a desperate fugitive the wide stone steps she had descended in glory two nights before.

She was now in the great hall. It was lit only by a single brazier burning low near the center of the room and casting giant, flickering shadows behind the statuary and the mounted hunting trophies that lined the walls. In daylight one took no notice of these stone images and animal heads, but in the silence and gloom of midnight, they seemed to Volanna a palpable and foreboding presence, as if granted some muted sentience during the hours of man's sleep. As Volanna crept into the hall, she felt the malignant eyes of every severed head upon her as if silently accusing her of violating hours that rightfully belonged to them. Her spine chilled, and the back of her neck prickled.

Fearing she would be seen by the serving maid, she moved silently from the stairway into the black shadow of a life-sized, eroded marble sculpture of a dying warrior brought to Valomar from the islands of the southern sea. The face, though eyeless and ruined like that of a decaying corpse, seemed to be watching her as if waiting for some false move or misstep to justify descending from his pedestal and giving chase. A stab of panic shot through her belly, and she moved away as quickly as she could. She felt certain the hideous head was turning to follow her, but she dared not look back to see.

She kept in the shadows near the walls and stole silently from table to statuary to pillar until she reached the kitchen door. With heart in throat, she eased it open just enough to peek in. A single lantern set on a stand near the far wall provided dim illumination of the large room. Seeing no sign of movement, she slipped inside. Directly across the room she could see the door that gave access to the moat, now closed. Cautiously she crept forward with her eyes focused on that door, the last barrier to her freedom.

Suddenly the door opened and the serving maid entered carrying a bucket of water. Volanna, utterly exposed, froze, and her eyes went wide with horror. She knew she was caught. But the maid only set her bucket down and turned to close the door; intent on her errand, she had not noticed Volanna. As the girl turned, Volanna jumped aside and crouched behind the cutting table. The maid emptied her bucket into a wooden tub, then went back outdoors to fill it again.

As soon as the door closed, Volanna stood and looked desperately around the room for a safer hiding place. Just above the cutting table was the hanging door of the innovative garbage chute Tallis had designed. Forgetting the odor and slime likely to accumulate within such a device, Volanna climbed onto the cutting table and into the chute, then gently pulled the door closed on her hiding place.

As she hid behind the closed chute door, Volanna was woefully unappreciative of the hygienic function of her father's invention and acutely aware of the assault it made on her nostrils. It seemed to her that the malodorous spirit of every scrap of fish, fowl, cabbage, onion, or cheese that had passed through that tunnel lived on in a reek that was almost making her retch. She did not notice that her feet were slowly slipping on the lumpy, waxlike coating of slime that covered the floor of the tunnel.

Just as the serving maid came back into the kitchen with another bucket, Volanna's feet lost their tenuous purchase on the floor of the chute, and she plummeted downward, screaming involuntarily as she slid. When the serving maid heard the scream, eerily muffled by the hollow tunnel and gradually diminishing as Volanna slid away, she dropped the bucket, emitted her own scream, and tried to run out of the kitchen. But she slipped in the spilled water and fell flat on her face, flailing and squealing like a hare in the jaws of a fox as she tried frantically to get up.

The guard on the parapet was overlooking the moat on the downstream side when he heard the scream. He ran toward the sound. As he leapt down the stairway toward the kitchen door, a gray-clad figure shot from the castle wall and plunged into the moat just below the post he had vacated. The maid's scream not only diverted the guard's attention, it covered the sound of Volanna's splash as well.

By the time the guard reached the kitchenmaid, she was delirious with terror. "It was the ghost of the castle, I tell you!" she blubbered. "I've heard it before, I have, and I've tried to tell everybody it haunts this place at night. But nobody ever listens. It was awful, I tell you— screechin' through the halls like the devil hisself was after it."

But as no one else had heard the sound and the maid was wont to report unearthly doings when on nighttime duty alone, the guard dismissed her fright as the product of an overactive imagination fed by the shadowed silence of the sleeping castle. He calmed her down and sent her to bed, and everything returned to normal.

Meanwhile Volanna swam frantically across the moat to where Brendal awaited in the shadows at the edge of the nearby trees. Then pulling herself from the water and scrambling up the bank, she dashed toward him.

"What took you so long?" he whispered in greeting. It was just as well the darkness hid the glare she shot at him in response. Both looked quickly back toward the castle, but seeing no signs of pursuit or discovery, they turned and slipped deeper into the trees to the place Brendal had tethered their horses.

He had her change of clothing ready—a plain brown tunic and breeches similar to the outfit she was wearing. She slipped behind a copse to change, then bundled up the wet clothing and gave it to Brendal to add to their packs. They then mounted up and rode away, picking up a narrow trail that would lead them away from the castle and the town and into the depths of Blackmore Forest.

CHAPTER SEVEN

LOST IN THE DARK

olanna and Brendal felt vulnerable and exposed on the open road, but they passed nothing more than an occasional farmhouse, asleep like the rest of the world with windows shuttered against the night like closed eyelids. Soon they topped a low hill and saw in the valley before them the gray expanse of Blackmore Forest, treetops wafting in the soft breeze like the waves of a vast sea. In less than a half hour they reached the forest. For the first time in her life Volanna found darkness more comforting than light. Her breath came easier and her wary muscles relaxed as the inky shadows enfolded them.

In moments their eyes grew accustomed to the shadowy world of the forest, and they began to weave their way through the trees single file, Brendal in front with the packhorse tied behind and Volanna in the rear. They talked little. Anything more than necessary warnings about low limbs and fallen logs seemed an affront to the gloomy silence around them. The stillness was broken only by the muted clop of the horses' hooves on the leafy forest floor and an occasional rumble of thunder, low and heavy like the growl of some distant creature. Once Volanna thought she heard the rustling of a large animal moving through the brush just behind them. She told Brendal about it, and he stopped briefly to listen, then dismissed it, saying, "It was probably just a deer."

For a time Volanna remained alert, but eventually the relentless rhythm of the plodding horse began to wear away the tension that had gripped her from the moment she had agreed to Brendal's scheme. As she relaxed, ramparts she had erected in her mind against rational thinking began to weaken and crumble, and thoughts she had kept at bay assaulted her with a vengeance.

What would her father do when they found her gone? She tried to picture him angry, bellowing curses and striking his scepter against the flagstone floor, loudly disowning his daughter and banishing her from Valomar forever. But the picture would not form, and she knew why. She had never seen her father lose his temper. His anger arose rarely and only in response to some deliberate violation of the law or in defense of a wronged victim; it was never because of a personal affront, and he was never out of control.

Even on the occasions when he had punished her with his birch switch—as for the time she and Kalley were caught trying to empty a chamber pot from her window onto a cat sleeping below—it was always with a calm detachment devoid of passion, with the clear intent of preventing a repetition of the offense. Soon afterward he would find or invent an occasion to pick up his little girl and embrace her in a cheek-to-beard hug that never failed to melt the hurt away. And such warm, fatherly embraces did not cease as she grew out of childhood. Her heart grew heavy as she wondered if she would ever again be warmed by those embraces.

She thought she knew exactly how her father would respond when her empty room was discovered: he would be crushed with grief. She could see the sadness in his eyes as she had seen it on the day messengers brought news of his brother's death three years ago. And she knew the cause of his grief would not be his ruined plans or compromised vow; it would simply be that he was certain a daughter whom he loved dearly had chosen a course that would place her beyond the possibility of real happiness.

As she thought of her father, she began to see for the first time that, as an owl is blinded by sunlight, she had been blinded by the glare of her desire. She looked into the unfathomable darkness of Blackmore Forest into which Brendal was leading her and saw that her choice to follow him had put real joy beyond her reach. She knew she could not hope to find peace of heart or freedom from guilt for the pain she was inflicting on those who loved her. In her imagination the path had not been dark at all, but filled with sunlight and laughter.

Volanna looked up through the tears now streaming down her face and saw Brendal's dim form ahead, slouched and swaying sleepily in his saddle. She knew she did not truly love him. How could she claim to be capable of love while betraying a love like that her parents had for her? Her willingness to walk away from their love so lightly and hurt them so deeply called into question her own capacity to love at all. To think she would be capable of loving Brendal deeply while turning her back on the deepest love she had yet known was outrageous nonsense, and with bitter regret, she now knew it beyond question.

"Brendal," she called hoarsely. He did not hear. "Brendal," she called again. He stopped his horse and half turned in the saddle.

"What is it?"

"I can't do it."

"Can't do what?"

"I can't go on. It's all wrong. I'm sorry, Brendal, I've made a terrible mistake. We must go back."

"Go back? You can't be serious."

"I am serious. Things will never work out between us as long as we are estranged from our families. We could never build a solid life together; we would have no foundation. I knew better, but I allowed myself to be blinded. I wanted something so much I would not let myself see the true cost. The price of our love is the killing of loves that have rightful claims on us already. If we are willing to treat those who love us so cruelly, it means that in our hearts, love itself is dead. It's like spending all of one's money for a wallet; the price renders the purchase useless."

"You are your father's daughter all right. The 'philosopher king,' they call him—full of fancy words but short on practical, strong-minded thinking. Now come on, let's get moving. The thunder is getting closer, and we want to get across the river before it rains." Brendal turned forward and prodded his horse.

Volanna's blood quickened at this unexpected slander of her father. She pulled up short and replied with heat in her voice, "If by weak-mindedness you mean commitment to the ideals of love and loyalty, then yes, I am my father's daughter. I inherited that imbecility. And I am going back. You do what you want." She turned her horse abruptly and began to retrace their steps at a canter. Brendal wheeled about, quickly rode up beside her, and roughly took her by the arm.

"No, you don't!" he growled.

"Let me go!" Volanna shouted, struggling and twisting to free herself from his bruising grip.

Brendal said nothing but took her by the waist and swung her onto his own horse as she flailed at him with elbows and fists. He clamped her tightly against his chest until for lack of breath she stopped struggling. Then turning his horse back the way they had been headed, he continued into the heart of Blackmore Forest. The two other horses followed closely behind.

"You can't do this to me!" hissed Volanna. "Abduction is a serious crime in Valomar. You could be imprisoned for years or even executed."

"By whom?"

"By my father, the king."

Brendal laughed. "Your father doesn't know it, but his days as king are numbered. I have nothing to fear from him."

"You are talking nonsense. My father is loved by all of Valomar. No one would think of doing him harm."

"You have not been keeping your dainty little ears open. Many in Valomar are convinced that your father is about to sell out our nation's independence on the madman's dream that Perivale's empire is about to be reborn. Such a catastrophe must not be allowed. A plan to prevent it is already in place, and as you will see very soon, you have a part to play in that plan."

"What do you mean?" Volanna was beginning to be alarmed.

"You will soon know."

They rode on in tense silence for half an hour more. Once or twice when Volanna felt Brendal's restraining arm relax, she tried to wrench free in the desperate hope she could escape into the woods before he could dismount. But each time Brendal's reflexes awoke and he roughly resumed his viselike grip.

The thunder became louder and more frequent, and the lightning drew closer. Soon it began to rain. Brendal pulled from his saddlebag a deerskin blanket, which he spread over his head and back, leaving Volanna uncovered. "Yours is packed in your own saddlebags," he said. "Since you have been a naughty little girl, you will just have to get wet." Volanna said nothing.

How long they rode in the drenching rain Volanna did not know, but ever afterward she remembered this night as among the most miserable of her life. She was soaked to the bone. Her saturated clothing clung to her skin like moss to a wet stone. Her hair became a sodden mass of dripping rings and mats. Only her back, pressed tightly against Brendal, was dry. She became chilled and began to shiver and sniffle.

But the worst of it was the change in Brendal. All pretense of love was gone. He dropped his graceful facade of courtesy now that it was no longer needed to secure her trust. He maintained a running monologue of complaint against her father and his stagnant policies. The army Tallis maintained was much too small. He had missed countless opportunities to annex portions of neighboring countries with very little political or military risk. He should allow more latitude for his subjects in certain areas of personal behavior and private pleasures. His taxation policies were much too timid; the citizens of Valomar were prosperous enough that their assessment could be doubled without serious protest. If he would aggressively mine the country's virgin reserves of silver, Valomar could build itself into the showplace and trade center of the Seven Kingdoms. Certainly there was no need for a kingdom with the potential might and riches of Valomar to become a vassal state to Meridan. If there was to be a new empire, a more progressive monarch than Tallis could see to it that Valomar, not Meridan, became its flagship state.

"And tonight we are taking the first step toward placing on the throne of Valomar a king with a clear vision of Valomar's potential," he said.

"Brendal, you are a traitor and a fool. Surely you don't expect me to help you in this futile and criminal rebellion. Let me go."

"You will help in this rebellion whether you wish it or not. I will not let you go. And you had best mind your tongue with me, princess. I do not enjoy being called fool or traitor, especially by one who has turned her back on her own father and mother."

Brendal's barb struck home, and Volanna sank into a heavy silence. The rain mixed with her bitter tears as it streamed from her brow and cheeks.

They came to the north edge of the forest. By the frequent flashes of lightning that lit the plain before them, they could see in the distance the tall oak and cypress trees that lined the River Tynor. Brendal stopped before venturing onto the plain and looked intently in all directions as if searching for something. Apparently satisfied, he rode into the clearing as the lightning flashed and was followed closely by a deafening clap of thunder. The moment of light illumined the plain like midday, and in that instant Volanna was sure she saw a figure on horseback on the rise just to their right. She had no idea who the lone rider might be, but she gambled that he could be a source of help for her.

"Help me! I'm being abduct—" she screamed at the top of her voice. Brendal's hand clapped roughly across her mouth, and quicker than thought she bit it. He jerked his hand away, then brought it back sharply against the side of her head.

"You little vixen!" he growled. "Do you mean to wake up the whole forest? I ought to throw you off this horse and leave you to the beasts you have undoubtedly roused."

"Please do!" retorted Volanna.

As they rode past the rise where Volanna had seen the other rider, she kept her eyes fixed to the crest where he had stood, hoping the next flash would reveal who he was. But when the lightning came, the figure was gone.

In silence they rode the remaining distance to the river and were preparing to descend the sloping banks into the ford when the lightning revealed another mounted figure. Again Volanna shouted until Brendal squeezed her ribs with such force that she could not draw breath. But the rider had heard and was now loping toward them. As he drew closer, she could see by the frequent flashes that he was an armored knight, and her hope of rescue rose. His shield was slung to the side of his horse, and she strained to make out the crest upon it. Brendal neither tensed, nor drew rein, nor gave other sign of alarm as the rider drew up beside them. And in the next flash of light, Volanna understood why. She was looking into the harsh, craggy features of Sir Borethane.

Borethane sat in his saddle utterly relaxed, oblivious to the rain. "You are late," he rumbled in a voice that without effort had the texture and force of a bullhorn. "And I think you have not had quite the cooperation from the princess that you led us to believe you would have."

"She came willingly enough, Father, but in the middle of Blackmore Forest she turned cowardly and tried to run back to papa. Now she insists that our marriage is off and that she will go on to Meridan like an obedient little daughter."

"She is a fool!" Borethane growled. "That means we must resort to our secondary plan immediately. Sir Thringal, Sir Laurenfel, and Sir Agualot were to be watching for you. They should have followed you at enough distance to avoid arousing the princess's suspicions."

"They are out there," replied Brendal, "and they may as well have announced themselves and ridden with us. They have been crashing about the forest like oxen in a pottery shop. We heard one of them behind us in the forest and saw Sir Laurenfel on a rise not far back."

"Incompetent bumblers!" rumbled Borethane. "And to think the future of Valomar depends on our working with such men. But enough talk. Dawn is little more than an hour away. We must get on with things.

"Your highness," for the first time Borethane addressed Volanna, "time is short, but to be fair I will spare a moment and give you a final opportunity to avoid the fate you have laid upon yourself by your unfortunate change of heart. Your royal position makes it impossible for you to appreciate the fact that your father's unenlightened policies have gotten Valomar locked in a course of cowardly regression. The country's only hope to keep pace with the future is for men with foresight and vision to gain access to the throne. We thought Brendal's marriage to you would give us that kind of access, so we set him to pursuing your hand. We assumed you would be the designated heir to Tallis's crown. And with you as queen, it would be only a small step to persuade the Hall of Knights to crown your husband king. With Brendal as king, the more progressive knights, such as Thringal, Agualot, Laurenfel, and myself would have a voice in enacting laws more favorable to Valomar's future.

"But Tallis's foolhardy vow to wed you, and along with you the entire Kingdom of Valomar, to the crown prince of Meridan both undid our plans and made the need for action more urgent. Therefore we quickly planned your elopement. Your marriage to Brendal would, of course, undo the wedding treaty with Meridan. And we believe your father, being of a forgiving nature, would eventually accept Brendal as a son-in-law and reinstate you as heir to the throne.

"On the other hand, we could not be certain that Tallis would let the matter drop so easily. He might arrange an extradition treaty with Lochlaund or secure permission to send a contingent of men after you and Brendal. That is why Thringal, Laurenfel, and Agualot are here. Not only did we watch the trail to defend you from pursuers, we are prepared to cross into Lochlaund to defend you against any attempt by Tallis' men to bring you home. Your refusal to honor your promise to wed Brendal does not weaken our resolve to undo Tallis's plan to sell out Valomar. However it does force us to take more extreme measures than we had hoped would be necessary. Brendal will now take you to the isolated cottage in Lochlaund that we had reserved for your wedding night. There he will do with you against your will what he would have done with your compliance had you been wed. A deflowered princess will be useless as currency to trade away Valomar's independence. The three knights and I will stay at the adjacent manor, ready to defend you against any attempt at rescue. In short, you will be held hostage until Tallis complies with our demands. And every day he waits, more and more of his men will defect to our cause. There are many in the Hall of Knights who are disaffected and tired of the lack of forward direction in Valomar.

"So you see, my dear princess, the fate of Valomar is in your hands. You can either marry my son of your own volition, causing little more harm than the loss of your father's pet dream and your own temporary estrangement from him, or you will be ravished by force, held hostage, and bring about a probable civil war, which will end in your father being deposed. It is your choice. Which will it be?"

"I would marry a leper before I would marry your son."

"Why you little—!" Again Brendal clapped Volanna fiercely on the side of the head.

"Stop it!" bellowed Borethane. "Save your violence till it's needed. The princess has made her choice. Let the consequences be on her head. On to the river, son. I will remain here and await our fellow patriots."

Brendal spurred his horse forward, and the packhorse and Volanna's gelding followed. They made their way down the slippery bank and into the water of the ford. They had just reached the center of the river when a deafening thunderclap split the air as a blinding bolt of lightning shattered the trunk of a towering cypress tree on the bank ahead. Brendal's horse screamed and reared sharply. It lost its footing on the river bottom and fell back with an enormous splash. Brendal lost his grip on Volanna as he was pitched into the water on the upstream side of the horse. Volanna fell to the downstream side. She immediately dived underwater and swam furiously with the current, determined to put as much distance as she could between herself and Brendal before she had to surface for air.

Brendal lost valuable seconds disentangling himself from the doeskin cape and fighting his way around the three panicked horses. When Volanna surfaced some thirty yards downstream, she heard a confusion of splashing and whinnying and the bellowing of the two men trying to guess the direction of her escape. She filled her lungs with air and dived again. This time she reached the place where the curving river entered the edge of the forest. She came up for air and heard the splashing of Brendal swimming some distance behind her and the angry cursing of Borethane as he rode along the bank and scanned the river for a glimpse of her swimming form. She dived under again and swam desperately. When she surfaced, she was hidden by the shadows of the trees along the bank until another angry bolt of lightning sundered the darkness.

"There she is!" shouted Borethane as he slid off his horse and clambered along the bank toward her. "Brendal! She's just ahead of you, where the river enters the forest."

Brendal swam furiously toward the spot.

At the sound of Borethane's shout, Volanna dived again and swam deeper into the woods. She hoped the blackness of the forest would hide her from further blasts of lightning. She was near exhaustion. She made her way to the far side of the river and ran her hand along the bank until she felt an overhanging cluster of tangled roots. She grasped a twisted root the size of her arm and began to pull herself out of the water. But the root gave way with a resounding snap, and she splashed noisily back into the river.

"Over there!" bellowed Borethane, pointing uselessly in the darkness, but Brendal had heard the splash and was already swimming toward it.

Volanna, realizing that silence had become more important than speed, made very little movement and let herself drift with the current. She stayed close to the far side of the river and kept as little of her head as possible above the surface. Brendal was rapidly closing the distance between them. She felt along the bank until she found another cluster of overhanging roots that covered a hollow in the bank. She refused to think about what kind of slimy, fanged, or coiled creatures might nest in such a hole and ducked under the roots, pressing herself into the narrow space and leaving only her nose and eyes above the surface.

She heard the snapping and cracking of roots as Brendal pulled himself from the water near the place where she had tried to get out. Across the river she heard the clank of Borethane's armor as he tramped along the bank looking for some sign of her. Brendal picked up a long, straight tree limb and began walking along the edge toward the place where she now hid, thrashing the underbrush and plunging the pole into the water, probing the spaces and holes between the roots and rocks.

"Curse this blasted darkness!" she heard him mutter. "She cannot have gone far, but without light to see by, she might as well be a thousand miles away."

Volanna heard Brendal's approaching footsteps and his probing pole as it raked and plunged along the bank. In a moment the roots above her head sagged with his weight, pressing her head downward until her nose was under water. His pole scraped by only inches from her face. Volanna prayed desperately that he would move on, or take at least another step, before she had to breathe. But instead he stopped, leaned on his pole, and called to Borethane.

"It's no use, Father. She could be right under our noses and we'd never find her in this darkness. We may as well go back to our horses and wait until morning."

"You don't seem to understand your position," Borethane answered. "With the girl in your possession you have bartering power for your protection. Without her you will be hanged or worse if caught. If we don't find the princess, you can never set foot in Valomar again. And by morning she could be completely out of our reach."

"But we have no idea which way she went. She could have gone on downstream, she could have climbed out on either side, or she could be hiding within earshot right now. To find her in this hour would be a matter of pure chance."

"We have no choice but to take that chance, thanks to your carelessness. One would think the tournament champion of Valomar could maintain control of a mere girl for—"

"You could not have done any better!" Brendal shouted. "A tree exploded twenty yards in front of us, and the stupid horse stood straight up."

"You shouldn't have let go of her for any reason. You have put our plans in great jeopardy."

"*Our* plans!" said Brendal bitterly. "You mean *your* plans. I don't know why I let you suck me into this plot of yours. All I wanted was the girl. You are the one who craves the throne of Valomar. You are the one who hatched this unworkable plot that has us all slogging around in the rain in the wee hours of the morning trying to find—"

"Don't you go blaming me for the rain."

"And don't you go blaming me for the girl's escape."

"Right now I'm blaming you for talking instead of searching. We've got to find that girl."

"How? Just tell me how!"

"Use a little common sense. We know she did not get out of the water; we heard her try it, and had she succeeded, we would have heard her thrashing through the woods. So she has got to be still in the river. It is not likely that in her state of panic she would have stopped and hidden, but if she did, your pole or the lightning would have revealed her by now. So she is likely downstream and surely not a great distance ahead. Swimming would be too noisy, so she must be drifting with the current. If we follow, she will make some sort of mistake or run up against some obstacle that will reveal her. Let's move on downstream. Continue your poling as we go. Now hurry! We've wasted too much time already."

With an obscene oath, Brendal jerked up his pole and began tramping downriver, probing the bank as he went. The root depressing Volanna's head sprang upward, allowing her mouth to break the surface, and she was able to draw her first breath in almost two minutes, which she did with a slight, involuntary gasp.

Borethane stopped. "What was that?" he asked. Brendal stood still, and they both listened. From a tree above they heard a soft, "Hoo-hooo."

"It's only an owl," said Brendal. "Is my brave father getting so jumpy he hears his prey in every sound and sees her in every shadow? Let us hurry, dear Father; we've wasted too much time already."

Volanna's lungs were burning for lack of air, but she dared not breathe deeply until the searching men had gone twenty more paces downstream. She remained in the water until she could no longer hear their crashing footsteps and angry cursing, then climbed up the bank and half stumbled, half crawled into the woods.

The thunder and lightning ceased, and the rain settled into a steady, unrelenting drizzle. Between the water dripping into her eyes and the darkness of the night, Volanna could hardly see. Brambles and thorns clawed at her legs and tore at her clothing. Low-hanging tree limbs snagged her soggy hair. Over and over she stubbed her toes on rocks and bruised her shins on fallen logs. She held her hands before her to protect her face, and they soon were raw and bleeding from scrapes and bumps against tree bark and boulders. More than once she heard some creature slipping through the brush or a menacing growl warning her away from some nest or lair.

Volanna was near the end of her strength. She wanted nothing more than to find a dry place under a rock overhang or a hollow bole where she could curl up and sleep until morning. She knew she could be passing within inches of many such shelters that would have been as welcome as her own bed had they not been hidden by the rain and darkness.

She had lost all sense of direction. For all she knew she might have circled and could be angling back toward the river, where she would meet her abductors head-on. She felt a growing urge to stop, lay herself down beside a tree, and just wait for whatever fate had in store. But she knew that to yield to such an urge could be fatal, so she stumbled on, wondering if the dawn would ever come.

Suddenly she tripped on a loose stone and sprawled on her face in a puddle of mud. Wearily she rose to her hands and knees. She crawled to a nearby tree and rolled over against it, panting from the effort and shivering with cold. She didn't think she could go on any further. Her eyes were heavy. She closed them for several minutes and would have fallen asleep but for the unrelenting torture of the rain.

When she opened her eyes again, she thought she saw a distant pinpoint of orange light. It was very dim, like the momentary glow of a candlewick after the flame has gone. The longer she stared, the more convinced she became that it was merely a trick of the mind brought on by fatigue. She closed her eyes again, counted slowly to ten, and then opened them. The light was still there. Her heart leapt with the first hope she had felt in hours. But after struggling stiffly to her feet and stumbling toward the light, she realized that it could just as easily signal danger as hope. It could be a fire that Brendal and Borethane had somehow managed to start in spite of the rain, or it could be a window in the cottage where Brendal had plotted to rob her of her maidenhood. But her desire for light itself, almost stronger than her craving for warmth and comfort, drove her forward.

She came to a muddy ravine separating her from the light she followed. She did not want to descend into the crevasse for it would mean she would lose sight of the light. She walked along it several yards in both directions, but finding no way to cross it, she finally half slid, half tumbled down the slippery side. In the bottom of the ravine she had to slog several steps through a thick, scummy mire before she could find a place to climb up the other side. After much sliding and grappling with slippery roots and loose stones, she managed to reach level ground again and sat gasping for breath as she searched eagerly for the light.

It was nowhere to be seen. In panic she got up and began to run. Unseen stones and whipping branches bruised and scraped her flesh, but it did not matter; she had to find the light. She ran until she could go no further, then sagged to her knees as cold despair numbed her heart. The light was gone, and so was all her hope.

She felt utterly alone, shut off forever from the warmth and light of love. There was no use in going on; with no light to lead her, she did not know how to find her way. She thought of the curse her mother said would follow in the wake of rebellion and knew she was receiving her just reward. She had turned her back on love; now love had abandoned her. Her folly had condemned her to wander eternally in this endless night, through this endless forest, borderless and unpeopled, tortured by this endless rain. Nothing else existed. Nothing else ever would. Wearily she fell forward on the wet earth and buried her face in her arms.

After a moment she thought she heard a distant sound. She lay quiet and listened. Soon she heard it again, a sound like that of an ax splitting a log. She looked up, and directly before her was the light— bright orange and not more than a hundred yards away. The hope she thought was dead leapt in her heart like a deer freed from a pit. She struggled to her feet and stumbled toward the light, whether as a moth to the flame or a ship to its haven she did not know. She only knew she could not do other than pursue the light.

As the muddy and bedraggled princess drew closer, she could see that the light came from the window of a cottage. Dawn was beginning to lighten the sky, and she could make out the dim outlines of a thatched roof overlaying a small room built against the bole of an enormous tree, obviously hollow and serving as part of the house. The window from which the light shone was cut into the tree itself. Blue smoke streamed from a stone chimney.

In spite of her craving for light and shelter, Volanna forced herself to be wary. This could be the cottage Brendal and Borethane had secured. She approached to within hailing distance but took care to remain concealed at the edge of the clearing surrounding the dwelling. She waited and watched. Presently the door opened and a tall man came out, picked up two split logs resting on a large stump, and then turned back toward the door. As he turned, Volanna saw his face, framed in a white, flowing beard. "The magician!" she whispered to herself. He showed no surprise when Volanna, afraid no more, emerged from her hiding place and stumbled toward him.

"Welcome, Dovey," he said as he took her by the shoulder and ushered her toward the door. "Come in. Come in."

CHAPTER EIGHT

JEPHTHAH'S DAUGHTER

An hour after Volanna entered the magician's cottage, she sat in a pillow-lined cane chair near the fire, which crackled cheerily in the stone fireplace. She was wrapped snugly in a woolen blanket and sipped a hot, honey-sweetened brew from a stoneware mug. She could not identify the mix of herbs it contained but found it soothing and restorative.

The newly risen sun streamed through the eastern window and glimmered on a large, orange, sleepy-eyed cat curled up on the hearth with its tail wrapped around its paws. The planked floor was covered with a woven rug, and the simple pine furniture was rough-hewn but sturdy and serviceable. One wall was filled with shelves sagging under the weight of hundreds of ancient books, all with leather bindings and gilt stampings. Her clothing, freshly washed, was spread to dry on a wooden rack beside the fireplace. The magician moved quietly about the room, finishing up the many little chores generated by Volanna's coming.

Immediately on her arrival, he had ushered her into the cottage's only other room—the one built into the hollow of the giant tree—and bade her sit on a three-legged stool while he filled a wooden tub, warming it with steaming water from a large pot that had been on the fire when she arrived. He gave her a towel and a blanket before withdrawing, and closed the curtain across the door. When she had undressed by the light of the lamp hanging at the window—the same lamp that had been her beacon in the forest—he asked her to give him her clothing through the curtain, and as she bathed, he washed the mud from them in a kitchen tub.

After Volanna had dried and wrapped herself in the blanket, she reentered the hearthroom to be met by the delicious aroma and welcome sound of sizzling bacon. The magician sat her in the chair near the fire, then on an oaken lap tray served the bacon—along with eggs, wheatcakes, and honey—which she ate ravenously. She had never enjoyed a breakfast more. When she was finished, the magician exchanged the tray for an earthenware jar of soothing balm. Once she had anointed her bruises and scratches, he gave her the cup of steaming brew and went about setting his house back in order.

With pots and plates washed and put away, the magician filled his own cup and sat down near the fire in a chair opposite Volanna. She looked into the face too wise to be young and too supple to be old. "I feel that I should know you—even that I have known you for a long time," she said. "Yet I'm sure I never saw you before your performance at the fair. I owe you a great debt for your shelter and kindness this morning, but—forgive me—I don't even know whom I should thank."

"You may call me Father Lucidis," answered the magician.

"You are not really a magician, are you, Father Lucidis?" she asked.

"I am sometimes called a magician just as you are sometimes called Dovey. That is, I am that but more than that."

"Somehow, I think there's no need to tell you who I am," Volanna replied. "I feel sure you know already."

"I do," said Father Lucidis. "You are Jephthah's daughter."

Volanna opened her mouth to correct him, but her tongue was arrested by the sudden realization that he was right. She remembered the story of the ancient warrior-judge Jephthah who, to secure victory in battle, vowed to sacrifice to the Master of the Universe the first living thing that met him when he returned home. He had expected to see cattle or sheep in his pastures or perhaps wild geese in the pond or a stag in the forest. But to his horror he encountered no living creature until the daughter on whom he doted ran joyfully from the house to embrace her returning father. The stricken judge felt bound to fulfill his vow, which he did after giving her thirty days to mourn with her virgin friends.

"Yes," said Volanna, "I am Jephthah's daughter. I am dead." She looked at Father Lucidis and saw that he knew exactly what she meant. Nevertheless she felt a compelling need to explain—to incarnate her jumble of thoughts into words whereby they could be displayed to bring order to the upheaval in her mind.

"The life I have known is over. The person I was and the person I thought I would become is dead, slain by my father's vow as surely as was Jephthah's daughter. The person I have been cannot live in the future that faces me. My life was built on hopes and expectations that are now all dead. Clinging to them would be like refusing to bury a corpse. My life would be contaminated by the decay of dead dreams and desires. I will find no happiness in fondling what might have been.

"To find any kind of peace, I must go to Meridan with no will of my own—no ambitions, no expectations, no wants, no wishes, no hopes, and no desires. That is really the only way to be happy, isn't it? I can see now that desire is the main source of our unhappiness. Desire leads us into most of our troubles, and desire unfulfilled is the source of all despair. The only way to find true peace is to root it all out, to pluck and scour one's life until absolutely no desire is left. Then we can serenely face whatever comes our way, because even the most miserable of futures will not wash away some sandcastle of foolish hopes and dreams."

Father Lucidis responded in his deep, soothing voice. "It seems to me that what you are willing to call happiness is merely the absence of unhappiness. You are willing to sacrifice the delight life offers if you can be assured of preventing despair, as if the best one can hope is to find the immobile point of balance between pleasure and pain, agony and ecstasy, failure and fulfillment, disappointment and delight."

"Certainly I wanted more from life than that," sighed Volanna. "Until last night, much, much more. But out there in the darkness of Blackmore Forest I learned the real truth about what life has to offer. It holds out delights with the promise of heaven, then snatches them away, leaving you in the outer darkness of hellish longing for the food you tasted but cannot have. It would be better not to taste delight at all but to live on in simple ignorance of bliss that cannot be.

"When I was a little girl, a holy man who lived alone in the Thorncroft Mountains came down into the city. He pronounced doom and destruction on us all if we didn't change our ways. 'You are seekers of pleasure,' he cried. He warned us that pleasure was a soap bubble that when grasped burst into nothingness. 'True peace is achieved through duty,' he said. Now I can see that he was right. Religions preach against the pursuit of pleasure for our own good. They would spare us the pain and despair that comes from pleasure thwarted. 'Die to yourself,' the holy man would cry. I didn't know what he meant, then, but I know now. Last night I died to myself, to all my dreams and desires. I had always hoped that when I crossed the river of death, it would be the Jordan and not the Styx. But it seems that I have crossed where those two streams merge into a single current. I have entered neither heaven nor hell, but limbo."

"Volanna, my dear princess—Yes, I know who you are. I even knew you were coming here. Didn't you wonder why I had water already boiling on my fire?—the holy man meant well, no doubt, but he was mistaken. Pleasure, delight, joy, ecstasy, and happiness are not evils. They are not temptations meant to tantalize or test you. You were created to delight in all the good that heaven and earth has to offer. It is right that you should desire what you were made to enjoy. To have no desire is to be a rind with the fruit eaten out—an empty shell living a meaningless life with no focus and no direction. Delight comes when desire meets its proper object. Joy comes when hope is fulfilled. Desire is the net with which one snares ecstasy."

"You pose a dilemma with no solution," said Volanna. "On the one hand, I am to desire the natural delights one is meant to enjoy, which for a woman surely includes love for a man. But on the other hand, I am to submit to my father's vow by renouncing forever such a love."

"Please forgive me, but I must correct you on this point," said Lucidis. "Your father has not asked you to renounce the love of a man. There is a man in your future, namely the crown prince of Meridan."

"But I do not love Prince Lomar," protested Volanna. "While I loved Brendal, my heart bloomed and all my life was bathed with joy. Now that I know his love was a mirage, my life stretches before me like an empty road in a barren desert. I will travel it without complaint but also without any hope of finding real joy."

"The future you chose for yourself has been thwarted," Lucidis replied, "but it does not follow that your future will be barren or joyless. Perhaps your father is offering you a greater future than you had chosen for yourself. The kind of love you had for Brendal you could experience with any man. The touch of fire, the beating heart, the tender look are simply the natural responses of the female to the male. The delight of blended bodies is an unfathomable wonder, but it is merely the gateway to the greater ecstasy of blended souls. The lesser is not denied when you choose the greater, but you may miss the greater if the lesser so fills your senses that the greater is obscured. With Brendal you would have waded ankle deep in the shallows of love. Your father believes that the prince will bring you a love of such depth that you both will immerse yourselves in it."

"It seems that you are asking me to trust my father's wisdom rather than my own senses—to substitute his will for mine. But why? How does that change anything? Can't his plans be frustrated as easily as mine? Why should I suppose that his Prince Lomar will prove less false than my Brendal?"

"Your father is doing the thing he is asking you to do. He is putting his trust in a power above himself—a superior, wiser, vaster power. He is convinced that the prophecy is rooted in the mind of the Master of the Universe. Your father is trusting your future to this power and asking you to do the same."

Volanna sighed, "What real choice do I have?"

Father Lucidis spoke gently but firmly. "You have the choice of either trusting your father and adopting his vow or living that barren life without hope or desire that you see for yourself—the life of the perpetual pessimist who wants nothing, expects nothing, and gets nothing. You can chance the longer, more perilous road to joy or take the safer road and close yourself up like a nerveless, cauterized wound forever immune to pain but also incapable of pleasure."

Volanna was silent for a long moment. Father Lucidis waited with quiet patience until she replied, "I will think on these things, but now I must return to my parents. I have treated them poorly, and they must be miserable with worry. I thank you from my heart for all you have done for me—not least for sharing your wisdom."

Volanna gathered her now dry clothing and went back into the tree room to dress. Father Lucidis gave her a comb and she did the best she could with her ratted hair. In a quarter-hour she was seated beside him in a sturdy cart pulled by a dappled farm horse pointed toward Valomar.

The exhausted princess swayed sleepily in her seat as the cart bumped along the uneven road, muddy and puddled from the night's rain. Soon they reached a fording place on the Tynor, and she was able to see across the river the oak- and juniper-covered hills of her homeland—soft, rolling, comforting, maternal hills that seemed to cuddle the cottages that nestled among them. She felt a pang of emotion that was hard to identify—a bittersweet longing, a melancholy yearning, a wistful pining—as she watched the lazy smoke curl from chimneys hidden in the folds of the hills. A wave of anticipatory homesickness washed over her. Once she journeyed to Meridan, would she ever see these hills again?

They arrived at Oakendale Castle in the middle of the afternoon, to be met by a distraught mother and a watching father who claimed he knew all along that she would come back. There were tears and embraces all around but no parental recriminations. King Tallis, who was indeed almost certain that his daughter would come to her senses before she went through with the elopement, knew that Volanna's conscience had done all the chastising she needed. Furthermore, he was extremely pleased with his daughter's decision to return. This one act showed him more about her character than her previous twenty years of unquestioning obedience. He was not, however, indifferent to the pain and disappointment that spurred her attempt to elope. In fact the matter had weighed heavily on him during the long hours since the discovery of her escape.

Volanna, weary to the bone, declined her parents' invitation to dinner, choosing instead a soaking bath, a light supper in her room, and an early bed. But before taking her leave, she requested an official audience with the king in his throne hall the following morning. Her request was granted, and she bade them a good-night.

Volanna was greatly ashamed of the distress she had caused Kalley, but her tearful apology and Kalley's quick forgiveness set things right again between them, and the unlikely friendship between the king's daughter and the serving girl prospered once again.

The sun was not yet down when Volanna undressed, slipped into bed and drifted into a dreamless sleep that lasted until well after sunup the next morning. By ten o'clock, however, she had breakfasted and dressed and was being ushered through the great, intricately carved, oaken doors of the throne hall of the king of Valomar.

"Her highness, the Princess Volanna," announced the footman. Volanna proceeded formally across the flagstone floor with regal grace, passing between the fourteen pillars representing Valomar's provinces as she approached the dais. King Tallis sat with bearded chin in hand, fingers drumming on the arm of the throne as he waited. His beloved daughter stopped before him and curtsied.

"What is the meaning of all this formality, Volanna? Why are you coming in here like some supplicant or ambassador? Why can't we meet in our chambers and talk with the normal privacy of a daughter and father?"

"Your Majesty, I am here on royal business, and what passes between us this morning should be witnessed officially and entered into the royal record," said Volanna.

"Very well," sighed Tallis as he signaled the royal secretary to approach. "So let it be written. But before I give you leave to state your business, I have an item of my own to clear with you." The king stepped down from the dais and stood facing his daughter. He put his hands on her shoulders and said, "My dear Volanna, since your escape I have thought much about how my sacred vow has become the source of great unhappiness for you. You know what a vow means to those of us who give our allegiance to the Master of the Universe. And you know that the purpose of my vow was to fulfill the prophecy to which I am utterly committed. It has shaped the policies of Valomar for twenty years. To break that vow is unthinkable.

"However, it has come to my mind that in one way, at least, my vow was as rash as that of the ancient Jephthah because it meant the enforcement of my will upon one who does not share my commitment to the prophecy, namely you, my daughter."

"But Father—" Volanna tried to interrupt.

"Pray let me finish, my dear," Tallis continued. "I have come to see that in a very real sense, my vow meant death to you as surely as did the vow of Jephthah to his own daughter. Although the ancient judge was stricken with grief at the folly of his vow, he did not waver in his resolve to carry out its terms. Frankly, I have never been quite certain that he was right in that resolve. It almost seems his dogged commitment to his vow was a selfish thing. His two choices were equally hideous: to sacrifice his daughter to his strong sense of principle, thus maintaining a legalistic integrity before the Master of the Universe, or to sacrifice his principle, disgrace himself before his people, and beg forgiveness from the Master. Perhaps Jephthah should have borne the consequence of his rash vow himself instead of inflicting it upon his daughter. Essentially, he chose to save himself at her expense."

"Father, if you will only listen to me, I—"

"Please, Volanna, I must tell you what I have concluded. I do not want to be guilty of the kind of rigid uprightness that places everyone around me in jeopardy of being sacrificed to my principles. I mistakenly assumed that you, being my daughter, would share my convictions. I thought of you as a satellite to me, held in willing orbit by the bond of inherited values. I overlooked the fact that you are not merely an extension of myself but a free person in your own right who must stand or fall before our mutual Master by the validity of your own choices. In short, I was wrong to make a vow that forced on you an unchosen destiny. I hereby release you from the obligation I have imposed upon you to comply with the terms of my vow."

"Father . . ." Volanna looked tenderly into the eyes of the king. She knew her father well and understood the full import of the sacrifice he was making. He had just offered up his own integrity, his hopes for his nation and the Meridanic Empire, and his hopes for a dynasty of kings who would carry on his bloodline, all for the love he bore for his daughter. "I have been trying to tell you, I have already decided to uphold your vow and wed the prince of Meridan. We must not break your vow and jeopardize our role in the ancient prophecy."

"Then you also believe in the prophecy?" asked Tallis.

"The prophecy is too great a matter for me to comprehend fully, but I believe in you, Father, and on the strength of that, I willingly obey the terms of your vow."

The heart of the king leapt for joy at his daughter's promise, but he choked back the pride that swelled in his throat and said, "The grace of heaven is that such commitments are credited as if they were dedicated to their proper object. In time you will come to know more fully the higher power that guides me and will place your trust directly in him, but for now your commitment to my commitment is enough.

"Now listen well, my daughter. There is one thing you must be very careful to remember. Whatever the cost, you must not marry the crown prince until the terms of the prophecy are fulfilled—until the Crown of Eden rests upon his head and the golden comet blends with the silver star. If you wed before these events occur, disastrous results will surely follow."

Volanna easily agreed, not suspecting the terrible anguish this promise would inflict on her.

Then Volanna informed her father of the plot against his throne that she had discovered in Blackmore Forest. King Tallis knew already that some conspiracy was afoot among the five knights. He had been awaiting some overt act on their part to give him cause for confrontation. Volanna's recounting of their traitorous plans for deposing him and their abduction and planned rape of his daughter gave him more than sufficient warrant to move against them.

Borethane and his fellow conspirators had counted on their revolt to create a groundswell of rebellion among the other knights in the hall. But they badly misjudged the country's loyalty to their good king, and now they found themselves isolated and outlawed. Knowing their cause to be hopeless, Sir Thringal and Sir Laurenfel surrendered and pleaded for mercy. They were duly tried and sentenced to prison. Sir Agualot attempted to escape into Oranth but was swallowed by the treacherous marshes that fester in that land. Sir Borethane made a proud but hopeless stand against the small contingent of knights sent to arrest him, choosing to fall by the sword rather than to live as a disgraced traitor. Brendal eluded all searchers sent to arrest him and escaped into the Graystone Mountains of Lochlaund and was not seen again in Valomar.

At the appointed time Princess Volanna, with a company of soldiers and attendants, set out on the seven-day journey to Meridan to meet her betrothed in his capital city of Corenham. Her mind was set, but her heart was heavy for she would not see her parents again until the week of the wedding, one year hence.

PART II
THE BLACKSMITH

CHAPTER NINE

THE REGENT

nticipation of Princess Volanna's arrival caused no small stir in Corenham. Meridan's capital city prepared like a bridegroom preening and dressing himself for the fair eyes of his bride. Tradesmen scoured their shops, put their tools in efficient-looking order, and carted off piles of accumulated rubbish. Merchants displayed their stock on spotless shelves and cleaned out long-neglected cabinets and forgotten corners. Couples whitewashed their daub- and wattle-cottages and put their children to work on the fences.

Up at Morningstone Castle, Lord Aldemar—appointed regent of Meridan after the death of King Alfron—was diligent in doing his part. He had the charwomen at Morningstone sweep and scrub until one could almost have eaten off the flagstone floors. Maids, pages, and scullery workers were enlisted to polish all the brass fixtures, beat and brush the tapestries, and wash all the soot and dirt from the ceilings and carvings. Outside, masons erected scaffolding around the castle walls and scraped away years of moss and bird droppings from the ancient stones and replaced the crumbling mortar between them. Carpenters repaired and refurbished gates, replacing cracked beams and scraping the rust from the iron reinforcements on the portcullis, dressing it all with a glistening coat of oil.

The regent's diligence in preparing for Volanna's arrival sprang from reasons other than his own highly developed sense of duty. Lord

Aldemar had been one of King Alfron's two closest friends (King Tallis of Valomar being the other) and his most trusted advisor. It was natural and expected that the Hall of Knights should have designated him regent, but it was a task he neither sought nor savored. He was a quiet man of strong convictions but not a public man. He much preferred the role of private advisor—a force behind the throne—than that of a man whose every act and decision affected the prosperity and security of the nation. Besides, he was getting tired. He was of an age when his days of service to the kingdom should be coming to an end, and he was ready to retire to the country with his wife and enjoy watching his garden and grandchildren grow. To him the coming of the new queen-to-be meant the day of his release was drawing nigh.

On becoming regent, Lord Aldemar had chosen not to reside in Morningstone Castle for at least two reasons: his natural humility prevented him from assuming the luxurious trappings of royalty, and he and his wife loved their own estate at the far edge of the city. Lady Aldemar strongly resisted the invitation to move their household into the huge royal castle.

As usual, Lord Aldemar's day began before sunup. On this particular morning he was aware as he took his breakfast that the servants were already up and about, disturbing the usual quiet tranquillity of his morning. Though he knew the reason for the early bustling and scurrying, he was convinced it was all unnecessary. The Princess Volanna was expected to arrive in Corenham tomorrow, and the plan called for her to reside at Aldemar's manor for two days: one day to rest from her journey and one to prepare for her presentation to Meridan. On the third day Prince Lomar would meet the princess at Aldemar's estate and escort her in a grand procession across Corenham to Morningstone Castle, where a suite of rooms was prepared as her resi-dence for the year before the wedding.

Because Lady Aldemar managed the manor impeccably, keeping it in a permanent state of readiness to accommodate any reasonable number of unexpected guests, Lord Aldemar protested that all the cleaning, refurbishing, restocking, and redecorating was an utter waste of time and energy. But his lady insisted that lodging such a guest as the kingdom's designated queen called for extraordinary preparations.

The regent left his estate just as the sunlight began to break between the peaks of the Dragontooth Mountains. As he descended the hill that his manor crowned, he looked out across Corenham, just becoming visible in the predawn twilight. The city was beginning to awaken. He could see the orange glow of hearth and candle in the windows of many cottages, and wispy columns of curling smoke drifted upward from their chimneys, breathing life and warmth into the chill morning air. Somewhere a rooster crowed, putting his whole being into the sound as though he were convinced that the sun could not complete its ascent without his call. In the distance Aldemar could hear the lowing of cattle as the sons of Halckane the dairyman, having milked their cows, now turned them into the fields for another day of grazing.

The advancing glow in the east, tinting the high clouds with brilliant tones of pink and orange, bore witness to the efficiency of the rooster's efforts. Across the city Aldemar could see the silhouetted towers and crenelated parapets of Morningstone Castle. The royal stronghold rose sharply from the crest of a granite mass known as Morningstone Hill, so named long before the castle was built because it had been the first point in the valley to catch the rays of the rising sun. Now as the regent watched, the first light of the morning struck the topmost tower of the castle itself. The hill had bequeathed to its namesake structure the ancient office of light sentinel.

Aldemar reached the base of his own hill and entered the streets of Corenham. The sound of his horse's hooves clopping along the cobblestones echoed from the bolted doors and shuttered windows of shops, inns, alehouses, and stables—some yet dark and still, others just beginning to stir. A quarter mile ahead, looming high over the roofs and treetops, he could barely make out the massive, shadowed form of the great monument to Perivale.

"Top of the morning to you, my lord," said a cheery voice from the door of the Red Shield Inn.

"And a good morning to you, Remmlet," replied Lord Aldemar. He turned his horse toward the opened door and the glow that silhouetted a rotund, aproned figure with a fringe of red hair framing a ruddy, bald head. Aldemar drew from his saddle pouch a large pewter mug, which he held toward the apple-cheeked innkeeper. Remmlet poured the mug full from his pitcher of steaming cider. Aldemar gave him the proper coin, saluted, and having completed his daily ritual with Remmlet, nudged his horse on down the street, sipping as he watched the Perivale monument loom larger and larger in the graying sky.

In a few minutes he reached the open expanse of Cheaping Square, the trade center of Corenham. Here local and traveling merchants set up temporary shop to sell or trade their produce, livestock, crafted goods, fabrics, and tools. A few enterprising vendors had already begun to erect their stands as Lord Aldemar passed among them.

The statue of Perivale was now fully visible on the far side of the square, dominating the view though yet over a hundred yards distant. The colossal image of the conqueror was the height of five cottages and carved from a single block of natural stone of the same color and texture as that of Morningstone Hill. The stone had not been brought to its present location for carving—indeed, there was no known method of moving a stone of such size. It was carved on the spot where nature placed it. A wide flight of steps made of native stone led up to the base of the statue, and a park, expertly landscaped and dressed, was built around it.

No one in Meridan knew how the sculpture would have looked in its final form for it had never been finished. The top half was a complete, perfectly formed image of the upper body of a man. He was muscular and nude, looking skyward, his eye following the near vertical line of his extended right arm. The hand at the end of the arm was opened and reaching. The left arm extended downward, the palm of the hand half sinking into the raw stone from which the torso emerged at the hips. The face was strong and noble, with features too definite to be anything but a portrait of the great Perivale.

In leaving the enormous statue unfinished, the sculptor had unwittingly created a visual metaphor for the changing fortunes of Meridan. When the country was prosperous and at peace, the mighty torso seemed to be struggling upward to emerge from his stony confinement. In times of national adversity, he seemed a tragic figure sinking into the shapeless, stony mass, his longing eye and aspiring arm reaching hopelessly toward the forever-unreachable heavens.

Often Meridan's kings had been urged to finish the sculpture, but others insisted it should never be completed. To them it was a convicting witness to the bane that brought Perivale's downfall. It was his Tower of Babel, erected in pride and thwarted short of completion, a monument to the futility of becoming too confident in one's own power. The sinking form of the unfinished image was deemed an appropriate symbol of unholy aspiration arrested by the mortality of the body returning to the matter from which it was formed.

To these interpreters of history, the meaning of Perivale's disappearance was clear, but the ultimate fate of the conqueror remained a mystery even yet, a hundred twenty years after the fact. The Crown of Eden had disappeared at the same time, as did the sculptor of the monument. And no trace of the king, the crown, or the artist had been seen since.

In time the acre surrounding the monument was adorned with flowers, hedges, junipers, stone benches, and flagstone walkways. It was duly christened Perivale Square, exactly as Perivale himself had intended. But the effect he had intended was marred by the half-finished statue. Instead of being a monument to a self-sufficient, all-conquering hero, it stood as mute testimony to his unexplained and humiliating end.

Lord Aldemar sighed deeply as he looked at the towering monument. His forebodings about Meridan's future under Prince Lomar were all too clearly expressed in Perivale's hopeless confinement in his stone trap. The regent's opinion of the young prince had never been good, and it was fast diminishing as the day of his coronation drew nearer. Aldemar wondered again, as he had wondered many times since Alfron's death, how a son could be so unlike his father. He charged Lomar's insolence and self-centeredness to the fact that the boy had been early orphaned. Alfron and his queen had both died within the same week, before Lomar had even been weaned. He was reared by nannies who spoiled him, partly because he was the royal scion and future king, and partly because their maternal pity compensated for his parental loss by gratifying his every want. But Lomar often exhibited darker, more ominous tendencies that could not be accounted for by mere leniency of his keepers.

While Aldemar entertained grave misgivings about the sort of king Meridan would have when Lomar came to the throne, not once did he consider using his powers as regent to prevent the prince's succession. He was a believer in the law and a servant of the prophecy. He had a strong conviction that once men began to bypass the law in order to accomplish some greater good, the result would be chaos, with every man becoming his own little king with his own set of laws. The law and men's acceptance of it was the mortar that held society together. His own misgivings did not give him the right to place his personal conviction above established law. If every citizen assumed that right, order would disintegrate.

But Lord Aldemar was also a patriot. It was his dedication to the welfare of Meridan that bound him to his office when retirement would have been far preferable. His dilemma was that while he was bound by his dedication to law to promote Lomar's succession, he was bound by his love for his country to find some way to protect it from the kind of rule he knew the capricious prince would impose. He had spent many hours in agonized meditation, searching for a way to preserve both Lomar's kingship and Meridan's welfare.

His best hope, he thought, was to strengthen the Hall of Knights. The legal powers of the Hall were not specifically outlined by written law. It functioned as a body that was partly legislative, partly advisory, and partly military. The knights of the Hall were for the most part landholders or warriors who had earned renown in Meridan for their influence, wisdom, or valor. Officially Meridan was governed by law, the king himself being executor of the law and subject to it. The Hall of Knights served to advise the king on all matters concerning law, including proposal and ratification of laws enacted by the king.

The purpose of this arrangement was to maintain a balance between monarch and subjects, preventing tyranny while concentrating enough power in the hands of a single man to ensure efficient government. In actual practice, however, this balance ebbed and flowed, waxing on one side while waning on the other, then reversing itself in another generation or under another king. Meridan had had kings who were virtual dictators, rendering the Hall impotent and useless, and other kings who were mere figureheads or lackeys to the will of a dominant Hall.

One became a knight by action of the king, although the ordination could be nullified by a dissenting vote of two-thirds of the Hall. Lord Aldemar felt certain that after his coronation, Lomar would bestow knighthood on his confidant Balkert. He fully expected that Balkert would become Lomar's chancellor, making him second in command in Meridan. Aldemar knew Balkert to be a devious and cunning man who accomplished Lomar's wishes behind backs and under tables. Aldemar had evidence that Balkert had already used Lomar's name to manipulate and scheme for his own purposes. Another of Lomar's cohorts, Sir Stundal, had been knighted three years ago—one of Aldemar's unfortunate appointments made at the urging of the Hall after Stundal's first tournament championship. Stundal, already captain of Lomar's guard, would undoubtedly become head of the military. It was a chilling prospect that did not bode well for the Kingdom.

The difficulty, as Aldemar saw it, was to infuse the Hall of Knights with enough power to keep Lomar in check but lacking the power lust to overthrow what was certain to be an unpopular monarchy. Given the fuel-and-fire nature of power and men, Aldemar was not at all certain the thing could be done.

Yet something had to be done, so when opportunity permitted, the regent had moved to add men of valor and integrity to the Hall. Seeking out men who would not be intimidated by Balkert's political machinations or Stundal's control of the military, Lord Aldemar had knighted five whom he trusted to remain loyal to the Kingdom. He had tried to knight others, but Meridan's most prudent men were wary of aligning themselves with the future monarch, whom they did not trust.

Only five good men, Aldemar thought as his horse began the ascent up Morningstone Hill. Of the forty or so most influential men in Meridan, there were only five that he knew to have unwavering integrity. The ancient city of Sodom was destroyed because it could not boast ten upright citizens. To the eyes of Aldemar, the future of Meridan looked dim indeed, and the need to strengthen the Hall continued to prod his thoughts.

Aldemar arrived at his office, a room opening off the great hall. He spent an hour signing parchments and issuing directives, then closed the office and again took to the streets of Corenham. Although he had appointed foremen to oversee the cleaning and repair of the city, he often rode through the streets to observe the progress for himself. With only three days left before the princess would proceed in formal procession across the welcoming city, his imposing, arrow-straight figure sitting atop his dappled gray charger was seen almost daily, inspecting, encouraging, suggesting, and urging the city to complete its dressing for the new queen.

On this particular morning, Aldemar chose a district immediately east of Morningstone Castle where most of the city's service shops were clustered. The stately regent rode slowly down the cobbled street, his keen eye observing the state of cleanliness and repair in each shop. As he approached the shed of Sorvan the carpenter, with its yards of stacked logs and squared planks, Aldemar breathed deeply, delighting in the smell of freshly sawed pine and oak. Sorvan himself was shaping a rafter beam, as loops like a maiden's curls spun from each sweep of the adz. He looked up and waved to the passing regent, who saluted in return and continued on.

Aldemar paused at the shop of Galvay the tailor and greeted the tailor's wife, who was sweeping the threshold.

"Has Galvay completed the prince's suit?" he asked.

"Oh, Lord Aldemar," she replied in a voice trembling at the brink of tears, "a terrible thing just happened, and I don't know what we're goin' to do." She went on to explain how Galvay had located a source of the finest oriental silk and velvet from a traveling broker and had mortgaged his tools to purchase enough fabric to cut the prince's formal apparel. She told him how she and her husband had let orders backlog while they spent over three weeks of long days cutting and crafting the royal garments. Aldemar's face darkened as the distraught wife told of that morning's fitting in Lomar's quarters.

"The prince told Galvay the suit looked like a feed sack and paid him less than a quarter of what they'd agreed on. When Galvay complained, that brute Stundal threw him out of the prince's rooms and slammed the door. I just don't know what we'll do," she moaned, dabbing at her brimming eyes with the corner of her apron. "It's bad enough we're deep in debt, but it's even worse because without our tools and loom—"

"Loom?" said Aldemar. "Do you mean to say that Galvay mortgaged his loom?" The tailor had invested his life savings to have the loom imported. It was his pride and joy.

"Yes, my lord," replied the good woman. "The cloth was fearful costly, and Galvay didn't see no risk, it bein' the prince's clothes and all, so he never thought twice about it. And it was such a beautiful suit, my lord, the likes of which has never been wore in Meridan."

"Who is your moneylender? No doubt he will give you some time to pay off the debt, which with your back orders, you should be able to do very quickly."

"That's just what I told Galvay when he came draggin' back from the fittin' at the palace. And for a moment we was cheered by the idea and thinkin' our plight, while fearful wrong, might not mean our ruin after all. But even as we was talkin' a little hope back into ourselves, who but Sir Benidah himself came poundin' at the door, demandin' either his money or his loom. An' he wants it today, m'lord. That was the agreement, he said: he would get his pay when Galvay got his money from the prince."

"Sir Benidah did this?" asked Aldemar. Was it possible that the wealthy Benidah had been drawn into Lomar's orbit?

"Indeed he did, my lord. Galvay tried to bargain with him and practically begged on his knees for more time, but ol' Benidah might as well have been deaf. An' it's not as if he needs the money. I don't understand it at all, m'lord. It's like money's got magnets in it, and when it starts gettin' clustered up like, its pull gets stronger and stronger until all the money around it gets pulled into it so the cluster keeps gettin' bigger and bigger and its pull keeps on gettin' stronger. Them like us that don't have much, what we have just gets sucked out of our hands by them that has too much already."

"Bring me a piece of parchment, a quill and ink, and a wax candle, if you please," said Aldemar as he dismounted. They entered the shop and the woman fetched the requested items. "What was the amount of your bill to the prince?" She gave him the figure, which he wrote on the parchment. He then signed his name to the document and impressed his signet ring into the candle wax at the bottom. He handed her the parchment and said, "Present this to the master of the exchequer today and it will be paid. Please comfort Galvay with the assurance that the government of Meridan is still one of fairness and law."

"Thank you, m'lord, thank you!" She could barely speak through her flood of grateful tears.

Lord Aldemar moved on. The tale from Galvay's wife was not unlike many he had begun to hear over the past several months from people who had dealings with Balkert or Sir Stundal. And now it seemed they were drawing other knights into their orbit. Something had to be done. The reek of curing skins assailed him as he passed the open door of Denning's tannery. In deference to his nostrils he nudged his horse to the other side of the lane where he stopped and shouted for the offending tanner to come out.

"Where is the door I ordered you to put on your shop?" Aldemar bellowed.

"It's almost ready, m'lord," replied Denning. "I'll have it hung by tomorrow, just as you said."

"See to it," said Aldemar as he moved on. "The smell of your shop is enough to cause the princess to revoke her vow."

Aldemar looked ahead where a small cluster of men had gathered in front of the shop of Wilmert the potter. They were talking, laughing, and stuffing their mouths with an amber-colored pastry. In the midst of the cluster stood "Ansel of the Honeycakes" and her winsome daughter Marcie, selling fresh-baked pastries from their handcart. Ansel was a handsome woman of some forty winters, and her daughter was less than half that age. Aldemar wondered how many men bought honeycakes for their taste alone and how many for a closer glimpse of the buxom lass. The daring sweep of the girl's loosely laced bodice was not likely to discourage trade.

Aldemar bought a honeycake and prodded his horse forward. As he drew near the end of the lane, which stopped at the end of the town, he heard the hard, bright sound of hammer on anvil ringing out from the shop of Bogarth the blacksmith. Aldemar had never lost his childhood fascination with the process of glowing metal made soft and malleable under a baptism of fire, to be reborn into the gleaming, hard shapes of tools and weapons. He pointed his horse toward Bogarth's shed.

Over the years the shop of Bogarth had become a gathering center for men of all classes—servants, shopkeepers, craftsmen, farmers, knights, noblemen, and on occasion, even a member of the royal family—as men waiting for horses to be shod or swords to be sharpened would loiter about, engaged in friendly colloquy.

Bogarth had inherited his trade from his father and would pass it on to his son Aradon. From childhood the burly blacksmith had observed the parade of humanity that passed through the shop and absorbed a diversified body of knowledge and an uncanny understanding of human nature. He was a man of unquestioned integrity, which he also inherited from his father. Often consulted by his peers for advice or arbitration, Bogarth was drafted to head the city's craftsmen's guild when strife within the organization threatened to destroy it. Bogarth did his duty but had no liking for the drudgery of administration and resigned from office after setting the guild right again.

Aldemar had considered Bogarth in his search for honorable men to fill the Hall of Knights. He had once broached the subject with the blacksmith, but Bogarth had laughed and rightly pointed out that many of the noblemen in the Hall would never accept a simple blacksmith as a peer. It was true that such an appointment would be highly unorthodox, yet Aldemar had never completely let go of the idea. He drew up at Bogarth's open-fronted shed to watch the big craftsman at work.

"What are we beating today, Bogarth, swords or plowshares?"

"Ah, Lord Aldemar!" boomed Bogarth. "It's neither. For six weeks we've made nothin' but gate hinges, cup hooks, ladles, and lattices. New princesses seem to be good for business. I say we should import one from every country in the Seven Kingdoms."

"And what, pray tell me, would we do with seven princesses?" asked Aldemar.

"Well, she's comin' here to get married, isn't she? We could find good husbands for six more like her, I'm sure. We could marry 'em off to young roebucks like my boy Aradon here who are too tongue-tied to do their own askin'." He nodded toward the tall, shirtless young man pounding steadily at a piece of red metal on an anvil in the back of the shop. "I don't know what to make of it, Lord Aldemar, I really don't. Look at him—muscled up like a horse, twice as strong as an ox, and not scared of man or beast. Why, one night last spring, he tracked down a horse that had escaped from our stall and fought off six wolves that had stalked the poor animal across the countryside and were closing in for the kill. But put him next to a hundred an' twenty pounds of eye-flutterin' female and his knees start knockin', his belly turns to jelly, and his tongue locks up. He gets all terrified like she was goin' to open up her mouth and swallow him whole."

"He actually may be wiser than the rest of us," Aldemar responded dryly.

"Ha!" exclaimed a loud female voice behind him. "If he was wise, he'd be married already." The voice belonged to Ansel, who had just stopped her cart in front of Bogarth's shop. Marcie stood shyly at her mother's side, glancing often at the young man working at the anvil in the back of the shed.

"There you go again, Ansel. I've told you over and over, Aradon's not ready to marry. He's only a boy," said Bogarth.

"Don't try to tell me that. He's twenty years old, and look at him. He's not a boy anymore, is he Marcie?"

"That he is not," sighed Marcie with obvious admiration as she watched the young blacksmith's rippling sinews dancing to the beat of his hammer and glistening beneath his forge-lit skin.

"All right, all right; he's not a little boy. But he's just barely a man, and he needs to taste a bit of freedom before some stalkin' female puts a noose around his neck and a ring in his nose," said Bogarth.

"Oh, horsefeathers!" Ansel exclaimed. "You men are all alike. You talk like bein' married is the same as livin' cooped up like a penned rooster. But I know better. My late husband, Collin, used to tell me he wouldn't trade me for a hundred girls like them in the Thirsty Eagle tavern. And I know he meant it too. But with his friends in the ale-house, he'd wag on the way you're awaggin' now, like the wedding bell was the clang of an iron gate shuttin' him up in lifelong misery. You roosters all crow like you got to have the run of the whole barnyard, but you always come back to roost in the comfort of the henhouse."

"I don't deny it, but he's not ready to roost yet. Give the poor lad a little time."

"And while he dallies around, all the ripest young girls are gettin' plucked. A man like him oughtn' to have to pick from the dregs; he ought to have first pick from Corenham's best and fairest. Now look at my Marcie here. There's not a more comely maid in the whole city. Where could you find a better match for your Aradon? But how long do you think a morsel like her will stay on the market? Come on, Bogarth, let's draw up the weddin' agreement between these two. He couldn't do better and you know it."

Bogarth held up his hands to ward off the woman. "Wait a moment now. You're talkin' to the wrong man."

"Don't be silly. You're his father."

"But he's twenty now, remember? Since I've made no weddin' contract for him, he's free to make his own."

"Then call him over here," demanded Ansel.

With a gesture of defeat, Bogarth called his son. Aradon laid aside his hammer and splashed his face and arms with water from the cooling trough. Looking wary and reluctant, he ambled over to where the three were standing. Aldemar, still astride his mount, continued to watch, the hint of a wry smile on his lips.

After exchanging greetings and giving Aradon a honeycake, Ansel got straight to her point. "Aradon," she said, "don't you think my Marcie is a comely lass?"

"Well, uh, yes, of course. I always have," replied Aradon.

"And I assure you that she is every inch as sound as she looks. Marcie, stand up here."

Marcie took her mother's hand and stepped onto an upturned crate. Then Ansel took a short iron rod from a nearby table and began to point out her daughter's salable features.

"Look at that fair face, Aradon: eyes brown like berries, lips red and full like rose petals, smooth, velvety skin lightly kissed with freckles. Open your mouth, Marcie. Look at those teeth, young man; every one white as pearls, straight as a picket fence, and none missin'. Look at that full head of shiny hair, the color of summer wheat. And look at this." Ansel lifted Marcie's skirt above the knee, exposing the girl's smooth, white thigh. "She's got good, sturdy legs and strong, smooth arms for the work in house or field from sunup to sundown. Yet she's soft and full of bosom and wide and round of hip for the work from sundown to sunup." Ansel laughed loudly as Aradon turned red as a cherry. Marcie merely stood on her wood-crate pedestal, looking at the abashed young man like a sailor at a tankard of ale.

Finally Aradon recovered his tongue. "She seems very, uh, well, I mean, if I were ready to marry, she would sure be, uh, well . . . I really need to get back to work now. Besides, I haven't anything for a bride price. I'll, uh, well, good morning, Ansel. Good morning, Marcie." The crimson-faced Aradon turned back toward his anvil, but Ansel grabbed his arm.

"When you're ready may be too late," she said. "Granval, the merchant from Rhondilar, is danglin' a bride price almost big enough to buy Morningstone Castle. But Marcie doesn't want to marry ol' Granval, and I can't say as I blame her really. The man is old enough to be my father and has rheumatism, gout, and a bad liver. And he wears a wig like a worn-out mop." Ansel leaned toward Aradon's ear and spoke softly, "She wants to marry you. And bride price or no bride price, to make my baby happy, I would consent. Yes, I would. Think of the robust sons and lusty daughters you two would spawn! But ol' Granval raises his offer every day, and I'm only a poor cakeseller, Aradon. I can't hold off an offer like that forever waitin' for you to make up your mind. Let's strike a deal today and let the old merchant look for his bedwarmer somewhere else. What do you say, boy?"

In truth, Aradon was attracted to the girl. What man would not be? And Ansel's tour of her scenic geography had quickened his blood. But he remembered the proverb his father had often quoted to him, "Fair face and rounded form count for nothing if the head is not wise and the heart not true." Marcie was fair—very fair—but what did he know about her head and heart?

As Aradon hesitated, Marcie decided to step down from the woodcrate. Whether what she did next was by accident or by design could not be known with certainty. The heel of her shoe caught between the slats of the crate, and with a cry of surprise, she lost her balance and fell toward Aradon. Aradon did the only thing he could do. He caught her in his arms, her face only inches from his as he clasped her against his bare chest.

But if the slip was indeed intentional, and if Marcie meant for this sampling of her soft embrace to tip Aradon's moment of indecision toward her, she miscalculated. Instead of clouding his rational judgment, it had the opposite effect. As he caught her, the thought came to him full force that he knew nothing about Marcie except that she was a woman, which was all she ever presented of herself. All her appeal to him was based solely upon their difference in sex. There had to be more.

"I'm sorry, Marcie," he said. "Now is not the time." He set the girl on her feet and returned resolutely to his anvil, somehow feeling he had survived a crisis.

The disappointed women left but not before Ansel clucked at Bogarth that his son would be sorry when Marcie was carried off forever to Rhondilar and wed to a man upon whom her abundant charms would be wasted.

"You might be surprised at how much heat can boil in old furnaces!" Bogarth bawled after them. Then he wolfed down the remainder of his honeycake and returned to his own anvil.

Lord Aldemar nudged his horse and rode on, muttering to himself, "Either that boy just passed up the chance of a lifetime or narrowly escaped a carefully set trap."

CHAPTER TEN

ṬḅE VELVET ṬRAρ

rince Lomar's four new Albustian stallions were ideal specimens of the breed: black as midnight and perfectly formed, as if sculpted by a master from glistening ebony. Lomar had bought the horses at an exorbitant price from eastern traders who had heard that the prince had a weakness for anything that would incite envy. The horses had not yet been shown in Corenham. Lomar had taken great care to keep them hidden in the royal stables, intending their debut to be the drawing of the royal carriage in the princess's procession three days hence.

Lomar wanted everything about the horses and carriage to be in top form on that day. But it was not the beauty or power of the four horses that interested him. Within his court was an aloof clique of five earls led by the snobbish Sir Grosefar, whose great passion was the acquisition and breeding of fine equestrian stock. Lomar knew that these men had nothing to equal his matched foursome. He could hardly wait to see their eyes pop like moonflowers above their gaping mouths as their bellies knotted with envy. He had the black, gilded carriage waxed and polished, the fittings replaced, and the wheels oiled until they turned at a touch and with hardly a sound. The tails and manes of the horses were brushed and trimmed in the current style, and their coats were oiled and curried until they gleamed like polished coal.

Balkert and Stundal had muttered to each other that the prince seemed more keen to present his new horses than the new princess.

And they were right. Lomar did not have high expectations of his coming marriage. It was a marriage arranged for political reasons, and he would go through with it but with no intentions of fidelity. He had already formed amorous liaisons with several women in Corenham that he fully meant to continue after the wedding. He knew that Volanna was rumored to be a great beauty, but all princesses were rumored to be great beauties, even if in reality they had faces that would curdle cream.

Lomar had commanded Sir Stundal and Balkert to drive his stallions personally to the blacksmith to be freshly shod. He would not trust the horses to the royal coachman, an elderly hireling of Lord Aldemar. The two men vigorously protested the humiliating order. They were prominent men high in the government of the kingdom and didn't wish to lower themselves to a servant's task. But their protests were to no avail.

The horses were fitted with canvas coverings to hide them from premature exposure and rigged to a light utility carriage. With heads down and eyes averted, the two seething men drove through the streets of Corenham toward Bogarth's shop.

"I am a knight of the Hall and jousting champion of the Seven Kingdoms, not the prince's lackey," complained Stundal through clenched teeth.

"I know, I know," replied Balkert. "Just be patient. We may have to bear a little humiliation now and then, but it will not go on indefinitely. Must I remind you that we are actually fortunate to have a prince who cares nothing for business? As long as we keep his itches scratched, we can continue to use his name for our own purposes. The further you get from Corenham, the weaker is Lord Aldemar's influence. With every day that passes we place more and more men in positions of power in the far reaches of Meridan—men who are beholden to us, not to Aldemar and not to Lomar. If we are patient, the time will come soon enough when most of the power is in our hands and we will no longer need to concern ourselves with our little spoiled prince."

"It better be soon. I'll not be treated as a lackey much longer," growled Stundal.

Stundal pointed out that the route to Bogarth's shop led them past the Eagle's Crown alehouse, or at least it would if he made a few advantageous turns. Since the day was warming, the errand was not urgent, and the two men were basking in a rare moment of freedom from the oppressive eye of their master, Balkert agreed. They found the alehouse and stopped to refresh themselves. Balkert drank little, but Stundal drained three generous mugs of strong ale before his companion insisted that they return to their errand. The two men left the house, Stundal on somewhat unsteady feet, and remounted the carriage.

"We've been coddling these horses too much," said Stundal as he took the reins. "Let's see what they're made of."

Balkert protested, but Stundal bellowed a command and cracked his whip, and the black team surged forward, almost tumbling the two men from their seat. Soon they were galloping down the street at a pace that would have been foolhardy even in open country. In the confined space of Corenham's narrow lanes, disaster was inevitable. As they roared across the cobblestones, alarmed vendors and pedestrians scampered out of the way before them. The carriage careened and swerved back and forth, toppling baskets, boxes, and racks of produce. Fruit and vegetables tumbled and spattered on the pavement. Goats and sheep, bleating in terror, broke away from their masters, running in all directions. Squawking hens, wings beating and feathers flying, darted among the churning legs of vendors and animals. One unfortunate goose got caught in the spokes of the carriage wheel, creating a spinning shower of white feathers before her mangled carcass was flung against a stack of pottery, causing a dozen pots to crash to the pavement. Above the chaos rang the angry cursing of merchants and buyers. But Stundal did not slow the pace. "I'll say this for the prince: he knows how to pick horses," he shouted to Balkert above the din. But Balkert, wide-eyed and white-knuckled, was totally absorbed in hanging on to his seat.

The team came to an intersection at the end of the street and tore around the corner, the carriage skidding and bouncing on two wheels as it followed. Immediately ahead, Ansel and Marcie were pushing their cart across the street, unaware of the approaching danger until it was right upon them. Stundal bellowed a warning, and the two women looked up and screamed. They jumped aside and tried to pull the cart with them, but they were too late. The team plowed into the cart, sending it bouncing and splintering along the cobblestones—cakes, wheels, and planks flying and spinning in every direction. The startled horses turned sharply to the side and reared, jerking the carriage to an abrupt halt. Stundal barely managed to retain his seat, but Balkert came tumbling forward and landed headfirst on the pavement between the horses.

After everything came to a stop, Marcie got carefully to her feet. She helped her mother extract herself from beneath an axle and the hub of a broken wheel. Neither seemed hurt except for minor scratches and bruises. Stundal sat for a moment catching his breath, then dismounted and stumbled toward the women, his face crimson with rage.

"What do you mean getting in the way of the prince's carriage?" he roared.

"You got no call to come flyin' through a crowded city street like you owned it," retorted Marcie, hands on hips, cheeks flushed and eyes flashing. "We coulda' all been killed."

"Listen, wench," growled Stundal, "I'll come down any street I choose, at any speed I choose, at any time I choose. You can either get out of the way or count on a short life."

"There wasn't time to get out of the way, you comin' round the corner like a crazed roebuck. By the time I knew you was comin', you was here. Look at what you done to our cart and our bread and cakes. And us just mindin' our own business. I hope you got the money to fix all this up again."

"I'll show you what I think of your cart and cakes." Stundal staggered over to the splintered cart, lying twisted and ruptured like a disemboweled animal. He kicked and stomped, scattering planks, loaves of bread, cakes, and buns over the cobblestones. Bread and pastries that could have been salvaged he ground into the pavement with his heel. With a scream of anger Marcie ran at him and clutched his arm to pull him away, but he slung her off like a rag doll, sending her sprawling across the pavement.

"Let that be a lesson to you wenches," he said as he scooped up the moaning Balkert, deposited him roughly on the floor of the carriage, mounted the seat, and drove away. Ansel and Marcie stood appalled, staring helplessly at the wreckage of their livelihood.

Finally Ansel spoke. "Well, we can't leave this mess in the street." They gathered the ruins of the cart and stacked them in the alleyway next to the clothseller's shop.

Stundal, partly sobered by the near disaster, slowed the horses to a less suicidal but uneven pace and drove directly to Bogarth's shop. Balkert lay on the floor of the carriage, his hand covering the egg-size lump on his head, moaning and cursing with each bump in the street.

When they reached the shop, Stundal demanded that Bogarth stop whatever he was doing and attend to the prince's horses immediately. As there were no urgent orders in the shop at the moment, Bogarth quietly complied. Aradon left the hinges he was making, and the two of them began to unhitch the horses. Balkert moaned, roused himself, and gingerly stepped down from the carriage to join Stundal on a bench near the open front of the shop.

"Beautiful horses," Aradon observed.

"To be sure," responded Bogarth. "But they're awfully skittish. And look how they're all lathered up. They've been driven mighty hard. I think we'd best work them together." One man held the horse by the bridle, stroking and soothing him with gentle words, while the other removed the old shoe, filed the hoof, and nailed the new shoe to it. This method almost doubled the time the job should have taken, which normally would have incited Stundal into a storm of rage. But he was sprawled on a bench, snoring in inebriated dissonance as his companion lay on the ground holding his head and moaning piteously.

As the two smiths prepared to shoe the last stallion, Aradon noticed that the hoof of its left foreleg was covered with blood. He gently lifted the leg and said to Bogarth, "This horse is badly injured. Look at this cut." He showed his father a ragged gash above the hoof, open and seeping blood.

Bogarth's face darkened. "Why are those fools drivin' this horse?" he growled. "If that wound is not treated soon and well, he may never

run again. Bring me hot water and strips of cloth. I'll get the salve."
Treating injuries to horses was not uncommon in Bogarth's shop, and
he kept the needed supplies on hand. Together the men tenderly
cleansed the animal's wound and covered it with a soothing, antisep-
tic balm.

"That should do it," said Bogarth. "You finish with the bandage,
and I'll start hitchin' things back together."

Aradon knelt and began to wrap the cloth strips around the
horse's lower leg.

"What in thunder do you think you are doing?" boomed a voice
above his head. Aradon turned and looked up into the livid face of
Sir Stundal.

"I am treating your horse," Aradon replied calmly. "He has a
nasty wound."

"I came here to get these horses shod, not to get white patches
stuck all over them. You can just take that right back off, smithy. In
three days these horses will draw the prince and princess in the welcome procession. Do you think I'm going to let that rag ruin the look
of an all-black team? Get it off—now!"

Aradon stood and looked Sir Stundal in the eye. "This horse will
not be able to draw a carriage three days from now. That leg will be
swollen and sore. The horse will hardly be able to stand his own
weight on it."

Stundal thrust his face into Aradon's and glared fiercely. "Listen,
smithy, don't tell me what to do with the prince's horses. Now, I'll tell
you just one more time to take off that bandage."

"I will not," answered Aradon, neither flinching nor moving.

Slowly and deliberately Stundal removed the whip from his belt
and let the coiled end drop to the floor, never taking his eyes off of
Aradon's face. "I warned you, smithy!" he growled as he stepped back
and lifted the whip to strike.

"Bogarth! Aradon!" called a genial voice from the open front of
the shop. "Shoe me up some shoes. I've got a horse that's almost barefoot. Or should I say barehoof? Oh, excuse me. I see you have a cus-
tomer already."

At the sound of the voice, Stundal quickly dropped the whip to his side as both he and Aradon broke their locked stares and looked toward the timely intruder. The young knight Sir Denmore stood in the entrance, grinning at them.

"Oh, it's you, Sir Stundal," said Denmore as his eyes adjusted to the shaded interior of the shop. "I see that I'm not the only knight prettying up the feet of his steed for the eyes of our fair new princess."

Stundal dropped his belligerence. It would not do to have a fellow member of the Hall catch him beating a blacksmith for treating an injured horse. At least not until Lomar became king. Then he would do exactly as he pleased and let his peers think what they wanted.

"I'll remember this, smithy," he muttered as he stepped away from the glowering Aradon. "Hurry up and get these horses back in their traces. The prince has been kept waiting long enough."

Sir Denmore tethered his horse and came into the shop. "What beautiful horses! They must be the prince's new Albustians I've heard all the rumors about."

"That is correct," said Stundal. "They will draw the royal carriage in the procession of the princess across Corenham."

"Ah, yes, she's rumored to be a rare beauty—a fair hand for our fair land. And according to the prophecy, her coming is the first of several events that will usher in the golden age of Meridan."

"Surely you're not swallowing all that mystical superstition," sneered Stundal.

"Stranger things have happened," answered Sir Denmore. "And you've got to admit, there's something uncanny about the way the predictions of the prophecy are playing out—the comet appearing on the night of Prince Lomar's birth, the Princess Volanna's birth on the same night, and the fact that the golden comet will converge with the silver star as the prince and princess are wed. Don't you think all that has meaning, Stundal?"

"Chance and superstition!" spat Stundal. "Any fool can dream up a prophecy and confirm it with coincidences, stars, tea leaves, or calf's entrails. Prophecies, miracles, and signs in the sky are for weak-minded dreamers and wishful thinkers. As for me, I believe only in what I can see, hear, or touch. All else is the stuff of fools."

"Ah, but Sir Stundal," Bogarth broke in, "the real fool is the fish that claims nothin' exists but its own pond, or the blind man who insists there is no such thing as light. Is it wisdom to deny that there might be a wider world out there beyond our own? There may be all sorts of powers and possibilities beyond what we can see and hear and touch. We oughtn' to close our minds to things beyond our reach."

"Listen, smithy, I'm here to get horses shod, not to be pounded with mystic philosophy. Get those horses hitched so I can get back to the prince's business."

"Just about finished," Bogarth calmly replied. "In fact, you can be on your way in just a moment."

He led the team from the shed and rigged them to the carriage. Balkert, who had hardly moved during the proceedings in the shop, arose sluggishly and grimaced as he eased himself into the carriage. Stundal pressed the prince's signet into the hot wax on Bogarth's bill of services, then climbed up beside his miserable companion and took the reins. He turned to Aradon with a look of unmitigated malice.

"I'm not forgetting your insolence, smithy. You want to know what happens to people who get in my way? Ask the cakeseller and her well-uddered daughter about what I did to them near Holgard the clothseller's shop. The next time we meet, I'll splinter you across the pavement just as I did their flimsy cart."

Before Aradon could reply, Stundal shouted at the horses and snapped the reins, and the carriage bolted into the roadway, almost tumbling Balkert and scattering a flock of honking geese being driven to market by an elderly woman.

"There goes Meridan's next general," observed Sir Denmore, "training for his coming role by making war wherever he goes. Come, Aradon, get my horse shod and we can spend a half-hour with the blades."

For over a year, Sir Denmore had bartered lessons in swordsmanship in exchange for horseshoeing. This arrangement had come about when Denmore noticed the gleam in Aradon's eye as the young blacksmith sharpened his weapons. "Would you like to learn to use that?" he had asked the boy one day as he watched him delicately run his thumb along the razor-sharp edge of his tempered broadsword. Aradon's response had been enthusiastic, and regular lessons had begun.

In truth, Aradon had a natural ability with the sword. This was clear to Bogarth and Denmore from the day of the first lesson. His reflexes were excellent, his strength enormous, and his speed was almost blinding. And he held the sword with an easy grace and balance such as could not be taught, even by the best of masters. What Denmore had expected to be halfhearted, short-term tutorials with a clumsy stripling grew into earnest training. After a few weeks of practice, Denmore had sensed that his pupil could soon better his master.

But today Aradon's heart was not in the swords. "Did you hear what Stundal said?" he asked. "Apparently he has smashed Ansel and Marcie's cart. Without it they have no livelihood. After I get your horse done, I'd better go find the cart and see if it can be fixed."

"Ah, the young would-be knight embarks on a quest to save his fair damsel in distress. No doubt his reward will be a dazzling smile, perhaps a kiss, or even her undying love and devotion. Does our fine, fair-haired hero harbor such high hopes?" said Denmore with mischief in his eyes.

"For a true knight, the deed accomplished is its own reward," replied Aradon with his chin in the air and his hand on his chest in a pose of mock heroism.

"Go on, Aradon. I'll shoe the horse," said Bogarth. "Take the wagon. You will have to gather up the cart in pieces." As Bogarth watched Aradon mount the wagon and drive away, he wondered which posed the greater danger: the sword or the girl.

"Well, what do you think, Bogarth?" Sir Denmore asked, as if reading the blacksmith's thoughts. "Is the boy being drawn into a web of wondrously wicked womanly wiles, or is he merely a disinterested but noble champion of the downtrodden?"

"I wish I knew," replied Bogarth, scratching his grizzled beard. "For the past six months Ansel has never missed a chance to parade Marcie in front of him like a farmer showin' a prize heifer. And lately they've been gettin' even more forward. Now they're openly pressin' the boy into weddin' the girl."

"Would that be so bad? She is quite a winsome lass."

"Ah, that she is, that she is, to be sure. If you judge the pea by its pod, Aradon could hardly pick better. But those two are comin' at him so strong I'm afraid they'll trap him before he really knows what he wants. And I can't quite read the boy's mind in this matter. Mostly I think their wavin' her wares in front of his eyes so forward-like is makin' him pull back. But sometimes I catch him lookin' at her out of the corner of his eye like he used to look at steamin' strawberry tarts in the baker's shop. I just don't quite know what he's thinkin'."

"I think I see what you're worried about. You're afraid the girl will offer a sampling of the fruit before he buys the orchard."

"Well, yes, somethin' like that," admitted Bogarth. "But, deep down, I know I shouldn't worry. I've done all I could to teach the boy to act gentleman-like with the lasses, so I've got to let him go and pray that my teachin' will be there when the temptation comes."

✍

Bogarth was right; Aradon hardly knew his own mind concerning Marcie. As he drove toward the site of their disaster, he tried to sort out his uncertain feelings. Like any healthy young male, he had more than an idle interest in women. He fully intended to marry. The warmth brought into his home by his parents' devotion to each other convinced him that wedded love was synonymous with man's happiness. But at the same time, he had witnessed enough of less perfect matches to know that marriage could also mean a lifetime locked in misery.

Fenstone the barber was a prime example. Fenstone was a highly intelligent and knowledgeable man whose restraint in the use of bleeding and leeching saved scores of lives in Corenham. Yet his wife treated him like an imbecile incapable of making a rational decision. Then there was poor Lela the cobbler's wife, who had to hide her meager earnings from selling eggs to keep her husband from spending every last farthing at the Eagle's Crown alehouse. And she often had to hide her three small children to protect them from his drunken rages. But to Aradon, the most pitiable was Corvin the bookseller, often cuckolded by a wife who treated his unwavering devotion as irritating foolishness.

No doubt Fenstone, Lela, and Corvin thought they were marrying the best of mates, mused Aradon. But either something had clouded their judgment or their mates had changed radically after the vows were spoken. Aradon knew such changes were possible; Fenstone's wife had been the meekest and most accommodating of women during their courtship. But as Bogarth had told him, a woman will often hide her true personality from her suitor until she has achieved her ends. "The clue to a woman's permanent disposition can be found in her treatment of others, especially parents, servants, and vendors," Bogarth had said. Had Fenstone been less blinded by his woman's face and form, he might have seen the truth during their courtship in her tendency to dominate every relationship she had except her relationship to him.

So what about Marcie? he thought. *What flaws might be lurking beneath that winsome surface that could wreck a marriage?* He had often watched her at a distance, laughing and bantering with the leering men who were her customers. He had little doubt that much of what was said in these exchanges was bawdy and coarse; he knew the men too well to think otherwise. Yet whenever Marcie crossed the threshold of Bogarth's shop, she was always so demure and maidenly it was hard to believe she was anything but pure as the morning dew. And perhaps she was. There was much to admire about her besides the fair face and stunning form. She was a diligent worker, she was always respectful to her mother, and Aradon had never seen her out of sorts or moody.

Aradon realized that his hesitation about Marcie was caused largely by the way she presented herself to him. Certainly there was nothing shameful about her lavishly feminine charms, but did she have to make those charms so visible? Couldn't her bodice be cut a few inches higher? Did the laces of that bodice always have to be loose and on the verge of undoing? Did she not know what Aradon could see or what he felt when she bent over her cart to hand him a honeycake? Did she really trip while descending the crate, or was it a calculated slip designed to force Aradon into close contact with her? He strongly suspected the latter—that she was trying to cloud his reason by enticing him into an intimacy their hearts and minds had not prepared them for. Yet he felt the heat rise in his face as he remembered her delicious warmth and softness within his arms.

Most of Corenham's healthy youths on the threshold of manhood would have taken immediate advantage of Marcie's invitations to intimacy, utterly uninhibited by such questions as Aradon pondered. What separated Aradon from the others was Bogarth. Aradon's behavior toward women, like his mores and views on almost everything, grew from seeds planted early by his father. Bogarth never missed an opportunity to expose his son to his personal view of life and the elemental facts about the world around him. From the time the boy was five until his voice began to crack, Bogarth had bartered for lessons from a tutor, who spent two hours a day, three days a week, teaching him reading, rudimentary mathematics, history, and the basics of natural science.

Among Bogarth's customers, there were two schools of thought concerning his education of Aradon. Most thought it a waste of time and money. "What's the point?" they asked. "He'll never be anything but a blacksmith. Can he beat a plowshare any better for knowing how to cipher? Will he shoe a horse any faster for reading of the wars of Perivale?" But Bogarth adamantly defended the practice. "A man needs to look outside himself just as a house needs windows. The mind gets all stunted and musty unless its got openin's to show what's beyond its four walls. To be sure, Aradon will live and die a blacksmith, but he'll not be a simpleton as well."

One patron, an educated immigrant named Heraklos, from the islands of the southern sea, applauded the hiring of the tutor but had open contempt for Bogarth teaching Aradon such a rigid moral philosophy. "You are enslaving the boy's mind," he had complained. "You should teach him to think for himself—to sift through the facts and make his own choices—and not dig channels in his brain that force his thoughts to flow to your conclusions. Your son will grow up to be like a trained horse with blinders, able to look only in one direction and respond only to one voice—the voice of Bogarth—which will echo in his head with your hopelessly narrow, archaic idea of truth."

Bogarth had replied, "You're assumin' there's no such thing as real truth; I'm assumin' there is. And if I'm right, a man's got to know what that truth is and pass it on to his sons and daughters so they won't waste their lives havin' to find it for themselves. Life is infested with thousands of dragons of deception lurkin' out there in the shadows, and I intend to give my boy a good weapon to fend them off with. It's my duty to hammer out the shape of truth early in his life, while the iron is malleable, so that when he's older it will harden true and strong."

Bogarth taught his son more than just the raw facts about the world around him; he gave the boy some sense of the meaning that emanates like an aroma from every created thing. Thus Aradon learned not only the elemental differences between the sexes but something of chivalry and masculine responsibility toward women as well. Surprisingly, the rough-hewn Bogarth had an uncanny ability to convey his own sense of awe and specialness—the "magic" as he called it—of the relationship between man and woman. As a result Aradon came to look at women not as fortresses to be stormed and sacked, or as fruit to be plucked and devoured, the core discarded, but as marvelous creatures of immense value, to be honored, wooed, and won courteously and gently. One must build trust, confidence, love, and commitment before tasting the ultimate intimacy.

Bogarth need not have worried about Aradon's succumbing to the velvet trap he thought Ansel and Marcie were setting. The iron had hardened strong and true in his son. To Aradon, it was unthinkable that his body would enter where his mind and heart had not opened the way. He sensed that to follow the voluptuous cakeseller's invitations to pleasure would be a lonely, isolating, selfish thing rather than an intimate sharing. His focus would be solely on his own pleasure; he would be using her body merely to satisfy himself. And the act would make him shamefully aware that he was a weakling incapable of mastering his own urges. Moreover, Marcie would sense that he was not truly interested in her; she would know she was nothing more to him than an instrument of pleasure. This, Bogarth had once told Aradon, was why so many illicit lovers loathed each other after their lust was spent. They loathed themselves for their own slavery to appetite, and the partner was a mirror in which they saw this truth unmasked. He had gone on to say, "The writer of the Eden story was not just bein' careless with words when he said that 'Adam knew his wife, and she bore a son.' He didn't just use his wife; he knew his wife. He knew her as he knew himself. Their souls and spirits were one, and it was neither an intrusion nor an act of selfishness for him to 'go in unto her.' Their bodies participated in the knowledge their hearts already shared."

Yet Aradon was aware as he drove toward the site of the wrecked cart that he looked forward to seeing Marcie. Was it possible that he was judging her too severely? The low-bodiced dress may have been the best she had. Or maybe she was innocently unaware of its effect on men. What he had interpreted as wanton flirting may have been simply an attractive, outgoing girl giving friendly service to her pastry buyers. Her fall from the crate into Aradon's arms may indeed have been accidental. "Yes, and I may be the richest man in Meridan," he muttered as he approached the site of the collision.

Aradon found the splintered remains of the cart stacked against the wall of the clothseller's shop. Ansel and Marcie were nowhere to be seen, however, and Aradon found himself strangely torn between disappointment and relief.

He loaded the pieces onto his wagon and drove directly to the shop of Sorvan the carpenter. Sorvan measured the broken parts and cut new ones as Aradon went on to his father's shop to fashion fittings to replace those that had been broken or twisted. Together Bogarth and Aradon reassembled the cart, and shortly after nightfall it was fully repaired. They returned it to the shop wall where Aradon found it and left it for Ansel and Marcie to reclaim in the morning.

"Don't breathe a word to them about who did this," Aradon instructed the clothseller as he and his father climbed into the wagon and returned home.

CHAPTER ELEVEN

THE WOUNDED STALLION

t was the day of Meridan's welcome for Princess Volanna. Almost every shop was closed. Families slept an hour later than usual, but before midmorning the route of the royal procession was lined with onlookers hoping for a glimpse of their queen-to-be.

Princess Volanna had arrived at Lord Aldemar's manor two days before. Lady Aldemar had taken the young princess under her own motherly wing and had made her as comfortable as possible in her unfamiliar surroundings. The matronly lady had adamantly shielded the tired girl from all official intrusion until she was well rested from her long journey. On the morning of her welcome Volanna had risen early, bathed and breakfasted, and donned a regal, ceremonial gown. Now Kalley was putting the finishing touches on her hair, chattering incessantly as she worked. Prince Lomar was to arrive at any moment.

"You're a strange one, Volanna," Kalley said as she coaxed wayward strands of her mistress's hair into place. "Any bride meeting her husband-to-be for the first time should be nervous as a cat in a kennel, and here you are acting like it's an everyday affair. For decency's sake you ought to be biting your fingernails—no, don't! It took me an hour to shape and shine them. But feel free to wring your hands, tap your feet, or chatter away on the verge of hysteria."

"I don't think there is room in here for any more hysteria.

Remember, the wedding is a year away. I'm only meeting the man today, not marrying him."

"It's almost the same thing," said Kalley. "You're promised to him, and from this day forward your lives will become more and more entwined. And you don't even know the man. You ought to be more curious—not that it would do you any good because the strange thing is, nobody will talk about him. The servants all turn mum when you ask what he's like. Even Lady Aldemar mumbles vague answers and changes the subject—I mean, when the subject is Prince Lomar—although she did hint once that he might be a little spoiled. I tell you, Volanna, there's something about Prince Lomar that no one wants to talk about. Haven't you noticed?"

"No, I haven't noticed because I haven't been prying information out of our hosts. As to Prince Lomar's being a little spoiled, that shouldn't be too surprising; he's an orphaned prince brought up by doting nannies. But remember, he is King Alfron's son, a descendant of Perivale, destined to be emperor of the Seven Kingdoms, soon to be a husband, and soon after, I presume, a father. He'll grow up quickly enough. But as you know, it doesn't matter what he is like; I have made a vow, and I will keep it. I am not my own, Kalley. My life is in the hands of my fate."

"Oh, I know all that. It's just that your calm acceptance of your destiny takes the fun out of what ought to be a time of excitement in any girl's life."

At that moment a maidservant entered and announced, "The prince has arrived, your highness. He will meet you in the sitting room at your convenience."

Kalley squealed and with flying fingers finished Volanna's hair and smoothed the cascades of her dress. In spite of herself, Volanna could not still the sudden fluttering of her stomach as she followed the servant through the hallways to meet her prince. She paused outside the waiting room as Kalley gave her dress a final smooth and fluff. Then the servant opened the door.

Prince Lomar was half sitting, half lying in a cushioned chair. He looked at Volanna with pale green eyes hooded with heavy lids that gave him a permanent look of cynical boredom. His hair was dark and brushed forward, rimming his forehead like hanging brush atop a granite knoll. His skin was pallid and soft, his frame thin but with the beginnings of roundness at the middle. He was outfitted in finery tailored to the cut of a foppish eastern design presently popular with young adults in the kingdom. After gazing at the princess for several seconds, he rose languidly from his seat, walked toward her with grace bordering on the effeminate, took her hand, and bowed as he pressed it to his lips.

"My dear Princess Volanna," he said in a thin but precise voice, "on behalf of the people of Meridan, I bid you welcome to our fair city and invite you to share the life of our people and the fortunes of our nation."

"Thank you, your highness, for your gracious welcome," she replied. Then she took his proffered arm so he could escort her to the royal carriage, and the procession to Morningstone began.

The procession was led by a mounted herald whose trumpet announced at regular intervals the approach of the royal couple. Following the herald rode the forty-two knights of the realm, resplendent in gleaming armor, with flying banners and elaborately skirted horses. Following the knights marched a retinue of sixteen marching guards commanded by Sir Stundal, who was mounted at their head, adorned in polished armor without helm, accented by a flowing green cape. Then came Prince Lomar and Princess Volanna in the gilded open carriage drawn by Lomar's magnificent quartet of black Albustian stallions. Regent Lord and Lady Aldemar followed the royal pair in their own carriage, and the rear of the procession was brought up by lesser carriages carrying government officials in order of importance.

The parade descended Aldemar's hill into the city, and the princess got her first look at her new home. Houses and shops stood clean and trim, with whitewashed walls and freshly thatched roofs that gleamed like brushed gold in the morning sun. Crepe banners hung from balconies, and multicolored flowers in earthen pots adorned the windows. Carved wooden signs, freshly painted and hung on bright hinges, identified the shops of merchants and tradesmen. The cobblestone street was clean-swept and lined on both sides with onlookers of both sexes and all ages, tiptoeing and craning for a glimpse of their new princess. As the carriage moved through the streets, the people shouted their welcome and waved bouquets and banners in homage. Volanna, greatly warmed by this outpouring of goodwill, smiled broadly and waved in return, much to the delight of the crowd. Lomar sat passively and scarcely glanced at the onlookers. He watched Volanna with a frown of disapproval.

"Your highness," he said, "the people will respect you much better if you display a bit more reserve. It is best to keep some distance between the common folk and ourselves."

"Surely you don't believe that distance breeds respect. Let's give them cause to love us as well as respect us," Volanna replied cheerfully, continuing her empathetic display of rapport with the crowd.

As the procession approached the Red Shield Inn, someone on the balcony shouted Volanna's name. She looked up to see the grinning face of Remmlet the innkeeper, his rounded torso decked with a tunic as red as his cheeks. He was surrounded by the smiling faces of the inn's cooks, charwomen, and porters. Remmlet gave a signal, and a red banner twelve feet wide and three feet high unrolled and dropped across the railings. *Welcomme Princesse Volanna* was painted on the banner in uneven but brilliant letters, along with a valiant attempt at a portrait of the princess as they had imagined she would look. Volanna laughed with delight and blew a gracious kiss to the innkeeper, who bowed deeply in return.

"Who is that man?" she asked Lomar. "I must send him my thanks for such a fine welcome."

"I really don't know," answered the prince. "How can I keep up with all the tradesmen and peasants in Corenham? As long as they do whatever they do, pay their taxes, and stay reasonably within the law, I leave them alone and they leave me alone. And we both like it that way."

"Oh, that's too bad. In Valomar royalty and commoners often mix with each other. My father says it does much to keep distrust from getting a foothold."

"Please, Volanna, please! They were born to their lot, and we were born to ours. Fate has ordained that their purpose for being is to serve us and ours to reap the fruits of their labor."

"Oh, no, no, Lomar! We are here to serve *them*. It is they who work to provide the products, produce, and services that keep the wheels of commerce turning. Our duty is to provide an environment for trade to flourish so men and women can live in peace and prosperity. That is the obligation and purpose of royalty."

"You sound like a pupil reciting a tutor's lesson. In Meridan we do things a bit differently. But you will learn all that soon enough. Now, look ahead of you. We are approaching Cheaping Square, and just to the right you can see the top of the statue of Perivale, my great-great-great-grandfather and the founder of the empire."

"Yes, I know of him," replied Volanna. "Remember that Valomar was once a part of Perivale's empire. I've heard of the unfinished statue, but I had no idea it was so perfectly huge."

As Volanna spoke there was a slight break in the even rhythm of the horses' hooves and an instant of hesitation in the pace of the carriage. "Is something wrong with your lead horse?" she asked.

"Just a rough place in the street," Lomar replied.

The team regained its rhythm and the carriage moved on. As they rounded the next curve, Cheaping Square came into full view, and above it towered the monumental mass of the famed sculpture.

"Oh, look at Perivale," said Volanna with awe. "He is trying to push free of the stone."

"Most people think he is sinking into the stone," replied Lomar.

"Oh, no. Look at his determined expression, the hope in his reach, the tension in the sinews of his arm. One who was sinking would have a look of defeat and despair."

"It sounds as though Meridan has gained an artist as well as a queen."

"No, no, my lord," laughed Volanna. "No artist, but one who loves the work of men's hands when they seem to touch the secrets of eternity."

Again the rigging clattered and the carriage jolted, this time enough to jerk the heads of the royal couple. "Lomar, I'm sure that horse stumbled again. Shouldn't we stop and see if something is wrong? He may have a loose shoe."

"Please, my dear Volanna, let the driver take care of the horses.

They get the best of care, and I'm sure nothing is wrong. It is certainly the street."

The pace smoothed once more, and the procession continued. As it approached Cheaping Square and the towering image, the crowds grew thicker and more demonstrative. Volanna continued to respond to their enthusiastic welcome with smiles and graceful waves, which incited them to redouble their adoration.

Volanna's first impression of Lomar was not as bad as her introduction and initial conversations might lead one to think. To be sure, she was dismayed by her first sight of him, but her father had repeatedly warned her of the danger of judging reality by surface appearances. She remembered from her childhood the woodsman whose horribly scarred face had sent her screaming until she learned that he had received his scars saving a neighbor's children from a fire. And there was the charwoman Beth, with her deeply creased forehead and a mouth drawn down in a permanent scowl, who was as fun loving and full of laughter as anyone in Oakendale Castle. Lomar could not help his hooded eyes or gaunt cheeks any more than they could help their unfortunate appearance. As to his indifference to his people, perhaps she could help him learn to appreciate them. His cynicism might yet be turned to good humor by the gentle influence of a loving wife. Such optimism may have had little basis in reality, but it made her future seem less foreboding.

For his part, Prince Lomar was agreeably surprised with what he saw in Volanna. He had not expected such beauty. In fact he could hardly keep his eyes from devouring this delectable morsel that had been dropped onto his plate. Yet he treated her with the same bored, condescending detachment with which he treated everyone. There had never been any need for him to woo or win the women he desired; the fact that he was the crown prince of the empire was always enough to bring any girl under his power. He showed little interest in Volanna's conversation for he cared nothing about what she thought or how she felt. It was not her mind or personality that interested him.

As the procession entered Cheaping Square, Lomar's right front horse began to stumble badly, this time slowing his pace and causing the carriage to veer to the right as the coachman fought for control.

"Lomar, that horse is limping. Something is wrong. We must ask the coachman to stop."

"Volanna, I told you not to bother about the horses. It is not your place."

As the carriage came abreast of the Perivale monument, the horses, trying to proceed at uneven speeds, jammed together, and the coachmen had no choice but to rein the team to a halt. Sir Stundal turned at the sound and shouted, "What in thunder do you think you are doing!" He trotted back to the coachman and drew up beside him.

"I had to stop the carriage," the coachman explained. "The right front horse has gone lame and could not keep pace. The team jammed up, so I stopped them before they pulled the rigging apart."

"All that horse needs is the whip. Now get him going!" barked Stundal. The coachman knew better, but under Stundal's hot glare, he picked up his whip and gingerly cracked it above the injured horse.

"Not like that," growled Stundal. "Give me that whip." He wrenched it from the coachman's hands and laid it sharply several times across the horse's back.

"No!" shouted Volanna, standing up in the carriage.

"You stay out of this!" hissed Lomar, grabbing her arm and jerking her back into the seat.

As Stundal's first lash landed on the back of the stallion, a figure watching from the pedestal of Perivale's monument leaped into the crowd and swiftly wove his way toward the royal carriage. Stundal raised his arm to strike again and felt the whip jerked from his hand. In surprise he turned to see the tall, powerful form and glowering face of Aradon, standing with feet planted wide apart, slowly coiling the coachman's whip in his hands.

Stundal was livid. "What is the meaning of this, blacksmith?" he bellowed, as he reached for his own whip.

"I warned you three days ago that this horse is too injured to be driven. You will ruin him if you continue. I will not stand by and let that happen," shouted Aradon.

"You think you can stop a royal procession to tell me how to treat the prince's horses?" replied Stundal. "Your impertinence is beyond belief! But in deference to our new princess, I will let your unforgivable intrusion pass for now. Just get out of this street and count yourself lucky you're not dead."

Stundal turned again to the injured horse and raised his whip to strike. In an instant Aradon leapt upon the big knight, grabbed hold of his cape, and pulled him to the cobblestones with a crash. Every onlooker gasped and stared in shocked silence at the spectacle of Stundal sprawled on the pavement. Slowly he raised himself to his elbow, wiped the trickle of blood from his lip and shouted to the guards, "Seize that man!"

Immediately the guards rushed toward Aradon. He sidestepped the first, who brushed by him and collided head-on with a lamppost. He rammed the second in the stomach with his shoulder and tumbled the man over his back to the pavement. He leveled the third with a fist to the face. He ducked under a wild swing from the fourth, then hammered him with a driving blow to the side that broke three ribs. The remaining guards fell back surprised as Aradon crouched and awaited the next attack. Volanna looked on in open-mouthed wonder, thrilling to the courage and power of the magnificent young man.

"What's the matter with you cockroaches?" bellowed Stundal, now back on his feet. "Can't the sixteen of you arrest one loutish blacksmith? I said seize him!"

Again the guards rushed Aradon, and after another flurry of ducking and punching, three more of them lay groaning and bloodied on the cobblestones. As the remaining guards regrouped, Aradon seized a sword from one of the fallen warriors. He leaped between the black stallions and began hacking at the traces. The injured horse was almost free when Stundal's whip sang through the air and wrapped several times around Aradon's neck. Aradon dropped the sword and clutched at the whipcord to keep it from twisting the skin from his neck as Stundal pulled him over the back of the horse and tumbled him to the pavement.

The guards were on him instantly, trying to pinion his arms to keep him from rising. Aradon pulled one arm free and managed to stand. With his right fist he pounded the face of the guard clamped to his left arm, crumpling him to the ground. But three more guards took the place of the one, and after another minute or so of struggle, Aradon was held fast in the grasp of four bleeding and panting guards.

Stundal stood before him, feet wide apart, his face contorted with rage. The crowd gaped in silence as the knight slowly pulled on his chain mail gauntlet, drew back his hand, and hit Aradon full force on the side of his face. Again and again he hit the pinioned blacksmith until blood poured from his nose and mouth.

Volanna was aghast. "Lomar, make him stop!" she cried. "He'll kill the poor man!"

"As well he should," retorted Lomar. "The idiot has ruined your welcome."

Stundal finally stopped beating Aradon, removed the gauntlet, and shouted to the guards, "Men, look about you at your fallen comrades." He gestured to the several moaning forms strewn about the pavement. "Are you going to let their humiliation go unavenged?" Two of the guards began to pummel Aradon as the others held him. He staggered and fell to the ground, and the guards began a frenzy of kicking and stomping on the now limp body.

"Stop!" Volanna stood and screamed. "Stop this at once!"

Lomar grabbed her roughly by the arm and again jerked her down to her seat. "What in the devil's name do you think you're doing?" he hissed.

"Stopping a murder, I hope."

"Sit down! If you can't act like a princess, at least act like a lady."

On hearing Volanna's shout, Stundal commanded the guards to stop the beating. They rolled Aradon, now unconscious, out of the roadway with their heels. Stundal commandeered a cart from a bystander, and seven injured soldiers were loaded into it. He ordered the owner to wait until the procession had passed, then take them to the infirmary at Morningstone.

Aradon had accomplished his purpose. The rigging that connected the injured horse to the prince's carriage was almost completely severed, and Stundal had no choice but to detach the animal. Lomar was outraged. The long-anticipated showing of his stallions was ruined. Volanna was angry as well but with a different cause. She was appalled at the brutal treatment of the horse and its rescuer. Nevertheless she continued to smile and wave at the crowd, while Lomar pouted and slumped in his seat, looking sourly ahead. Throughout the remainder of the parade the two had nothing to say to each other.

The crowd stared in shock as the procession passed, wondering what could have caused the disarray that met their eyes. The corps of guards—or what was left of them—was bloodied, tattered, and limping. An incomplete team of three horses pulled the royal carriage, much of the rigging dragging and clattering across the cobblestones. Sir Stundal's cape was torn, his lip bloody, and his armor dented and scratched.

A deadly pall dampened the rest of the ceremonies. When the procession arrived at Morningstone, Prince Lomar read his speech of welcome with a wooden detachment relieved only by occasional overtones of sarcasm. Volanna's speech of response was gracious but subdued. At the high dinner the two hardly spoke to each other, and the guests and officials, sensing the tension, engaged in forced conversation that never fully flowed. Neither the entertainment of minstrels and tumblers nor the dance restored life to the festivities, and as soon as it was socially proper, the guests began to slip away.

As evening fell, all that remained with the royal couple were the castle servants, Lord and Lady Aldemar, and Sir Brevemont, the kingdom's minister of internal affairs, who with his family had taken up temporary residence in the castle to serve as chaperones.

The rooms of Prince Lomar and those of Princess Volanna were well secured and in opposite parts of the castle. They were separated by an open courtyard, meaning that in effect the two lived in different structures. Nevertheless, Aldemar, with his strong sense of propriety and his equally strong distrust of the prince, had insisted on installing a chaperone.

Lomar, warmed by the wine and mead of the banquet, saw the emptying of the hall as a fine opportunity to initiate the seduction that had burned in his imagination since the moment he first laid eyes on Volanna. He turned to her with his most charming smile and said, "Perhaps the princess would care to accompany her prince to the balcony." Volanna did not care to do any such thing, but knowing they needed to relieve the tension between them, she agreed. They walked to the balcony and looked out over the parapet at the starlit city of Corenham.

"It seems that you and I have not made a good beginning," said the prince.

"No, we have not," agreed Volanna.

"I'm sure that neither of us wants to let what happened today drive a permanent wedge between us. A single incident on our first meeting should not sour the relationship that has been imposed upon us by our fathers."

"Yes, you are right. We must recover from this stumble and take our first step again."

"I am happy that you agree. I have been reminding myself that you are new here. You don't know us, our customs, or our expectations. This must be a difficult time for you—uprooted from a lifelong home, thrust into the midst of total strangers, and finding yourself the focus of the entire kingdom from the moment of your arrival."

"Why thank you, your highness, for your sensitive understanding," she replied with a slight softening of the tension in her voice.

"Of course, your highness. Please forgive me for allowing that understanding to bloom so late. I should have realized from the start how different life in Valomar must be from life in Meridan. I made the error of assuming that certain things were common to royalty everywhere, forgetting that outlying provincial kingdoms such as Valomar would lack some of the sophistication we take for granted in Meridan."

"What do you mean?" asked Volanna, wary again.

"Just that I forgive you for your, uh, undignified behavior today."

"What undignified behavior?" An edge returned to her voice.

"In the carriage, of course. I hate to mention it now, but surely you know what I mean—bouncing around in your seat, grinning like an imbecile, waving like a clock with a broken spring—"

"You mean you think response in kind to the warm welcome of your people is undignified behavior?"

"Well, I didn't mean to put it in quite that way, but with your provincial background, you probably didn't know any better. What I found more difficult to understand was your yelling commands to the captain of my guard as if you were the prince yourself—commands in opposition to my will, I might add. In Meridan no lady does such things, especially not a princess. I would have thought the same were true even in places such as Valomar."

"Yes, Lomar, it is the same in Valomar. No one has the right to counter the will of one in authority. But in Valomar not even the king has the right to ruin a wounded animal or beat a brave, innocent subject senseless. And if that sort of thing is allowed here, then all your boasting about Meridan's superior sophistication is merely wind, and this is in fact a barbaric kingdom."

"There are some things you just don't understand," replied Lomar. "The people of Meridan have looked forward to your arrival for months. The whole city has been virtually rebuilt for you. A holiday was proclaimed so they could turn out to welcome you, and those four horses were my own contribution to your welcome. Bearing you to Morningstone Castle was their first public use. That lumpish blacksmith ruined everything. He wrecked the procession, injured six or eight guards, humiliated my most loyal knight, and now it seems, has driven a wedge between myself and my queen-to-be. His beating was less than he deserved."

"It certainly was. What he deserved was honor. He saved your horse."

"Can I just stand by and let any lout in the kingdom appoint himself guardian of my livestock's health?"

"Apparently someone needs to be their guardian. Even I could tell that something was wrong with that horse, and I told you so. But you did not care. A courageous young man was beaten almost to death, and you did not care. Your only concern was your image— how you and your parade looked in the eyes of your people, about whom you do not care. Don't pretend the parade was for me. You've already shown that my enjoyment of it only ruined it for you. The problem between us is more serious than a simple misunderstanding or my failure to comprehend your culture. We have deep differences on things more basic. We appear to have a long and rocky road ahead of us. At this point I hardly even know how to begin, but I'm sure that further discussion tonight will merely drive the wedge deeper between us. Let's part and address the problem at a later meeting, after we've had time to think things through."

"Very well," Lomar sighed. "Good night, my princess."

The prince reached for Volanna's hand, but she had already turned and was walking down the hallway toward her rooms, her dress swishing with the briskness of her pace. He looked after her, frowning with frustration at this rare failure to bring a girl quickly under his spell. But his greedy eyes followed the graceful movement of her splendid figure and the frown melted into something like a smile, or perhaps more like a leer, as he muttered, "I'll not wait a year, my dear Volanna."

CHAPTER TWELVE

THE EMPTY VISION

Aradon pulled himself up to a sitting position and eased his back into the plump, down-filled pillow at the head of his bed. He winced as a stab of pain shot through his cracked ribs. His cheek and jaw were purple with bruises and one eye was swollen almost shut. His head no longer throbbed, and he could move without groaning now, a significant improvement over three days ago, after the incident at Cheaping Square.

When Bogarth had brought him home unconscious, his mother, Faeren, had bathed him, dressed the cuts and abrasions she found, and put poultices on his worst bruises. He had awakened that evening with a throbbing head and a high fever. After accepting a few sips of a healing brew of spiced mead, he had fallen into a natural sleep but had then endured a fitful night filled with wild dreams and hallucinations. By the second day his fever was almost gone and the pain had subsided. Faeren spoon-fed him a savory, warm broth, and he began to recover rapidly.

Now he gingerly felt the bruises on his face and torso. He was carefully testing the movement of all his limbs, toes, and fingers when his mother entered the room with a full bowl of steaming stew.

"I'm not hurt too badly," he said. "Nothing seems broken."

"It's bad enough, and it could have been worse," she replied. "That brute Stundal almost killed you, and he might have done it had the new princess not intervened."

"Did she indeed?" Aradon had not known of this. In fact, he had neither seen nor heard the princess, so intently was he focused on the maltreatment of the stallion. "Perhaps she is cast from a different mold than our local royalty. I will have to find some way to thank her."

"You will do no such thing," said Faeren. "You must stay away from Morningstone Castle altogether. You managed to humiliate the castle guard and the next general of the army, and you ruined the princess's royal welcome procession. You don't need to go poking your face in places that could remind the wrong people of your affront to them. They may not think beating you to the edge of the grave was enough."

"But, Mother, I was not trying to humiliate anyone or ruin anything. I was just trying to save a mistreated horse who was in great pain and very near permanent ruin."

"Oh, I know, Aradon, but why must you make it your task to do these things? If the thousands of people watching felt no need to interfere, why not you as well?"

"I suppose it was because something needed to be done and no one else was doing it. Someone had to. I just happened to be there."

In truth Faeren was very proud of her son. When her mind was freed from worry over his injuries, she would be glad that he had had the courage to confront one of the kingdom's most powerful men for a just cause. But like all mothers she fought a battle within herself between the desire for her son's safety and the desire for his uncompromised honor. She was ever trying to believe in a universe where the two were not mutually exclusive.

Before she married Bogarth, Faeren had been the personal attendant of Alfron's queen. As a high servant in the palace, she was well educated for a woman of her day and was a consummate practitioner of impeccable etiquette and precise speech, traits she tried to transmit to her husband and son. She had more success with the son than the husband. She left the queen's service four years before the birth of Prince Lomar, having fallen in love with the truehearted blacksmith she met at Meridan's harvest fair. She was cherished and well treated, and never once did she look back with longing on her former life in Morningstone Castle.

"I think I'll be able to get back to the shop in two or three days," said Aradon, hoping to ease his mother's concern.

"Not for a fortnight," she replied firmly. "If you had to go out and get yourself hurt, you picked the perfect time. Everything in Corenham that needed smithing was done in the last few weeks, and no one has a farthing left for anything but shoeing and repairs. At the moment there is not even enough work to keep your father busy. You lie back and rest."

Faeren took Aradon's empty bowl, straightened his bedclothes, and left him to himself. The young man stretched, settled contentedly into his pillow, and gazed out the open window by his bed. In spite of his injuries, he felt that delicious sense of well-being that comes to one when all needs are met and the mind is at peace. The morning sun streamed through the window, and a fresh, gentle, spring breeze brought in the delicious scents of new-mown hay and morning glories. Looking outside he could see the cluster of tall, thick oaks where he had often climbed and played as a child. Past the oaks he could see five hundred yards across a sunlit valley that cradled a clear, sparkling stream. His eyes grew heavy as he watched a shepherd boy singing lustily as he drove a flock of bleating sheep up the valley toward the meadows beyond.

Shortly a creaking, horse-drawn cart came into view, piled high with golden straw and looking like a shock of windblown hair on the head of a country lass. As Aradon gazed languidly, he realized that the straw was indeed hair, and that a head, complete with face and features, existed below it, and beneath that the neck and bosom of a winsome young woman. With a start he realized he had drifted into that listless twilight between sleep and wakefulness and that he was looking at the face of Marcie, who was standing at his window with her shapely arms folded on the sill, looking like a master portrait in a rustic frame.

"You startled me," said Aradon as he pulled the sheet over his bare chest. "I suppose I was dozing a bit."

"I'm so sorry," said the girl. "I should have knocked at your door and let your mum bring me in proper. In fact, I tried that three days ago when you was first hurt, an' she said you was too bad to see anyone. I was afraid she wouldn't let me in again today, and I so wanted to be sure you was really mendin'. You see, I feared you was dead when those awful soldiers kicked you like that, and I . . . I . . ." Here the fair cakeseller bit her lip and turned to hide the brimming moisture forming in her eyes. She disappeared for a moment as she bent down outside the window, then reappeared holding a plump, golden honeycake. "I brought you somethin'," she said, brightening the morning with a smile like sunrays breaking through a cloud.

"Thank you, Marcie," said Aradon as he reached for the honeycake, forgetting his injuries until a sharp stab of pain made him gasp and grimace, stopping his arm in midreach.

"Here, I'll hand it to you," she said, leaning forward into the room, seemingly oblivious as her already precarious bodice gaped open, giving almost total exposure to her generous bosom. But Aradon was not oblivious. He quickly averted his eyes to the cake in her extended hand. It seemed to him that Marcie lingered in her provocative pose long after he had taken the cake, but he doggedly kept his focus on the pastry, taking his first bite as she watched with unabashed adoration.

"Mmmm, delicious!" Aradon mumbled through a full mouth.

The smile spawned by his approval was a wonder to behold. Then, as Aradon devoured the honeycake, she turned sober and said with fetching shyness, "I thought it was wonderful the way you pulled Sir Stundal off his horse."

"I'm afraid he got the last blow," said Aradon ruefully.

"To be sure—him and them sixteen ruffians he calls guards!" she replied with indignation. "But there's six or eight of them that'll sure remember you."

"I hope they will forget me. I'm not looking for a rematch."

"But Sir Stundal had it comin', what you did to him. Him and that weasel Balkert have been bullyin' their way around this town ever since the prince brought them here. The people in Corenham have been talkin' about what you did more than about the comin' of the princess. It's the most happy and excited I've ever seen people aroun' here. The only thing that would have made them happier was if the big lug had broke his neck!"

"Well, I'm thankful that he did not, or mine would now be hanging from a gallows."

"What happened to you was almost the same. We all thought you was dead after them brutes got through with you. But I'm sure glad you're not. Well, I better go before your mum finds me here."

"You don't need to sneak around to the window, Marcie. Next time come to the door. My mother will let you in now that I'm mending."

With that Marcie said a quick good-bye and slipped away. Long after she left, her fair face and ravishing form lingered in Aradon's idle mind like the afterimage on the retina of a closed eye. She was beautiful, certainly the fairest maid he knew. And it seemed apparent that she cared for him and did not want to marry the aging widower from Rhondilar. *Why am I so hesitant about her?* Aradon wondered. *Why don't I take what seems to be the best match I could make and be happy with it? What is it I'm looking for that seems to be lacking in her?*

Thus musing, Aradon again drifted into sleep, and again he dreamed—not the dissonant nightmare of a fevered delirium but an idyllic dream set in an arcadian landscape of lush grass, crystal streams, gold and purple mountains, and rich, viridian trees. He was standing in the cool shade, dressed in his finest clothing. At his side stood his father and mother, also handsomely dressed, both looking intently at him with obvious concern.

In a moment he heard the sound of oboe, lute, and timbrel, although he saw neither players nor instruments. Then he became aware of a lavishly gowned, female figure walking gracefully toward him. In another moment he could see that it was Marcie, glowing with Edenic health and bedecked in the splendor of a white wedding dress fit for a queen. As she approached she beamed upon him her beatific smile. She laid her hand upon his arm, and a warm thrill ran through him. Together they turned to face a robed holy man whom Aradon had not noticed before. He began to chant in ceremonial tones, but Aradon heard not a word. He was entranced by every feature, every detail of the glowing creature beside him—the hair like sunlight, the cheeks flushed with a dainty tint of rose, the soft, red fullness of her lips, the lavish convexities of her figure. His trance was broken by the voice of the holy man.

"Do you, Aradon, take this woman to be your bride in troth for as long as you both shall live?"

"Do you, Aradon?" asked his father.

"Do you, Aradon?" echoed his mother, intense concern showing on both their faces.

Do I indeed? thought Aradon. Misgivings flooded his mind. *How can I know?* He looked at the clergyman, his mother, his father for the answer, but they merely stared the question back to him.

"I must look into the matter," Aradon said, then he started to walk in a small circle around Marcie. But as he circled, she kept herself turned toward him at all times, ever smiling, ever dazzling in her unearthly beauty. He walked faster in order to get behind her, but she merely turned faster to keep her face toward him. He tried suddenly reversing his direction, but she was too quick for him. Finally he stopped and faced her at arm's length. He took her by the shoulders and slowly turned her around.

She had no back. She was merely a facade, a shell, a mask. He could see the reversed contours of her face, her arms, her breasts, her torso as if looking on the inside of a halved walnut shell. He turned her face to him again, and the emptiness was now apparent. The eyes were almond-shaped holes through which he could see the landscape beyond. The cheeks were lumpy and glossy like painted mâché, the smile stiff, fixed, and masklike. In surprise he let go of her, and she toppled to the ground with a clatter. The noise made him start violently, and he awakened from his sleep to find himself in his bed, curtains blowing in the breeze and a broom lying across the wooden floor.

Marcie continued to visit Aradon every morning as he recovered, bringing him her largest honeycake each time. She never came to the cottage door but always appeared at the window—and only when she was sure his mother was out of the room.

CHAPTER THIRTEEN

EDEN IN THE FOREST

fter four days Aradon was up and about the house, although with some pain and limited movement. In a week he was restless, and he determined not to spend another day cooped inside the walls of the cottage. After a hearty breakfast he announced to his mother that he was going to his father's shop.

Bogarth was happy to see his son up but adamantly refused to let him at hammer and anvil. "There's not enough work that I need your help yet," he said. "And there's no need to be puttin' mendin' muscles to use too soon. Wait a few more days."

With a full, warm day ahead and nothing to do, Aradon picked up a sturdy walking stick, stopped by the feed bin, and scooped up a small sackful of corn, then headed down the trail toward Braegan Wood. On the trail he met several small groups of villagers and farmers carting their produce to Corenham. As always, young milkmaids and shepherdesses eyed the striking young man, some furtively with deep blushes and quiet sighs, others with open gazes of unabashed awe. More than once other members of a group stared at Aradon and turned to their companions to whisper behind cupped hands that this was the man who had dared defy Sir Stundal.

Aradon, oblivious to his sudden notoriety, continued happily toward his beloved forest. He had never been infected with the superstitious fear of the woods that had haunted its name since the disappearance of Perivale. Indeed, even as a child he had been drawn to the ancient forest, wondering what mysteries and enchantments might be hidden within it. He had first ventured into the edge when he was barely twelve years old, and now he knew many of its trails and streams by heart.

As he entered the woods, he stopped and looked around him, wanting to experience with all his senses everything the forest had to offer. He loved the refreshing coolness of the air, the muted browns and grays of the tree boles, the gray-green moss hanging from the limbs, the lichen-covered stones, and the patchy green seas of gently waving grass. He loved the fresh scent of sap and blossom, as well as the musty aroma of dried leaves. Most of all he loved the awe-filled sense that time itself yielded to the magic of the forest.

He breathed deeply and walked on. An early summer breeze rustled the translucent leaves above him, creating an undulating dance of sunlight on the grass. Birds of every kind twittered in the branches overhead, and bushy-tailed squirrels moved in graceful waves along trunks and limbs. Wildflowers of every hue opened their blossoms to the embrace of wooing honeybees. Butterflies, bright and iridescent, flitted about like flying flowers. As Aradon walked through this wonderland, he remembered listening spellbound to traveling minstrels in his father's shop who told stories of fantastic lands populated with fabulous creatures, and he thought, *No world they can conjure from their imaginations is more enchanted than the real one we live in every day.*

Occasionally he stopped and scattered corn on the path around him. Birds, squirrels, hares, chipmunks, and wood mice scampered about his feet to claim their shares. A pair of wrens even took kernels from his hand, and a yellow-eyed grackle perched atop his head, wings spread for balance as it bobbed and swayed to the rhythm of Aradon's footsteps.

As he went deeper into the forest, the trees grew larger, taller, and closer together. The woods became darker as the overhead foliage grew so thick that the sun was shut out almost entirely. Only occasional breaks in the topmost branches allowed slanting beams to descend like transparent columns, illuminating patches of grass and brush with glimmering brilliance. Aradon paused in one of these oases of sunlight to refresh himself with a cool drink from a crystal-clear, meandering stream. Often he had wondered about the source of this stream and had been tempted to follow it until he found the spring that spawned it. *Why not today?* he thought. He had the time. So he left the familiar trail and struck out along the banks of the little brook.

Although the stream curved and angled to find its way between boulder and bole, following it was fairly easy for Aradon. After a while he came to a fork. A brook equal in size to that which he had been following tumbled away to Aradon's right. The stream above the fork was wider and deeper.

As he continued, he noticed that the scale of the forest was changing. The trees were enormous, almost twice the height and girth of any he had seen before in Braegan Wood. Here there was little decay on the forest floor and the green of the grass and brush was deeper and more luminous. The birds and small animals now ran ahead as if escorting him, he thought, to some place he seemed destined to go. Aradon felt that he was walking into some arcadian dream—an echo from the ancient Eden that flourished untouched in the heart of Braegan Wood.

Aradon stopped. He heard a sound. It was a constant, even noise like that of wind rustling the leaves of trees. But the gentle breeze that barely moved the treetops was not enough to generate such a sound. And what he heard was not diffused throughout the woods as the rustle of a breeze would be; it seemed to come from some definite point ahead. Aradon continued on and the sound became louder. Soon he rounded a bend in the stream and parted the branches of a bush that blocked his path. He stopped short and drew a deep breath.

The stream he had been following spilled out of a deep, wide pool, clear as glass and dappled with splashes of sunlight that streamed through the leafy branches arching above. The bottom of the pool was clearly visible and covered with smooth, flat stones the size of clamshells. Clustered sprays of green waterfern swayed gently beneath the surface. The banks sloped evenly toward the water and were covered with short, tender grass. Several ancient oak trees stood

at the water's edge, drawing nutrients from the pool with deep, probing roots. At the far end of the pond, forty or fifty yards from where
the awestruck Aradon stood, was a craggy ledge some twenty feet
high and covered with blooming vines. Down the center of this ledge
plunged an effervescent waterfall, the source of the rushing sound
that had drawn him forward.

Aradon parted the hedge, removed his shoes, and walked down
the gently sloping bank, his feet delighting in the delicious coolness
of the grass. Then he removed all his clothing and plunged into the
cool water. For the next hour he swam and soaked in the pool. For
much of that time he sat on a stone beneath the waterfall and let the
sparkling cascade massage his healing bruises.

Greatly refreshed, he finally stepped out of the water. Suddenly
he realized that he was moving freely and painlessly and looked down
at his legs and torso. To his amazement, all his bruises were gone. He
found a patch of sunlight on the grass where he lay on his back,
closed his eyes, and let the gentle breeze caress his moist skin as the
sound of the waterfall and the calling of the birds lulled him into that
twilight world between wakefulness and sleep.

He did not know how long he lay suspended in this delectable
stupor before he realized that another sound had intruded upon his
idyll. He opened his eyes and listened. *Hoofbeats!* Silently he rose, and
crouching to stay hidden, crept up the bank and peered over the bushes
that rimmed the pond. In a clearing perhaps eighty paces away stood
a magnificent knight, armored in gold and mounted on a splendid
white charger. The knight stood in one of the descending shafts of
sunlight. His armor flashed and shimmered as the massive horse
tossed his head, splashing his white mane about his neck like foam on
the crest of a wave. Aradon could not see the knight's face for his
helm was in place and the visor down. The distance and the reflecting sunlight prevented him from reading the blazon on the shield.

The knight turned his horse to face the place where the gaping
young man hid. To Aradon's great surprise, he raised his arm and
beckoned for Aradon to follow him. Then he turned and rode slowly
into the forest. After a few paces, the knight stopped and repeated the
beckoning signal. Aradon tore his eyes away, found his clothes and

pulled them on, then plunged into the woods to follow the golden knight. The mounted warrior moved at a pace that kept Aradon from closing the distance between them but took care to stay just within his sight. But after less than a quarter-hour, he entered a dense growth of trees and disappeared.

Aradon followed until he came to the edge of a grassy, oval clearing. He looked for the knight but found him nowhere in sight. Aradon stopped, unsure of which way to go.

The branches arching above the clearing met overhead, closing out all sunlight except for a single shaft that lit the base of a massive oak at the far end of the oval. The light shone on a cluster of gnarled roots webbed with a layer of clinging, greenish moss. Topping this mossy covering was a whitish mass, which from this distance Aradon took to be a clump of cottonwood seed like the many he had seen throughout the forest. Although he could see no hoofprints in the grass, he decided the knight must have crossed the clearing, but he found himself strangely hesitant to follow.

He could not identify any specific cause for his uneasiness. Perhaps it was the uncanny silence, or maybe it was the absolute stillness of the grass and leaves. He felt some sense of presence hanging in the air that made the hair of his neck stand. After a moment he dismissed his fear as silly and decided to walk into the clearing. But before he proceeded, he thought he should remove his shoes. If asked why he should enter the clearing barefoot, Aradon would have been hard-pressed to give a reason. He might have articulated some answer that had to do with not wanting to disturb the quietness of the place, but in truth his shoes would hardly have added any sound. Nevertheless he thought he should remove his shoes and did so, then stepped silently into the clearing. As he neared the great tree, he had the uneasy feeling that something was not natural about the mossy roots at its base. But he shrugged it off and continued.

Suddenly the roots moved. Aradon stopped short and stared in wide-eyed amazement. What he had taken for a mossy covering over the roots was not moss at all but a wrinkled, tattered robe. The white mass above it was not cotton but a headful of white hair. The forms beneath the moss that he had taken for roots were the arms and legs of an old man, calmly sitting against the tree and observing Aradon's gaping stare.

The two looked at each other, Aradon tense with wonder and surprise, the other with relaxed serenity and a touch of amusement. As Aradon stared, he revised his first impression of the seated figure. The man was not old—not with those clear, sea-blue eyes, the glowing, supple skin of his face, and the apparent strength and grace of the body beneath the ragged robes. And the whiteness of the beard and hair was not the lank whiteness of a dead thing drained of color but an almost shimmering whiteness that seemed to draw its brilliance from the total spectrum of light. There were lines in the face, not the ravaging furrows of wear or worry or sorrow but the embellishing underscores of wisdom and deep character—lines of definition rather than decay. No, he was not old; strength and vitality exuded from every aspect of the man. Not old yet somehow ancient. The face and eyes, for all their apparent youth and health, carried a weight of wisdom and vision that could only come through a massive accumulation of years.

"Aradon," The man spoke with a resonant voice like the ringing of a bell. "I have been waiting for you. Pray do sit down. I have something to say."

Without taking his eyes off the young but ancient being, Aradon sat on the grass. Later, when he thought back on the incident, he wondered why he was not more wary, why he trusted the man enough to relax his guard and comply with his wishes without suspicion.

"Who are you?" he asked. "How did you know my name? How did you know I was coming?"

"Please, my son, one thing at a time," the man replied. "As to knowing who you are, I have known you from the day you were born and even before. How did I know you were coming? Why, my dear boy, you have been on your way to me for most of your young life. Who am I? I have many names, but you may call me Father Verit."

Such answers only raised more questions, but Aradon bore them patiently, correctly assuming that he would get only what information Father Verit chose to reveal, and that in his own time. "Very well, Father Verit," said Aradon. "What do you want of me?"

"Are you familiar with the prophecy concerning the rebirth of Perivale's empire?"

"Yes, sir. Everyone in Meridan knows of it."

"We are on the eve of its fulfillment," said Verit, "and you, young Aradon, are to be one of the agents that brings that fulfillment about."

"I?" asked Aradon in wonder. "I am merely an apprentice blacksmith. What have I to do with such things as prophecies and empires?"

"The choices you make within the next few months will shake thrones and move armies. But you should not count that as exceptional. Every man and woman born, if they only knew it, make decisions and commit acts daily with consequences that spread like ripples through time, working untold effects on the shape of the future for generations to come. Since you know the prophecy I presume you also know the story of King Perivale."

"I know somewhat of it."

"I must tell you some things about Perivale that you don't know—some things, in fact, that only one other person now alive knows, and that person is an enemy who must be stopped if the prophecy is to be fulfilled."

"What enemy?" asked Aradon.

"I'm speaking of the ancient creature Morgultha."

"Morgultha? But Perivale defeated her over a hundred thirty years ago. Even if she survived the war, she would be long dead by now."

"I'm afraid that is not so," replied Father Verit, shaking his white head slowly, causing a slight shimmer at the edges of his hair as if the movement dislodged infinitesimal particles of light. "She is very much alive and has a plot in place that must be thwarted if the prophecy is to come to pass."

"What is she then? Surely no human who was an adult five generations ago could be alive still. She must be of some other race—something like the Nephilim of ancient times my father told me about."

"There were races of rational creatures other than man before the ancient flood—hideous, hybrid creatures sired by unearthly beings upon human women. But those races are gone. In fact, the purpose of the great flood was to cleanse the earth of such monsters and the evil they had wreaked upon it. No, Morgultha was born human."

"She is a witch, then?"

"Yes, she is that. From early in her life she has been driven by an unquenchable lust for power. She knew that the kind of power she wanted could not be amassed in a normal life span, so she made a pact with invisible beings of darkness and traded her soul for a body preserved by hellish necromancy from the ravages of time and disease."

"Then she is immortal."

"No, she remains human. Her unholy contract preserves her from natural decay, but she can be killed like any other mortal. She has studied the black arts and has mastered many hidden magical powers, but do not make the mistake of exaggerating the scope of those powers as many do in fear and ignorance. Evil is always limited. Morgultha has the power to change her form into that of another creature, for example, or at least to give the illusion of such a change. And she can project some of her sensory and communicative powers into the illusion. But she cannot know your mind, or the future, or see beyond the range of her own natural eyes. No evil can have any power over you that you do not choose to give it."

"Where has she been all this time? Where is she now? What is this plot of hers? What can be done to stop her? Who is going to—"

"Wait a moment, wait a moment, son. Some of your questions I can answer and some I cannot. But if you will be patient, I think I had best start at the beginning and tell you the whole story."

So Aradon stretched out on the cool grass as Verit settled back against the tree and told the following tale.

"Long before the rise of Perivale, Morgultha had achieved the first step of her evil ambitions. With help from her allies of the dark, she amassed a hideous army of ghoulish creatures, pieced and patched from the parts of dead men and animals. With these foul troops she had subdued the kingdoms of Sorendale, Vensaur, Rhondilar, and Oranth. Now she was launching an attack on Lochlaund. On her head rested the ancient Crown in which was set the Stone of Eden and—"

"Is it true that the Crown has magical properties?" Aradon interrupted.

"The Crown does convey power to its wearer, but as you will learn in a moment, that power does not always benefit the head on which it rests. The Stone of Eden is a fabulous jewel like none ever mined from the bowels of the earth. It is said to be the only thing in Adam's hand as he was expelled from Eden. You see, the task of Adam in paradise had been to rule the earth and have dominion over it. The Stone of Eden was the talisman of that task. But when Adam fell from created perfection, he forfeited to the dark creature that seduced him his right and power to rule.

"Adam knew the stone could never again mean what it did in Eden. He sensed that its power could consume or corrupt him now that he had lost his intimate connection with the Master of the Universe, so he left it untouched. He was like a child who had driven the chariot confidently from his father's lap, but he knew better than to take the reins alone. Adam feared the stone, yet he could not part with it.

"When Adam's son Cain joined his brothers to bury his father, he found the stone among Adam's possessions and knew immediately what it was. Indeed, no one who laid eyes on it could help knowing it was not of this fallen world. It retained the capacity to reflect to human eyes a hint of Eden's original dazzling spectrum. You see, just as there are sounds that no human ear can hear, there are also colors that no human eye can see. The spectrum visible to us includes only seven distinct hues, but there are colors both above and below these that Adam's prefall eye was capable of seeing. The Edenic stone still refracts a hint of that wider spectrum just beyond our visual range. You cannot quite see these colors when looking directly at the stone. They tease and elude the eye like those slight movements you can often see better in the periphery of vision than when you focus on them.

"But I digress. Cain understood something of the purpose of the stone, so he secretly carried it away to the isolated land where he had settled his people. There he forged a crown of pure gold, in which he set the stone. He wore that Crown in the hope of reclaiming his father's lost dominion over the earth. The Crown has rested on many heads between Cain and Perivale, some whose names you would know, such as Nimrod, Melchizedek, Solomon, Nebuchadnezzar, and Cyrus, and others hidden from the light of history. How it came into the possession of Morgultha does not presently concern us. Suffice it to say that she got it by devious means.

"Morgultha intended to use the Crown to gratify her unholy lust for conquest. She knew there was enormous power in it, but she did not clearly understand its nature. In fact the significance of the Crown is simply that it enhances, strengthens, amplifies, exposes, and develops more fully the innermost attributes that dwell deep in the heart of the person wearing it.

"Morgultha, as I have said, had long since given herself up to the lust for dominion over the kingdoms of men. The Crown fanned that spark into a firestorm that burned out all balancing attributes that could have brought reason to her ambition. She was no longer under her own control. She became a slave to the power she coveted and could not let it go. It devoured her humanity until all that was left of her was a hollow shell driven by raw ambition.

"After Lochlaund fell to Morgultha, she turned her attention to Valomar. The king of Valomar and King Landorm of Meridan realized that neither kingdom could withstand Morgultha's army alone. They made a mutual defense pact, and when Morgultha invaded Valomar, King Landorm came to Valomar's defense.

"At this time Perivale was a knight in the service of King Landorm. When Landorm was slain in the first battle, the demoralized troops of Meridan and Valomar were put to flight. But Perivale stepped into Landorm's place and rallied both armies. After days of desperate fighting, he turned the tide and began to drive Morgultha's forces into retreat. You know all this, of course—how Perivale pushed Morgultha out of Lochlaund, Sorendale, Vensaur, and Rhondilar.

"In a terrible final battle, Perivale overcame Morgultha's hideous troops. She was captured and held prisoner in a tent on the battlefield. In her right hand she clutched the Crown of Eden. Perivale demanded that she give it to him, but she would not. He ordered his men to take it, but they could not pry her fingers from it. So Perivale commanded his men to hold out the offending hand. Then he drew his sword, and after warning Morgultha, he cut off her hand. The severed member fell to the earth still gripping the Crown and had to be destroyed finger by finger to free it. The Crown bears the imprint of Morgultha's fingers to this day.

"While arrangements were being made to transfer Morgultha to the dungeon of the castle in Meridan, she escaped in the night by means of an illusion. Perivale and his knights pursued her, but they lost her trail in the labyrinths of the swampy caverns of Rhondilar. No one knew what became of her, whether she perished in the caves or fled to another land.

"Perivale was acclaimed high king of all the Seven Kingdoms, and the Crown of Eden was placed upon his head. He set up his throne at Maldor Castle in Meridan. At first things went well for him. His victory over Morgultha had made him extremely popular in the Seven Kingdoms and extremely feared by their neighbors. Trade flourished and the kingdoms prospered.

"But in time the Crown began to reveal Perivale's weakness. The fatal trait did not show itself at first because it was almost dormant. But it was there—a seed planted but not sprouted, a cloud on the horizon no bigger than a man's hand, a weakness so small that it might never have become visible had not the stone in the Crown drawn it out."

"The Crown is an evil thing, then," said Aradon. "It searches for the evil spark within its wearer, then fans that spark into a flame that consumes him."

"No, Aradon, the Crown is not evil. It gives added strength to the traits its wearer chooses to nurture, whether good or evil. It amplifies those near-silent strings of the heart that he chooses to pluck. King Solomon might never have discovered his passions for opulence and women had not the Crown given these tendencies opportunity for expression. On the right head the Crown would as readily cause courage, patience, or kindness to blossom. Unfortunately it is the tendency of most men who wear crowns to give vent to illicit passions or self-indulgences, ones that might never surface were not gratification made possible by their access to power.

"At times the Crown has even affected its wearer physically, causing inner traits to become visible in his body. After Cain had worn the Crown for years, it was said that his skin and muscles hardened and became as stonelike as his heart—so stonelike, in fact, that a spear once used in an attempt to murder him merely bounced off his chest and fell to the ground broken. The appearance of Morgultha herself shows the effects of wearing the Crown. It began to wither her body even as it sucked the humanity from her soul. Had she worn it longer, she would have become a virtual walking skeleton. On the other hand, it is said that after Melchizedek wore the Crown for many years, he became a head taller and his features took on the appearance of a young god, which was a true reflection of his enormous, godlike spirit.

"As you can see, the effects of wearing the Crown of Eden cannot be predicted. It had placed no mark on Perivale's body at the time he disappeared, but it had taken its toll on his inner self. Perivale's downfall was pride, the most common of men's vices and the seminal one. It is the tinderbox vice that ignites all others, the vice that makes a man think he is his own god, the worthy recipient of praise, pleasure, wealth, and power. Not long after Perivale took the Crown, his pride began to be the spring from which all his actions flowed.

"After Perivale secured peace in the Seven Kingdoms, he had no more worlds to conquer. He began to turn his attention toward embellishing his own world. King Landorm's Maldor Castle became too small and unimposing. He planned a castle like no other in the Seven Kingdoms and chose Morningstone Hill at the northern edge of the village of Corenham as the site. He began construction in the second year of his reign.

"At the same time he undertook lavish steps to make Corenham the showplace of the empire. He paved its streets and built bridges, parks, and monuments. He began to purchase tapestries, sculptures, paintings, and earthenware from traders across the world. And he decided to establish a monument to himself that his people could not ignore. He thought the natural stone jutting from the earth about a quarter mile from Morningstone might be carved into a godlike sculpture in his own likeness. He found a young sculptor on the great peninsula that juts into the southern sea who, it was said, could make stone breathe.

"With the coming of the sculptor, Morgultha saw an opportunity to regain the Crown. The artist made many preliminary models of Perivale in various poses before he began to carve the actual stone. She bargained with him for one of these images, life-sized and heroically proportioned, which she took into the caves of Rhondilar, deep in the roots of the Dragontooth Mountains. There she had a hundred duplicates cast in bronze. These she animated with a spell that gave them a semblance of life and skill at battle.

"The sculptor was half finished with the monument when Morgultha coerced him to reveal where the Crown was kept and to deliver it to her at an appointed place in Corenham when the king rode out into battle. Perivale was posing for the sculptor in the newly completed Morningstone Castle when news came that a band of a hundred alien warriors had captured a village some forty miles north of Corenham. Perivale was restless and battle-hungry, and his longing for glory caused him to make a fatal mistake. Against the counsel of his most prudent advisors, he took only fifty warriors to meet the invaders. He could imagine the tale sung in the halls and alehouses of the Seven Kingdoms of how the great warrior-king and a few valiant men crushed an invading army twice their size. But instead, Perivale's men were routed, not merely because of the bronze warriors' superior numbers but because of the strange and unsettling thing that happened when one of them was cleaved in the side or sliced through the neck. While fighting, Morgultha's warriors looked and moved exactly like living men. But the moment one fell in battle, the spell was broken and his appearance reverted to that of cast bronze. Perivale and his knights were terrified by the eerie transformation. By the time they recovered their courage and rallied, their losses left them hopeless of victory. They were cut down one by one until only Perivale himself remained alive.

"Perivale was in terrible anguish over what he had done to his men. In his pride he had led them to certain death. For the first time he looked into the face of defeat, and he could not cope with what he saw. He stared with horror at the mangled bodies of his men and the scattered, metallic remnants of his foes, and a cold, irrational fear gripped him, a fear that for the first time in his life he could not master. Instead of plunging into the battle and ending his life with a heroic stand, he dropped his sword and fled in terror toward the nearby abandoned Maldor Castle. The twenty bronze warriors that remained gave chase as darkness fell.

"That night a sound like the crack of a thousand thunderbolts was heard over all Meridan. A dam on the river near Morgultha's caves crumbled, and the plain of Maldor was flooded. It has been a swampland ever since. Maldor Castle began to sink into the ooze like a block of tallow in a boiling pot, cracking and splitting apart as it went down, until finally the entire lower level—throne room, dining hall, courtyards, and scullery—was beneath the mud. It kept sinking until it hit bedrock, and there it rested half-submerged and atilt, with massive breaches sundering its stony walls.

"You know the rest of the story. The next morning the villagers found all fifty of Perivale's men slain. There was no sign of Morgultha's bronze warriors, and there was no sign of Perivale. He had disappeared and was never seen again, nor was his body ever found. The sculptor disappeared as well, leaving the clay model of Perivale shattered and the great statue itself unfinished."

"If Morgultha now has the Crown, why hasn't she used it?" asked Aradon. "Why hasn't she drawn on its power to attack Meridan again?"

"I did not say that Morgultha got the Crown."

"Then the sculptor must have got it and run away with it."

"I did not say that either. The fact is, the fates of the Crown, Perivale, the sculptor, and Morgultha have remained a mystery ever since their disappearances. Now we are on the eve of the prophecy's consummation, and either the Crown will be found and the prophecy fulfilled, or it will not be found and Prince Lomar will claim the prophecy to be fraudulent. He will take the throne by simple right of succession. But without the Crown he will fail to unite the Seven Kingdoms and Meridan will strangle in the grip of a tyrant."

"Why are you telling me all this, Father Verit? I do not see how I can possibly fit into these great plans and schemes. If I am to do something, please tell me what it is so I can get it done and get back to my father's shop."

"It is not that simple, young Aradon. There is no specific task that you can complete and then wash your hands of further responsibility. You have already committed a deed that will draw you into the web of the prophecy. In a matter of days, you will be asked to make a choice that will draw you even deeper, and from that choice will come other choices. Your decisions at each juncture will either draw you into the very heart of the prophecy or expel you from it altogether."

"But I have no idea where to start—or even if I want to be a part of it," said Aradon. "I am utterly without direction. I might inadvertently make a decision that causes the prophecy to fail. Can't you tell me something of what I am to do? Where to start? What sort of thing is expected of me?"

"No, I cannot," replied Father Verit, "but I can assure you that you need not worry about the prophecy. It will not fail. It will be exactly fulfilled down to every word, every letter, every comma, every period. A great paradox of the universe is that while the prophecy is fixed and unalterable, its fulfillment will come about through the utterly free and unfettered choices of individuals acting independently and without concern for it at all. Aradon, you can no more stop the prophecy than an ant can stop a charger. The question is, Will you have the courage to play the part intended for you or will you choose the easier, safer path? The prophecy will not fail. The only question to be answered is, Will you fail?"

Aradon was silent, looking vacantly at the grass and idly spinning the stem of a wildflower between thumb and forefinger. Finally he spoke. "When I came here today, I thought I had found the most beautiful place in the world, a place almost outside of time, a place that must be much like Eden itself before Adam's fall. But at this moment I wish I had never found it. I want nothing more than to be a simple blacksmith like my father. I want to marry a winsome girl and live a simple life with a cottage full of children. But you cloud my future with talk of terrible choices fraught with danger and involving great people and unearthly powers. These are things I want no part of, but you say they are things written into my destiny. Surely I was better off before I knew of all this."

"But remember," Verit replied, "that Adam's Eden was not just a place of beauty; it was a place of decision. It is as true for you as it was for him: Eden can be retained with the right choice or lost with the wrong one. I will not hide the truth from you, Aradon. Soon you will be called on to make a decision as bitter as that of Adam. He had to choose between his beloved Eve and his beloved paradise, and along with paradise, his connection with his maker and his purpose for being. He chose Eve and lost all else. Not one year hence you will face a choice no less agonizing—a choice that will pit your heart's deepest desire against nothing less than your honor. If you bear the pain and choose rightly, you will win paradise. But yield to your own desire and you will lose all. I have told you all you need to know. Now you must return to your home and take up your life."

"I feel that I may need to talk with you again. Will I find you here?" asked Aradon.

"Be assured that you will always find me when you need me."

With that Aradon bid the ancient one farewell, retraced his path through the forest, and returned to his parents' home.

CHAPTER FOURTEEN

The CONSCRIPTION

On the day after his excursion into Braegan Wood, Aradon returned to the anvil. His bruises were completely healed, much to the amazement of his parents. To Aradon the healing itself seemed no more fabulous than the other things he had witnessed in the forest. There was still little work being brought into the shop, so Bogarth and Aradon spent much of their time cleaning and repairing equipment. Once or twice, Aradon started to tell his father about his meeting with Father Verit, but he found himself strangely reluctant. He feared that Bogarth would not believe his story of the golden-armored knight, the young-looking old man, or the incredible things he had told Aradon. But Bogarth was wanting to talk as well. Questions about Aradon's overnight healing kept rolling in his mind and pressing at his tongue. Finally he sat on a bench where Aradon was sorting nails and motioned for his son to stop work.

"I thought you might like to tell me where you went yesterday," said Bogarth.

"I went into Braegan Wood, just as I often do," replied Aradon.

"I know that; you told us as much last night. But you're not tryin' to pretend that nothin' strange happened to you in there, are you?"

Aradon hesitated. "Father, do you think it possible that a person could age without getting old? I mean, could a person look very young, with fresh skin, bright eyes, and a strong body, yet somehow have a look about him that made you know he was extremely ancient?"

Bogarth stared hard at his son, a quizzical look on his face that Aradon interpreted to mean, "You must have got more bruises on your head than we knew."

"I know it sounds strange," Aradon continued, "but what I mean is this: Could a person be very old without being wrinkled and with-ered, yet have the look of age in a good way? This is very hard to explain, but I—"

"Son, why don't you just take your time and tell me everything you're thinkin'. I'll listen."

So Aradon told Bogarth the entire story, hesitantly, shyly at first but with increasing confidence and animation as he got into it. He told of discovering the Edenic pool and bathing in it, finding after-ward that his bruises and pains were gone. He told of seeing the golden-armored knight who beckoned him to follow. He told of the cathedral-like clearing with the feel of holiness hovering about it and of the moss-covered roots of the great tree that resolved themselves into the young-looking old man who introduced himself as Father Verit.

Here a distant look came over Bogarth's face, and he turned away from Aradon and gazed out the window, but he continued to listen as his son told the story that Father Verit had told him of Morgultha and Perivale and how the Crown of Eden was lost. And finally, how the Crown would soon be found again and come to rest on the head of Alfron's son. When Aradon finished his story, he stopped, watch-ing his father's profile and wondering at the faraway look in his eyes.

"And what does all this have to do with you?" asked Bogarth.

"Well, after Father Verit told me these things, he said something most strange. I remember his very words: 'The choices you make within the next few months will shake thrones and move armies. But you should not count that as exceptional. Every man and woman born, if they only knew it, make decisions and commit acts daily with consequences that spread like ripples through time, working untold effects on the shape of the future for generations to come.'"

"Did he tell you what he meant by that?"

"No. I asked, but he would tell me nothing specific. He simply said that very soon I would start making decisions that would lead me deeper into the prophecy and that a time was coming when I would have to make a choice as wrenching as the one Adam made in Eden."

"Everybody makes that kind of choice every day," said Bogarth. "Adam chose to bring evil into a world of good, and every choice we make is whether to bring good back into this world of evil or let Adam's choice stand unchallenged."

"Do you think that is all he meant?" asked Aradon. "Just that I will be making the same kind of choices that people make every day? I must say that when he spoke the words, he seemed to mean more than that."

As Bogarth was not quick to answer, Aradon continued. "In fact, as I think back on it, I begin to wonder if I really saw these things at all. Though they looked as real and solid to me as yonder anvil, could they have been merely phantoms I conjured up from my own imagination? Maybe I got bruises on my brain that aren't yet completely healed."

Bogarth shook his head slowly. "No, what you saw was real enough. There's too much evidence for it. Namely, the healin' of your ribs and bruises. And your story has the ring of truth about it. It has details and thoughts in it that you could hardly have dreamed up. I've heard enough stories in this shop to know the truth from a lie when I hear it."

Aradon was visibly relieved. "What do you think it all means?"

"I really can't say. It seems that this Father Verit thinks you're about to get sucked up into things involvin' kings and crowns and sorcery and battles. And I've wondered sometimes if you didn't have the same sorts of ideas prancin' around in the back of your head—to become a squire, or soldier, or maybe even a knight. Denmore says you're almost good enough for it. While I'm not thinkin' for a moment that your story is in any way untrue, I suppose you could find it natural to interpret Verit's words to fit your own ambitions."

"I'm not aware of any real ambitions of that sort. That is, not since I used to play knights and barons with stick swords and lances."

"I'm not so sure about that," said Bogarth. "When I watch you duelin' with Denmore, there's a bright gleam in your eye that makes me think such ambitions may still be lingerin'. But let me tell you this, son," Bogarth picked up the six-pound hammer laying on the bench. "When I get too old to lift this hammer, it will be yours, this and all that goes with it. The Master of the Universe has been good to you. You'll be startin' your life with a trade and a shop to practice it in. I've told you already that I'm savin' the three acres behind this shop for you to build your house on. I'd advise you to start buildin' it soon and get on with findin' a girl who loves you to help you fill it full of huggable little duplicates of yourselves. This is what happiness is about, son. You can outfit yourself in armor and weapons and ride the world over questin' for adventure, but all that makes life livable is right here under your nose, in this shop, on yonder acreage."

"I agree with you, Father. Indeed, I told Verit the same thing. But he seems to think my destiny lies elsewhere. What should I do about his claim that I will do something to bring about fulfillment of the prophecy?"

"You don't have to do anything. If the prophecy is real, it will play out to its predicted end no matter what you do. I advise you to forget the whole thing. If you have a role to play, you needn't go lookin' for it; it will find you. Get back to your own life and let greater powers than ourselves deal with the likes of kings and crowns and prophecies."

"But what if I'm drawn in?"

"Just keep your head down and your nose in your own business and maybe you won't be. You could fulfill your part of the prophecy by doin' somethin' so natural and common that you'd not even be aware of it, like the squirrel that thinks he is hidin' acorns but is really plantin' oak trees. The little things you do can grow into big results. So, you don't need to go lookin' for the big important things. Remember, your first duty is to your neighbor, not to your kingdom. It's like your mother always told you, 'Just eat what's set in front of you; don't go askin' for what's not on the table.'"

"Except she would never say *askin'*, would she?" grinned Aradon.

Bogarth glared at his son. "You go bringin' grammar and diction classes into this shop and I'll go lookin' elsewhere for someone to take it over."

Aradon turned serious again. "Father, I need to ask you one more question." He ran his hand nervously through his blond hair. "You spoke just now of finding a girl to marry. I, uh, what do you think of, uh, Marcie?"

Bogarth's heavy brows knotted, and he scratched his beard as he spoke. "Well, I'd say that I've seldom seen a book with a better cover, but I'd advise you to read her story pretty carefully before you think of puttin' her on your shelf. I can't blame your eyes for rovin' in her direction, but if I ever again see you gawkin' at her the way you did that day when Ansel showed her off like a butcher sellin' a side of beef, I'll cool your fire just like this." Bogarth grabbed his son by the hair and shoulders and dunked his head in the cooling trough. Aradon came up dripping and sputtering just as Sir Denmore walked into the shop.

"I'm sorry I missed the baptism," said Denmore. "But I see that I missed only half of it. You've baptized the boy's head but not his body, which is the opposite of what you should do, don't you think, since it's our bodies that pull us into most of our sins."

"Why does everyone always go puttin' down our bodies?" retorted Bogarth. "Is it our bodies' fault that we swell with pride or trample everyone in our paths pursuin' our ambitions or speak rudely to a stable hand? These poor bodies do their share of sinnin', no doubt, but I'll wager that three-quarters of what the body does is on orders from the head. I think I baptized the right end."

"Maybe you did at that," said Denmore. "Indeed, you may need to go ahead and dunk it a dozen more times to keep it from swelling up like a pumpkin. Have you heard the talk about the town? The name of Aradon is filling the air like seed blowing off a cottonwood tree."

"I've heard enough of it," said Bogarth.

"The entire incident at Cheaping Square has been repeated and embellished in every tavern and shop in the city. I just heard a man from Oranth telling that 'Haradorn the blacksmith'—they don't always get his name quite right—took up a hammer and killed sixty men with it. They are talking of little else."

"Don't you go fillin' the boy's head with delusions of grandeur," boomed Bogarth. "I just told him to forget about all that, and here you come undoin' everything I said."

"I didn't come to lay oral laurels on the lustrous locks of our latest luminary," said Denmore. "I'm merely a menial messenger sent to march master Aradon to a meeting with a very important person who desires an interview with the lad."

"What person?" asked Aradon.

"I am not at liberty to reveal the name or the place," replied Denmore, "but I assure you that the man is honorable."

"Give the man my thanks, Denmore. But I'll decline the invitation."

"Aradon," said Denmore with gravity, "I have orders to compel you to come, though if that is what I must do, I think I will take momentary leave to fetch a score of knights to assist me. I don't want to be laid up for a fortnight like Sir Stundal's guards."

"You'd better go with him, Aradon," sighed Bogarth. And under his breath he muttered, "Mark my words, no good will come of this."

Aradon saddled a horse, and Sir Denmore escorted him to the far side of the city into narrow streets where he had never been before. Near the end of a dusty, unpaved lane, they came to a daub-and-wattle structure that had obviously begun as a single hut, but rooms had been added to it in seemingly random fashion until now it sprawled like a sleeping hound. Most of the whitewash was gone, and much of the daub had sloughed away, revealing the reeds of the inner walls. The timbers were cracked and sagging. Above the door a lopsided, wooden sign hung by a single rusty hook and bore letters faded almost beyond recognition. Aradon could barely make out the words, *The Musty Tankard.* They entered the door to the pungent odor of sweat and stale wine. When their eyes adjusted to the dim interior, the proprietor, a bony man wearing an apron that looked as if it had not been washed since the tavern was built, motioned toward a door at the back of the room.

They made their way past the few patrons, and Sir Denmore opened the door and stood aside as Aradon entered. Sitting at a table awaiting them was Lord Aldemar. With a wave and a brief word of thanks, he dismissed Denmore, leaving Aradon standing alone to face the stern countenance of Meridan's regent.

Aldemar looked hard at the young blacksmith, then in a voice low and firm, he said, "You, Aradon, son of Bogarth, ruined a critically important procession that had been months in the planning. You humiliated the crown prince of Meridan. You decimated the garrison guard. And you embarrassed its captain. What defense do you make for such behavior?"

Aradon, caught utterly off guard, explained the condition of the horse and told of urging Sir Stundal three days before the procession not to work the animal until his injuries healed.

"Why you?" demanded Aldemar. "Who appointed you guardian of the prince's stallions?

"No one, my lord, but at the moment I thought this stallion needed a guardian."

"If Sir Stundal, the coachman, the stable keeper, and others saw fit to let the horse work, what made you think you had the right to countermand them?"

"I was not thinking of my rights or theirs, sir. I was thinking of the horse. Had they driven him all the way to Morningstone, he would have been ruined for life."

"You are an expert on horses then?"

"Not an expert, sir, but I know a little. My father and I treat them often at the shop."

"Did you not know that attacking the head of the prince's garrison could land you in prison for years?"

"I was not thinking about that at the moment either, my lord, though I did think of it later. At the time nothing seemed to matter but getting that horse out of the traces."

Lord Aldemar relaxed his foreboding demeanor and said, "I praise you for your bravery, Aradon. There are few men in the kingdom who would dare stand up to Sir Stundal as you did. Your courage has made you the people's hero for the moment, but it has also earned you some powerful enemies in high places. Fortunately you seem to have the favor of the new princess, and that may be enough to protect you for now, at least from overt harm. The prince is still out of favor with her after the incident with the horse. But beware, and watch your back." Aldemar offered Aradon a chair, then began to speak in earnest.

"I fear that evil times are ahead for Meridan. I have been trying hard to keep King Alfron's ways intact, but it gets more difficult every day. The men the prince has chosen as his companions and confidants do not like what they see as the backwardness of my regency. Alfron's ideals mean little to them, and they are trying hard to push the kingdom into adopting the values and mores of the kingdoms across the water, which they see as more progressive. They have long pushed me to bend any laws that interfered with their goals, and when I refused, they set themselves on a course to win a majority in the Hall of Knights in order to get those laws changed.

"Meanwhile, behind my back they are ignoring whatever laws don't please them and getting more and more blatant about it. For example, just before the arrival of Princess Volanna, Prince Lomar's men not only cheated Galvay the tailor out of his proper fee for the prince's suit, they also conspired to take his loom, which they could have sold for a handsome profit. And I have strong evidence that they are wreaking havoc with the rule and taxation in the border villages of Meridan, where it is difficult for our armies to patrol. I fear for Meridan and the Seven Kingdoms when Prince Lomar comes to power. I will not touch the prince, who succeeds to the throne by legal right, but his men must be brought under control and some balance restored to the leadership of Meridan if the country is to be saved. We need more brave and true men of strong conviction who are willing to place the welfare of the kingdom above the interests of self.

"You, Aradon, are obviously this kind of man—one who is willing to sacrifice self for a right cause. I brought you here to urge you to become a servant of the kingdom—to train as a warrior with the expectation that if you train successfully, you would become one of the knights of the Hall. I have known your father for most of his adult life; he is a brave and honest man with a true heart. And I have observed how carefully he has passed on this infinitely valuable legacy to you. I am convinced that you would be a valuable and incorruptible addition to the Hall."

Aldemar explained the details. Aradon would be trained at a place called Ironwood, the estate of his deceased brother in the kingdom of Vensaur, a half-day's journey on the far side of Braegan Woods. The training would include jousting, swordsmanship, proficiency in all weapons, and archery. Aradon would live on the estate during the training. The project would be kept strictly secret, for if Balkert or Sir Stundal got wind of it, they would certainly find some way to stop it. The training would be daily, all day, for six days of every week. Aradon would be allowed three days at the end of each month to come home and visit his parents. He would also be granted brief times away for emergencies or other unexpected needs. Ordinarily the training of a knight took eighteen months or more, but since Aradon was already proficient with the sword, it might be shortened to under a year, making knighthood possible before Lomar's coronation.

"What do you say, my boy? Are you willing to become a servant of Meridan?"

"I am very sorry, sir. What you offer is a fine opportunity for one with warlike or political inclinations, but it is not the path I have chosen for my life. It would take me away from my father's work. He needs my help, and he expects me to train to take his place."

"I fully understand. No one with a heart for right would willingly choose warfare or politics as his lifework. But sometimes one must choose not what he prefers but to obey the call to sacrifice. As I have told you, the future of the Seven Kingdoms is at stake, and the welfare of the thousands of citizens who would suffer from its collapse should be placed above the private hopes of a single tradesman. Let me ask you not to form your answer yet but to take time to think it over and talk of it with your father. Give me your answer in three days."

Aradon agreed, and Lord Aldemar granted him leave from the interview.

❧

"What kind of regent does that man think he is?" boomed Bogarth when Aradon told him of his meeting with Lord Aldemar. "Stealin' the kingdom's finest young men for what he calls the welfare of the country! Doesn't he know that the country exists so that such young men can pursue their trades and raise their families?" The blacksmith ranted, pacing back and forth in his shop, waving his arms in emphatic punctuation and occasionally slinging a scrap piece of metal clattering into a corner. Aradon kept to his anvil, his head down, diligently beating out the blade of a scythe. After a few minutes, Bogarth took up his own hammer and pounded furiously at a wagon hook he was repairing for Halckane the dairyman, muttering all the while.

When he allowed himself to think objectively, Bogarth saw the wisdom of Aldemar's proposal, and that was his problem. His wishes for Aradon's happiness clashed with what he knew to be the good of the kingdom, and it took him a little time to come to terms with the kinds of choices he knew must be made in a fallen world. He dearly wanted his son to live a simple, uncomplicated life of domestic tranquillity. And the boy had been given a wonderful talent for blacksmithing that would be utterly wasted if he responded to Lord Aldemar's plea. Yet he could see that fate was pointing his son in another direction—that forces above him were moving the boy's future beyond his control. He quit punishing the wagon hook and told Aradon the decision was up to him. "Whatever you decide, you have my blessin'."

For the next two days, Aradon took long walks deep into Braegan Wood. Bogarth never asked him where he went or what he did there, but when Sir Denmore returned three days later, Aradon was ready with his answer. He would go to Vensaur to enter training as a warrior. Bogarth knew that his son had made the right decision, the only one a man of honor could have made. But he could not help but mutter under his breath as Sir Denmore rode away, "No good will come of this."

One week later Aradon left for Vensaur to begin his training, taking with him a letter of introduction from Lord Aldemar. When Ansel and Marcie came to the blacksmith's shop on the following morning, they noticed his absence and asked Bogarth about it. He explained vaguely but truthfully, as he did to all who asked the question, that Aradon was working on a long-term project in Vensaur and would return in several months. Marcie could not hide her disappointment. Her eyes brimmed as she turned away, causing Bogarth to add in spite of himself that Aradon would return for three days at the end of every month. As he watched the women push their cart away, he muttered to himself, "Now, why did I have to go and tell them that? I'm gettin' all soft and sentimental in my old age."

CHAPTER FIFTEEN

ENCOUNTER IN HELL

Volanna saw nothing of Prince Lomar during the two days after her disastrous welcoming procession and banquet. She was both relieved and disturbed: relieved because his company was unpleasant to her; disturbed because he was her betrothed, and like it or not, she must do her part to repair the breach between them.

She understood that in many kingdoms, couples whose marriages were arranged for economic or political reasons had no expectations that love would ever grow between them. The songs of minstrels and troubadours told of husbands and wives stepping outside the bonds of arranged marriages to find love in furtive nighttime liaisons with mistresses and knights who had too much time on their hands. But in the courts of Valomar—and under the late King Alfron, the courts of Meridan as well—such dallying was strictly outside the bounds of propriety and morality. Mates expected to find love and commitment in the arms of each other, whether or not the marriage was arranged. Love could be learned and practiced because it was a commitment of the will, not a thing that stormed the emotions with irresistible force. Volanna fully expected love to blossom in her relationship with Lomar, but she knew already that he was a desert in which she might wander long before finding such a bloom. The journey had best begin now. And though her dream of a marriage bonded by a deep love was now threatened, she refused to let it die. She might yet find the key to loving Lomar if she put her heart into it.

As Lomar's betrothed, Volanna had no real duties, and she was beginning to wonder what she would do with her days at Morningstone. She spent one day touring the castle under the direction of Sir Brevemont, but as there had been no balls or banquets in the great hall she and Kalley had taken their meals together in her rooms. She was glad when a page brought her a note from Lomar inviting her to a banquet the next evening. It was to be a small, intimate affair designed to introduce Volanna to his inner circle of friends. The banquet would be held in "little hall," a more private dining hall Perivale had built for smaller gatherings that would have been engulfed by the cavernous great hall.

In spite of her misgivings, Volanna prepared for the banquet with anticipation. She hoped to make new acquaintances from which friendships could grow. When the time came for Lomar to escort her to dinner, he knocked on her door.

"My princess looks dazzling tonight," he said when she opened the door. "In fact, there is no woman in Meridan with half your beauty. I can assure you that every lady at the banquet will utterly hate you."

"Hate me? Why?" asked Volanna with surprise.

"For your beauty, of course. Envy will eat right through their hearts."

"Why would anyone envy beauty? It's not a thing that one achieves or deserves; it is merely a gift that comes with no merit attached."

"Nevertheless there'll not be a woman here tonight who would not kill to have your beauty or kill you for having it. I tell you this in warning. Be prepared to hold your own tonight, or they will eat you alive."

Volanna, now apprehensive about the evening, entered the dining hall on Lomar's arm. There were no more than twenty people in the room, about an equal number of men and women, all young, all lavishly dressed in styles the likes of which Volanna had never seen. The guests were clustered in groups of four or five, chatting and laughing until they saw the royal couple enter. All talk ceased. The men stared at Volanna as if they had never seen a woman before, while the women looked as though the door of fortune had just been slammed in their faces. One woman, a beautiful girl with lustrous brown hair tied with crossing ribbons of lavender silk, examined Volanna with a chilly gaze. For a moment her darkened eyelids narrowed in open hostility. Then she turned again to her group and resumed her conversation.

Lomar escorted Volanna directly to the woman. "Princess Volanna, I have the great pleasure of introducing you to Lady Larensa, countess of Hampshield, and daughter of Sir, uh, Sir Whomever."

"Daughter of Sir Benidah," supplied Larensa, casting a look of feigned exasperation toward him. "Welcome to Meridan, Princess Volanna." She made a halfhearted attempt at a curtsy, which Volanna acknowledged with a slight tilt of her head.

"What a lovely dress your highness wears tonight," said Larensa. "I haven't seen one like it in seven years." The ladies in the circle tittered quietly, and some of the men rolled their eyes.

"Thank you," said Volanna, choosing to ignore the insult. She looked aside at Lomar, who raised his eyebrows and shrugged slightly as if to say, "I warned you."

"Larensa, would you be so kind as to introduce the princess to her new friends?" asked Lomar.

"Of course, your highness. They can hardly wait to meet her." Larensa's voice clearly conveyed the opposite. She made the introductions, each of which Volanna acknowledged graciously and with a smile. Some of them she had met at the welcome banquet. She remembered Sir Stundal, Balkert, Lady Wilda, the Earl of Widmont, Sir Fentamore, Sir Grosefar, the Earl of Brevant, and Lady Gwynnedd.

When Larensa completed the introductions, Volanna addressed the group. "I thank you for your kind welcome. May the future prosper from our newfound friendship." The men applauded lightly, and the women curtsied as if doing so were an embarrassment.

"Shall we gather at the table?" said Prince Lomar. As they made their way to their seats, Volanna noticed the tapestries that hung from the stone walls. All were springtime scenes of men and women—

handsomely dressed, strolling through gardens, talking together in private, dancing, and courting as plump amoretti hovered about. Volanna took her place at the elaborately carved oaken table between Prince Lomar and Lady Wilda, and the servants brought in the food. As the banquet began, so did the chatter and laughter. Volanna understood little of the talk or the humor, which seemed to center on private jokes, innuendo, sarcasm, and ridicule of all fashion outside their accepted conventions.

"Lomar, I just love your suit," said the young Earl of Brevant. "Be a good fellow and tell me who made it and where you got the fabric. I simply must have one like it."

"Maybe you'd rather have one like Sir Denmore wore to the welcome banquet," said Sir Grosefar.

"I could hardly believe he wore that same suit yet again. Did you see the thin places on the knees and the frayed threads on his sleeves?"

"It's no wonder. He's had the suit for two years," said Brevant.

"At least," said Widmont. "I remember him wearing it at my vows, and that was three years ago."

"He's young enough to know better," said Gwynnedd.

The servants kept all wineglasses full, which was no easy task. For a while Volanna was ignored by all but Lomar, who repeatedly urged her to refill her own glass, but she repeatedly refused. Finally Larensa turned to her and said, "Forgive us, your highness. We have completely forgotten that you were here; you are so quiet. How rude of us. And this banquet is in your honor. Please, tell us something about yourself."

"There's really very little to tell," said Volanna. "I am the third of three sisters; I was blessed with no brothers. I suppose I have lived the plain, simple, ordinary life of a king's daughter."

"Don't you think her highness has a charming accent?" said Lady Wilda. "I just love to hear the brogues of these people from the hill country. It's so quaint."

"Surely a woman with your beauty has attracted a lover?" said Gwynnedd. "Some handsome, young, dragon-killing, maiden-rescuing knight who rode in on a white horse and swept you off your feet?"

Volanna blushed slightly. "There was one who showed interest, but he proved false."

"What a surprise!" said Larensa, her voice oozing sarcasm. "Being false goes with being a man like smelling bad goes with being a skunk." She made no attempt to hide from Volanna the barbed glance she shot at Lomar. Lomar smiled and said nothing but held his wineglass toward the serving maid to be filled yet again.

"Tell us what it was like growing up under the great and wise King Tallis," said Sir Grosefar, putting an ironic twist to the words "great" and "wise."

"I couldn't have had a better father," said Volanna. "He was always good to me and—"

"Oh, come now, your highness. You don't have to defend Tallis in front of us. Word has got around about how he treated you—that he made you do your own chores, take care of your own clothes, and even feed goats and chickens. You can't claim that a king who would do such things to a princess is a good father, can you? But maybe it was all rumor with no truth about it."

"It's all true enough," said Volanna. "My father thought we should learn to work. My sisters and I worked in the barnyard, swept our hallways, helped in the kitchen, and even—"

"In the kitchen?" exclaimed Wilda. "You mean you had to bake and fry and—and—whatever else one does in a kitchen? I've hardly even been in ours."

"I wouldn't know what to do with a broom if I had one." Gwynnedd sounded almost proud of herself.

"You could ride it," Stundal said with a malicious smile. The group laughed, and Gwynnedd raised her arm as if to hit him, but he caught her by the wrist and pulled her giggling toward him.

"You must be terribly glad to get away from all that, your highness. I think it's shameful that a king would treat his daughter like a common slave," said Wilda.

"Oh, no, you misunderstand. Father did not treat me like a slave. He loved me, and I knew it. I didn't mind doing chores. In fact I miss having something to do."

"You've got a real jewel of a princess, here, Lomar," said Larensa.

"Where would you ever find another so versatile? Equally at home sitting on a throne or a kitchen stool, prattling at balls or bawling at cattle, sweeping kings off their feet or sweeping out sculleries."

Volanna could not miss the heavy sarcasm, and her face burned like an ember. Lomar leaned toward her and said in a low voice, "You are blushing, my dear. See the smug look on Larensa's face? She wants to hurt you. You don't want to let her know the shoe pinches."

"But why does she dislike me so?" asked Volanna.

"Oh, she treats everyone that way. You'll get used to it."

"I'm not sure I want to," said Volanna.

Lady Wilda had been eavesdropping. She cupped her hand and whispered in Volanna's ear, "Larensa is smarting from being displaced. She was Lomar's mistress for almost a year before you came. No other woman has lasted so long."

Volanna reddened again, this time in shock, not only over Lomar having a mistress but also at his friends feeling so free about telling her of it.

"Maybe King Tallis has to work his daughters because he can't afford servants," said Grosefar. "He doesn't bring in near the money he could. Everyone knows Valomar sits on the richest lodes of silver in the Seven Kingdoms. But he strictly limits the mining of it. The man is a fool."

"When you think on it," responded Fentamore, "it is very like King Tallis to make his daughters work like commoners. It's all part of the old code of honor and equality left over from the days of King Landorm. Tallis has refused to change with the times. He's riding into the future facing the wrong end of his horse."

"Or maybe he *is* the wrong end of his horse," said Stundal. Everyone laughed, and Gwynnedd giggled and snuggled against him.

Volanna reddened again, this time with anger.

"Your highness," said Balkert, "you needn't be upset that we take issue with your father's policies. We take issue with those of Lomar's late father as well. Indeed, Tallis and Alfron were cut from the same cloth. Both were dedicated to preserving the old ways. But no one can keep the sun from rising. The future will come, and it's futile to resist it. Each of us faces a time when we must choose our own paths, even if it means breaking away from the paths our fathers set us on."

"You'll have to forgive Balkert," said Lomar. "He can't talk without making a speech, and he's always too serious. But you'll get used to him."

"I never did," said Stundal. Again Gwynnedd giggled and snuggled.

"Your highness, please forgive me for pursuing the matter," said Balkert to Volanna, "but we merely want to help you escape from your father's influence so you can be free to choose your own path."

Volanna replied, "But if I can see that my father is on the right path, the freedom you insist I should have allows me the choice to follow him, does it not? If you demand that I break away from his path to follow yours, your so-called freedom is a sham."

"I can see that you are your father's daughter," said Balkert.

"I have been told that before, and it's very strange that each time it is with the intent to insult. But I want everyone here to know that I am honored to be called the daughter of King Tallis. Lomar, may we leave now? You and I have things to discuss."

"Of course, my dear. Will you please excuse us, my friends?" Lomar stood and held Volanna's chair, and they walked out of the little hall into the corridor.

Volanna was visibly shaken. "We must find a place where we can talk."

"We can go to my chambers," said Lomar. "In fact, I have something there I want to show you." Volanna agreed, and they went up the stairway to Lomar's rooms, where he seated her on a pillowed couch and called for a page to bring glasses of wine. "It will help steady you," he said. When the servant returned, Lomar handed Volanna her glass and after dismissing the page, sat on the couch beside her. Volanna took the wine and sipped it slowly.

"I have never in my life been through anything quite like tonight," she said. "I cannot see why you surround yourself with such people. Surely there are others in Meridan who would make much better companions."

"They were just having their own kind of fun. They enjoy the give-and-take of the sort of biting wit you heard tonight."

"I felt the bite, but I missed the wit. Tonight the clear message to me was that I do not fit into their circle. I am excluded by my beauty, my clothing, my speech, my parentage, and my hands being tainted by common labor."

"When they throw such barbs at you, they expect you to throw them back. You will learn."

"I think there is more to it than that. I'm convinced that Lady Larensa hates me."

"Of course. And I told you why," said Lomar. "Simple jealousy."

"Of my beauty or my position? I was told that Lady Larensa was your . . . your—"

"Whatever she was to me, it is all in the past, just as your own failed love is in the past. A woman like Larensa, who is reasonably beautiful, will always be jealous of a woman like you, who is exceptionally beautiful. It is that simple. Larensa will never like you unless you scar your face and become withered or fat. You'd best learn to meet her wit head to head with wit of your own. You're capable of it. You showed a little wit once or twice tonight."

Volanna smiled. The wine was beginning to calm her. "Thank you, Lomar. But I don't think anything I said tonight had any effect on Larensa."

"Your wit is too gentle, just as you are." Lomar reached around her and rested his hand on her shoulder. Volanna stiffened involuntarily, but allowed his hand to stay. "But there's much to be said for womanly gentleness," he said as he moved his hand downward toward the bodice of her dress.

She thrust his hand away, stood abruptly, and walked swiftly toward the door. Lomar jumped from his seat and moved in front of her. "I'm sorry," he said. "Perhaps I was moving too fast. Don't leave yet. You have not seen what I wanted to show you."

"Then show me and let me go."

She remained standing near the door as Lomar went into the adjacent room. In a moment he returned. "I want you to meet Belze," he said. Draped around his neck and shoulders was a snake, a constrictor of mottled gray and brown, the thickness of Lomar's arm and almost eight feet long.

Volanna screamed in terror. "Take it away! Please, take it away!" But Lomar merely grinned and sat casually on the couch. "Please, Lomar! I can't stand snakes! She backed toward the door and fumbled with the bolt behind her, never taking her eyes off Lomar and the snake. But the door was locked. She looked at Lomar with pleading eyes as he drew the key from the purse on his belt and held it up for her to see, grinning all the while.

"You may as well sit down," he said. "There are a few things you need to understand."

Volanna saw that she was trapped. Trembling, she sat in a chair across the room from Lomar and the serpent.

"No doubt I was being too hasty," he said.

"One year too hasty," said Volanna. "There will be no intimacy between you and me until we are wed. None. Not of any kind."

"Surely you are not serious. We are already pledged in marriage; what is the point of waiting for the redundancy of a vow?"

"A betrothal is not a marriage. Until we are married, you keep your hands and everything else to yourself."

"Why on earth do you hold on to such an archaic, legalistic code of morality?"

"Because that code was given to us as absolutes to guide our behavior by the Master of the Universe himself."

"Oh, Volanna, Volanna. Do you still believe in that old nursery tale? No thinking person today believes in an uncreated being who has lived always. And without such a being, you can have no absolutes."

"Something had to be here forever. Things cannot just appear from nothing any more than you can unpop a soap bubble."

"Your father has conditioned your mind to where you cannot reason objectively. Look at the world, at nature. What kind of mind would have made things the way they are?"

"A mind that wanted his creatures to be deliriously, ecstatically happy. This world was made to be wonderful, beautiful, harmonious, and delightful."

"Then how do you explain that bug carcass on the floor yonder? There lies the true story of nature. Everything dies. Everything is wasted. Nature is like a suicidal millstone, continually grinding everything, including itself, to powder. Whatever you build wears out or falls apart. Order crumbles into chaos. And we humans cannot escape it. We are nothing but little lumps of dirt and water temporarily arranged into sinews, viscera, and bone, and have no more importance than a tree, a stone, a dog, or that dead bug in the corner. We spend our lives in a cycle of futility, consuming and eliminating, aging and decaying all the while. And we all end just like that bug."

"If you really believe that, what reason can you find to go on living? How do you muster the will even to get up in the morning?"

"I have found that the only way to make life bearable is to spend every waking moment bringing pleasure to the eye, ear, tongue, and flesh. What others think of me is not important. It doesn't matter one whit whether what I do makes them happy or unhappy, as long as it pleases me. I exist only for self, and my life, be it short or long, is dedicated to experiencing as much pleasure as I can pack into it."

"But what about love? Don't you believe there is pleasure in love? One who loves finds a deeper, more satisfying delight in selflessly abandoning his own desires for the sake of his beloved. Don't you expect to have any of that kind of love for me?"

"Love is merely a euphemism for lust. We feign selflessness and call it love in order to get pleasure. You, Volanna, are nothing to me but an instrument of pleasure. I do not love you any more than you love me, nor do I expect it. In fact, I am aware that everyone around me hates me—my people, my friends, my servants, even my snake. In spite of your talk of love, even you hate me."

"No, no, Lomar, I don't hate you. I . . . I want to love you and—"

"You do hate me, Volanna. I can see it in your eyes—in the look of disgust that you try to hide and in the way you stiffen when I touch you. But I don't care. I have power over the people of Meridan because I am their prince. I have power over my pet Belze because I am larger than he is, and I can twist and shape him as I wish. You may resist me now, but I will soon have the same power over you, and I will have my way with you with or without your acquiescence." Lomar took the body of the snake in his hands and twisted, causing the reptile to jerk and writhe in pain.

"Stop hurting that snake!" she cried.

"Ah, the goodness of one who believes in absolutes is a wonderful thing to behold, is it not? The snake repels you, yet in your goodness, you do not want it hurt. Understand this, Volanna: you and I are nothing alike. Inflicting pain does not bother me at all. I know from experience that the time will come when I will tire even of a delectable morsel such as you, and I will casually and without pang cast you aside for some newer, more stimulating pleasure, all to keep that little, almost invisible spark called self alive by continually giving it new things to feel and experience."

"But there's the prophecy, Lomar. You are forgetting the prophecy. How could it be fulfilled unless the Master of the Universe is guiding it along? The prophecy proves that all you are saying is wrong. There is a reason to believe in absolutes."

"To me the prophecy means nothing. I doubt that there is a shred of truth to it. But as long as others believe it, I will use it to my own ends. The fabled Crown of Eden means nothing except that if it does come to rest on my head—if it even exists at all—it will simply increase my power and thereby give me more access to pleasure."

"But if the prophecy proves untrue, you may not inherit the throne of Meridan even though you are Alfron's son. Some think that if the Crown does not appear when the two stars meet, the line of Perivale will be broken and Meridan will be free to choose another king."

"Yes, I know that if the prophecy fails, some think they can prevent my succession. But I am taking strong steps to secure it. Balkert and Stundal are, shall we say, reorganizing local governments in the villages on the edges of Meridan beyond the effective reach of Lord Aldemar. And they are working their way inward. By the time the stars meet, I will already have most of Meridan under my control."

Volanna was horrified at what she was hearing and now fearful even of being alone in the room with Lomar. She arose from her chair and backed toward the door, looking at him all the while as if he were some monstrous creature about to spring. "I must go now. Please unlock the door for me."

Lomar stood and moved toward the door, the serpent still draped about his shoulders. Volanna shuddered and moved away. "You are right to fear me," he said. "Faith in absolutes gives one a conscience, which is a restraining influence on man's deepest impulses—all of which are, by your standard, base and despicable. Without absolutes I am utterly without conscience, and though I will let you go tonight, remember as you walk out my door that whether or not you are in my presence, you are never safe from me." He opened the door and stood aside as she slipped through it. "Good night, my dear."

Volanna, shaking uncontrollably, hurried down the dimly lit hallway, descended the stairs, and crossed the commons to her quarters.

ᴊ

Lomar was angry and frustrated. He had not intended to reveal so much of his inner motivations to Volanna this soon. He had hoped to wait until she came around to his thinking and that of his companions. He was sure that after spending enough time in their presence, she would align with their attitudes and behavior just as ducks tend to face the same direction when they sleep. Had he been able to wait until she made this alignment, she would not have been so shocked. But her stubborn clinging to her archaic mores had provoked him. Who was she to withhold herself from him? He was the crown prince of Meridan and was not accustomed to such refusals. It didn't matter, though. Whether by persuasion, deception, or coercion, he would have his way with her, and he would not wait much longer.

The only pleasure he got from the evening was the spectacle of her panic at being trapped in his room. He had not got what he wanted from her tonight, but he had planted the seeds of fear of him in her mind, seeds that he would nurture until they sprouted into full-fledged terror and loathing. That would make his final conquest of her all the sweeter.

The satisfaction of that thought did not lessen his anger, however. He was smarting from being spurned and burning from his unslaked lust. "She's a stupid woman, Belze," he murmured to the constrictor. "She doesn't know what she missed tonight."

Just as he threw the snake roughly into its cage, a knock came at his chamber door. He opened the door to a courtesan whom he had invited to come to his room an hour before midnight. He had completely forgotten. He had arranged the assignation over a week ago—before he had planned the banquet for Volanna. The girl gave Lomar a smile that spoke volumes of promise and pressed herself against him, but he was now in no mood for the likes of her. He flung her away rudely and ordered her out of the room.

Closing the door firmly behind her, Lomar threw himself heavily onto the couch and began to brood. His fixation on the princess had made him dissatisfied with other women. After several more glasses of wine, he disrobed and stumbled into bed with wanton images of Volanna burning in his mind.

Lomar slept fitfully. He tossed and turned till the sheets twisted about him like a cocoon. Long after midnight he opened his eyes for the twentieth time and decided it was the moment to act. He was the prince of Meridan, and she was his betrothed. Why was he conforming to her wishes? He didn't have to ask. He didn't have to wait. He could simply take what he wanted.

He arose from his bed, stalked out of his chambers, and crept through the castle and across the commons. When he arrived at Volanna's door, he tentatively pressed against it. It opened. He entered silently and looked toward her bed, where he saw her sleeping form, a vision of unearthly beauty as she lay bathed in the moonlight from the window. Carefully, stealthily, he advanced toward her. As he neared her bed, she turned toward him, yet asleep. He stopped dead still, not daring to breathe. Then she opened her eyes, and seeing him standing over her, sat bolt upright and screamed in terror.

At her scream the floor began to rumble and shake as if giant beasts were stampeding through the castle. Lomar struggled to keep his balance as he saw cracks appear, widen, then gape open like pits into a glowing underworld. He stared in horror as huge, grotesquely formed hands, knotty and clawed and covered with hair, reached up from the cracks, clutched at his legs, and began to pull him under the floor. He kicked and fought and struggled furiously to free himself. A huge, winged shadow darkened the crumbling floor around him, and he looked up to see an enormous bird, stark and black against the pale moon, flying into the open window. The bird settled to the floor and transformed into a tall, black-robed figure of a woman.

Lomar awakened from his nightmare to find himself on the floor beside his own bed, panting, sobbing, and struggling with the bedclothes that were wound tightly about his legs. Looming above him was Morgultha, a black silhouette outlined by the moonlight streaming through the window behind her.

"Who is this before me, wallowing in lust while the Crown of Eden remains unfound and Perivale's empire remains unclaimed? Is this the son of my own body whom I placed in a position to make the kingship of Meridan virtually inevitable? Is that who now grovels on the floor, his mind inflamed with dreams of wanton pleasure while my carefully laid plans of power lie gathering dust?"

"What do you mean coming in here like this in the middle of the night?" demanded Lomar.

"I have come with a warning," said Morgultha. "You are about to destroy the web I have woven together for over a century, and I will not allow it. I now have you positioned to gain the Crown of Eden for me without having to build an army or fight a battle. But you are not doing your part. You have failed to begin the program of power with which I have charged you."

"I'm doing my part to take the throne. You know what I've got Balkert and Stundal doing in the far villages of Meridan."

"It may not be enough. I have shown you the path to more subtle powers, but you have failed to learn the black arts I have tried to teach you—arts that could call up powers of the dark that would make our own position unassailable. Your pampered life as Meridan's prince has left you capable only of gratifying your own wants, which include nothing but clothing, horses, games, food, and wenches. And the coming of the princess has further diverted your attention. Enormous power is within our reach, but you can do nothing but grope about for your own little pleasures."

"What is the point of power unless it gets you the pleasures you desire?" Lomar retorted. "What greater good can one do for himself than gratify the senses? What does power add to the meaning of life that sensual pleasure doesn't give?"

"If you want to dabble in pleasure while almost unlimited power is within your grasp, that is your own affair. But confine your dallying to palace chargirls and village wenches. You must keep your lecherous hands off Princess Volanna. If you bed her before the Crown settles on your brow, you will lose the kingdom. Your subjects have little love for you as it is, and there are many—including the princess herself, I'll wager—who would cry foul if you violate the terms of their precious prophecy. Deflower the princess and you will be thrown out of Morningstone and out of the line of Perivale quicker than you can blink an eye."

"Why should I help you with your power lust when doing it takes me away from my own pleasures? Who makes the rules that say I should deprive myself of my wants in order to give you what you want?"

"The power you disdain makes its own laws. Ultimately there are no rules but those that power makes and enforces. I intend to be the one who makes the rules, not the victim of rules imposed on me by someone else."

"Fine," said Lomar. "To each his own. Go after all the power you want. Just leave me out of it. What I want lies asleep even now in a chamber across this castle. I don't need Perivale's Crown to get her, nor do I intend to wait for it to turn up, if it ever does."

"I've been too long at setting the stage to let you thwart me now," Morgultha replied. "And don't imagine for one moment that maternal love will save you. I humiliated myself by subjecting my body to a male in order to conceive you, and I did it for one purpose only: to give me access to that Crown. I do not intend to let you make that humiliation meaningless. I will have that Crown, Lomar, and putting you on Perivale's throne is my means of getting it. You will hold your lust in check and play your part in my plan, or I will see that the nightmare you just experienced comes true. It was the shadow of a reality that I can bring about."

As Lomar watched, the blackness of Morgultha's robe and hair seemed to dissolve into smoke while her tall form collapsed to the floor. And without realizing just how it happened, he saw in her place a huge blackbird, piercing his soul with eyes so yellow they almost glowed. The bird then spread its black wings, flew out the window, and disappeared into the full moon.

Lomar sat trembling, a cold sweat beading on his forehead. After a moment, he crawled back into his bed, pulled the covers over his head, and curled up into the sheet like a shrouded corpse, quaking and moaning until he sank into a pit of dreams infested with hideous creatures crawling up from caverns in the floor and enormous black-birds with eyes of fire shrieking all about him.

CHAPTER SIXTEEN

DUNGFACE

hy did you come 'ere, boy? If all you intend to do is loll about, you should 'ave stayed 'ome with your mother."

Aradon lay on his face in the dirt, a cloud of dust churning about him and a voice above his head grating in his brain like a sledge dragging on a gravel road. He felt the nose of his horse nudging his shoulder. He rolled over and raised himself on his elbow, spitting dirt and straw from his mouth.

"Stand up, boy. This is no time for a nap."

Aradon got to his knees. Dirt and pebbles cascaded from inside his tunic. He stood, steadied himself, and looked into the granite face of Sir Hardwicke, the battle-scarred veteran who was the master of the school at Ironwood.

"I wonder if you're capable of learning at all. If a dumb old wooden soldier can knock you about like a baby, what's going to 'appen when you face a real man?"

As Aradon's head cleared, another sound invaded his dirt-filled ears—the sound of laughter from eleven other trainees watching the newcomer take his first spills.

Aradon glared at the quintain and wondered if redemption were possible for the man who devised it. It consisted of a horizontal bar of wood with a battered shield attached to one end and a sack of sand about the size of a melon to the other. The bar was set like the cross of a *T* atop a vertical pole about seven feet high. It pivoted on a vertical axle inserted through a hole drilled through the bar halfway between the shield and the sandbag. Set atop the axle, which protruded some twelve inches above the bar, was a rusty, battered helmet. Aradon had never seen a quintain before and had no idea how it worked. When Sir Hardwicke had put him on his horse, given him a lance, and told him to ride hard toward the shield and hit it solidly with his lance, Aradon had put himself wholly into the task and hit the shield squarely in the center. Suddenly a sharp blow to the back had sent him tumbling from his horse. He had not known what hit him. Now, however, the arms of the quintain, still spinning, told him the whole story: the force of his blow had spun the shield around, bringing the sandbag hard against his back as he rode by.

"Shall I get my mother's pony for you?" Hardwicke yelled. "The woman's almost eighty years old, and she can ride faster than that. Now do it again, and this time see if you can get that 'orse of yours up to something more than just a trot."

Aradon tried again. And again. And again. Each time faster but each time with the same result—sprawled in the dirt, bruised and scratched and dazed. Finally he charged the quintain at a full gallop and hit the shield solidly. As the bar spun around, he ducked low against the horse's neck, and the sandbag swung just above his head. He turned with a grin on his face and trotted in triumph toward Sir Hardwicke. But Hardwicke took up a pole with a wad of padding tied to the end of it and rammed it into Aradon's shoulder, knocking him yet again from his horse. He landed facedown in a pile of horse dung, causing his companions to howl with laughter.

"We've got a new name for you, blacksmith," cried Unther, the son of a nobleman from the harbor city of Kerrigorn. "Dungface!"

"Never, never, never duck!" barked Hardwicke. "The one important thing you've got to learn is speed, speed, speed! You've got to outrun the sandbag. Do you hear me, boy?"

"Yes, sir," said Aradon, sitting on the ground and wiping the dung from his face.

"Stand up when I talk to you." Hardwicke prodded him with the stick, and Aradon stood shakily. "What did I say was the one important thing?"

"Speed."

"What?"

"Speed!"

"Just speed? Is that all?" Hardwicke stood almost nose to nose with Aradon, but he bellowed as if he were in the next county.

"Speed, speed, speed!" Aradon yelled back.

"Now, get on that 'orse and show me some speed."

Aradon slowly mounted and took up his lance. He abandoned all caution and spurred his horse until it reached a full gallop. But at such speed he could not hold his lance steady, and when he reached the shield, he missed it altogether and fell into the dirt yet again from sheer anticipation of the impact.

His fellow trainees brayed with laughter and one of them, a bull of a man with a shock of red hair, jeered, "Is that a new strategy, Dungface? You think maybe you can win battles by just riding past your enemy and whiffing him off his horse?"

Sir Hardwicke walked up to Aradon. "Do you remember what is the most important thing?"

"Speed, speed, speed," said Aradon.

"No! No! No! The important thing is accuracy." (Hardwicke pronounced it "accura-see.") "Accuracy! Accuracy! Accuracy! What good is speed if you can't 'it the shield? What did I say is the most important thing?"

"Accuracy! Accuracy! Accuracy!" bellowed Aradon.

"If only you could do it as well as you talk it. Maybe what you need is a bit of a demonstration." Hardwicke turned to the young redhead and said, "Llewenthane, come show the boy how it's done."

In a single fluid motion, Llewenthane took up a lance, vaulted onto his horse, and galloped full speed toward the quintain. He hit the shield solidly, spinning it like a potter's wheel, but when the sandbag came around, Llewenthane was five feet past it. Aradon looked on with wonder.

"You see how it's done, boy?" Hardwicke said. "What two things does Llewenthane 'ave that you don't 'ave?"

"Speed, speed, speed and accuracy, accuracy, accuracy," said Aradon, dully.

At last the sun touched the tops of the pines in the west and Hardwicke called a halt to the day's training. The twelve trainees walked the two hundred yards to the river, stripped off their grimy clothing, and plunged into the cold water. After letting the stream massage their bruises, they scrubbed their clothes clean and dried off by walking naked back to Ironwood's common hall.

The hall was a large, rectangular building with a vaulted roof beamed with pine logs and covered with thatch. This was their home for the duration of the training. Each man had his own deerskin cot, all lined up side by side against the long wall. At the end of the room was a stone hearth. Tables for food preparation stood nearby, and pots and utensils hung from the wall.

The tired but clean trainees donned the clothing they had washed yesterday and lined up at a serving table near the hearth as kitchenmaids filled their plates.

"To the end of the line, Dungface," growled Llewenthane as he pulled Aradon from the serving table and shoved him roughly away.

Aradon did not respond. He was low man in the pecking order, and he knew it. All the others had been in training for weeks at least, some for months, and two of them—Llewenthane and Unther—for over a year. The men were sons of noblemen or knights of Meridan's Hall—except Llewenthane, who was from a small village in southern Meridan, and Anffwyn of Wyddcroft, who was the son of a merchant. Llewenthane was their acknowledged leader, however, due to his longer tenure, greater skill, and natural bravado. He was a loud, blustering man, though at times he would sit quietly apart from the rest with a wistful look in his eye as he stroked a gold ring with an emerald setting that he wore on his finger. All the men had formed friendships within the group, and none felt disposed to reach outside these bonds or below their stations to enfold the bumbling blacksmith newcomer. But on this first night, Aradon was much too tired to care. He just wanted to eat his supper and get to his cot.

The men took their filled plates to a long, rough-hewn oaken table with side benches set in the center of the straw-covered, dirt floor. Aradon found a place at the end of the table next to Anffwyn and asked him, "Where do we get our drinks?"

"Over there." Anffwyn pointed to a barrel in the corner near the hearth.

Aradon left his bowl of stew on the table, drew a tankard full of ale, and returned to his seat. He scooped a heaping spoonful of the stew into his mouth. Suddenly his mouth was afire as if he had filled it with hot metal. His eyes watered, his face turned red, and he spewed the burning stew to the floor. Gagging and coughing like a dying man, he grabbed his tankard and gulped down several swallows before he stopped to gasp for air.

"Is the stew too hot for you, Dungface?" asked Unther with exaggerated concern. "It seemed fine to me."

"I thought it quite good myself," said Anffwyn.

"I suppose we've got to find some milder food for our city boy blacksmith. Derena, bring Dungface another bowl of stew, and leave out all the spices." The serving girl filled a bowl from the same pot and brought it to Aradon. He ate silently, vowing never again to leave his meal unattended.

When Aradon finished his supper, he was much too fatigued to defend himself against the banter and laughter of his companions and walked slowly and stiffly to his cot and eased himself down onto it. He had never been so tired. Every bone ached, the whole surface of his skin was sore, and he had bruises on his arms, sides, legs, and shoulders that could hardly bear his touch. Wearily, he undressed, eased himself into a prone position, pulled the coverlet over his shoulders, and was asleep almost instantly, completely oblivious to the continuing chatter of his companions.

It seemed only minutes before he heard Sir Hardwicke bellowing in a voice like nails caught between grindstones, "Why did you come 'ere, boy? If all you intend to do is loll about, you may as well 'ave stayed 'ome with your mother. Stand up, boy. This is no time for a nap. Come on out to the field. I've got a few things to teach you, though I wonder if you're capable of learning at all."

Wearily and painfully, Aradon rolled out of bed and followed the voice through the darkened hall, now lit only by the orange embers in the hearth. He passed through the door and made his way to the training field, which was brightly lit by a ring of torches mounted on poles.

"Come on, boy. Quit your lollygagging," called the ruin of a voice, though Hardwicke himself was nowhere in sight.

The quintain loomed stark and huge within the ring of light. Aradon approached it slowly, warily, and saw to his horror that inside the battered helmet was a human head bearing the craggy features of Sir Hardwicke.

"Come on, boy," yelled the head. "Remember, speed, speed, speed. Accuracy, accuracy, accuracy."

Aradon found himself mounted on his horse with a lance in his hand. He galloped hard toward the quintain, but instead of aiming at the shield, he pointed his lance directly at the head of Hardwicke. He made solid contact, and the head went bouncing across the earth.

Aradon had just raised his arms in exultation when suddenly a blow to his back knocked him to the ground. He jerked violently awake and found himself sprawled on his cot, thrashing at the coverlet. Hovering for a moment between the dream and reality, he looked about for any sign of Hardwicke, but he saw no one other than his fellow trainees asleep on their cots, barely visible in the dying firelight. He wrapped the coverlet about himself and fell asleep again.

Shortly he again heard the terrible bellowing of Hardwicke's voice. Convinced that he was dreaming once more, he didn't even open his eyes but turned over to reenter the oblivion of sleep. But suddenly his cot tilted sharply and dumped him to the floor. He looked up at the bulky form of Llewenthane, looming black against the light of a new fire in the hearth.

"Why did you come 'ere, boy?" said Llewenthane in a fair imitation of Hardwicke. "If all you intend to do is loll about, you may as well 'ave stayed 'ome with your mother. Stand up, boy! Can't you see it's morning?"

Aradon could see that his companions were already scrambling from their cots and pulling on their clothes. Facing down the threat of mutiny from his stiff joints and sore muscles, Aradon followed their lead. He could smell bacon sizzling and see the kitchenmaids bustling about the tables near the fire. Hardwicke came into the hall and paced about, fresh and vigorous as if he had been up for hours, barking orders and taunting the men for their sluggishness. In the distance a rooster crowed as if trying to reclaim his rightful role as the first to greet the dawn.

Aradon managed to pull on his clothing and stumble to the breakfast bench to join the others. After finishing a hearty breakfast of eggs, bacon, bread, and honey piled generously on their plates, the twelve trainees went out to the field just as the first light of the sun turned the jagged peaks of the Dragontooth Mountains to golden fire.

For Aradon the day was a dismaying repetition of the previous one. As were the day after and the day after and the day after. He spent much of his time on the ground, dust filling his lungs, dirt and straw filling his mouth and clothing, and Sir Hardwicke's voice filling his ears with derision for his ineptness. His first experience with other weapons was at least as disastrous as his first efforts with the quintain. The first time he swung a mace-and-chain at a shield hanging by two ropes from a high tree limb, the chain wrapped around his neck, and the heavy, spiked ball pounded against his shoulder, throwing him yet again to the earth.

"Dungface," shouted Llewenthane, "if the ball's too heavy for you, we can get the women to sew you one made of cotton."

After the laughter subsided, Hardwicke again called on Llewenthane to show Aradon how the mace was to be wielded. The burly young man took the handle, swung the mace around his head a few times, then brought it crashing against the shield, which flew backward a good five feet. Llewenthane continued to whirl the mace with an even rhythm so that each time the shield swung forward, his mace was there to meet it. He hit it again and again, causing it to dance in the air like a leaf on the wind. When he finished, Llewenthane gave Aradon a look of smug disdain, flung the mace-and-chain at his feet, and walked away.

Aradon's life as a blacksmith had given him no occasion ever to use a battle-ax, a spear, a crossbow, or a dagger. And his first attempt at each was awkward and unpromising. He had used a longbow a few times, having done a little hunting in Braegan Wood with his father and Rolstag, but he soon found that most of his companions had

completed enough training to outshoot him four times out of six. He
began to wonder if his decision to train had been a mistake.

After a week most of the soreness was gone from Aradon's
muscles, but while his bruises healed quickly, new ones kept replacing the old. He was still isolated from his fellow trainees, who
adopted only two attitudes toward him: taunting him mercilessly or
ignoring him altogether. And they continued to torture him with
little tricks. One night they filled his cot with cattle dung, and
Aradon thought himself fortunate that it was dried and easily
brushed away. One morning he found his clothing tied in knots,
earning him five extra rounds at the quintain as punishment for being
late to the field.

One night after Aradon had fallen asleep, Llewenthane brought
in a spider that he had caught in a bowl. The creature was covered
with brownish gray hair and had a leg span well over half that of
Llewenthane's hand. The men gathered silently about Aradon's cot as
Llewenthane took the spider in his fingers—though huge and
hideous, it was harmless if handled properly—and placed it on
Aradon's arm. He was sleeping with the side of his face resting on his
hand, and when Llewenthane nudged the spider forward, it began
crawling along Aradon's arm toward his face. Llewenthane tickled the
sleeping man's nose with a feather, and Aradon opened his eyes to see
the hideous creature approaching, now less than eight inches from his
nose. He jumped to his feet in panic, slung the spider across the hall,
and fled from the cot, knocking three men to the floor and running
headlong into a supporting post. He sat dazed in the dirt and straw,
shuddering at the lingering image of the many-eyed monster creeping toward him with mandibles working and palpi probing the surface of his arm.

Llewenthane looked down on Aradon with disdain. "Look at
him, men; he can't ride, can't aim, can't handle a mace, can't eat a
man's meal, and he's afraid of little bugs. I say that Dungface here is
just not much of a man and not likely to become one."

Llewenthane and the others walked away, and Aradon crawled
back onto his cot, angry and humiliated. He had an inordinate fear
of spiders. When he was a child, a spider much like Llewenthane's

had crawled into his tunic and bitten him painfully several times before his mother could get him out of his clothing. He had never forgotten the look of the hideous creature as it fell to the floor, where it lay dying with its segmented legs flailing in the air before they curled slowly inward like a clutching claw.

Two weeks passed, and Aradon was convinced he was making no progress at all. About the time he thought he was making headway, Hardwicke would place a new challenge before him. Just as he learned to hit the quintain squarely and outrun the sandbag, Hardwicke paired the trainees against each other to joust in the lists using blunted lances. The other men had engaged in these exercises several times before, but it was Aradon's first attempt. Hardwicke outfitted them in armor—helmets, gauntlets, plate armor for their torsos, and chain mail for the rest of their bodies. He would not allow his trainees to use plate armor on their arms and legs, for as he explained, to encase one's limbs in metal tubing limited movement too much for any form of battle except jousting. "And there's another danger in plate armor that warriors don't think about," he said. "On a midsummer day the 'eat inside can roast a man alive. Plate armor 'as killed more men than it 'as saved. Chain mail is 'ot enough, but at least it can breathe a bit whereas plate armor can't."

Aradon, now fully armored, sat on his mount facing Llewenthane, who stood ready at the other end of the list.

"Just think of Llewenthane as a quintain," said Hardwicke. Then he gave the signal, and the two men galloped toward each other. Aradon aimed his lance directly at Llewenthane's shield, but Llewenthane's lance caught firmly on his own breastplate and swept him from his horse. The big redhead laughed and shook his head as he circled around his fallen opponent. "Go home to mother, Dungface. You're not doing any good here."

That evening as Aradon sat at supper, exhausted, bruised, isolated, and ignored except for an occasional insult, he watched his companions chatting, laughing, joking, and bantering—all but Llewenthane, who sat gazing into the fire and fingering his ring—and he longed to be a part of them. Why wouldn't they accept him? He thought Llewenthane might be right. He was doing no good here.

Why not face the truth? He was simply inept at weaponry. He had misinterpreted Father Verit's meaning, and Lord Aldemar was mistaken about his potential. No one noticed as Aradon left the table to lie on his cot and fall asleep.

CHAPTER SEVENTEEN

speed and accurasee

he Ironwood trainees arose late for it was a seventh day, which meant there would be no training. Each man was on his own to entertain himself, go as he pleased, or simply stay in the hall and rest. Some wanted to practice at their weapons, but Hardwicke strictly forbade it. "It's not that you don't need the practice," he had told them, "but you'll do much better in the long run if you take a little time off at regular intervals to let what you've learned seep into your bones." The men formed into their usual groups and disappeared, some going into the nearby village, some into the fields to hunt, and others to the river to swim.

Aradon had wasted his previous free days wandering about the compound and trying to stay out of the way of his companions. He was determined not to waste today. He calculated that his pond in Braegan Wood was no more than three hours distant on horseback, and he decided he had no better way to spend the day than to go there. He asked Derena to pack him a lunch, which she did gladly. She had gazed often upon Aradon and was happy to do anything that would draw his attention to her. He took the lunch and rode into the forest to his pond, where he spent four or five hours swimming beneath the waterfall and lying on the grassy bank to dry. He fell asleep thinking of his parents, the feel of a six-pound hammer in his hand, the sizzle of hot metal in the cooling trough, and not infrequently, the fair face and figure of Marcie. His trips to the pond became a weekly habit, and for several weeks, they were his only solace.

One morning as the trainees were gathered on the field, Sir Hardwicke picked up a shield and drew his sword from its sheath. He turned to Aradon and held the shield to his face. "This is a shield," he said. "Its use is simple. You keep it between yourself and the sword of your opponent." He dropped the shield to the ground and held the sword in front of Aradon's nose. "This is a sword." He pointed to the hilt, "You put this end in your 'and—," then he pointed to the blade, "—and this end in your opponent's belly." Hardwicke turned to the rest of the group. "As I 'ave told all of you but the boy, 'ere, dueling with the sword is like no other kind of warfare. Brute force or wild abandon won't win for you at swords. Sword fighting is an art, and a complex one at that. It is the most important art a knight can learn." He distributed to each man identical swords, all edges blunted (although even blunts could inflict painful wounds), and had each drop his gauntlet into a basket from which it would be drawn to determine pairings for practice dueling.

When Llewenthane found that he had drawn Aradon's gauntlet, he was livid. He stalked over to where Sir Hardwicke stood. "You know I've won every duel here for the past six months, and that blacksmith doesn't even know which end of a sword to hold. How will we ever perfect our skills if you keep having us play nursemaid to this bumbling know-nothing? Put me up against Unther and send this baby home."

"You've got a short memory, don't you?" replied Hardwicke. "Little more than fourteen months ago, you were just like 'im."

"Like him?" thundered Llewenthane. "I was never like him."

"Ah, but you were. The new ones always learn from the older ones. You came in 'ere stupid and awkward, just like the boy. And you 'oned your own skills against those who were better than you. Now you've got to pass that favor on."

"My skills are wasted on this idiot. He's never going to be a warrior and you know it as well as I."

"Enough, Llewenthane! You drew his gauntlet, and rules are rules. That is all." Llewenthane turned and stalked away, grumbling and muttering to himself.

Sir Hardwicke called out the first pair, set them facing each other, and said, "'ere are the rules. A sword striking anywhere on the opponent's breastplate, leg, or 'elmet scores a point. If your opponent falls to the ground, you get a point. Three points wins the match. Or the first to draw blood wins the match, or the first to lose 'is sword loses the match. No strikes to the face or 'ands. Anyone who violates the rules faces me. Do you all 'ear?"

The men grunted their assent, and the duels began. The first two combatants were Orreld of Surrifax and Anffwyn. Anffwyn took his opponent in about five minutes with three strike points, but Aradon noted that he was a little clumsy and his guard was so poor that he had given his opponent several openings that the man simply lacked the skill to take. The next two pairs were less skilled than Anffwyn, and their matches even more awkward. Aradon and Llewenthane were called next. They donned their helmets, took up their shields, and faced each other.

"Dungface," Llewenthane called in a voice all could hear. "Surely you've been told that I'm the best swordsman here. Why humiliate yourself again? Give Sir Hardwicke your sword, admit you made a mistake coming here, and go back home to mother. Your stupidity is holding back the rest of us."

"Today I will beat you," said Aradon.

The ten watching men looked up in surprise, then burst out laughing. Llewenthane was first shocked, then livid with outrage. In an angry frenzy he jerked the emerald ring from his finger and held it up for all to see. "You see this ring?" he shouted to Aradon. "It is pure gold, set with an emerald the likes of which you've never seen. If you defeat me, this ring is yours. If I defeat you, you go home."

"Agreed," said Aradon. "Get your guard up."

Llewenthane rushed Aradon, swinging his sword furiously. Aradon parried easily and stepped aside as his opponent fell to the ground. "One point for the boy," shouted Hardwicke, grinning. The big redhead got up, glaring at Aradon all the while. This time he attacked with more caution, using a thrust, parry, and feint sequence, but Aradon was ready and met each stroke sharply with his own blade or shield. Llewenthane changed tactics and swung first at Aradon's head, then at his legs in an attempt to confuse his defense. But again Aradon deftly parried every blow.

Llewenthane increased his speed, hoping Aradon's reflexes could not match the flurry of blows he rained on him. But after several minutes of this, he had not even shaken Aradon's defense. He fell back panting, looking hard at Aradon in consternation. Immediately Aradon attacked, his sword moving like lightning, and Llewenthane stumbled backwards under the sheer power of the blows, which he barely managed to ward off. Aradon deliberately dropped his shield, and Llewenthane took the bait, swinging hard at Aradon's head. Aradon ducked and thrust the point of his sword hard against Llewenthane's breastplate, much to the man's astonishment.

"Point two for the boy," shouted Hardwicke, greatly surprised but enjoying the duel immensely. The onlooking trainees stared in silence, unable to believe what they were seeing.

Llewenthane stood for a moment staring at his opponent with dismay. Slowly his features hardened, and with a great bellow of rage, he charged, swinging furiously with all his strength. Aradon fell back from the onslaught, still parrying deftly and keeping his shield in place. But the heel of his shoe caught on the edge of a mole trench, and he stumbled backward, splaying his shield wide to keep balance. Immediately Llewenthane's sword landed hard just above his knee on his exposed thigh.

"Point one for Llewenthane," shouted Hardwicke.

Heartened by his success, Llewenthane charged again. But this time Aradon held his ground. Their blades had rung against each other for three or four minutes when Aradon employed a trick Sir Denmore had often used against him. With a quick turn of the wrist, Aradon's blade caught Llewenthane's at the end of its stroke and twisted the sword from his hand.

"The match goes to the boy," shouted Hardwicke. He called to Llewenthane, who stood immobile and stunned, staring at his empty hand, "Are you sure you can't learn anything from the newcomers?"

Slowly, without looking up, Llewenthane twisted the ring from his finger, gazed at it for a long moment, then extended it toward Aradon. When Aradon took it, Llewenthane turned and walked away, his head bowed in humiliation. He did not join his companions but sat down on a nearby stone and stared at the ground. No one shouted, no one cheered, no one commended Aradon for his victory. They merely gaped in astonishment.

Hardwicke called for the next pair and the dueling continued until all matches were complete. Then he spent the rest of the day working with each man individually, correcting defects he had observed during the matches. As the sun began to set, Hardwicke dismissed them, and the trainees headed for the river to bathe, each one subdued and awkwardly silent in the presence of Aradon.

A little of the old banter returned at the dinner table, but it was a mere shadow of the chatter of the nights preceding. They seldom spoke to Aradon—that had not changed—but they did not taunt and ridicule him either. Llewenthane hardly spoke at all but ate his dinner in silence. And when anyone spoke to him, he answered shortly, his dejection plainly showing. Unther, the nearest thing to a rival that Llewenthane had, secretly rejoiced in Llewenthane's humiliation, seeing in it his own opportunity to become the group's unofficial leader. He decided to press his advantage.

"What's the matter, Llew? Did our little Dungface hurt your feelings?"

Llewenthane stood abruptly, fire flashing in his eyes as he glared hard at Unther. But the flame quickly died, and he sagged visibly, then turned on his heel and stalked from the hall. The men looked at each other in uncertain silence. They spoke little, feeling uneasy and insecure that the order they had known for months had been upset. After dinner was over, Llewenthane still had not returned. When the men gathered around the fire to sip their ale, tell stories of girls and conquests, and sing an occasional ballad or drinking song, Aradon slipped out the door unnoticed.

As he wandered toward the training field, he saw the dark figure of Llewenthane sitting on the same stone where he had rested after his defeat. Aradon walked toward him and stopped ten feet from where he sat.

"Llewenthane, it is not merely your defeat this morning that is bothering you, is it?"

"Get away from me," Llewenthane growled. "If you came to gloat, I suppose you've earned your right to it. Get it done, and get out of my sight. But if you came to give sympathy, I don't need it—certainly not from you."

"Indeed, I have no sympathy to give you. After all you have put me through since I came here, I cannot pretend I am sorry about what happened today. But I didn't come to gloat either."

"Why did you come?"

"For the truth. I want to know the meaning of the ring I won."

Llewenthane sighed deeply—a long, broken sigh that sounded almost like a sob—but he said nothing and kept staring at the ground beneath his feet.

"Tell me, Llewenthane."

After a long moment the dejected warrior lifted his head and spoke in a muted and unsteady voice. "Two months before I came here, I pledged to wed a girl in my village. We thought of having the wedding before I left, but we knew it would be better to wait; the taste of love would only make us thirst for more, and my stay here would be miserable for the longing of her. On the night before I left, she gave me the ring. It was an heirloom, handed down for generations from mother to daughter. She told me to keep it with me at all times for if ever I was parted from it, she would know that my love for her had died."

"And has it?" asked Aradon.

"No. Not in the least," he replied.

"Then why did you—"

"I did not think it even remotely possible that you would give me a challenge today. I thought the ring was perfectly safe. Of course, now I see that I did a rash thing, and I must bear the cost."

"You may have the ring back." Aradon extended it toward him.

"No! It is yours," Llewenthane retorted with heat in his voice. "You won it fairly. My rashness is not your problem."

"My father once told me that the weaknesses of each are the burden of all. You must keep the ring. I do not need it, and it is the key to your happiness."

"I pledged the ring to you, and I always keep my pledges."

"You have kept your pledge in giving me the ring. Isn't it now mine to do with as I will?"

"It is," said Llewenthane.

"My will is to return it to you. Do not deny me the right you just granted me—to do with the ring as I will." Again he held the ring in the palm of his hand and extended it toward Llewenthane. Llewenthane looked up for the first time, saw the bright sparkle of green moonlight dancing on the stone, and hesitantly, gently took it from Aradon's hand.

"I thank you, Aradon," he said in a voice choked with emotion. It was the first time he had ever uttered Aradon's name.

"I will not tell anyone of this," said Aradon. "You may keep the ring in your purse, and our friends will be none the wiser." Llewenthane nodded with gratitude, and Aradon returned to the hall.

As Aradon started toward the serving table the next morning, he heard the voice of Unther just behind him, "Out of my way, Dungface!" Unther grabbed him roughly by the shoulder and shoved him aside.

Aradon turned toward him, fire in his eyes, ready to spring, but Llewenthane was already there. His fist cracked against Unther's jaw, tumbling him to the floor. Llewenthane bent over the dazed man, waving his fist in his face. "I don't want to hear anyone ever calling Aradon that name again."

And no one ever did.

ℒ♥

The duel with Llewenthane was a turning point for Aradon. From that day forward, he faced the task of learning weaponry with new confidence. He learned quickly, and in a few weeks he moved abreast of the others in almost every category. Though it took days of painful repetition and countless falls before Aradon mastered the simultaneous tasks of jousting—holding a shield, controlling his mount, aiming his lance, balancing for impact, and deflecting his opponent's lance—master them he did, moving up continually in the weekly rankings.

Sir Hardwicke, however, never let up on Aradon. The moment

Aradon thought he had mastered a skill, Hardwicke would detail every defect and push him as hard to correct them as if he had learned nothing at all. Indeed, while Aradon knew he was doing well among his fellow trainees, he often wondered just how his newly acquired skills would play against those of experienced knights outside the compound.

After a little more than three months, Lord Aldemar visited the compound for a day to observe the progress of his trainees. To show the skills of his men, Sir Hardwicke held a tournament among the twelve to determine the best in every category—crossbows, long-bows, spears, mace-and-chain, battle-ax, jousting, and swords. To the surprise of no one, Aradon won at swords. To the surprise of some, he also won at spears, crossbows, and longbows, was a close second at the battle-ax, third at mace-and-chain, and fourth behind Llewenthane, Anffwyn, and Unther at jousting.

After the tournament Sir Hardwicke dismissed the men for the day. The warriors-to-be removed their armor and made for the river as stableboys attended their horses. Lord Aldemar and Sir Hardwicke walked slowly toward the hall.

"What do you think, Hardwicke? Are not some of these men ready for knighthood?"

"Llewenthane, Anffwyn, and Unther are already at least as good as 'alf the knights in your 'all, m'lord. I say you can present their names for knighting at any time."

"Why do you omit Aradon? He won today's tournament, did he not?"

"That 'e did," replied Hardwicke. "The boy is doing wonderfully well. In fact, I'd say 'e's the most apt pupil I've 'ad in twenty years, though 'e does 'ave a persistent style defect in 'is jousting. You've got a real jewel on your 'ands there, but 'e's still a bit rough around the edges. Let me keep 'im a bit longer, m'lord, and I can make 'im into a finely cut diamond. I'll work that little defect out of 'im and send back to you a knight the likes of which you've never seen."

"I can believe it," replied Aldemar. "Judging by what I saw today, I think I've never seen anyone with more natural talent."

"Natural talent!" boomed Hardwicke. "By the roots of my beard,

I'll swear that there's no such thing as natural talent at any art or skill. People like to call 'igh proficiency 'natural' to excuse their own failure to do what it takes to learn. What you call natural talent is always the result of strong desire combined with good training and 'ard practice. If you want to learn something strongly enough to sacrifice what it takes to learn it, learn it you will. Given normal intelligence and 'ealth, of course. Forgive me, sir, I didn't mean to raise my voice. You just touched one of my sore spots."

Aldemar laughed. "The blame is mine, Hardwicke. I should have remembered. I've heard that speech before, you know. How long ago has it been, now?"

"Thirty-seven years, my lord."

"By the grace of the Master! Has it been that long? Sometimes it seems only a few months; yet at others, it seems almost a lifetime."

"You were my first really great pupil, sir," said Hardwicke.

"Was I indeed? You certainly didn't let me think it then. I thought I was a bumbling fool making no progress at all. I still remember the first words you spoke to me: 'Why did you come 'ere, boy? If all you intend to do is loll about, you should 'ave stayed 'ome with your mother.'" Aldemar's imitation of his old master's speech was gentle and full of respect, and both men laughed at the memory. "As you know, Hardwicke, in time my life veered away from the warrior's path you set me on, but you taught me two things that I have found beneficial in almost everything I do."

"What things, m'lord?"

"Speed, speed, speed and accura*see,* accura*see,* accura*see.*"

CHAPTER EIGHTEEN

TLE KITCLENMAID

After Volanna's distressing encounter with Lomar, she returned to her chambers. She was upset and knew it would be long before she was able to sleep. She thought of calling in Kalley so she could pour her anguish into her friend's sympathetic ear, but she knew Kalley would be asleep by now.

As Volanna's handmaid, Kalley had to rise early each day for the next fortnight to attend all-day training for her service at Morningstone. Kalley had wondered whether such long training was needed, but the head chamberlain had soon convinced her. In order to serve the princess efficiently, she must learn her way about the castle and memorize the names, specialties, and locations of all the primary servants—those in charge of such things as the kitchen, cleaning, upkeep, clothing, posting, paging, and a score of other services of which Kalley had not even heard. She must know how these services worked and how to gain efficient access to them.

Volanna disrobed and slipped into bed. For a while she stared out the window at the bright, full moon as Larensa's insults and Lomar's threats echoed in the chambers of her mind. Turning toward the opposite wall did not help. Her eyes remained wide open, staring at the cold moonlight shining on the stones. The image of Lomar with the hideous serpent sliding about his shoulders arose in her mind, and she shuddered. She felt trapped in a web of evil and isolated by the envy and snobbishness of Larensa and the other ladies of the court. She was utterly baffled by her treatment at their hands—or rather, their tongues.

In Valomar Volanna did not incite such jealousy among women—at least, not much. It wasn't merely that they sensed her beauty to be so overwhelming as to make her virtually unapproachable by all but the most intrepid of men. They seemed to regard her as an eloquent statement of the femininity they shared with her. They were proud of her beauty for it inspired them to glory in their own womanhood, to delight in being feminine, and to take pride in its differences from the masculine. It was as if Volanna's beauty placed her at the hub of femininity, whereas most women lived at the rim where the feminine did its magic where it was most needed, with the reality of husbands, housework, and babies—bringing delight, magic, poetry, and completion to a world that would otherwise be a dull and plodding place.

Volanna knew that she was beautiful just as she knew that apples were red. It was a mere fact. But under the tutelage of her parents, she had managed to avoid the tendency toward conceit often found in beautiful women. Humility did not consist of her denying the obvious truth that she was beautiful; it was a matter of her treating her beauty as an objective reality rather than as a measure of her worth. Beauty was a gift—not one given for her own benefit but given for the delight of others. It seemed that the Master of the Universe had selected a few women to bear momentarily the weight of untainted beauty so that in them men and women could see beyond the corrupting blight of the fall and glimpse something of the original ideal infused into all creation.

But it seemed to Volanna that her beauty had become a curse to her in Meridan. And as the shadows of this evening's encounters with Larensa and Lomar troubled her sleep, she found herself wishing for a plain face and a flat, angular body that no woman would envy and no man would crave. She knew that plainness did not inhibit happiness. There always seemed to be a man who found just what he wanted in the homeliest of women. Either he saw within her features the beauty that nature intended but somehow missed, or he found a deeper beauty that his love drew to the surface, where it transformed her plainness into something desirable. As the old proverb said,

"Every woman is thrice beautiful: in the moonlight, as a bride, and in the eyes of her lover."

I must find some way to fill my days so I won't go on brooding like this, thought Volanna. Larensa and her friends had disdained her for her work in the kitchen of Oakendale Castle as if it were a shameful thing. Well, why not justify their disdain? In the morning she would dress in a servant's shift and apply for work in the kitchen of Morningstone. Word of her doing such a thing was sure to get around the castle, but Volanna did not care. Inside Lomar's circle she was sure to become prey to the predatory gossip of Larensa and her ladies. To them, her kitchen work would be nothing short of scandalous. It might even cause them to exclude her from their company altogether. *If only it would,* she thought.

Heartened by the simple act of making a plan, she finally relaxed. Her eyes grew heavy as she stared at the moonlit wall, and just as they were about to close, she thought she saw the shadow of a huge blackbird flit across the stones. She thought it odd for a bird to be flying about at such a late hour, but she was too sleepy to dwell on it and fell into a deep slumber.

☙

"But your highness, it is not fitting," protested Hilbront, chief cook and head of the kitchen at Morningstone Castle. "You are a princess, soon to be a queen. Your royal hands do not belong in cake batter or dishwater." He did not say what he thought, that she would be hopelessly in the way in his kitchen. Someone would have to show her every procedure and teach her the use of every utensil, not to mention that she would demand only the lightest tasks and require pampering and deferential treatment, completely disrupting the order and schedule of his realm.

"In your kitchen I am not a princess, I am merely Volanna, another servant under your orders. And if you are worried about my lack of experience, you needn't be. I have done this before."

"But, your highness, how would I explain it to Sir Brevemont or Lord Aldemar? They would have me pilloried for presuming to treat you as a servant."

"I will make it clear to them that this is my own idea and that I insisted on doing it. Now, please put me to work. I'm not leaving until you do."

Hilbront sighed and shrugged his shoulders. "Very well. Come with me."

He handed her an apron and a rag to tie about her head. Then she followed his rotund form as he led her into the kitchen. All the servants stopped working and gawked at the princess as she passed through. They recognized her face but were shocked and baffled by her attire and wondered what she could be doing in their kitchen. Hilbront led her past rows of hanging ham hocks and cheeses the size of large pumpkins. He pushed aside two huge sides of beef so they could pass, leaving the carcasses swinging behind them like giant pendulums.

Three women were kneading large lumps of bread dough on the dough board in the rear of the kitchen, laughing and chattering among themselves as they worked. They looked up as Hilbront and Volanna approached, and their eyes grew wide with surprise as they recognized the princess. They immediately turned from their boards and curtsied. Hilbront glared at them. It was going to be just as he feared.

"No, please. Don't stop your work," said Volanna. "You mustn't curtsy or treat me differently from any other worker. Forget my rank, and let me work beside you." She might as well have asked a sparrow to forget that a peacock had invaded its nest.

"Of course, your 'ighness," mumbled one of them as they all curtsied yet again. They turned back to the dough board and began kneading once more, keeping their heads down in silence. A bearded man with longish brown hair and a ragged tunic set a large bowl of bread sponge on the board in front of Volanna and bowed deeply.

"Please, don't bow to me while I'm working here," said Volanna. The man said nothing, just nodded and bowed again before he turned away.

Volanna sifted flour onto the sponge and vigorously stirred it in until it became dough thick enough to knead. Then she plunged her fingers into the dough and began massaging it in and out, turning it over and over with soft patting sounds against the board. Often she paused to add a sprinkling of flour to the lump, and soon her hands and arms were white with the powder. A spot or two even found its way to her face.

She tried to start conversations with the workers at her side, but they were too shy of her to engage. She hardly got more out of the women than their names, which they mumbled so quietly that she was not sure even of them. Nevertheless she was happy just to have something to do and delighted in the feel of the dough in her hands. Her heart floated above the dark thoughts of Lomar and Larensa that had burdened her mind through the night, and she remembered her happy childhood days in the kitchen at Oakendale. Completely unaware that she was doing it, Volanna began first to hum, then sing an old folk tune she remembered from those days:

> *She thought her kisses would hold him so well,*
> *And kissed him from sunrise until the night fell,*
> *But she lost her dear love to a maid in the dell,*
> *Who baked him the tarts that he loved, oh, so well.*

The workers about her looked at each other in silent wonder, but Volanna sang on, utterly oblivious to them.

Most of the time Hilbront sat at a table near the huge hearth, which spanned most of one wall of the kitchen. Servants and cooks came to him continually for orders and reported to him the progress of their work. Occasionally he would push himself out of his chair and waddle around the kitchen, inspecting, commanding, and tasting the results of the workers' efforts. Volanna noticed that these rounds created a wave of increased diligence among the workers, though as Hilbront passed, it dissipated into a wake of glares and angry gestures at the man's wide back. Often Volanna heard him curse and yell at some servant for laziness or incompetence, and she realized that the man was a tyrant and the servants all hated him.

Nevertheless she was enjoying her work. After kneading the dough, she separated it into several strips, which she then deftly twisted together and placed on the board for the bearded servant to take to the oven. Her companions watched with sidelong glances and again looked at each other in surprise. The princess was skilled and efficient. Where could she have learned it?

With the bread in the oven, Volanna turned to the girl beside her and asked, "What do we do next?"

"Well your 'ighness, we are going to clean and dress the chickens you see on yonder table. I suppose you should be asking 'ilbront what 'e 'as that you can do." The girls made for the table, which was piled high with three dozen or more fat chicken carcasses, all headless and plucked. Volanna followed and joined them on stools surrounding a large wooden tub on the floor. Before they could start their work, she heard the shuffling feet and hard breathing of Hilbront coming up behind her.

"Your highness," he said, "surely you don't intend to soil your hands cleaning these chickens. You have no idea of the mess or the smell. It's the worst job in the house. Let me take you over here, where you can help wash potatoes for baking."

"Hilbront, I'll do just fine right here. Please stop being so concerned about me. I am not a fragile ceramic doll."

Hilbront looked at her as if he thought that was exactly what she was, but he sighed and shrugged and waddled back to his table as the girl next to Volanna handed her a chicken and a sharp knife and watched to see what she would do with it. Without hesitation, Volanna slit open the carcass and raked the contents into the tub, then plunged her hand into the cavity to scrape away the residue from the sides. With sure, deft strokes, she cut off the feet and handed the fowl to the silent, bearded man who stacked it with the others to be washed and roasted.

Again she tried to engage her companions in conversation, but again to no avail. While they were surprised and awed at her skill and diligence, and it was clear that she was not going to play the princess or condescend to them; nevertheless, they were still suspicious. Why was the future queen of the Seven Kingdoms doing dirty, menial work in their kitchen? Royalty simply did not do such things, and they could make no sense of it.

Volanna tried chatting with the bearded man who was washing

and stacking the chicken carcasses, but got no response at all. "Do you think he didn't hear me?" she asked the girl sitting beside her.

"Oh, 'e 'ears all right, but 'e can't talk, though 'e 'as a tongue. Born that way, or so I 'ear. And 'e may be one of the moonlit ones, if you catch my meaning. You know, a bit slow in the 'ead. All 'e does is wash and clean and carry things. We all call 'im 'Mute.'"

When all the chickens were cleaned, Volanna went out with the other girls to the well, where they washed the slime from their hands. The silent man lifted the tub of offal by its handles to take it out to the hogs. But he slipped in some of the stuff that had missed the tub, and he fell hard to the floor, spilling most of the foul contents across the flagstones. The edge of the tub landed heavy on his hand, and he sat gripping his bleeding fingers as Hilbront huffed up and stood behind him with his fists on his hips and his eyes glaring.

"You idiot!" he yelled. "I don't know why I keep such a half-wit as you in my kitchen. Just look at what you've done!" In a spasm of anger he picked up the tub and dumped the remaining offal on top of the mute's head. It ran down his face and neck and dripped to the floor. "Why are you just sitting there? Get to your lazy feet and clean up this mess." Hilbront threw the tub to the floor beside the man and waddled away.

Volanna returned from the well just in time to see Hilbront pour the slime onto the mute's head. She was furious. Her face went crimson and fire flashed from her eyes. She marched straight to Hilbront, forgetting all about her determination to be subservient to the chief cook, and all the princess within her surged to the surface. "Don't you care that he is hurt?" she spat at Hilbront. She turned to the mute, helped him to his feet, and sent one of the girls back to the well for clean water. She took a rag from the table and cleaned the blood from his fingers, which did not seem badly hurt, then bound the rag around his hand. She found another rag and began to wash the slop from his head and clothing.

All work stopped as the servants, as well as Hilbront, looked on dumbfounded.

"What is this man's name?" Volanna asked of the girl who had worked beside her.

"I'm told 'is name is Olstan, your 'ighness," she replied.

"Olstan," she said, "do you think you can still work?" Olstan nodded and she continued. "If you will get a shovel and a mop, we can get this floor cleaned in a matter of minutes." Olstan nodded again and fetched the tools. Then the two of them scooped the offal back into the tub and mopped the floor clean. She took one handle of the tub as Olstan took the other, and together they carried it out and dumped it into the hog trough.

The moment they were out the door, the workers turned to each other and the room began to hum with chatter about the spectacle they had just witnessed. Immediately the voice of Hilbront cut through the noise, "Why are you slackers standing around doing nothing? The show is over. Back to work, all of you!"

When Volanna returned, she walked straight toward Hilbront, her eyes still flashing fire and her hands balled into fists. He stood as she approached but did not bow, uncertain whether it was Volanna the princess or Volanna the servant who approached him. But when she spoke, all doubt vanished. "These workers are servants of this castle just as you are. They are not your dogs, to be kicked about and treated any way you wish. Today is not the last you will see of me. I will work in this kitchen at will, and I tell you this, Hilbront: if ever I see you treating one of these servants as you treated Olstan today, I will use what influence I have with Lord Aldemar to have you discharged." She flung her apron to the table before him and walked out the door.

Volanna worked often in Morningstone's kitchen. Her solicitude to Olstan and the dressing down of Hilbront destroyed a wall between her and the kitchen workers but erected in its place a pedestal. They had regarded her with suspicion; now she was their idol. From that day on, it was clear that they adored her with a fierce loyalty, but she was as isolated by their worship as she had been by their timidity. She was unable to form any real friendships among them. In their awe for her, they could not accept themselves as her equals. Still, the kitchen diversion lifted her spirits and did much to make life in Meridan bearable.

On days when she did not work in the kitchen, she read from her books or explored the castle with Kalley. Once she had Kalley request a carriage and they drove into the streets of Corenham. But she found that such excursions required complex preparations—the rigging of the horses and carriage, a guard of four mounted men, and the attendance of a coachman and doorman dressed in their finest suits. Volanna did not attempt such a trip again.

There were state dinners hosted by Sir Brevemont and his lady, with Lord Aldemar presiding as regent. Volanna did her duty and attended all such events on the arm of Prince Lomar. At such functions she met most of the lords, knights, and ladies of Meridan's court, and she sensed that many of these men and women were quite different from the few that Lomar had selected to surround himself. She watched some of the ladies across the great hall as they laughed and chatted with their friends. She hoped some of them would approach her for conversation, but it seldom happened. Those who did not know Volanna assumed she was like the others in Lomar's clique, and they wanted no part of it. When Volanna took matters into her own hands and approached one of these ladies, Larensa, Wilda, or Gwynnedd always followed and hovered nearby, ready to interrupt and steal Volanna away before the conversation took flight. Lomar was determined to keep her isolated from outside influences.

Lady Aldemar seldom attended court events at Morningstone, but she often invited Volanna to her estate for dinner. Volanna learned to love Lady Aldemar as she would a grandmother, but she longed for a friendship among her peers.

While Volanna found ways to make her days more bearable, she found no defense against the nights. After work in the kitchen or attending a banquet or one of Lomar's dinners, and after Kalley left her chambers and Volanna undressed and slipped under the covers, a black curtain of loneliness would descend and wrap about her, isolating her from the world of love and happiness. She felt as if she was sinking alone into an abyss, an underworld where she was aware of nothing but herself, engulfed in darkness devoid of the sound of another voice, the touch of another hand, the sight of another face. She thought of her mother and father, two kingdoms away and snug in their own bed, wrapped in each other's arms. She thought of her two sisters, each enfolded by the love of good husbands and happy children. Tears welled in Volanna's eyes, and she wept. She was home-sick—bitterly, wretchedly, inconsolably homesick. And it was a sickness for which she could see no cure.

She tried to sleep, but her mind persisted in turning her misery over and over like a miner examining a lump of ore. At home in Valomar when she was wrestling with some dilemma, she would ride into Blackmore Forest and spend a day among the streams and trees, which seemed to still her mind and release it from the self-defeating pressure to search for solutions. Why couldn't she do the same here? She had heard evil tales about Braegan Wood and knew that few people ventured deeply into it. But as she put little stock in such rumors and had no tendency toward superstition, she thought an excursion alone into the forest would do her good. Her troubled mind accepted this plan of action and released its grip on her misery. She fell asleep and did not wake until morning.

CHAPTER NINETEEN

A Meeting in Eden

Before the first rays of sunlight touched her window, Volanna awoke, her heart filled with anticipation. She rang for Kalley.

Over breakfast she told her friend of her plans for an excursion into Braegan Wood. Kalley was apprehensive; she, too, had heard the tales of evil about the great forest. But in the end Volanna prevailed, and Kalley helped her by getting a lunch packed and ordering the stable keeper to saddle a good mare. Volanna dressed in the plain skirt and bodice of a servant, and after swearing Kalley to secrecy, mounted her horse and rode out toward Braegan Wood just as the morning sun broke over the tops of the trees.

The deeper into the forest Volanna rode, the less reason she saw to fear it. Indeed, she thought it the most beautiful place she had ever seen, and her weighted spirit began to soar at the sight of the great trees regally dressed in rich, green foliage, the sunlit grasses waving in the breeze, and the seas of wildflowers delighting her nostrils with their sweet scent. This place was more verdant and rich with color and texture and aroma than her wildest vision of Eden. She wandered deeper yet, until the path narrowed where the trees grew taller and the underbrush thicker. Her horse now had to pick its way through the flourishing undergrowth and around the occasional great stones that stood like holy monuments among the trees.

Suddenly an animal jumped up ahead and bounded away through

the brush. It was only a deer, but the horse jerked violently in panic and began galloping headlong through the forest. Volanna tried to rein the mare to a halt, but she could not. She bent forward and clutched the flying mane to keep from falling off. Low branches swept by her like the arms of a quintain, and she hugged the horse's neck to avoid them. The horse came fast upon a stream and stopped short, tumbling Volanna over its neck and into the water. The splash startled the mare yet again, and she galloped away into the forest, leaving Volanna sitting shoulder-deep in the stream.

Volanna was unhurt. She stood and waded out of the water, her clothing soaked and dripping. She looked around her and saw that she was near the point where the stream flowed out of a clear, placid pond fed by a majestic waterfall. For a moment she wondered if she would be able to find her way out of the woods but decided she was in no hurry to try. She was drawn by a strong yearning to linger in this beautiful place.

It was a warm, summer day, but in the coolness of the forest, she was beginning to chill in her wet clothes. She took all of them off and spread them on a bush to dry, then yielded to the invitation of the clear pool and plunged into it for a delectable swim. Half an hour later she stepped from the water greatly refreshed, and a gentle breeze set her skin to tingling with delight. She found a sunlit place on the grass just to the other side of a great oak, where she lay down to dry.

She intended to stay awake. Every one of her senses was tuned to a heightened awareness she had not known before. The forest had them dancing in ecstasy with every color, every sound, every aroma, every caress of the breeze. She did not want sleep to rob her of a moment of it. But lulled by the music of the birds and the steady rush of the waterfall, she let an unbidden drowsiness overtake her and fell asleep like a Venus in an Olympian forest.

The sound of a splash brought her instantly awake. She sat up and peered around the tree to see the cause of it. A man was swimming in the pond. She must get out of this place before he saw her. But her eyes lingered a moment longer for he was a magnificent-looking man, young and strong, with a face and physique like her vision of Adonis.

She kept low so he would not see her above the tops of the bushes, gathered her clothing, and dressed quickly. She began to ease away from the pond, taking care to keep the huge oak between herself and the swimmer. Suddenly she stopped short. Moving slowly across the path in front of her was a fat, mottled brown-and-black snake. She screamed and ran instinctively back to the pond.

The swimming man heard the scream and came toward the sound as fast as he could stroke. He reached the shallows and waded splashing toward the great oak until he looked up and saw the young woman standing in front of it. He stopped, embarrassed, and tried to cover himself with his hands, then hurriedly plunged back into the water to hide his nakedness. Volanna now recognized the swimmer as the man who had saved Lomar's stallion at the welcoming procession.

"Is anything amiss?" he called. "I heard a scream."

"Nothing is wrong," Volanna replied. "A snake frightened me. You go ahead and swim. I will wait behind this tree."

"Wait for what?" he asked.

"For you to finish swimming," Volanna replied. The snake had made her apprehensive about trying to find her way out of the woods alone. Now that she had identified the young man, she no longer feared him and hoped he would escort her back to Corenham.

"I've had enough swimming for today. Wait behind the tree, and I'll get out."

She started to walk around the tree but found herself reluctant to return to the vicinity where the snake might be lurking. "Uh, I think I'll wait here. I'll just sit on this stone, turn my back, and close my eyes."

Aradon swam to the bank where he had left his clothes and got out of the pool. He dressed and came to the stone where Volanna sat. "You may open your eyes now."

Volanna opened them and gazed up at the man standing above her. Sunlight glistened on his golden hair and the light of the pool flashed in his guileless blue eyes. His forehead was broad and intelligent and his jaw strong and firm, as if sculpted by the hand of a master artist. He was quite tall, and his well-proportioned body was lean and hard. His powerful shoulders looked as if they could bear the burden of Atlas. Volanna forgot herself and stared entranced. Was this the god of the forest? Another image of ecstasy to delight her dancing senses? Or had she somehow been transported back to Eden to meet the primeval Adam in his natural home?

Suddenly she realized she was staring and he had said something to her. "I, uh, oh, yes, of course. You'll have to forgive me. I shouldn't have screamed, but I have an irrational fear of snakes."

He smiled, and all her troubles evaporated like mist at sunrise. "I understand irrational fears," he said. "With me it is spiders. I suppose everyone has some kind of monster he can't face."

Volanna thought it could not be true. This man who had challenged Sir Stundal and wrecked half the castle guard could not be afraid of anything. He was merely trying to ease her embarrassment about her fear. And he was succeeding very well.

"May I sit down?" he asked.

"Oh, of course," she replied, and he sat on a stone opposite hers.

"I am Aradon, son of Bogarth the blacksmith. I am an apprentice to my father, though I'm presently working on a long-term project in Vensaur."

She was happy to find that apparently Aradon did not know who she was. So much the better. "I am Dovey. I work in the kitchen at Morningstone Castle."

Aradon was enthralled by the vision before him—the dark, cascading hair with auburn highlights sparkling in the sun, the deep blue eyes rimmed with dark, curling lashes, the exquisite outline of her oval face, the fullness of her delicate lips, the smooth, white pillar of her neck, the perfect, womanly form, and the entrancing grace of every movement—she was like no woman he had ever seen. He had to force himself not to stare at her in rapt wonder and succeeded only partially.

"You must think me a silly coward, afraid of my own shadow," said Volanna.

"If you were a coward, you would not have come into this forest. You are one of the few people in Meridan I've ever known to set foot in it. May I ask what brings you here?"

"I needed some time to think, and I needed to get away from everyone to do it. I just stumbled into this place, so to speak. And what brings you here?"

"I spend most of a day here almost every week. Today I'm on my way from Vensaur to my parents' home in Corenham. I couldn't resist stopping for a short swim."

Volanna stood up. "Could I beg of you a favor? Would you be so kind as to escort me back to Corenham? I'm not sure I could find my way alone."

"Gladly," replied Aradon. "But must we leave now? I've not yet eaten my lunch. Perhaps you would share it with me. I assure you, there is more than enough."

Volanna was hungry. Her own lunch was on the runaway horse, which she did not mention to Aradon. "I will be most pleased to dine with you, m'lord," she said with a playful curtsy.

Her smile left Aradon weak in the knees, but he recovered quickly and took momentary leave of her to fetch the lunch from his horse, hidden beyond the bushes a quarter of the way around the pond. He ran the entire distance as if he feared she were some kind of heavenly apparition that might vanish if left unattended. He returned with the bulging wallet Derena had packed, along with a blanket, which the two of them spread on the grass. Then with a parody of a courtly bow, Aradon invited her to sit with him on the blanket, where he spread the contents of the wallet between them.

They ate and they talked. Aradon, who was usually so tongue-tied with girls that his father told him that there must be a dam somewhere between his brain and his tongue, found the sluice gate lifted, and words flowed in torrents. Volanna found it so easy to speak with him that she had to watch her words carefully to keep from saying things that would reveal her identity. As they ate their meal, several small animals—a pair of squirrels, a hare, a dozen or more different birds, and even a yearling deer—came up to the edge of their blanket without fear, obviously expecting to be fed.

"A moment ago you called me a lord," said Aradon. "Well, here is my court. My lady, meet Hermes and Penelope." As he spoke, he tossed a handful of hickory nuts to the squirrels. "And he of the twitching nose and longish ears is Sir Hopper." He called the names of the birds as he flipped tiny pieces of breadcrumbs to each of them.

Then he glanced all about him as if looking for something. "Someone is missing," he explained as he held a couple of crumbs in the open palm of his upraised hand. He whistled lightly and called, "Thimble and Needle, where are you?" The next moment a pair of gray wrens no larger than his thumb flew down from somewhere in the tree above. They alighted on his palm and began to peck at the crumbs. Aradon lowered his hand to where Volanna could see the birds and smiled at her across his palm.

She was enchanted—by the smile as well as the birds. "How did you ever get them to trust you?"

"I did nothing. They seemed unafraid of me from the day I first came here."

"Do you think they would eat from my hand?"

"Let's try it. Put a few crumbs in your palm and slowly bring it next to mine." She did as he suggested, and when the little birds finished the crumbs in Aradon's hand, they hopped over into Volanna's and continued eating unfazed. She smiled with delight, and Aradon was intensely aware of the brief touch of her hand to his.

When the wrens had consumed the last crumb, they flew from her hand and perched on a low branch above them. "I'm impressed with your courtiers, m'lord. They are much more amiable than those of Morningstone's court."

"It sounds as though you've had some unpleasant contact with some of them."

"Occasionally," she replied. "They're not the sort of folk I'd choose as friends. I much prefer to be in the kitchen." She thought she had almost said too much. She must be more careful.

"I've had a bit of unpleasant contact with them myself."

Volanna had to bite her tongue to keep from saying, *I know, and you were magnificent.* "Is that why you are working in Vensaur?" she asked.

"No. I've been sent there by someone who thinks I should take up another trade instead of blacksmithing. Lately I've been sort of getting the feel of the land." Aradon had vowed secrecy about his training in Vensaur and could not let her probe into this area of his life, so he turned the question back to her. "Have you ever considered taking up an altogether different trade?"

"Oh, yes, I've thought of it," she replied. "But my parents, their parents before them, and their parents before them have always worked in castles. I suppose I'm doomed to follow their path."

"May I be so bold as to ask what drove you into the forest to think?"

She looked away, and her face clouded. She paused long before replying, "I'm sorry, I really cannot tell you of it now." Suddenly she stood and pointed toward the fading light in the west. "Oh, dear! Just look at the sun! By the time we get to Corenham, it will be almost dark. Where has the time gone? Don't you think we should leave at once?"

Aradon hated for the day to end, but he distributed the remainder of the food to the animals and led the enchanting maiden to his stallion. He mounted, then took her hand and pulled her up behind him. Again, he was intensely aware of the touch of her hands as she reached about his waist and held him while they rode away.

It was dusk when they came into the edge of Corenham. The western sky still glowed above the mountains, though the sun was no longer visible. Lamps shone orange in the windows of cottages, giving them the look of living souls. Most of the shops were closed, and people in the streets were returning to their homes, their bright lanterns waving and bobbing in the near darkness.

One of these lanterns was borne by Ansel, returning home with Marcie at the end of the day. Aradon was so enamored with the girl at his back that he did not even notice the two cakesellers as his horse walked past them. But Ansel recognized Aradon by his voice and looked up to see the woman riding behind him. She was as stunned as if a hammer had hit her on the head. She left Marcie with their cart and told her to take it on home, she would be there shortly.

Ansel followed Aradon through the streets, hoping to identify the girl who shared his horse. The near darkness and the peasant's clothing Volanna wore prevented Ansel from recognizing her. Nor would it have occurred to her to guess that she was the princess. It would have been absurd to think she and the blacksmith could have been together. But even by the dim light of the passing lanterns, she could see that the girl was extraordinarily beautiful and a threat to her hopes for Aradon and Marcie. But who was she? She followed and watched as Aradon came to Cheaping Square and halted. She drew near enough to listen to their exchange of words.

"Yes, Aradon, we must part now. I can walk home from here."

"But there is no need. I can take you safely to the postern gate of the castle. It is dark, and you have no light."

"But there is light enough for walking. Besides, there are so many pedestrians with lanterns that the streets look like a plague of fireflies. I'll be in no danger at all."

In the end Volanna prevailed, and Aradon reluctantly helped her from his horse.

"May I see you again?" he asked as she turned to go.

Volanna hesitated, then turned back to him. "How often do you go to the pond?"

"Every seventh day."

"I can promise nothing. But perhaps a time will come when we will meet there again."

Aradon watched her as she walked into the street and mingled with the crowd, then he turned toward his own home and rode slowly, his mind soaring as if on a cloud with the fair image of Dovey.

Immediately Ansel began to trail the girl, hoping to find some clue to her identity. She followed her all the way to the postern gate of Morningstone Castle, and in the light of the lantern set on a nearby post, got a fair view of her face as she turned and looked around before she opened the door. Ansel's jaw dropped in surprise. The face bore a strong resemblance to the new princess. But surely it could not be. It made no sense to think the future queen of the Seven Kingdoms would indulge in trysts with a blacksmith. Yet she knew that Prince Lomar had many liaisons with young chargirls, milkmaids, and barmaids all over Corenham. He had even taken her own daughter into Morningstone for a night once or twice. Wasn't it likely that the princess was of the same stripe? Why shouldn't the hen claim the same privileges as the rooster? Ansel's doubts began to diminish.

&v

That evening as Kalley brought dinner to the chambers of the princess, she was full of questions about Volanna's day in Braegan Wood. Volanna told her everything—of the unearthly beauty of the forest, of the runaway horse, and of Aradon, whom she identified as the man who saved Lomar's lame horse in the procession.

"I wish you could have met him, Kalley. He is only a blacksmith, but he's as mannerly and courteous as any nobleman in my father's court. And he had humor and wit, but his wit is nothing like that of Lomar's circle. Never once did I hear him malign people for their clothing, their manners, their taste, or even for their mistreatment of him. And when he looked at me, I could tell that he thought me beautiful, yet it seemed that he saw more than just my beauty; he really seemed to see *me*."

As Kalley listened, she became alarmed. "Volanna, you must not allow yourself to be drawn toward this man," she warned. "You could be hurt beyond recovery."

"Oh, it's nothing like that," Volanna assured her. "I have merely made a new friendship, the first since I came to Meridan with a person my own age who seems to think and talk like my friends in Valomar."

"Yes, and a friend who just happens to look like a sculpted god and who looked at you as if he thought you a goddess from heaven."

A warm look came into Volanna's eyes, and her entire face seemed to glow. "Yes, he did look at me that way," she said, "and I did not mind it at all. In fact, I enjoyed it."

"Volanna! That is not like you at all. You've never shown any conceit about your beauty, though how you have avoided it I'll never know. Now you are saying you liked it when this poor man drooled over you."

"No, you misunderstand. He didn't drool over me. I don't like it when men look at me as Lomar does, as if I were a prize morsel in a meatseller's stall. I know that some women want men to look at them that way, but it makes me feel dirty, as if their looks carry some kind of contamination that clings to whatever part of me they stare at. Yet

for a woman to feel delight when her beauty is properly enjoyed simply as beauty seems appropriate. And Aradon's enjoyment of my
beauty seemed as proper as his enjoyment of the waterfall. He could
enjoy the fall for what it gave him in its white purity, its graceful
descent, its merry roar, without thinking he had to plunge into it and
try to drink it all."

"And I suppose you were gazing at him the same way?"

"No, not really in the same way," said Volanna. "Have you
noticed that what women find attractive in men tends to center on
their strength? The hard contours, the broad shoulders, the firmness
of the jaw. Men are the vessels of strength as women are the vessels of
beauty. Indeed, Father was right when he said that both sexes admire
strength in men and beauty in women because it is the ideal of creation. When Aradon gazed at my beauty, I found myself enjoying my
beauty in much the same way he did; I enjoyed it through him. You
might say I enjoyed his enjoyment of it. I delighted in the fact that
the Maker had created me to be a vessel of delight. I think that is the
way women are meant to enjoy their own beauty—through a man's
enjoyment of her, as if it is her gift to him—a gift she passes on from
the maker of all beauty."

Kalley looked blank. "I know you hate to hear it, but you *are*
your father's daughter, you know. Try all you want to shake me from
the trail with your high-blown talk about beauty and strength and
ideals, but I warn you, this man is a dangerous spark whom you must
not let anywhere near the dry kindling that now fills your heart. You
must not go into the forest anymore. He may be there again, and only
trouble can come from this."

"I will almost certainly go into the forest again, and whether I
encounter Aradon matters little. The forest itself is worth the while.
All the darkness of my future is dispelled when I am in it. And if the
blacksmith is there, you needn't worry; I am firmly committed to my
vow, and I keep a barrier erected in my mind that will prevent the
intrusion of love."

"You underestimate the force of love's battering ram," was
Kalley's final word on the subject.

Before Kalley left for her own quarters, Volanna extracted a

promise that she would tell no one of this or future meetings with
Aradon. For if the tryst were known, he could be in great danger.
Volanna disrobed and slipped into bed, and in spite of her resolve, she
fell asleep with visions of Aradon's golden hair and godlike form filling her mind.

☙

The next day Ansel went immediately to the Eagle's Crown alehouse,
where she knew she could find Sir Stundal five mornings out of seven.
She entered the darkened room, and when her eyes adjusted, she saw
him sitting at a table, a tankard in his hand and two empty ones on
the board. He was laughing and bantering with two of the barmaids.
It was not a busy morning at the tavern.

Ansel hastened over to him. "Sir Stundal, could we talk private-
like?"

Stundal turned and glared at her, already a little bleary-eyed even
though it was an hour till noon. "What do you want, cakeseller. I've
told you already, I'm not paying for your carelessness."

"No, no, it's nothin' about that. The cart is all fixed and rollin'
again, and I'm willin' to let bygones go by. Could we get alone just
for a moment like?"

"Why should I want to get alone with you? Though if you
bring your daughter, that might be another story." The two barmaids tittered.

"You might go achangin' your mind if you knew what I know.
But no matter. Someone else will pay me dear for what I've got to
say." With that Ansel turned and began to walk toward the door.

"Wait a minute. Come on back," growled Stundal. He shooed
the women away and kicked out a chair for Ansel to sit on.

"Thank you very much, your lordship," she said as she sat opposite him. "As I said, I know somethin' that the prince hisself would
pay me dear to tell him. But I'm thinkin' it might help me and you
both if you paid me and delivered the message yourself. That way I
get the shillings and you get to look like you're out here doin' a fine
job lookin' after the prince's well-bein'."

"I don't know what you're trying to pull, cakeseller, but I suggest that if you have something to say, you'd best say it or you just might find your flimsy cart smashed beyond repair next time."

"No, sir, if you're not payin', I'm not talkin'. I'll find me a knight with a bit more foresight—or a bit more money." Ansel got up and turned to leave, but Sir Stundal grabbed her roughly by the arm and flung her back into the chair.

"Listen, woman, I don't pay for what I can't see. You talk, and if I think what you say is worth it, I'll pay you five crowns. If it is worth nothing, consider yourself lucky that I let you out of this hole alive. Do we have an agreement?"

"Oh, very well," sighed Ansel. "The end of the story is simply this: I think the prince's betrothed has been meetin' Aradon the blacksmith somewhere out in Braegan Wood." Stundal glared at her with mounting incredulity as she recounted seeing Aradon come into the city at dusk with a beautiful woman riding behind him on his horse. She told of their parting at Cheaping Square, of following the girl to the servant's gate of Morningstone, and of the glimpse of her face by the light of the lantern, which convinced her that the girl was the new princess.

When Ansel finished her story, Stundal glared at her a moment longer then began to laugh. "Ansel, I'm tempted to pay you not five, but ten crowns for such a story. I couldn't have made up a better one myself. Where did you get such a preposterous notion? Why would you ever imagine that the future queen of the Seven Kingdoms would stoop to having a tryst with a mere blacksmith?"

"Why is that so strange-like? The future king of the Seven Kingdoms has them all the time with girls all over the kingdom."

"Including a few with your own daughter, as we all know. Come now, cakeseller, everyone knows that bees choose what blossoms they want from all the flowers, but blossoms never choose the bees that come to them. No crowns for you, woman. Get out of here and let me get back to my business."

Ansel left without payment but not without determination to find some other way to thwart Aradon's unlikely alliance with the princess.

CHAPTER TWENTY

ThE PARTING

W hen Aradon returned to Vensaur, he was alert and focused as long as he was on the training field. In fact, Sir Hardwicke thought he detected a new vigor and energy in the way the young man performed his exercises. But the moment Aradon's mind relaxed, the image of Dovey arose unbidden and filled his thoughts like a scented breeze from Eden. During the next fortnight he visited the pond three times, always with the hope that she would be there.

He was twice disappointed, but on his second visit he sat on the stone where he had first seen Dovey and absently trailed his fingers across the surface of the rock as he gazed dreaming into the pond. His fingers slipped into a small cavity in the stone and felt a piece of rough bark. Absorbed in his reverie, he pulled it from the hole and idly turned it over in his hands before he realized something was scratched on the inside surface. He looked closely and made out the words, *Next week, Dovey.* She had been here. She was coming back. His heart lifted like a bird on the wind.

True to her promise, on his next visit she was there. She sat on the same stone and wore the same plain skirt and bodice as before. As he parted the high bushes and entered the clearing, she looked up and saw him. She smiled broadly and her cheeks flushed as she arose from the stone and took a step toward him before she checked herself and sat down again. But in that moment Aradon knew that she was as delighted to see him as he was to see her. And he was nothing less than ecstatic.

This time each of them had brought lunches, which they spread on Aradon's blanket and shared. Again they fell into easy conversation, and the only impediment to its flow was the caution Volanna had to observe to keep from revealing her true identity. She deflected all specific questions about her past and gave him only vague generalities about her present. She wanted the relationship to remain unaffected by the barrier that her royalty would erect.

Again they forgot the time and had no thought of parting until the sun touched the tops of the trees. Volanna had come on a horse—one she had borrowed, she told Aradon truthfully enough—and she could make it back to Corenham well before nightfall. But before Aradon would let her go, he extracted a promise that she would meet him here again the following week.

"If I am not prevented," she said as she rode away.

She did return to the pond the following week, and the week after, and for several weeks after that. As a result Aradon and Dovey became very good friends. At least, this was how Volanna described the relationship to Kalley. Indeed, Volanna was surprised at how much she and Aradon had in common. In spite of the great difference in their social stations—unknown to Aradon, of course—they discovered that their parents shared an identical code of honor and a deep commitment to aligning their lives with the Master of the Universe. She told Kalley that she was happy to find at last a citizen of Meridan with whom she could enjoy a simple friendship without fear or distrust.

But for Aradon, the relationship quickly grew past mere friendship. He was overwhelmed by the intensity of the joy he felt in her presence. These were his first deep feelings for a girl, and some of them took him by surprise—the pounding heart, the thrill of touch when their hands accidentally brushed, the delight of holding her waist as he helped her cross a stream, the difficulty in keeping his eyes off her, the desire to hold and protect. Lying at night on his cot, he thought much on these feelings and others as well.

He thought of Marcie and the very different kind of feelings she had stirred in him. He remembered her white-hot embrace when she fell from the crate and the momentary flush of desire at the display of her bosom at his window. He wondered why Dovey did not produce the same stirrings. As he mused on it, the answer came to him. Marcie presented herself in a way intended only to arouse lust and offered nothing more of herself than a means of slaking it. Beyond that she was a featureless wilderness.

Dovey, on the other hand, presented herself not merely as female but as *feminine,* which went far deeper than mere bodily appeal and captivated Aradon's entire being. Everything about her was delightful. Even common things such as honor, courtesy, humor, friendship, conviviality, when drawn from the deep well of her femininity, were transformed into glorious wonders that charmed Aradon to no end. Desire for her was there, no doubt, but so diffused within these other enchantments that he could not isolate it from them. Dovey was a many-branched tree that Aradon would delight in climbing before he even thought of plucking the mysterious bloom hidden deep within her leaves. He sensed the bloom would wither and die in his hands if he tried to pluck it too soon and isolate it from the nourishing branches in which it was hidden.

Aradon had found in Dovey exactly what he wanted, and in finding her, his future took firm shape in his mind. Visions of knighthood faded and gave way to the simple charm of domesticity. He would complete his training in order to fulfill his duty to Lord Aldemar. He would do whatever deed he was destined to do to play his part in the prophecy. Then he would bring Dovey back to the acres at the edge of the meadow and begin his family.

The very shape and dimensions of his cottage began to form in his mind. As he rested between bouts on the training field, he sketched the outlines of it in the dirt with a twig, often erasing a line and retracing it until it matched the image in his head. He would first build a single room with a stone hearth and space for a table, bed, and cupboards. He would locate the cottage strategically within the trees so that he could expand it with additional rooms as needed. When he had the plan firm in his mind, he split a quill, borrowed ink and a small parchment from Derena, and sketched the house in fair detail. When he was satisfied with his artistry, he folded the parchment and put it inside the pouch in which he carried the gold locket his mother had given him when he left for Vensaur.

When Aradon arrived at the pond on the next seventh day, Volanna was sitting on her stone waiting for him. As she gazed at him approaching, she realized how much she always looked forward to seeing him and how taken she was by his tall, manly shape, finely chiseled face, and golden hair. She began to realize that Kalley's fears might have been justified. But while she fully acknowledged affection for Aradon, she was convinced that she was not in love with him. She would not allow such a thing to happen for she remained firmly committed to her vow.

They spread their lunches on the blanket and began to eat and talk as usual. Or almost as usual. Volanna noticed that Aradon seemed uneasy and distracted. Even a little tongue-tied, she thought. He was as amiable and courteous as always, and he responded well enough to her conversation and questions, but he was unable to initiate much conversation of his own, though he seemed to be trying.

"Have you injured your tongue, or am I beginning to bore you?" she asked.

"You could read Coradane's entire treatise on curing hog diseases and I would not be bored by a single word."

Volanna reddened slightly at the declaration. "Then why are you so mum? Surely you have not exhausted your store of knowledge."

"I did that in the first two minutes we met, but it never stopped me from talking." He drew a deep breath and continued, "I have been thinking of late, and I, uh, I . . . that is . . . well, I have been thinking about what I'm going to do with the rest of my life, and I, uh, well, do you intend to have a family?"

"Not until I am wed."

"Of course, I didn't mean . . . that is, uh, I do too . . . hope to have a family, that is, uh, when I am wed. When my father grows too old to work the shop, I will take it over. But even before that I plan to build a cottage on the three acres behind the shop and, uh, get married. Lately I have been thinking about just how that cottage would look, and I have made a sketch of it. Would you like to see it? Maybe you could suggest some improvements."

Volanna suddenly became alert and wary. It did not take much intuition to sense the direction Aradon's conversation was taking. She must try to divert him. "Oh, I doubt that I could help you. I don't know much about such things."

But Aradon had already retrieved the sketch from his pouch and had it unfolded on the blanket before her. "Here is how it will look at first," he said, pointing to the drawing as he spoke. "It will have only one room, but one large enough for a table, a bed, and a cupboard. Notice how I have placed it among the trees. There is space here between these trees for another room, and here for yet another, and even another could come out to here. And, if there were more, uh, children yet, I could add another room or two in this area facing the meadow."

"Do you expect to have a family or an army?"

Aradon blushed. "Well, uh, that won't depend entirely on me, will it? What about you, Dovey? Do you ever think about marriage?"

"Yes, I think about it. But now is not the time for me."

"Nor for me, just yet." Aradon sensed that she was pulling back and he reined in his intentions to lessen any sense of pressure she might feel. "I have promised to perform a certain civic duty first, but when that is done, I want to get on with the life I have chosen."

Volanna looked troubled and could not meet his open gaze.

"Have I said something wrong?" he asked.

"Aradon, more than once since we met I hinted to you that there is something deep and troubling in my life that I can hardly bear. I regret to say that this trouble has not left me, and I fear that it never will. Please, let's not speak of the future just now. Such talk only serves to bring the weight of my burden down on my heart."

"I have told you before that I wish you would tell me of this burden so I could help you bear it."

"Someday I will. Indeed, someday I must. But today I cannot."

Aradon saw the sadness in her face and longed to hold her and melt it away. What could there be in her life to cause such pain? Surely he could help her if she would only open her heart to him. Suddenly the thought of Father Verit came to his mind. He remembered Verit's parting words, *Be assured that you will always find me when you need me.* He needed Verit now, and he could be found only minutes away. "Dovey," he said, placing his hand on hers, "I know someone who can help you. Someone who helped me once and promised help anytime I needed it."

"No one can help me, Aradon."

"Don't be too sure. This man is like no one you have ever seen before. You may find what I'm about to tell you hard to believe, but please hear me out. At first you would think this man to be very old, and indeed I believe he is perhaps centuries old. But as you look on him, you see that in another way he is not old at all. His eyes are bright, his face is young, and his body is healthy and strong. Yet his hair is pure white, and his eyes have a look of wisdom that could only come from an enormous accumulation of years. He is kind as well as wise, and he lives in this forest, not far from here. We can walk there in a quarter-hour."

She listened with increasing interest. She was sure that Aradon had just described the magician, Father Lucidis. "What is this man's name?" she asked.

"He called himself Father Verit. Come, let's go see him." Aradon stood and extended his hand to her. Volanna did not know what to make of the different name, but she was sure that Aradon had encountered Lucidis or another just like him. After a moment's hesitation, she took his hand and Aradon led her into the forest. They picked up walking sticks along the way to help them through the luxuriant underbrush and up the rise toward the place where Aradon was sure Dovey would find relief from her burden.

As they neared the cathedral-like clearing, Aradon slowed their approach, expecting the feeling of numinous awe to descend on them as he had felt it on his first visit. But there was no such feeling. The features of the clearing looked the same, yet they did not. They were not tinged with the same sense of holiness as before. Aradon thought the lack was likely in him rather than in the place. This was his second visit, and perhaps he had become inured. The freshness of the first experience could not be recaptured for him, but perhaps Dovey felt it. He looked at her as she gazed about the opening. If she felt anything extraordinary, she gave no sign of it.

"Is this the place?" she asked.

"Yes," he answered in a muted voice, trying to respond appropriately to the sense of awe he remembered. "In fact, you can see him now." Aradon pointed to the great tree at the far end of the clearing. "There he is; sitting just to the left of the huge tree."

"Where? I see nothing but moss and a cluster of cottonwood seed clinging to a tangle of roots."

"Those things are not what they appear to be. Come closer and you will see."

As they approached the tree, Aradon watched to see just when he would discern the face and form of Father Verit within the roots and moss. But it did not happen. They arrived at the tree only to find that the roots and moss and seeds were only roots and moss and seeds, nothing more. Aradon looked all around the tree and into the forest beyond for some sign of Father Verit, but after several minutes he realized his search was futile. The man was not to be found. He came back to the place where Dovey stood watching, deep in thought. "You must think me the biggest liar or the biggest fool in Meridan," he said. "I suppose there is no way you can believe that I was telling you the truth."

"I know you were telling the truth, Aradon. I suppose it was not meant that we should find him at this time. Maybe on another day."

Aradon was grateful for her declaration of trust, but he wondered if she wasn't merely trying to soften his humiliation. *Why isn't Verit here? He promised to help whenever he was needed. And Dovey needs his wisdom desperately.*

With dampened spirits they began to make their way back toward the pond. For most of the walk, both were silent, Aradon with consternation and humiliation and Volanna with sorrow and guilt.

She knew that Aradon had fallen in love with her, and he would be utterly crushed when she told him she was promised to another. *Why had she not foreseen this? It was because of her own selfish need,* she thought. In her desperation for companionship, she had treated Aradon as if he were nothing more to her than the stick in her hand, to be leaned on when needed, then discarded. She had shielded herself against love with her vow, but Aradon had no such defense and no inkling that one was needed. Stabs of pain pierced her heart as she grieved over what she had done to him.

She must hide the truth no longer. When they returned to the pond, she would tell Aradon everything so that he could tear her from his heart and begin to look elsewhere for one to help him fill his cottage. He would be terribly wounded, but better now than later. She should have told him the first day they met. She would tell him the truth, then she would get out of his life and they would never meet again. She knew it was the way things must be, but she was not sure her heart could endure it.

As they reached the pond and sat upon the blanket, she searched for the gentlest words to bear the awful truth to him, as if somewhere in her vocabulary she could find syllables that would pierce him less than others. But before she could muster the courage to speak, Aradon took her hand in both of his and said, "Dovey, perhaps I cannot drive away this pain you bear, but I want to do all in my power to help you live with it. I want you to become my wife. Perhaps in time you could—"

"Oh, Aradon, I cannot! I cannot! I am promised in marriage to a man chosen by my father. I should have told you the day we met. Please forgive me." She withdrew her hand from his and found within her palm a locket with a golden chain. She could not look at him but kept her head down, gazing at the locket as great, hot tears welled from her eyes and fell upon it.

Aradon was stunned. He sat for a long moment staring at her, utterly still, utterly silent, as all joy drained from his heart.

"Who is this man?" he asked.

"It doesn't matter. You would not know him," she replied in a voice weak and trembling.

"Do you love him?"

"I . . . I will learn to love him, I hope. But it doesn't matter; I have vowed to my father that I will marry him." She looked at the locket and caressed the chain for a moment before holding it toward Aradon. "Here, you must take this back. I cannot keep it."

He made no move to take the locket. "No, I want you to have it. I had hoped to give it to you as a pledge of betrothal, but now I give it as a pledge of my—my friendship. If ever you should find yourself in need of any kind, send that locket to me and I will move heaven and earth to come to you. Even after you are wed to another."

Overcome by the strength of his hopeless devotion, she clutched the locket in her hand, too tearful to speak. After a long moment she found enough of her voice to say, "Please forgive me for what I have done to you. It was selfish and cruel of me. I wish I had foreseen that this would happen."

"There is nothing to forgive. You are right, of course. I am deeply hurt, and I know the pain I carry from here will linger long. But I would rather bear it than to have missed the joy of these past few weeks. That will stay with me the rest of my life, and I will always be grateful for it."

"I thank you for that, Aradon," she said as she stood. "We must part now, and we can never meet again."

Aradon's heart grew heavy with grief, which welled up into his throat and choked off all possibility of reply. He watched in silence as his Dovey walked along the bank of the pond and beyond the ring of bushes, then mounted her horse and rode into the forest. He stood staring after her long after she had disappeared. Then he gathered his blanket and began his return to Ironwood.

Had Volanna prodded her mare as she should have, she would easily have come out of Braegan Wood before dusk. But she took no notice of her speed and let the horse move at its own pace. She stared straight ahead, heedless of the forest darkening about her. Once she thought she heard a sound some distance behind her, but when she stopped and turned, she saw nothing to cause alarm and rode on.

Moments later she heard it again, a low, rhythmic rumble that did not cease when she stopped her horse and turned to look. This time she saw the cause of it. A man on horseback was riding hard toward her. Quickly she wheeled her horse about and urged it to a full gallop. She did not know how far she was from the edge of the forest, but she hoped she could make the cottage of Rolstag the huntsman before the rider overtook her.

But when she looked again, she saw that the rider was closing the distance quickly, and in moments he drew up beside her. He reached toward her and she tried to fight him off with her free hand. He caught her wrist, then reached around her waist and pulled her from her horse and set her on his own in front of him. He slowed his mount and let Volanna's horse run on into the woods. She tried to scream, but he clamped his hand so firmly over her mouth that she could not even open it. She tried to look at his face, but the darkness was now too heavy to reveal his features. He briefly removed his hand from her mouth, but as she opened it to scream, he stuffed a rag into it so roughly that she almost gagged. Then he clasped her firmly about the waist and spurred his horse into an easy trot.

"Does this bring back old memories, your highness?" he said. "You and I are about to take a little journey."

Volanna went rigid with fear. It was the voice of Brendal.

CHAPTER TWENTY-ONE

PRISONER OF MALDOR

We seem to have a penchant for nighttime rides together, do we not?" Brendal's icy voice struck terror in Volanna's heart as they rode along a narrow road toward the northeastern parts of Meridan. "You thought me dead, didn't you? Well, I'm far from it, no thanks to you. Your fickleness that night cost other lives, though, including that of my father and some of the finest patriots of Valomar. And I cannot forget that."

The gag in Volanna's mouth was almost unbearable. She feared it would make her choke but she could do nothing about it. Brendal's arm was clamped around her, pinning her own arms firmly to her side. True to his nature, Brendal could not help but boast of his exploits and the high schemes he was a part of.

"You thought our plot to take Valomar from your father was nothing more than a futile plan concocted by a few ambitious bumblers acting on their own. There was more to it than that. Much more. It was part of a larger plan masterminded by an ancient being of supernatural power and wisdom, and there are similar plots developing in the other kingdoms of Perivale's empire. It is all carefully planned and organized. Balkert is working in the far reaches of Meridan, using Prince Lomar's name and Sir Stundal's men to take over village governments one by one. When Lomar comes to the throne of Meridan, the plots working in all the Seven Kingdoms will mature and those kingdoms will be coerced into submission by Meridan's superior power.

"Aren't you curious about where I have been all this time? Oh, you can't talk right now, can you? Is the gag in your mouth comfortable enough?" Brendal laughed and continued.

"When the plot to take Valomar failed—and it would not have failed had my father been more patient and waited for the timetable of the master plan—I escaped through Lochlaund and Rhondilar to Maldor Castle, in the abandoned swamps of northern Meridan. That is where the mastermind of the plot has taken residence. There I reported the failure of the coup in Valomar and began participating in the plot to take Meridan. For now I am acting as Balkert's agent in the villages, but when Meridan and the five other kingdoms are firmly under our control, we will march against Valomar and overthrow King Tallis. As a reward I am promised your old home, Oakendale Castle, and the throne of Valomar. And if you are worried about your immediate safety, you needn't be, for I want you alive to witness your father's humiliation and execution when he is deposed. I will let him live long enough to see me sit on his throne, then I will slay him by my own hand, with you as witness.

"By tomorrow night you will be the guest of the Mistress of Maldor and will meet face to face the genius behind the great events now stirring."

For the rest of that miserable night, Volanna endured the gag in her mouth, Brendal's confining grip, and his running monologue on the plot to take the Seven Kingdoms. She did not know how much of what he said was true, but she knew some of it was for it matched things she had heard Lord Aldemar relate at the dinner table at his manor. They stopped once near dawn, and he took the gag from her mouth on the promise that she would not scream. As far as she could tell, a scream would be useless in this wilderness; she had not seen any sign of life for miles. He fed her from the food in his saddlebag. Then they mounted and rode on.

Shortly after midday, they veered from the road, if such an overgrown trail could be called a road, and entered a swampland of gray, muddy earth, splotched with tangles of gray-green grass and infested with putrid pools of water covered with a pale green scum. Sickly, malformed trees clustered here and there, masses of dead brush and twisted branches clumped about their roots. Volanna wondered if it would be possible to find a solid path through the swamp, but Brendal seemed to know the way and guided his horse without a misstep. Here and there she saw great webs within the dead brush, some of which spanned the length of a horse. The centers of the webs narrowed like funnels, and now and then she would glimpse a hideous gray or brown form huddled within, sometimes with a hairy, segmented leg or two protruding forward. Volanna remembered legends she had heard in childhood of enormous spiders said to infest the swamps of Maldor, guarding some mysterious evil that haunted the ruined castle. If such legends were to be believed, the swamp hid spiders large enough to snare and devour large animals or even men.

Just before dusk she saw the listing mass of the infamous Maldor Castle looming ahead. The abandoned ruin lay atilt in a basin of mud mottled with islands and ridges of damp, spongy earth. The walls were riddled with great fissures and cracks. Some of the towers and walls had crumbled away. She knew from the legends that half the castle was sunken beneath the swamp and filled with mud and water. The castle must have been very large indeed, she thought, for some of the walls and towers that remained jutted above the ground to a height of three or four stories.

Brendal brought Volanna inside the walls of the castle through a door that had once been a second floor window of a wall tower, now crumbled into a shapeless maw. They dismounted, and a silent servant took the horse. Then Brendal ushered her through another door that had formerly been a window and into the keep.

At once the tilting floors and walls disrupted her sense of balance. As they walked through the hallways, she stumbled on a floor that seemed flat but was actually slanting upward in front of her. She found it difficult to walk straight, often bumping into walls or furniture. When she leaned to conform her posture to what her eyes told her was vertical, she had to reach for a wall to keep from falling over. Walking up a spiral staircase behind Brendal took great concentration; she found herself leaning toward the center of the spiral at one moment, then away from it after taking two or three more steps. As they continued, she began to feel dizzy and a little queasy.

The unsettling effect was heightened by Brendal's utter disregard of the slanting surfaces, taking on the tilt of the floors himself as if it were normal. He noticed her discomfort with satisfaction. "If you stay here long enough, you will take on the same tilt as the castle without even being aware of it."

Brendal remembered when the off-plumb floors and walls had ravaged his own sense of balance, especially when he was in the presence of his mistress Morgultha. Whenever she walked or sat, she had taken on the tilt of the floor, while Brendal had to stand true to the earth's gravity, making him seem out of plumb with the listing castle. In some rooms the tilt was so severe that he had not been able to walk at all but had been forced to crawl on the floor to quell his rising nausea. But now he had taken on the same tilt himself, and the skewed orientation of the castle seemed normal to him.

He took Volanna up another winding stairway, coated with dust and occasionally veiled by the funneled webs that stretched like sheets across two or three steps at a time. More webs hung from the walls, floating in the air like wisps of coagulated smoke. When they reached the top of the stairway, they faced a wooden door reinforced by rusted iron bands. Brendal chose a key from his belt, opened the door, and stood aside for Volanna to enter.

"This room will be your home for the next few months. I hope you are pleased with the accommodations."

The room was large but spare. The only furniture was a bed. Once it had been a fine piece of furniture, its great posts intricately carved with dancing dryads and fauns entwined within flourishing vines and leaves, but now it was cracked and broken. A straw mattress was covered with a rough woolen blanket, eaten with several holes. Volanna walked over to the room's single window, pushed open the wooden shutters, and looked out. In the darkness she could barely make out the swampy ground three floors below. Escape seemed out of the question.

Just as Volanna closed the shutters, a very tall woman entered the room. Volanna shuddered when she looked at her. She was pale of face, with cold, almost colorless eyes in which there glimmered no hint of a soul. The fingers of her left hand were long and white, almost skeletal, and her right arm was hidden in the folds of her black robe. Without bothering to identify herself, the woman began speaking in a voice almost as deep as a man's.

"Welcome to Maldor Castle, Princess Volanna. Though you may not think it at the moment, I mean you no harm. Indeed, I am holding you here only temporarily—as a 'courteous prisoner,' if you will—and it's all for your own good. I will hold you until your marriage is imminent, then release you to fulfill your wedding plans. You will be treated well, even though not with the luxury to which you are accustomed. I shall give you a change of clothing, which will be the dress of a servant much like that which you presently wear. Your food will be plain but adequate."

"Why are you holding me?" asked Volanna. But the woman ignored the question and left the room, taking Brendal with her and locking the door behind them. Volanna ran to the door, opened the food window that had been cut into the heavy door, and called into the stairwell, "Why are you holding me? Please tell me! Why are you holding me?" There was no answer but the scuffle of descending footsteps followed by a closing door and the scraping click of a rusted lock.

As they walked away from Volanna's prison tower, Brendal turned to Morgultha. "I still don't think we should have brought the princess here. She will be missed, and no stone will be left unturned until they find her."

"Nonsense," Morgultha replied. "They will look everywhere but here. Everyone thinks Maldor is abandoned except for the wraiths that haunt it. Besides, many minds will harbor the suspicion that Volanna escaped to get away from Lomar, and as many will wish her success. The search may be more halfhearted than you think. But even if there is some risk in holding her, it is less than letting her remain at Morningstone to inflame Lomar's rampaging lust and distract him from his purpose. The fool! Even the prospect of unprecedented power is not enough to subdue his insatiable appetites. I know Lomar. I've watched him all these years, ever since I placed him in the queen's crib. Trust my word, Brendal, if we leave Princess Volanna in Morningstone, he will find a way to work his will on her.

"Balkert—who is supposedly part of our plot—could do more to restrain Lomar, but it is becoming more obvious every day that he wants the prince to fail so he can make his own play for power. We must watch that man; he is a pawn who makes moves like a queen the moment you take your eyes from the board. No, Brendal, the girl had to be removed to ensure that Lomar does not violate her and void the terms of their sacred prophecy. The common people of Meridan love their new princess as much as they detest their crown prince. It would take only a small misstep for him to lose the willingness of the people to allow him to be crowned."

Volanna, exhausted by the forced journey, fell upon the mattress without undressing and slept until morning. As the rising sun began to glow through the decaying shutters, a knock at the door awakened her. Twice she asked who was there, but the only answer was repeated knocking. As she awakened more fully, she wondered why anyone would knock at all. The door was locked from the outside, and the food window—obviously a recent addition—was accessible from inside or out. She went to the door, opened the little window, and looked out. To her great surprise, she found herself looking into a face she recognized instantly.

"Olstan!" she cried.

His finger went quickly to his lips to urge her to silence. He handed her a bowl of stew, a dry crust of bread, and a mug of milk, then bowed low and left. She could hear his footsteps descending the stairway. Volanna wondered what he was doing in Maldor and thought it likely he had been brought to serve here because of his inability to tell others of what he saw. He continued to serve her at each meal for the next two days, and he occasionally managed to slip her a piece of fruit or a small bowl of nuts.

As the time grew near for her breakfast on the third day, Volanna heard the faint sound of a voice in the stairway. She went to the door, opened the food window, and found that she could hear quite clearly the voice of the woman in black. The door at the foot of the stairway had apparently been opened, and the round stairwell conducted the sound like a trumpet. The mistress of the castle was giving instructions to Olstan for a journey into Corenham to carry a message to Balkert.

Volanna had already formed something of a plan, and Olstan's journey would give her the means to implement it. She took Aradon's locket, and with a small knife she had hidden in her skirt, scratched on the back of it, *Maldor*. When Olstan arrived with her meal, she handed the locket to him with instructions to take it to a certain pond in Braegan Wood. She described the stone with the hole in it and told him to place it there. She began to give him instructions to find the pond, but he made it clear with nods and hand signs that he knew the place, much to Volanna's surprise. He placed the locket in the pouch on his belt, bowed deeply, smiled at Volanna, and left.

CHAPTER TWENTY-TWO

THE STOLEN BAIT

When night fell and Princess Volanna had not returned from her weekly excursion into Braegan Wood, Kalley became worried. Very worried. Volanna had said she would return before sundown.

Kalley waited until the moon rose above the eastern horizon, huge and orange like a baleful, unblinking eye, before sending a swift courier to Lord Aldemar with a message that the princess was missing. Aldemar chose not to upset his wife with the ominous news, telling her instead that he was needed at the castle to attend to some overlooked but urgent detail.

When he arrived at Morningstone, Kalley was waiting for him at the door of his office. She looked worried and distraught. Once they were seated inside, Lord Aldemar began to question her. He wanted as much information as she could give, but her frequent hesitations and care in choosing her words told him there was something about the disappearance she was unwilling to reveal.

"Are you sure the princess left the castle alone?"

"Yes, your lordship. I saw her leave myself."

"Do you know where she went?"

"Well, not exactly. Only to some pond in Braegan Wood. Maybe you could search all the ponds in the forest."

"I don't think you realize how huge Braegan Wood is. It covers almost a tenth of Meridan. There must be hundreds of ponds within it, some of which have not seen man for over a hundred years. Most of the people have a superstitious fear of the forest, though apparently the princess does not share it."

"No, my lord. In Valomar she loved Blackmore Forest. She used to spend entire days there."

"Is that the whole of it? Did the Princess Volanna ride out this morning simply to indulge her love of the forest?"

Kalley hesitated. "I, uh, I think there was more to it than that, sir. She felt a strong need to be alone."

"Tell me, Kalley, was the princess unhappy for any reason?"

"Yes, sir. She and Prince Lomar are not getting on well. In fact, they have quarreled—rather severely, I think—and Volanna has not been sleeping well. She often goes into the forest to get alone so she can think about her life and come to terms with the way things are."

"Do you think she is so unhappy that she might have run away?"

"She is unhappy enough, but she would not run away. She is stubbornly committed to the vow she made to her father, and I'm sure that Perivale's army itself could not prevent her from keeping her word."

"Is it possible that someone else may be involved in any way?"

Kalley reddened. "Uh, what do you mean, sir?"

"I mean anything that you can tell me. Does she have any enemies? Any friends who could be helping her escape, maybe even against her will, thinking it to be for her own good?"

Kalley fell silent and dropped her eyes, unable to meet the regent's stern gaze. She would not betray her mistress in the matter of her friendship with Aradon. *Suppose Volanna's despair had led her to run away with him?* she wondered. Was there any way for her to find happiness in her future with Lomar? Surely she would be better off hidden in a humble cottage somewhere with the honest blacksmith. "I cannot answer that question, sir," she finally answered.

"Kalley, I know you love your mistress and you would not withhold any information that could help us find her. It is important that you tell me all you can. Even a tidbit that seems insignificant to you might provide just the clue we need to pick up Volanna's trail."

"I understand, sir. I think I have told you all I can."

After a moment of hesitation in which he considered pressing the girl hard for what she was apparently hiding, Aldemar said, "Very well, Kalley, you may leave. But if you think of anything that you haven't told me, please come to me immediately, day or night. Do you understand?"

"I do, sir." With that, she stood, curtsied to the regent, and left for her room.

After dismissing Kalley, Aldemar summoned Prince Lomar to his office. It took a third summons delivered by two armed palace guards before the prince appeared in Aldemar's doorway, his hair rumpled and his tunic wrong side out, obviously thrown on hastily. Though the hour was not late, the prince had apparently been in bed—and not alone, the regent knew. Hallway talk among palace pages sometimes reached his ears, and he was well aware of Lomar's wenching habits.

Lord Aldemar ignored the scowling face of the prince. Rising from his chair, he bowed to the son of his old friend and spoke with proper formality, as if no unpleasantness had ever passed between them.

"Your highness, if you will be so kind as to take a chair at the table, we have an emergency to address."

"You forget who I am, Aldemar," Lomar spat across the oaken table. "You think I am at your beck and call any time of day or night."

"No, you forget who you are," said Aldemar calmly. "You are the prince of Meridan, not its king."

"But when the stars meet next spring or the Crown is found or whatever prophetic nonsense these superstitious simpletons are waiting for, I will be the king. You seem to forget that I will be your king as well. Do you think I will forget how you have pushed me and made demands on me and humiliated me as if I was your underling?"

"I have merely pushed you to learn your duty and demanded that you do it. The humiliation is of your own making. It is brought on by your resistance to the authority that I must impose to force you to your duty. As a matter of fact, I would not have called you on this occasion, but we are facing a crisis of the utmost urgency, and I need to know what help you can be in resolving it. The Princess Volanna is missing."

Lomar dropped lazily into the chair and swung a leg over the arm. "And that should matter to me?" he said. It did matter to him for she was his path to the throne, but he was in no mood to let Aldemar know it.

"I should think you would have some concern for the safety of your betrothed. According to her maidservant, you and the princess have quarreled recently. I thought you might have some insight into her state of mind, her intentions, her—"

"I know nothing about what happened to our uppity princess, nor do I care," interrupted Lomar. "If she wants my concern, she can show a little more interest in my concerns. As it is, she cares nothing for what pleases me."

"I can only imagine what it must take to please you. Please, forgive my intrusion into your pleasures. You may return to your rooms." Aldemar rose and bowed to the prince.

"Remember this, my dear Lord Aldemar," Lomar's voice was cold with contempt. "You are presently the regent of Meridan, and I am only its crown prince. But the balance of power is all on my side. Your sworn duty is to preserve Meridan for me and present the throne intact when my day arrives. But I have no sworn duty to protect you. Indeed, when my day comes, you will be like a mouse in the paws of a cat. And mark my words, Aldemar, I will remember and repay every humiliation you have imposed on me in the name of your duty." Lomar stood, sauntered to the door, opened it, and paused. "Just remember, in less than a year I will be your king." He punctuated his parting threat by closing the door sharply behind him and stalking down the hallway.

Aldemar shook his head and sighed, then went out into the commons to the stableman's quarters and asked him about the horse Princess Volanna took. The man described the dapple-gray mare and told of how he had saddled the horse and helped the princess to mount, but he knew nothing more. Aldemar questioned other servants as well, working long into the night, desperate for any clue that would help him trace Volanna. But it was to no avail.

At daylight he called for Rolstag the huntsman to assemble a band of men to search Braegan Wood. He knew within reason that there was little likelihood of finding her there. Rolstag himself would search the forest diligently, but few others would venture deeply into its fabled depths. He sent riders out on all roads from Corenham to put out the word that Princess Volanna was missing and offered a generous reward of one hundred crowns for finding her.

It occurred to Aldemar as well as Kalley that Volanna might have run away, even that she might be better off. But it was his duty to find her. He feared for her safety, and like his wife, he had come to care for the girl as a daughter.

☙

Before the day was an hour old, word of the missing princess had got around to most of Corenham. Ansel and Marcie heard of it at the shop of Darcel the wineseller, the first stop of their route. Though she hid it well, Ansel was elated at the news. It meant the threat to their hopes for Marcie and Aradon had apparently been eliminated, at least for the moment. But it suddenly occurred to her that Aradon and Volanna might have run off together. When they reached the blacksmith shop, they found to their relief that Aradon was at his anvil just as he usually was on the last three days of the month. The two women continued their route with hope renewed that somehow Aradon would come to realize that he and Marcie belonged together.

Ansel knew that Aradon was not oblivious to Marcie. Like Bogarth, she had seen him stealing sidelong glances at her daughter, and she knew that the gleam in his eye was more than just the reflection of the fire in his forge. "The boy just needs a little nudge," she muttered to herself as they pushed their near-empty cart toward home at the end of the day. And he needed to be nudged soon, she thought. The princess may not be lost forever. She could turn up at any time, and the apparent liaison between Aradon and her could be resumed.

Ansel thought long and hard that night while she and Marcie mixed and kneaded the dough for tomorrow's pastry. As they were cutting and shaping the dough into cakes, she stopped and turned to her daughter. "Marcie, I know how we can get that blind Aradon's eyes back on you where they belong."

"I reckon we'd about have to tie him up so he couldn't turn his head and me stand right in front of him since the princess came around," said Marcie.

"No, no, nothin' like that. I mean it. Tomorrow's the first day of the month, and Aradon's leave will be over. We've watched him enough to know which way he goes when he heads back to Vensaur. He follows the stream that runs by Rolstag's cottage into the edge of Braegan Wood. I have an idea, so you listen close and Aradon's as good as yours. And it's so simple. You know the crook in the stream just inside the woods? All you need to do is be bathin' there when Aradon passes by."

"Bathing? You mean without my clothes on, Mother?"

"Of course without your clothes on, girl. That's the whole point. When you've had as much experience with men as I have, you'll know what I'm gettin' at. Haven't you seen the way Aradon looks at you when you bend over your cart to hand him a cake? Didn't you see him blush when I put you on that crate and showed you off to him?"

"I know. I wish you hadn'ta done that. I felt like a cow at an auction."

"I was just doin' what Heraklos says his ancestors did on the islands of the southern sea. When they had a beauteous slave girl to sell, they'd strip her down and put her up on the block for all to see. Then those rich noblemen would bid double or triple what the girl was worth. If I could've put you on that crate naked, I could have got Aradon snared right then and there. That's just the way men are."

"And if I go bathin' in the stream, what will happen then?"

"What will happen then? Where are your brains, girl? You know what will happen then. Get that body of yours all doused and glistenin' out there in that woods and there's no way Aradon can resist you. He'll be in that water like a duck after a waterfly. Nature will take care of the rest, and in two or three months we can tell him you're with child. And you know Aradon. We may get him to slip off his principles a bit tomorrow, but at heart he's an honorable man just like his father. He will own up to what he's done and marry you."

"What if all that happens just like you say, but I don't get with child?"

"It really doesn't matter. If you claim it, he will believe it. And if you are with child, so much the better. But if you're not, you can get sick and just say you lost the baby. By then it won't matter because you'll already be married."

"But that—that wouldn't be fair to Aradon. I mean, you say he's honorable and all; shouldn't we be honorable too? I don't feel right makin' him marry me that way."

"You won't be makin' him do anything. When he plunges into that water after you, you'll both be wantin' the same thing, and what he's doin' won't be any more honorable than what you're adoin'. It's all just a game nature plays by her own rules with men and women as the pawns."

In the end Marcie agreed to the plot, and the women put the cakes on the boards to rise overnight and went to bed. Ansel slept very well that night, but Marcie tossed and turned.

&

When Lomar told Sir Stundal of Volanna's disappearance, he remembered what Ansel had told him of the tryst in the woods between Volanna and Aradon. He had given no credence to her story at the time; the very idea was ludicrous—that a lout such as Aradon would attract the eye of the future queen of the Seven Kingdoms. Yet Volanna had disappeared. And he had heard from talk at Bogarth's shop that Aradon had been working somewhere in Vensaur, returning at regular intervals to visit his parents. Strange as it seemed, the two could have been meeting somewhere. He thought it might be worthwhile to check into Ansel's story, just to follow all leads. Besides, he could use the hundred-crown reward. Stundal thought the best plan would be to have Aradon watched. If there was anything to Ansel's report, Aradon might lead him to a clue. He sent one of his guards to Bogarth's shop, telling him to have his horse shoed, and while he waited, to find out all he could about Aradon's activities.

The guard returned to Stundal two hours later with news that Aradon was making preparations to leave home the following morning and return to Vensaur. He was not able to find out where Aradon went or what he did in Vensaur. "Do you want me to follow him?" asked the guard.

"No, I'll handle this myself," Stundal replied.

Shortly after sunup the next morning, Stundal watched Bogarth's cottage from behind a copse in the meadow just beyond it. He saw Aradon walk from the cottage to the adjacent stable and emerge fifteen minutes later leading a chestnut stallion, saddled and packed as if for a short journey. Aradon mounted and rode out. Stundal let him get well along the trail, then mounted his own horse and followed at enough distance not to be noticed.

Aradon seemed to be in no hurry. He allowed his horse to walk at an even pace as he picked up the trail by the stream that flowed out of the forest near the cottage of Rolstag the huntsman. In little under a quarter-hour Aradon reached the woods. Stundal continued to follow, but as other travelers thinned out on the trail, he dropped back to stay out of Aradon's range of vision. Soon after Aradon entered the woods, he heard splashing in the stream ahead and a clear soprano voice singing a country folk tune.

> The milking maid was pale and wan,
> Because she loved the cobbler's son,
> Who loved the girl who kept the sheep,
> Who loved the boy who sailed the deep,
> Who loved the girl upon the shore,
> Who loved the boy who swept the store,
> Who loved the girl who poured the wine,
> Who loved the boy who pruned the vine,
> Who loved the milkmaid, pale and wan,
> Who loved the milkmaid, pale and wan.

Aradon knew that some young woman must be bathing in the pool at the bend (he had accidentally come up on such a scene before), and for an instant he was tempted to ride up quietly and get a glimpse of her. But his better judgment quickly thrust the thought away, and he turned aside from the trail to take a familiar shortcut through the woods.

CHAPTER TWENTY-THREE

THE SUMMONS

radon sat on the stone near the bank of the pond and stared at the word Maldor scratched into the gold back of the locket in his hand. How could it have gotten into the hole in the rock? Who could have put it there? What could it be telling him about Dovey? He could solve none of these riddles, but his course of action was clear. He had told Dovey to send him the locket if ever she was in need. This was a summons, and he dared not ignore it. The location was the sunken Maldor Castle, which made no sense to him at all, but he had no other thought than to go to Maldor and give what aid she might need.

He left the pond without taking the time to swim or eat his lunch and rode back to Ironwood. He immediately searched out Sir Hardwicke and told him that he must take leave for a few days, then he began preparations for his trip. He prevailed upon Derena to pack him enough salt beef for three days—knowing she would pack for five—and gathered his sword, a long length of rope, a bow, a quiver of arrows, and his small amount of money. He packed it all as compactly as he could on his horse and left for Maldor at dawn.

⚜

Aradon had been on the road for most of two days, and he was nearing the Plain of Maldor. At the village of Garvane, a few miles back, he had asked the innkeeper about the distance and approach to

When Stundal arrived at the same place moments later, he also heard the splashing and singing. Like Aradon, Stundal knew the meaning of what he heard: a woman was bathing in the stream ahead. Thus distracted, he failed to notice where Aradon's hoofprints veered aside from the trail.

Stundal slowed his pace as he rode toward the sound. He stopped some distance away, tethered his horse, and approached the stream quietly on foot. He kept his head low and crouched behind the tall brush at the edge of the stream. Carefully parting the branches of the bush that hid him, he saw a sight that made him forget all about Aradon. Marcie was bathing alone in the clear, flowing water.

Marcie, who had dimly seen a figure approach through the brush, did not consider the possibility that her watcher could be anyone but Aradon. So she played to her audience, swimming luxuriously and wading into the knee-deep shallows near his hiding place to give him an unhampered view of her.

Stundal endured several minutes of the girl's performance as he quietly undid the laces in his clothing. Then he rose from his hiding place and waded with long, splashing strides into the water. By the time Marcie realized the watching man was not Aradon, it was too late; he was only a few steps away. She tried to run, but the calf-deep water tugged at her legs like groping tentacles. Stundal quickly caught up with her, and as he grabbed her arm, she screamed.

"Don't do this," Marcie cried, "I beg you."

"Who are you trying to fool? I've watched you for nearly a quarter-hour. That was not a bath; it was a performance. An invitation," Stundal said. "You knew I was there all along."

"But I thought you was somebody else."

"As you can see, there is no one else. You and I are the only ones in this forest."

Marcie twisted and kicked and thrashed and screamed, but to no avail as Stundal easily scooped her up and carried her to the bank.

Maldor Castle. The innkeeper was incredulous that anyone would venture into that foul, swampy waste.

"There be creatures out there that will make yer blood run cold."

"What kind of creatures?" Aradon had asked.

"Spiders, man. Spiders the likes of which ye've never seen before. There be spiders in that swamp with legs that would span this room."

Aradon's blood had indeed run cold at the innkeeper's warning, but he told himself that superstitions of the countryfolk often had no source but legend. The Plain of Maldor, with its strange history, provided natural fodder for such legends. He hoped he had no more to fear from Maldor than he did from Braegan Wood, also a breeding ground for irrational fears and superstitions, ones Aradon knew to be unfounded.

The innkeeper had told Aradon that there had been no roads to the abandoned ruin since before his father was born. There was only a vague, treacherous trail, mostly overgrown and nearly impossible for a stranger to follow. Nevertheless he had given Aradon directions, telling him to follow the road he was on until he reached the dry tree. There he should turn north into the swamp.

Aradon was now watching for the dry tree. He knew by the increasing flatness of the land and the gray dullness of the foliage that he was nearing the place where he must leave the road and find the boggy semblance of a trail. The trees about him were growing knotty and stunted, their sparse limbs hanging with dead moss that had the look of dry, rank beards. Soon he saw on the horizon the skeletal limbs of a great, dead cypress tree and knew it for the landmark the innkeeper had described. When he drew abreast of the dry tree, he turned his horse from the road and eased it into the dank thicket.

Aradon kept his horse moving in a northerly direction but allowed it the freedom to weave from side to side in search of sound footing. The ground was treacherous, and more than once the horse stepped onto a crusty surface that looked solid but gave way to a thick, gray sludge. Each time the animal managed to pull away before sinking too deeply to extract himself, but after two tedious miles, he stepped into a bog so thick it bound his legs and he could not get out. Aradon dismounted and managed to pull the horse to solid ground, after which he led the animal as he picked his way around the festering pools and rotting stumps, testing each step before he put his weight down on it.

From the moment he had entered the marsh, he had seen enormous spider webs clinging like shrouds to the dead underbrush. Now one of the webs bridged his path, and in the narrow funnel of it he could see a bloated, gray spider huddled into a knot the size of his fist. With a loathing that made his skin crawl, he drew his sword and hacked his way through the web. He twisted the sticky fibers around the spider, trapping it in its own snare, and crushed it with a stone. He did not want to foul his sword with it.

In the late afternoon a fog began to settle over the swamp. As darkness descended, he often saw the movement of some large but indistinct creature creeping low through the brush and slipping into the water as he approached. After sundown the fog settled to the ground, and looming above it on the horizon, standing stark against the lurid twilight, he saw the listing silhouette of Maldor Castle. The cold light of a full moon shone down from above him, giving the ground-hugging fog an eerie, phosphoric glow, as if the plain itself were possessed with some kind of earthbound spirit.

As Aradon approached the ruined castle, he was awed by the enormity of it. It towered huge and black above him, the tilt of its walls ominous and threatening, as if at any moment it could roll toward anyone who encroached upon it and crush them deep into a swampy grave. He secured his horse to a dead willow and eased toward the ruin, looking all the while for signs of life and a safe way to enter. He began to circle the castle, taking care to stay hidden among the trees and underbrush.

To all appearances the castle seemed abandoned. There was no movement, no lights in the windows, no smoke from the chimneys. But he kept circling and was finally rewarded by a dim light in a single window high in a tower on the northwestern wall. As he watched, a woman came to the window, looked out briefly on the dead landscape, then closed the shutters. Aradon's heart leapt within him. It was Dovey. Aradon thought of approaching the wall and throwing pebbles at the window, but he dared not risk the exposure yet and remained hidden in the brush, well away from the walls. With renewed energy he continued to circle the castle, looking for the entrance.

A rustling in the grass at his feet stopped him suddenly. He looked down and froze in horror. Crawling across his path was a swollen, gray spider with a leg span of over two feet. The spider, surprised at Aradon's approach, turned toward him, raised up on six of its hairy legs, and waved its two frontal appendages toward him in a menacing warning. Involuntary panic seized Aradon. He turned to run and fell headlong into a fetid pool. He splashed wildly across it and crawled out, panting furiously as he regained his composure, then steeled himself and eased forward again, his heart pounding against his chest as if trying to escape its confinement.

As he reached the north side of the castle, he saw an opening in the wall, gaping and black, and after looking warily about for signs of life, he crept into the clearing and made his way toward it. He never reached the door. A rustle in the dry weeds behind him made him turn, but his reaction was too late to ward off a sharp blow to his head. Everything went black as he slumped into the weeds.

Aradon awakened lying flat on his back on cold stone. It was dark except for the pale light of the moon shining through a window twelve feet above the floor. His head throbbed as if a spike were being driven into it. He was cold, and his clothes were damp. He heard the rustle of rats scampering about the cell, and by the light of the moon shining on the wall, he could see ragged, funneled webs hanging from the ceiling and in the corners, some containing the same bloated spiders he had seen in the swamp, though not as large. He felt for his sword, but it was missing. He closed his eyes again and shuddered. He gingerly touched his bruised head and tried to think. He remembered his mission and his approach to the castle, and he realized someone must have heard his splashing in the pond when he ran from the spider and captured him from behind.

After a few more minutes he tried to stand, moving slowly to accommodate the protest of his aching head. Once he managed to get to his feet, he took a step, but he almost fell again, losing his balance to the slant of the floor and the tilt of the walls. He knew he was inside Maldor Castle.

When morning came, a silent servant brought him a breakfast of dried bread and a mug of stale mead. Aradon tried to communicate with the man but without success, and judged him to be either idiotic or mute. He had little stomach for the food but ate all of it to keep up his strength, then lay again on the bare floor and began to doze.

"Who are you, and why were you stalking this castle last night?"

Aradon awoke at the sound of the voice and looked toward the cell door. A tall, sturdy man not four years older than himself peered through the bars. He was finely dressed and armed with a sword.

"I was lost, and I hoped I might find a place to sleep. I thought this castle was abandoned," answered Aradon.

"You are lying," said Brendal. "No one comes into this boggy waste without purpose. I ask you again, what is your name and what are you doing here?"

"If one answer doesn't please you, why should I think a second will do better?"

"Your insolence is poorly considered. You are the one in the cell; I am the one with the key. However, I will not press for an answer at this moment for I have other matters to attend today. But I have sure ways of loosening tight tongues. You have until tomorrow morning to reconsider your stupid silence. Then I will return and force an answer in ways you will find most unpleasant. Good day, fool." Brendal turned and walked away as Aradon eased his pounding head to the floor and dozed once more.

He awoke again to a sharp tapping on the bars of his cell and looked up to see the mute servant slipping his afternoon meal into the room. After eating he felt much better and began a systematic check of all the stones in the wall that were within his reach. Low on the wall opposite the door, he found a crack the width of his finger, and two or three of the stones around it were loose enough that, with a little effort, he could move them slightly. He found that the mortar between these stones was loose and brittle. Well satisfied with this discovery, he left the stones and spent the remainder of the day resting and sleeping.

After night darkened his cell, he went to the loosest stone and tried to work it back and forth. He had little success at first. Then he removed his belt, and with the edge of the brass buckle, he was able to scrape out much of the mortar. Minutes later he could move the stone by about the thickness of the leather of the belt. After half an hour, he had it out and had begun to work on the next. The second went faster, and in less than two hours, he had removed six stones, making a black hole in the wall just large enough for him to crawl through. He knew that the opening might lead him nowhere or into a swampy maze of dead-end corridors, but he could see no other possibility of escape.

He replaced his belt and crawled through the hole into absolute darkness. Reaching about him, he could feel walls on either side and knew he was in a narrow corridor, so he arbitrarily chose a direction and began taking careful, probing steps, holding his hands before him.

When his fingers plunged into the dry, clinging fibers of a thick web, he jerked back and shuddered. He fought down his welling revulsion and worked up the will to hack his arm into the web and step through it. But as he stepped through the one web, he stepped into others. Apparently he had stumbled into an infestation of the creatures. Panic began to rise and push against his caution until he lunged forward, flailing wildly into the webs. Immediately he felt the crawling legs of the spiders creeping over his head, back, legs, and arms. He fought frantically to get them off, clawing at his hair, twisting, jumping, slapping furiously all about his body as he careened down the narrow passageway with all caution forgotten. He tore through layer after layer of the odious webs until his foot found no floor beneath it and he felt himself sliding and tumbling downward on a decaying stairway.

CHAPTER TWENTY-FOUR

KING OF THE SPIDERS

Aradon found himself sprawled on a flat, stone surface, panting heavily. After giving himself a moment to collect his senses, he realized there was now enough light that he could barely make out the shapes of the walls and steps around him. He looked up and saw the source of the light. Feeble rays of moonlight were seeping through a crevasse little more than six inches wide. By this pale light he could dimly see the gray shadows of several spiders creeping about the floor. He stood quickly and kicked them aside, then looked about him.

The stairway down which he had fallen was coated with a thick padding of moss and slime, which had softened his fall. Nearby he could just discern the black, conical shape of a torch protruding from a sconce in the wall and wondered if it could be lit. He took the torch out of its holder and loosened some of the material at the burned end, then laid the torch across a step so it extended over the edge of the stairway. Then he took out the flint and steel he carried in a small pouch under his shirt and began striking them together near the material he had loosened. It took several tries before a spark could ignite shreds of the torch material, but at last Aradon was elated by the small, flickering promise of a flame, which soon grew into a dim but stable blaze.

The spiders scurried away from the light and disappeared into the many cracks and crevasses in the floor and walls. By the light of the torch he could see that he was on a landing which opened into a stairwell that spiraled downward into a circular tower. He was hesitant to descend further under the castle as he was likely to encounter nothing but more mud and stale water. And the object of his quest was in the other direction, high in a tower above him. But he had no other choice than to take the one opening available.

Holding the torch aloft, Aradon followed the stairway downward until it ended and he found himself facing a thick, wooden door, wedged tightly shut, apparently for ages. He hesitated to open the door, as there was likely to be nothing on the other side but sludge or water, either of which could be fatal if it trapped him in the stairwell. But again he could see no other choice. He found a sconce to hold his torch, then began to push at the door. He dared not pound on it for fear of rousing whoever lived in the upper floors of the castle.

After a few minutes of pushing and bumping with his hands and shoulders, he managed to open the door about six inches. He retrieved his torch and peered inside. The air was stale but dry. Somehow the room had remained intact and impervious to the seepage from the swamp that surrounded it. Encouraged, he opened the door further to let in more breathable air. The creaking hinges echoed in the darkness like a groan from a dry, hollow mouth. He slowly stepped inside, holding the torch above him.

Aradon looked down a columned hall, long and narrow, with a high, vaulted ceiling. Webs floated lank from the columns and ceiling, but none contained live spiders, though dried, shell-like spider carcasses still hung from some and littered the floor. He took another cautious step into the room and stopped short. His jaw dropped and his heart froze at what he saw before him. Along the sides of the hall, set between the columns, were two rows of seated, unmoving figures, perhaps ten to each side, their forms vaguely visible through massive shrouds of spider webs. At the far end of the hall, facing Aradon, was a single figure seated on a massive throne elevated high on a three-tiered dais. This figure also was shrouded in webs, and its head seemed massive and out of proportion to its body. Its right hand gripped a scepter, which rested on the floor among its robes.

For a moment Aradon stood frozen by the unearthly sight. The only movement in the room was the pounding of his own heart. When he regained his courage, he moved carefully toward the nearest of the shrouded figures. He brushed away the webbing from the head and was startled to find beneath it the face of a man so lifelike that at first he thought it was alive. On further examination he realized it was made of bronze, but it was so perfectly formed and natural in expression that it seemed awake. He moved to the next figure and found another face exactly like the first. The features of the face were familiar to Aradon, and he wondered where he had seen them before. The third figure was also the form of a man and had a face exactly like the first two.

Suddenly he remembered where he had seen this face. It was an exact likeness of the face of Perivale on the huge monument at Cheaping Square. He knew there was a great mystery here, but he would think on it later. He passed by the rest of the seated images and went straight to the figure on the throne. With a sense of dreadful awe, he mounted the dais and reached out to wipe away the veil of webs from the massive head.

To his horror the head bobbed forward. *It's alive!* Aradon thought and jumped away so suddenly that he dropped his torch. The room went black. In the darkness he heard a rustling about the figure on the dais, followed by something clattering and rolling at its feet. Dead silence followed. Aradon dared not breathe for a long moment, but when he heard no more movement, he felt cautiously about the floor until he found the torch and relit it with his flint and steel.

When he looked again at the figure on the throne, his heart leapt to his throat. The head was missing. He looked to the floor and saw a round, webby mass lying near the feet of the figure. Cautiously he kneeled and wiped the webs away and stared into the hollow eye sockets of a human skull. He stood and brushed away the webs from the hand that gripped the scepter and found beneath them the bony fingers of a skeleton.

Aradon thought back on his first impression of the enthroned figure and wondered why it had seemed to have such an enormous head. The fallen skull was of ordinary size, so what could have caused the impression of mass? As his mind churned on the puzzle, he thought he could guess the answer. His heart began to pound, his breath came faster, and he found that his hand trembled as he waved the torch about, searching the floor for the thing that must have been set atop the skull.

Then he found it: a shapeless mass of ragged webs. He picked it up and brushed the webs away until he uncovered a round rim of dull gold that rose into three peaks on the front, the center peak being the tallest. And set deeply within the face of the center peak was a stone from which emanated a hint of colors that Aradon had never before seen or imagined. He gazed with awe on the treasure in his hand. "The lost Crown of Eden," he whispered.

Aradon looked again at the skull, then at the headless skeleton enthroned in decaying finery. "So this is the end of the great Perivale," he said quietly, "once emperor of the Seven Kingdoms, now king of the spiders."

Aradon tore a strip from a rotting tapestry on the wall, wrapped the Crown within it, and tied it to his belt. He found on the same wall a somewhat rusty but serviceable sword in a leather scabbard, which he took and strapped on. He checked the walls around the hall, looking for another way out. He knew it was futile to return the way he had come in. He found a door to the right of the throne and pushed hard against it. It would not budge, but when he began to hack at it with his sword, he found the wood rotted enough that he could make good progress. He splintered two of the boards in the door, only to find a solid wall of oozing mud behind it.

He hacked through the mud wall until he had made a breach in it almost two feet deep. Suddenly the wall gave way, and a rush of water came surging in. He watched helplessly as the flow of water gained momentum and began to tear away the other timbers in the door. Soon the entire door came crashing in, and the stream became a torrent. Aradon splashed about the room, searching everywhere for some other exit. He found none and realized he would soon have to swim, as the water would be rising over his head. Already it reached his thighs and covered the laps of the web-shrouded bronze figures.

His only hope of escape was to swim against the current through the door where the water was coming in. With the water swirling about him now at chest level, he held the torch high and waded toward the door. Before he reached it the water lapped at his chin and he had to stand on the tips of his toes. He placed himself directly in front of the door, looked at it steadily to be sure he was properly aligned with it, then pitched the torch away and plunged forward in darkness. He stroked hard against the rushing current, hoping he was aimed toward the now invisible door. In moments he felt the wall and began groping for the door. He found the top of the frame, now a foot or more underwater, and reached inside it through the rushing current and hooked his arm around the other side. Holding on with all his strength, he began to hook his leg around the frame when a great mass of balled weeds and roots swept against him and dislodged his foot, stretching him out into the current like a rag caught on a stem. He managed to hold on to the doorframe and with a mighty effort, doubled his body forward and pulled himself through the door. With lungs bursting, he came up to the surface on the other side.

He caught his breath as he treaded water. He did not know what kind of place he was in; he might be trapped in a mud-sealed room with no way out. In minutes he realized there was enough light that he could see a little. It came from a vertical fissure that ran from the top of the high wall down to ten feet or so above the surface of the water. The crack was narrow at the bottom—no more than six or eight inches wide—but its width increased to a foot or more as it neared the ceiling. If he could climb up that crack, using it for hand- and footholds, he might squeeze through at the top and climb down it the same way on the other side.

He swam to the wall just beneath the fissure and examined the stone surface. Some of the stones were cracked, with parts missing, and some had been loosened and jutted a few inches inward. Others jutted outward. He thought the stones were uneven enough that he might grip them to climb the wall and reach the fissure. He took hold of a jutting stone just over his head and pulled himself out of the water. Then slowly, carefully, he made his way up the wall until he could hook his arm into the bottom of the fissure and pull himself up to it. Grasping the edges of the crack with his hands and wedging his feet into it, he moved steadily upward until he neared the ceiling, where he managed to place his entire body within the fissure and rest.

He looked out on the moonlit marsh and saw that the ground outside the castle was only about twenty feet below him. He breathed deeply, glad to be out of the foul-smelling murk of the castle's bowels. Growing beside the fissure only twelve feet from the wall was a cypress tree that topped out just over Aradon's head. About four feet below where he stood, a strong-looking limb jutted out from the trunk and almost touched the wall. He eased himself outside the crack and jumped to the limb, then climbed down the tree to the marshy ground.

Aradon found his horse where he had left it and placed the Crown of Eden in the saddlebag. He took out the rope and made his way back to the window where he had seen Dovey. Along the way he picked up several pebbles and a stick of waterlogged wood about a foot long and three inches in diameter. The window was dark and shuttered when Aradon reached it. He took one of the pebbles and threw it against the shutters. He had to hit the window four or five times before he saw it open and the face of Dovey appear above him.

"Who is there?" she asked.

"Not so loud," Aradon whispered. "It is Aradon. I've come to take you away."

Dovey could not clearly see the figure beneath her, standing as he was with the moon at his back, nor could she identify the whispering voice with certainty. But with a few more whispered exchanges, he half convinced her of his identity, then tied the stick to the end of the rope and threw it into her window. She took the rope and tied it low around a bedpost. Her misadventures in Meridan had made her wary, so as the man climbed up the wall, she held her knife against the rope, ready to sever it if the face that appeared at the window was other than Aradon's.

When Aradon looked over the sill, she was overjoyed. She helped him into the room and threw her arms around his neck, completely forgetting her resolve to distance herself from him. She pulled the blanket off the bed and gathered it under her arm, then held tightly to Aradon as he grasped the rope and rappelled down the side of the castle wall. They picked their way through the marsh until they reached the horse and packed the blanket on it. Aradon placed Dovey in the saddle and began to lead the horse out of the swamp, picking his way around the treacherous bogs in the waning moonlight.

They seldom saw the giant spiders, though they heard them moving through the dry grass, sometimes plopping softly into the water ahead of them. Once or twice, when the moon reflected its image on the surface of a pool, they could make out the shapes of spiders in the water, one with a leg span of six feet or more, its bloated body half emerging from the scum on the surface and the top joints of its legs protruding upward like the unthatched beams of an abandoned house.

Aradon was appalled at the monstrous creature. "Look at that," he whispered with a shudder. "I would never have believed that spiders could grow so huge." He began to fear that the innkeeper's warnings may not have been exaggerated.

After they had put the castle a good distance behind them, Dovey told Aradon she must stop to heed the call of nature. She dismounted as Aradon made his way several paces further and stopped to wait on the other side of a large clump of decayed logs and brush. Suddenly Aradon heard a series of sharp splashes followed immediately by Dovey's scream. He bounded around the brush to see an enormous spider—its bloated, hairy body almost the size of a fattened cow, its clawlike legs as thick as a man's, covered with sparse, thorny hairs and spread in a span of well over nine feet. Its fanged mandibles were clamped tight on the edge of Dovey's dress, and it was pulling her into the murk as she fought desperately to get back upon the bank, screaming all the while. Aradon splashed into the water to face the monster and slashed furiously at the fang that snared Dovey's dress. The creature flinched backward and the cloth ripped free, plunging Dovey into the water. Aradon grabbed her arm and flung her to the bank.

"Run, Dovey!" he cried as the spider turned on him. The creature raised itself upward until its hideous cluster of milky eyes looked down on him from a height of seven feet or more. It balanced itself on its back four legs and clawed and pulled at Aradon with its front four as he slashed and hacked at them in a fury. Water and black murk from the creature's wounds splashed about in all directions. He managed to cut through one leg but he found that fighting the giant multiped was like taking on several opponents at once. The monster's three other legs pulled him toward its fangs, which were the size of goat's horns and dripped stringy globules of yellow slime. Beneath the fangs lurked a gaping maw, deep, black, and foul behind the creature's clicking mandibles.

Aradon could not fend off the simultaneous attacks of the multiple legs, mandibles, and fangs. While he hacked at the leg that drew him inward, the spider snared Aradon's left arm in the vise of its mandibles and sank one of its fangs deep into his flesh. He thrust hard several times at its eyes until it flinched backward and relaxed its grip enough for him to pull his arm away, ripping a six-inch gash between his wrist and elbow. He took his sword in both hands and rammed it with all his strength into the spider's mouth. The creature convulsed, rolled slowly onto its back and sank into the slime as its seven remaining legs curled sickeningly inward like a closing claw, almost exactly as Aradon remembered the dying spider of his childhood. For a moment the only sound was of Aradon gasping for breath and an uneven bubbling from the slain creature as it slowly collapsed in the water, expelling air from its breath holes.

Aradon was badly shaken, bleeding, and wary. He looked at Dovey, who stood on the bank trembling.

"You did not run as I told you to do," he said.

"Where would I run? Is there any safe place in this swamp? I thought myself better protected here with you than running out into the dark among these infested pools."

Aradon nodded. "You're right."

"I thought you were afraid of spiders," said Dovey.

"I have never been more terrified in my life," Aradon replied with a shudder.

Volanna looked at him with wonder. She could not remember Brendal ever admitting to fear of any kind. This man was like none she had met before. "Yet you faced this thing you feared and overcame it. My father used to say that courage is not the absence of fear but the will to do what must be done in spite of it. I think you just proved him right. You may find that you conquered more than just a spider tonight."

"It would comfort me to think you are right, but believe me, I never want to face a spider like that one again."

Aradon was exhausted, but he dared not take time for rest, and he did not want to stop again in this hellish swamp. Again he lifted Dovey onto the horse, and they made their way toward the road.

CHAPTER TWENTY-FIVE

The Night of the Wolves

radon was sure he and Dovey would be followed at daybreak. He thought their pursuers would expect them to take the shortest route to Corenham, depending on their lead to get them there before they were overtaken. Once on the road, he would mount the horse behind Dovey in order to increase their speed. Yet he knew that with two of them on one horse, they could not achieve the kind of speed they would need to outdistance pursuit. He decided that they should take a more circuitous route to Corenham, one that would lead them around the northeastern edge of Meridan through several small villages. When they got to Evenshire, they could turn west toward Corenham. He had been in this country before on trips with his father, and he knew something of the road.

Thus when they reached the dry tree where Aradon had left the road two days before, he mounted behind Dovey and turned the horse east, away from Garvane, the village where he had asked directions to Maldor Castle. They traveled until dawn, then left the road to find a hidden place by a stream where they could camp and rest before they took up their travel again at sundown.

Aradon killed a pheasant with his bow and arrow, and Volanna cooked it by turning it on a makeshift spit over a fire. As they ate, he asked her why she had been abducted and held at Maldor Castle. She answered truthfully that she did not know. She told him of her abduction as she left Braegan Wood, of her meeting with the black-robed woman in Maldor, and of what the woman had said—that she was being held for her own good. Always she omitted any parts from her account that would reveal her true identity. Aradon could make no sense of it. He fell quiet as he turned the puzzle over in his mind, looking for some reason for this elaborate, apparently preplanned abduction of a mere kitchenmaid.

Volanna slept on the blanket while Aradon kept watch, then Aradon slept as she watched. When Aradon awoke late in the evening, his arm was swollen and painful. Volanna cleaned the wound with water from the stream, then cut a strip from the hem of her dress to wrap it. To bind the wrapping to his arm, she drew from a pocket in her dress a silk kerchief, striped in rich blue and white.

"That's an expensive looking kerchief for a kitchenmaid," Aradon said.

"It was a gift from a noblewoman," she explained.

At sundown they went back to the road and continued their journey. They rode throughout the night and encountered no difficulties, although they did hear wolves howling in some of the wooded areas as they passed through. Volanna went tense, but Aradon reassured her.

"Wolves are really cowards. They are like bandits or rowdy boys. They do their bad work in packs where they can pool their meager courage into enough mettle to act. They pick only on weak, injured, or isolated animals that can hardly give them much fight. And they are as afraid of fire as if it were a beacon of hell. Keep a blaze going in your nighttime camp and you're as safe from wolves as if you were snug in your own cottage."

As morning approached, they rode into Northmere, the first village on their route. They found an inn, its kitchen just beginning to open, and took breakfast there. As they ate, the tables around them began to fill with farmers and tradesmen who came to take their breakfast before they began the workday.

At the table next to Aradon and Volanna sat a farmer, wizened and grizzled and with multiple patches on his threadbare tunic and leggings. He shook his head sadly and said to the merchant sitting across from him, "Have ye heard about poor Dunwain?"

"What have they done now?" said the merchant.

"Gone and ruined him for sure, they have," replied the farmer. "Took his farm, they did. And him with a wife and a wee one acomin'. Said his crops came in so good-like that he owed half his makins in taxes. When he couldn't pay up, they put him off his land with nary a penny nor a means of makin' one."

"Where did they get the idea that Dunwain made a good crop last year?" said the merchant. "He got the same kind of backward weather as the rest of you farmers. His grain got hardly a drop at planting, and at harvest his fields were so wet he couldn't get in them without bogging up to his knees."

"Ye know it, and I know it, and that devil Brendal knows it. But do you think that makes a whit of difference? It's like what happened to ol' Egrond last week. Brendal said he owed more tax than Egrond's paid in ten years. Took his ox and wagon, they did. Only ones he had too. What he'll do, I can't imagine."

"Why the prince put Brendal over this country is a great mystery. Between him and that weasel Balkert, we'll all be ruined before it's over."

They heard other stories as the tables filled with breakfasters. They were all similar, all of growing oppression by the prince's appointed overseer Brendal—stories of exorbitant taxation, the seizure of lands, and the confiscation of their finest animals.

Aradon's arm was beginning to throb, and he felt himself chilled, though the room was overly warmed by the fires of the kitchen. "I'm feeling a bit feverish," he muttered into Dovey's ear. "I would like to stay here at this inn and let my arm heal a little, but I think it's unsafe for us to stop in daylight without putting more miles behind us. Let's go." He paid for the breakfast and they rode south out of Northmere just as dawn began to break.

Once well away from the town and the farms that surrounded it, they left the road and entered a wood huddled at the base of a low mountain. They rode deep into the thicket until they found a grassy area several paces from a stream, sheltered by a large boulder and a tall oak tree. As they dismounted and spread the blanket on the grass, a wolf howled far up the mountain. Volanna tensed, but Aradon paid

no attention and began to gather a pile of dead sticks and small logs
for the fire they would need later. He readied some of the wood for
burning and set the rest to the side.

Aradon's fever was rising. He found that even the light exertion
of carrying wood left him breathing hard and unable to stand steady.
He half sat, half fell to the grass beneath the tree.

"Dovey," he said, panting. "You go ahead and sleep. I'll keep
watch."

"First, we need to look at your arm." She sat beside him and
undid the bandage. The arm was red and swollen, and the wound
looked hot and angry. "We must cleanse this wound in the stream,"
she said.

She helped him stand, took his good arm over her shoulder, and
walked him to the stream a few paces away, where she eased him to
the ground and bathed his arm. She cleaned the bandage and draped
it across a limb to dry, then tore another strip from the hem of her
dress and wrapped his arm again. She wished she had some healing
farlae leaves to pack against the wound, and she thought it likely that
she could find them in the woods. She would search after she finished
attending to Aradon, who was now shivering with the fever. With
greater difficulty, she got him back on his feet, walked him to the
grass beneath the tree, and covered him with the blanket. But his
shivering did not stop.

Volanna realized that Aradon would not be able to keep watch.
Indeed, his eyes were closing even now, and she knew the fever would
not allow him to stay awake at all. She sat beneath the tree watching
him writhe and moan as he slept. Sweat poured from his forehead
and soaked his hair. Three times she took the rag she had hung to dry,
soaked it in the stream, and bathed his head and face with it, but he
did not awaken. She searched the area about the tree for farlae plants,
but having heard the howl of the wolf, she would not venture beyond
where she could see Aradon.

She continued to sit and watch. Occasionally she heard small
creatures rustling though the grass about them, and again she heard
the howl of a wolf and thought it sounded nearer than before. When
she got hungry, she ate some of the salt beef she found in Aradon's

food wallet. At times she got very sleepy and stood to walk about the tree until she felt alert again. As the afternoon grew warm and the air was still and the woods quiet, she did drift into sleep, and when she awakened the long shadows told her it was late evening. As the wood darkened, she took the flint and steel from his pouch and lit the wood he had prepared.

As the darkness deepened, Volanna sat under the tree beside Aradon and dreaded the night. She wondered if she should have left him alone and gone for help, but now that night had fallen, that was out of the question. She sat beside him and gazed at the flames that lit a circle of twelve feet or so about them. She prayed all the while that Aradon's fever would break and his arm would begin healing. She could not bear the thought that he might die.

She bolted upright at the sound of a great crashing in the woods just behind her, followed by galloping hooves diminishing into the distance. Aradon's horse had run away, and in the next moment she understood why. She heard something in the darkness, a soft rustling in the underbrush just beyond the reach of the firelight. She looked in the direction of the sound, and staring back at her from the blackness were two yellow, almond-shaped eyes. A wolf.

Volanna sat straight up, unable to look away from the glowing eyes as she reached across Aradon and slipped his sword from its scabbard. She leaned back against the tree again, but her eyes never left the pair that watched her from the darkness. Then with a chill of horror, she realized that two more eyes stared at her beside the first pair. She looked around the blackness outside the circle of light and counted over a dozen pair of the baleful eyes glowing in the firelight, looking directly at her. She went rigid with fear and could do nothing but look continuously all around the circle, from one pair of eyes to the next, as if her staring at them would keep them at bay.

After a while she realized that the wolves had crept closer as the fire burned lower. Slowly she eased herself up from the grass and with sword in hand made her way warily to the pile of wood and threw the rest of the logs onto the fire. She wished she had gathered more wood during her idle daylight hours for it was clear that her supply would not last the night. As the fire blazed up, the wolves backed deeper into the darkness, but they did not leave.

The revived fire lasted less than two hours before it burned low again, and once more the wolves crept in, staying just outside the reach of the diminishing light. Volanna found a few dozen small stones and hurled them at the yellow eyes. More than once she apparently hit one of them for it would turn or back away, but only momentarily. The fire flickered, then sank into orange embers, and the wolves stepped out of the brush and moved toward Aradon and Volanna, the shapes of their ears and backs clearly visible in the pale moonlight. Volanna could easily have climbed to safety in the tree behind her, but she would not leave Aradon alone on the ground. She stood and stepped across his prostrate form and faced the wolves.

The sword was too heavy for her to wield with one hand, so she gripped it in both and held it low before her, waving it toward the wolves. She was protected at her back by the tree and the stone, but the wolves moved in on her from three sides, snarling and baring long, white fangs. She turned continually, keeping Aradon behind her, keeping the sword at the animals' eye level and sweeping it slowly back and forth to keep them at bay as they closed the circle about her. She saw that she would not long be able to hold them off on all fronts at once. As she forced back the wolves that approached on her right, two on her left moved close enough to nip at her dress before she could turn and thrust the sword to back them away. No sooner had she dealt with these than those on her right moved in again, their low growls ending in sharp barks as they brought their jaws together with hard snapping sounds.

In a frenzy born of desperation, she gripped the sword and jumped suddenly toward the wolves, shouting and screaming as she swept the blade back and forth with all her strength. The startled wolves retreated a few paces but then held their ground. The largest of them, apparently the pack leader, broke from the others and moved toward her. She lifted the sword and with all her might brought it down toward the creature's head. But the blade struck hard on an overhead limb and flew from her hands, landing on the grass twelve feet away. The wolves surged forward. With no more means of defense,

Volanna turned and threw herself across the unconscious form of Aradon and braced herself for the ripping of fangs in her back.

She heard a frenzy of growls and snarls as the wolves approached, but this was followed by a confusion of sounds—yelping, scuffling, soft thuds against the earth, and finally the rustle of a scampering retreat accompanied by a disordered thrashing about in the under-brush. And then silence. She started to look up, but another sound stopped her—the sound of some large creature moving through the woods toward them. She forced herself to look toward the noise and saw the shadow of a huge beast breaking through the brush. She buried her face in Aradon's hair and clung to him in desperation, waiting for sure death to follow.

Volanna felt a gentle hand on her shoulder, and slowly she looked up into a bearded, moonlit face. Two wolves lay still nearby, each with an arrow protruding from its side. Tears of relief flowed from her eyes as she stood and embraced the welcome form of Olstan. The beast she had feared was nothing more than Aradon's runaway horse, which Olstan led by its reins.

Olstan tied the horse to a tree and immediately set about to gather more wood and build up the fire. He removed the pack from his back and took from it a thin blanket, which he handed to Volanna with hand motions indicating that she should sleep. He would stand watch for the rest of the night. But she shook her head and told him of Aradon's desperate condition.

"Can you help me make a torch?" she asked. "Before I sleep, I want to find some farlae leaves to draw the poison from his wound."

Olstan signified that she should stay by Aradon and the fire, which now crackled with a hearty blaze, while he searched for the leaves. He was not gone more than ten minutes before he returned with a pouch filled with the healing herb. Olstan indicated that they should get Aradon to the stream and bathe him in the cool water to reduce the fever. Volanna agreed, and though Olstan was not a large man, he lifted Aradon alone, carried him to the stream, and placed him on the bank.

By the light of the moon they undressed him and immersed all but his head in the shallows, letting the flowing water cool his fever.

After some time they drew him out of the water, and Olstan dried him with his own blanket and covered him with the other as Volanna crushed the farlae leaves and bound them to his arm. Then Olstan carried Aradon back to the fire and laid him gently on the grass. As dawn lightened the eastern sky, Aradon rested quietly. Volanna breathed a prayer of thanks and fell asleep on the grass beside him as Olstan stood watch.

CHAPTER TWENTY-SIX

PURSUIT

radon awakened in the late morning. Volanna, who had awakened earlier and had since been sitting nearby watching over him, was overjoyed. Olstan was away from the camp hunting for their breakfast.

"Welcome back to the land of the living," said Volanna as he opened his eyes and looked around.

"How long have I been away?" he asked.

"One day and one night. I was afraid you might not come back at all," she said with a slight quiver in her voice.

Tentatively, he lifted the blanket that covered him. "Why am I, uh, where are my clothes?"

"They were so foul after your battle with the spider that I had to burn them," she said with a straight face.

"You had to burn them? You mean, you undressed me? What will I wear?"

Volanna laughed and told him the whole story of the wolves, the coming of Olstan, and of their cooling his fever in the stream. "I did not burn your clothes. I washed them in the stream this morning as I bathed, but they are not yet dry. The sunlight will get the job done soon, and until then, the blanket will just have to do."

Olstan returned with two plump rabbits on his belt, and in less than an hour the three of them were eating, Aradon still the captive of his blanket. When they had finished, Aradon demanded, "Dovey, bring me my clothes—wet or not. I'm tired of this blanket." She checked his tunic and leggings and found them dry. She handed them to him and turned away as he dressed. When she turned back, he was standing on his feet, though he was yet somewhat wobbly.

Throughout the rest of the morning, Aradon walked about the woods to regain his strength, using a strong, straight limb as a staff for support. Volanna walked with him, and as they strolled by the stream, he was quiet for a long while, as if deep in thought. Finally he asked, "Do you have any idea how Olstan found us, and why he has stayed to help us?"

"I don't know how he found us," she replied, "but I'm sure he is helping us because I once helped him when we both worked in the kitchen at Morningstone. None of the other servants knew much about him—where he lived or where he came from. Most thought he had been abandoned as a child. Others thought his parents had died. No one knew where his home was, though some thought he lived in the forest."

Aradon seem relieved. "I am glad to hear that he has reason to feel loyalty to you. I've been concerned that he might have been sent to follow us by the woman in black you met in Maldor Castle. Yet I wonder how he found us. It seems unlikely that he just happened to stumble on our camp while on some other errand. We're not on a road that leads to any place significant."

"I wonder if he didn't follow us simply to help us—a guardian angel of sorts, you might say. I have no reason to doubt his loyalty. It seems he has twice proved it already in carrying the locket to you and saving us from the wolves. And now he is providing our food."

"No doubt you are right," said Aradon after a moment's reflection. "If he were a scout or a spy, he likely would have contacted his masters by now."

Aradon and Volanna continued to talk as they strolled about the woods. They were still mystified by her abduction, and though they considered many possibilities, they could find no reason for it. Volanna privately suspected it was Prince Lomar's doing—some scheme to isolate her from the protection of Lord Aldemar and the society of Corenham in order to coerce her into succumbing to his will.

The stroll was tiring to Aradon, and more than once he stopped to rest on a stone or log. By early afternoon he was exhausted, and they retraced their steps back to the tree.

Olstan was gone. They looked everywhere in the vicinity of the tree, but found no trace of him. And the horse was missing as well.

"We may have absolved your friend too quickly," said Aradon.

Volanna did not answer. She was unwilling to believe that Olstan had left to betray them, yet at the moment she could find no better explanation. Aradon dropped himself to the ground and leaned against the tree. "Well, we dare not stay here long. We must leave this camp and make our way through the woods. Our only course is to keep traveling after night falls, though now we will be afoot and without bow or arrows. But I don't think I could travel twenty feet at the moment. I must sleep for now. We will start walking when I awaken." Volanna sat down beside him as he closed his eyes and began to drift into sleep.

Half an hour later he felt a hand gently shaking his shoulder. "Aradon, wake up. I hear hoofbeats," whispered Dovey.

He sat up, suddenly alert as his chestnut stallion came into the clearing with Olstan on its back. Olstan dismounted, grinning, and held up seven or eight quail for them to see. By eloquent hand signs he indicated that he had ridden to a meadow near the base of the mountain where he had stalked and flushed the birds. Aradon was ashamed of his doubt. Olstan began to clean the quail as Volanna prepared a fire. Aradon started to rise to help them, but Olstan would not allow it, so he sat and watched them work until the meal was ready. As they gathered beneath the tree and ate the quail, Aradon thanked Olstan for all he had done for them and invited him to accompany them to Corenham. Olstan accepted with a nod. They finished their meal and rested until nightfall, then resumed their journey under the cover of darkness.

Olstan insisted that the weakened Aradon ride the horse while he and Volanna walked. Aradon's pride resisted such an arrangement, but he was in no condition to prevent it, so reluctantly, perhaps even a little sullenly, he mounted the horse with Olstan's assistance, and they made their way at walking pace down the moonlit road. After traveling three or more hours, Volanna began to tire and slacken her pace. Olstan stopped the little procession and insisted by signs that she should ride on the horse with Aradon. She protested, expressing sympathy for the poor animal, but again, Olstan prevailed. She mounted behind Aradon, and the feel of her arms about his waist was dear to him. Near dawn they topped a hill and saw in the distance the village of Evenshire.

They camped just outside the village until morning, then entered to find an inn and take their breakfast. Aradon was shocked at the condition of the town. Roofs of cottages sagged, and the thatch was thin and often rotting. The timbers in many of the buildings had lost their whitewash, and the daub in the walls was cracked and crumbling. Fences missing slats looked like gapped rows of neglected teeth, gates hung unlatched by a single hinge or none, and goats and geese and hens roamed the street at will. The few people they met on the street were rudely dressed, mostly in undyed woolens, ragged and held together by many patches.

"I came through Evenshire less than three years ago, and it looked nothing like this," he said. "What could have happened here?"

Although the town's one inn had no sign to identify it, the fugitives found it easily by the aroma of bacon drifting from its open door, along with wispy traces of blue smoke. They entered and found an empty table, where they sat on the split log bench and ordered bacon, eggs, honeycakes, and mugs of cider. As they ate, they overheard more stories of the same kind they had heard in Northmere.

One farmer, speaking to the man at the table with him, told of having his only horse confiscated for taxes he could not pay. "An' me with five wee ones to feed too. That harness doesn't fit my body nary as well as it did my dray, but it's mine to wear now."

As he was speaking, a young woman, pale and thin, entered the room with two small children, a girl about four years old and a boy just over two. The children huddled close to her, hiding in the patched, frayed folds of her gray woolen skirt. The clothing of the little ones was so shapeless and ragged as to be hardly identifiable as clothing at all. Aradon watched as the woman made her way with lowered head and unsure steps to the kitchen where the innkeeper was stacking dishes and spoke to him in a voice too low for others to hear.

The innkeeper would not look at her but shook his head as he kept working. "I'm sorry, Mavery, I can't do it anymore. I've been feeding ye for weeks, now, and I'm running low myself. Ye've got to find help somewhere else."

Aradon saw the despair in the woman's eyes as she turned to leave, and as she passed their table, he stood and asked, "Would you care to breakfast with us?"

"I can't pay," she said.

"It doesn't matter. Please join us."

With only a little hesitation, the woman sat at the table with the three travelers. Aradon ordered additional food for his three guests, and as they ate, the woman told her story.

"My husband was a dairyman," she said, "and a right good one he was too. We had five good cows with udders like washpots, and I helped him with the milkin', and he supplied many in this village with milk, cheese, curds, and cream. Then came Lomar's man Balkert and this man Brendal with him, tellin' us how he would be collectin' our taxes now. Brendal saw how we was doing well, so he put our tax at five times what it had ever been before. When we couldn't pay up, he came and brought three men, all big and rough-like, to take our cows, and Crennan—that's my husband—started fightin' to keep them away. Brendal had him arrested and locked him up in the prison, where he's been for nigh on two months now. You'd think they'd done enough, just takin' my man, but Brendal put a torch to the thatch on our cottage, and it burned to the ground with everything we had in it."

Mavery dabbed at her eyes with a corner of her ragged sleeve. Volanna tried to help the little boy by cutting his bacon and honey-cakes into bite-sized morsels, but her efforts were in vain for he stuffed his mouth until his cheeks bulged like a chipmunk's, and she wondered how he would chew it all. But chew it he did, and when he finished, his plate was clean, but his hands, cheeks, and mouth were a sticky mess of honey and crumbs. Volanna called for a bowl of water and scrubbed him clean, causing an outburst of giggles as her cloth tickled his face and neck.

"He tickles easy," said the little girl, "but not me. I'm too big."

Volanna's hand darted out and caught the girl's arm, and she applied the washrag to her face as she had to her brother's, causing a second outburst of giggles that turned the heads of everyone in the inn. After the giggling subsided and the faces were clean, Aradon resumed his questioning.

"Where did you live after they burned your house?"

"Brendal's men left the cowshed standin', and that's where the children and I have been livin', though we go out most every day to beg for our food. Everyone was good and generous for a while, but now there's many people what Brendal has done in too, and they don't have so much to give anymore."

"Why hasn't your husband been tried or released?" he asked.

"We used to have trials regular when Balkert came 'round—if you could call them trials—but he's not been seen here for some three months, and Brendal says he can't hold court. He's only got authority to tax. So I suppose Crennan'll stay in prison till Balkert shows his face 'round here again, and who knows what will happen then."

"What about the sheriff? Farragan is his name, as I remember. My father knows him. Lord Aldemar appointed him years ago. Surely he would not hold your husband without trial."

"I went to Farragan, but he's too fearful to act without Balkert's givin' him leave."

"Where is this prison?" asked Aradon, his anger rising.

"In Hallifax, the next village south, a half-day from here," she answered.

Aradon gave the woman half the money he had left, and Volanna gave her the blanket she had taken from Maldor Castle. She kissed the children, hugged the poor woman, and whispered a word of encouragement in her ear. Then Aradon, Volanna, and Olstan left the inn and took the southward road toward Hallifax, leading the horse behind them.

Once outside the village, Aradon insisted that Dovey mount the horse and ride. "We will have to walk in daylight for about two hours; the next wooded area is six miles from here. It's all farms until then."

"No, you ride, Aradon. You don't have your strength back yet."

"Walking will help me regain my strength."

"Not if you push yourself too soon. Don't try to impress me with your heroic endurance."

"I'm not trying to impress you with anything. I'm just trying to be reasonable. Look at you. You have to take two strides to my one. It will take you twice the energy to walk the same distance."

"Not so, you big lug. It takes you twice the energy to lift those big feet."

"You're spending more energy talking than it will take me to get to Hallifax. Now get on that horse."

"Who are you to tell me what to do? I'll walk if I want."

Aradon threw up his hands, expelled an exaggerated sigh, put his head down and kept walking. Olstan rapped his staff on the road to get their attention, and when they looked at him, he held his hand palm downward about three feet above the road, pointed back to the village, then pointed at them and shook his head.

"What are you trying to tell us?" asked Aradon.

They both watched as he repeated the gestures, then Volanna laughed. "He's telling us we're acting like children." Olstan nodded and grinned.

Aradon laughed as well. "And so we are. Why don't we all three share time on the horse. We'll all need the rest before we get to Corenham." They drew straws, and Volanna was the first in the saddle. Aradon helped her mount, and they went on their way.

Just as they approached the end of the farm country, they met a herder coming toward Evenshire driving a dozen milk cows before him. Aradon stopped the man and bargained for the fattest of the twelve and paid him with the last of his money.

As the herder went on his way, Aradon turned to Olstan and said, "You can see the beginning of the wood ahead of us. There's a stream deep in the trees on the right side of the road. We can make camp there. After we get settled, I will take this cow back to the mother in Evenshire."

Olstan took his arm, and with a series of gestures made it clear that he would take the cow back to the village as Volanna and Aradon went on into the wood to set up camp. Aradon agreed on condition that Olstan would take the horse, which would cut his time in half or better. He took the bow and arrows from the horse, then he and Volanna parted from Olstan and went on to find their camping site.

They chose a small, grassy clearing in a grove of oak trees fifty paces from the stream. "I'll take first watch," said Aradon. "It's mid-morning now, and Olstan could be back as early as an hour past noon. We can find a midday meal and trade watches when he comes."

Aradon gathered wood as Volanna slept, then nocked an arrow in his bow and sat with his back to a tree where he could overlook the clearing between the trees and see to the stream, keeping watch over Dovey.

Aradon thought about Olstan. Perhaps he had been wrong to allow the man to take on such a mission in broad daylight. Suddenly he remembered the Crown of Eden in the horse's saddlebag. He had been so absorbed in the journey and the presence of Dovey that he had not until now even thought of the Crown. He wondered what he should do with it. Give it to Father Verit or Lord Aldemar, no doubt. The thought struck him that this finding of the Crown of Eden might be his part in fulfilling the prophecy. The more he thought on it, the more he concluded that indeed, he had fulfilled his duty. He knew that the Crown figured somehow in the fulfillment of the prophecy, though he could not explicitly remember its role. When they arrived in Corenham, he would go to Lord Aldemar and turn it over to him. Then he would get on with his life. A slight apprehension grew in him as he thought of the danger to which he had exposed the Crown by leaving it in the saddlebag of the horse Olstan was riding. Perhaps he should have removed it, but it was futile to be concerned about it now. At the moment there was nothing he could do.

He gazed at Dovey as she slept and felt his heart move into a deeper cadence. She slept on her side with her cheek resting on her hands. *How could any creature on earth be so perfect?* he thought. Even in the abandon of repose her form had a grace about it that could not have been improved had she carefully placed each limb, each strand of her flowing hair. *Why did such beauty exist?* he wondered. Heraklos had told him it was merely nature's means of inciting lust to propagate the race, but Aradon knew that this was not the truth, or at least, not the whole of it. He thought of couples he knew who did not possess beauty but did possess a cottageful of wee ones. He looked at Dovey's exquisite form and knew that his delight in her had nothing to do with lust. If their relationship ever found a way to grow beyond where it was at this moment, deeper, more intimate desires would come upon him, no doubt. But whatever the future held, he was presently tasting a heaven of ecstatic delight simply feasting his eyes on her and could die happy without ever asking for more.

His eye lingered on the velvet freshness of her perfect face. It caressed the delicate outline of her lips, moved up the exquisite line of her nose, and traced the evenly arched eyebrows. He stared in wonder at the long, dark lashes, now closed, giving her the look of a sleeping Eve, freshly created, a masterpiece lovingly shaped by the hands of her maker, waiting to be awakened into life. He was aware that his heart was beating faster and his breath was coming deeper, and he wondered how much of such ecstasy he could bear.

As he watched, Dovey's eyes opened and looked straight into his. Aradon stopped breathing. Neither of them smiled, neither moved so much as a single muscle as both gazed deeply and unabashed, without blinking, without looking away, as if into the very soul of the other. Warmth and contentment flowed along the beams of their gaze, and within that unguarded moment they nourished each other from the deep store of affection they had held closed within the centers of their beings. After a long moment, her lips curved into a gentle smile, which lingered as she closed her eyes to sleep once more, and Aradon began to breathe again.

As he sat and waited, three wood hares wandered into the range of his bow, and two of them ended up skinned and hanging from an overhead limb.

Volanna awakened not long after noon. "Has Olstan returned?" she asked.

"No, but it may be a bit early to expect him yet. We can go ahead and get our meal ready. He should be here by the time these hares are cooked."

They made a fire and roasted the meat, but Olstan did not arrive. "He may have had more trouble finding Mavery's farm than we expected," said Aradon as they sat on the grass and began to eat. "Though he does seem to have an uncanny way of finding things, as he found us at our camp and the pond in Braegan Wood."

"He is certainly not the idiot the workers at Morningstone assume him to be," said Volanna.

"Yet I wonder why he chooses to remain with us. Surely he needs the wages he earned at Morningstone and Maldor."

"One reason, I think, is simple loyalty. I have done him a good turn, and I suspect that kindness is a rare thing in his life. Then too, I suspect that our including him in our journey has given him a sense of belonging, which is likely the nearest thing to friendship he has ever experienced. He has always been shunned by the other servants, who never bothered to look beneath his handicap to find the man of intelligence that Olstan is."

                          *

Just as Aradon had thought, Olstan had no trouble finding the cow-shed that sheltered Mavery and her two children. He delivered the cow, and the woman was overwhelmed with gratitude. Immediately he got back on the road toward Hallifax to make his rendezvous with Aradon and Volanna in the woods near that village. Just as he passed the last farm and could see the woods ahead, he heard the sound of hoofbeats approaching swiftly behind him. He turned to see three riders coming toward him at a full gallop and moved to the side of the road to let them pass. But instead they reined their steeds as they drew abreast of him, and one of them reached out and seized him by the tunic and threw him from his horse. Brendal looked down on Olstan as he picked himself up from the road.

"Fine gratitude you've shown Balkert for giving you a job. You helped our prisoners escape. Where are they?"

Olstan stood silent.

"I forgot that you are a mute and an idiot. Very well. Where did they go? Point the way," Brendal demanded.

Olstan looked at Brendal evenly but made no move. Brendal drew his horse close and hit Olstan hard across the face with the back of his gauntlet. Blood streamed from Olstan's nose. "I know you can hear. Now, you show me where I can find the princess and I will leave you alone." Olstan did not move. Again Brendal hit him hard on the face, knocking him once more to the road. "Are you going to show me now, or shall I hit you again?"

Olstan got to his feet shaking his head vigorously and pointed down the road in the direction of Evenshire. Brendal drew back and hit him a third time. "You are lying. We just came from Evenshire, and the villagers already told us that two men and a woman took breakfast there and got back on the road toward Hallifax. We know they never arrived in Hallifax, for Stenwilde here just came from that village. And we know they've been camping in the woods at night. I don't know why you're not with them now, but my guess is you were on your way to meet them at their daytime camp. I think I'll just let you continue your journey. We will follow about twenty paces behind, which is an easy shot for Manawyn's bow should you decide to bolt into the woods. Get on your horse."

Olstan mounted and prodded his horse toward Hallifax. Brendal and his two men followed, Manawyn with an arrow nocked in his bow. When they reached the trees, Olstan veered into the thicket to the left of the road, knowing that Aradon and Volanna had camped to the right. He rode in an erratic path until they came out of the woods on the southeast, looking out toward the sea. He turned and faced Brendal and shrugged his shoulders.

"He's led us wrong, Sir Brendal," said Stenwilde.

"We're wasting our time on this idiot," said Manawyn. "Let me kill him on this spot." He raised his bow and aimed the arrow toward Olstan.

"No, take him, and come with me," said Brendal.

Manawyn and Stenwilde seized Olstan and followed Brendal as he rode back into the center of the woods. He approached an ancient oak tree with a trunk round as a wagon wheel and stopped.

"Tie him to this tree," he ordered.

They threw Olstan's back against the tree and tied his arms to the trunk. When they were convinced he could not escape, they stepped away, and Brendal said, "You are reaping the reward for your traitorous disloyalty. Since you can't call for help, no one will ever find you here. What do you think will happen to you? Will you starve? Or will the wolves eat you first? Maybe the ants will feast on you before the wolves arrive. Or maybe the crows will come and pluck out your eyes. Meanwhile, we will search the woods on the north side of the road. Come, men." Manawyn and Stenwilde mounted their horses, and leading Aradon's horse behind them, followed Brendal back to the road.

CHAPTER TWENTY-SEVEN

The Return of the Princess

Aradon awakened in the middle of the afternoon. Volanna had finished bathing and now sat on the grass grooming her hair. Aradon watched her, thinking that her every movement was the very incarnation of grace. After a moment she glanced at him and smiled.

"So you've decided not to hibernate after all."

"My fur hasn't grown long enough yet. Has Olstan returned?"

"No, he hasn't. I can't imagine what is keeping him."

"Nor can I," said Aradon. "I may as well bathe. Then we can discuss what we should do." He walked up the stream until he was hidden by the brush, removed his clothes, and slipped into the water. He washed his leggings and tunic as he bathed. The day was warm enough that he could simply wear them as they dried.

He had just pitched his clean clothing to the bank and begun to swim about when he heard Dovey scream. He splashed from the water, thrust himself into his leggings, took up his sword, and ran toward the camp. Two men were dragging Dovey toward their horses as she fought them like a panther, kicking, scratching, and pummeling in a frenzy until they pinned her arms behind her.

"Let her go!" Aradon bellowed as he rushed toward them.

Manawyn released Volanna, drew his sword, and turned to face Aradon. With a few quick strokes, Aradon left him on the ground, bleeding heavily from the side, and rushed toward Stenwilde. Stenwilde drew his sword and turned to defend himself. After a short duel Aradon dealt the man a blow that cleaved his torso from neck to heart.

"You will pay for this," said an angry voice above him.

Aradon looked up and saw the man who had questioned him in the cell at Maldor, mounted on his horse not twenty feet away with a naked sword in his hand. Brendal spurred his horse toward Aradon, intending to make short work of the matter.

"Aradon! Run!" cried Volanna. She knew that Brendal was the jousting champion of Valomar and was sure Aradon would have no chance against him.

But Aradon stood firm. Brendal rode directly at him and slashed at his head in a swift, wide arc, but Aradon dodged to the side as Brendal passed. Brendal turned and charged again, once more trying to lop Aradon's head from his body, but once again Aradon dodged. Brendal turned to charge a third time. To Volanna's horror, this time Aradon made no move to dodge but stood his ground. As Brendal approached, Aradon crouched and then sprang up, ramming his shoulder into Brendal's horse's chest, jarring it sideways enough to throw Brendal off balance, causing him to check the stroke of his sword and grab for the reins. At that moment of imbalance, Aradon jumped to Brendal's side, clutched his cape, and pulled him to the earth. Brendal jumped to his feet with sword in hand and immediately charged at Aradon, bellowing like an angry bull. Aradon engaged Brendal's sword with his own but was tentative and defensive, retreating from his opponent's rapid strokes as he studied the man's style and tendencies.

Volanna looked on terrified, her hands clasped in fear and anguish. She had watched Brendal duel before and saw no way for Aradon to survive the man's skill. Yet the match continued, with Brendal advancing aggressively but finding himself unable to penetrate Aradon's defense. Soon Aradon began to feel confident that Brendal had exhausted his tricks, and he knew he could hold his own.

Gradually Aradon became more aggressive, and fear began to show in Brendal's eyes. Volanna looked on, and her anguish gave way first to astonishment that Aradon was still in the fight, then to a thrill of wonder at his power and skill. After a few minutes Brendal became desperate and his strokes lost their discipline, until finally he left an opening that Aradon exploited with a strong thrust toward his heart. Brendal recovered and brought his sword back to ward off the blow, but Aradon's blade sliced through the thumb and two fingers, and Brendal's sword flew through the air. Brendal dropped to the ground, writhing and rolling on the grass as he clutched the bleeding wound. Aradon stopped Brendal with his foot and put his sword to the injured man's throat.

"Where is Olstan?" he demanded.

"I don't know who you're talking about," said Brendal.

"You lie," said Aradon. "You have his horse. Where is he?"

"Dead," Brendal snarled.

"Then so are you," Aradon growled and raised his sword to strike.

"No, wait!" pleaded Brendal. "He's not dead. I'll tell you where he is."

"You will do better than that; you will take us to him," said Aradon.

Volanna took her knife and tore strips of cloth from the tunic of the dead Manawyn and bound the wounded side of Stenwilde. Aradon bound Brendal's maimed hand then tied his wrists together. As he finished, Brendal spit in his face.

"Bind his mouth," said Volanna, "as he bound mine when he abducted me from Braegan Wood." She feared that Brendal would reveal her identity to Aradon.

Aradon wiped the spittle from his face with Brendal's cape, then tore away part of it and stuffed it into the angry man's mouth. He helped Brendal mount his horse and laid the wounded Stenwilde across his own. He plundered Brendal's saddlebags and found his purse, a large one of doubled leather and filled to capacity. Volanna retrieved Aradon's tunic from the bank of the stream and helped him slip it on. Then she mounted Aradon's horse, Aradon took the horse of the dead Manawyn, and Brendal, with nods and grunts, led them to the road and into the woods on the far side of it, where they found Olstan tied to the oak tree.

Aradon cut Olstan free as Volanna told him of all that had happened since their parting. Olstan mounted Stenwilde's horse, laid the wounded man in front of him, and they made their way down the road toward Hallifax. They arrived at the village two hours before sundown and found the inn, where Aradon secured a room for Stenwilde and instructed the keeper to care for him until he was well. When he asked the innkeeper the cost of these services, the man rubbed his chin and looked at Aradon from the corners of his eyes.

"Ummm, I could hardly do all ye've asked for less than two crown," he said.

Aradon went to Brendal's horse, took four crown pieces, and held them up for Brendal to see. "The man will love you for your generosity," he grinned. Brendal glared at him helplessly. Aradon dropped the coins into the innkeeper's hands and said, "As soon as the man can walk, send for Sheriff Farragan to take him off your hands."

The man looked at the money in his palm and his eyes went wide. "Ye can be sure I will, my man. Ye can be sure."

"Where can we find a barber?" asked Aradon. The innkeeper directed him to a shop on down the street. Brendal screamed with pain as the barber sewed together the flesh where his fingers were missing, cauterizing the remaining wound with a hot iron rod. After the barber bound up what remained of the hand, Aradon paid him twice the amount he asked, again with money from Brendal's purse.

They emerged from the barber's door, mounted their horses, and after asking directions to the prison, made their way down the street. By now a crowd of curious villagers had gathered and followed them, wondering at the sight of their oppressor brought into town as the wounded captive of a young stranger. They arrived at the jail, a stone building with its wooden door locked and bolted. The sheriff was not there.

Aradon turned to the crowd. "Does anyone know the whereabouts of Sheriff Farragan?"

"I heard tell he went over Daverton way this mornin'," said one. "Won't likely be back until tomorrow."

Aradon looked over the crowd. "Is there a carpenter among you who would like to earn a crown?"

A stocky man of middle age stepped forward. "Depends on how it's to be earned," he said.

"First I want you to break down this door. Then when my business here is finished, I want you to repair it," said Aradon.

"I'll repair it once the damage be done, but ye'll have to do the breakin' yourself," the carpenter replied.

"Very well," said Aradon, "if I may borrow your ax."

The carpenter went to his cart and returned with the ax, and with a few strokes Aradon splintered the wood around the lock and pushed the door open. He found the sheriff's keys hanging on a nail and walked into the short corridor lined on either side with filthy cells smelling of sweat and urine. "Which of you is Crennan?" Aradon called.

"I'm Crennan," three or four voices answered simultaneously. They had seen the keys in Aradon's hand.

"What is the name of your wife," Aradon called.

"Mavery," called a thin man with a ragged beard and unkempt hair who looked intently at Aradon through the bars of the cell. After trying three or four keys, Aradon opened the cell and let Crennan walk out, using his sword to keep the other seven or eight men inside.

After leading Crennan from the jail, Aradon went again to Brendal's purse, scooped a handful of coins from it, and dropped them into Crennan's hand. "Spend tonight in the inn and get yourself cleaned up, then get home to your wife and little ones. They need you badly."

After gushing his gratitude, Crennan said, "If it's all the same to ye, sir, I'll be headin' on home afore the sun sets tonight. It's been two months, ye know." With that the man made his way through the crowd and down the road toward Evenshire.

Aradon took the reins of Brendal's horse and turned him so that he faced the crowd. "Do you know who this man is?"

The crowd responded mostly with grunts and nods. A matronly woman spoke up, "He's the very devil, he is, though he wears the name of Sir Brendal."

Another responded, "He's Prince Lomar and Balkert's man. They put him over us to rob us into the grave."

"And he's almost done it too, he has," said another.

"Where is your mayor?" asked Aradon.

"We haven't had a mayor in well nigh half a year," said the woman. "Stoufford yonder was our mayor, and a good one he was too." She pointed to a gray-haired man leaning on a staff at the edge of the crowd. "But then Balkert came and told us we didn't need a mayor anymore 'cause Brendal was taking on the government of all the villages from Northmere to Lenshaw."

"Stoufford," called Aradon. "What will happen to Brendal if I lock him in this jail?"

"Well, one thing's sure," said Stoufford. "Unless you put him in a cell by himself, he'll not last till mornin'. Most every man in this prison was put there by Brendal and not one of them for any crime but poverty. When he went to sleep tonight, they would see to it that he never woke up."

"Is that what should be done with him?" asked Aradon.

"It's terribly temptin', and there'd be a certain justice to it," sighed Stoufford. "We'd all get fine satisfaction seein' Brendal get his end at the hands of those he has oppressed. But it would hardly be worthy of us as citizens of Meridan. I say the right thing is to lock him up in a cell by himself."

"What would Farragan do if he returned and found Brendal in his prison? Would he take him to Morningstone for trial?"

"Farragan's a good man, but Brendal's had a hold on him. I think now that Brendal is ruined, Farragan will likely become his own man again and do the right thing."

"Very well," said Aradon. "Here are the keys to the jail. Lock Brendal up in a cell by himself." He threw the ring to Stoufford, who caught it and said, "I will do as you say. But would you please us by tellin' your name. We would honor the man who has lifted a great yoke from our necks."

"Your gratitude is honor enough," replied Aradon. "I deem it best not to reveal my name to you, as you have witnessed me breaking into property belonging to the kingdom and performing acts that rightfully should be performed only by properly appointed officials. If you are called to witness to what you have seen, you can honestly say that you don't know the name of the perpetrator of these crimes."

"Correcting injustice is hardly a crime, young sir," said Stoufford.

At a word from Stoufford, three or four men removed Brendal from his horse and locked him in a cell of Farragan's jail.

For the rest of the evening, Aradon, Dovey, and Olstan went into the various shops of the village to purchase provisions for the remainder of their journey, always paying generously with the money from Brendal's purse. Most of what they bought they gave away again as they encountered hunger and poverty at every door, though they did keep two of the blankets they bought at the shop of the weaver. They bought five pounds of cheese from a cheeseseller who came down the street straining in the harness of his loaded cart.

"Don't you have a horse to pull your load?" asked Volanna.

"Nay, miss, though I did before Brendal took it. Land tax, he called it, though I barely have enough land for the shed that cures my cheeses. I buy all my milk from the dairyman."

Aradon led Brendal's horse to the man. "This can hardly be the same horse, but perhaps it will do," he said as he handed him the reins. The man protested that he could not buy the horse, and when Volanna made it clear to him that it was a gift, he was speechless with gratitude. Olstan helped him rig the horse to his cart, and the happy man gave them at least six or eight more wedges of cheese, which they accepted and later gave to three widowed beggar women living in a hut at the edge of the village.

As the sun went down, Aradon turned to Volanna and Olstan and said, "Since we have dealt with our pursuers, we no longer need to travel under cover of darkness. Let's stay at the inn tonight and ride on toward Lenshaw in the morning. My horse needs a shoe, and I can get it done here before we depart."

His two companions agreed, and they secured a single room at the inn. They all slept fully dressed, Volanna in the bed as Aradon and Olstan spread their blankets on the floor.

Once during the night Aradon awakened; something was crawling on his leg. He turned back his blanket and found a spider the size of his shoe heel. He scooped it up and pitched it out the window, then went back to sleep.

When morning came, the three travelers took their breakfast in the common room of the inn. As they finished, Aradon asked directions to the blacksmith of the village.

"We don't have a smith anymore," answered the innkeeper. "Brendal jailed him two months back, and the poor man died in prison, he did. His widow lives near the edge of town toward Lenshaw."

They found the shop, and Aradon bargained with the widow to let him fire up the forge and use her late husband's tools to shoe his horse. He borrowed brushes for Olstan to use in grooming and combing out the burs and grass from the manes and tails of their two newly acquired mounts.

As the two men went about their tasks, the widow came out to sit on a nearby bench with her granddaughter, a toddler of less than two years. The lonely woman wanted to talk, and the baby wanted to play. Volanna accommodated both as she sat on the bench beside them. Soon the woman was filling her ear with words that had been pent up for weeks with no receptacle to pour them into. And the baby, shy at first, quickly warmed to Volanna's smiles and "peeka-boos" and soon was climbing over and about her like a kitten with a mother cat. Dovey often glanced toward Aradon, thrilling to his strong profile, the glistening forge-light on his chest and shoulders, and the power in his arm as he pounded the orange metal into a shape that would fit his horse's hoof.

Aradon could not resist stealing several glances toward Dovey, his heart warming as he watched her smile and laugh at the toddler. More than once his glance met hers, and each time both blushed lightly and quickly looked away. Volanna scooped the child onto her lap and sang a silly rhyme as she bounced the giggling girl on her knees:

> *Jumping, hopping, bouncing, dancing,*
> *Sir Higity on his horsey prancing,*
> *Up and down over hills and streams,*
> *To seek the little lady of his naptime dreams.*

Aradon stopped beating the anvil and listened entranced by her warm, clear soprano voice. Hope began to rise again in his heart that he could find some way to win her for his own.

In an hour Aradon's horse was shod and he had cleaned the forge and put the tools back in order. As he finished, Olstan brought up the other two horses combed and gleaming. He remained mounted, holding Volanna's horse by the reins as Aradon gave the widow most of the money remaining in Brendal's purse, keeping only enough to purchase a meal and a room in Lenshaw.

The poor woman thanked him profusely and said, "Ye two make a most beauteous couple, ye do. I don't know that I've ever seen yer equals. And it's a beauty that has nought to do with your fine-formed bodies and wondrous faces, though fine and wondrous indeed they be. I can see beyond these things, I can—always could—in the way the child takes to the lass here and in yer generous ways, young sir, and in the way ye put yerself to yer work. Now, I can give ye nothin' proper for what ye've given me here in this bag, but I can give ye a bit of old woman's advice if ye're of a mind to take it."

She paused, and Volanna picked up her cue. "Yes, please tell us."

"Ye two genuinely love each other. I can see it in yer eyes and in yer hearts. But ye're shy of lettin' it show. Don't be so foolish. There'll come a time when one of ye no longer has the other, and then it'll be too late, and ye'll wish ye'd always said what was in yer heart while it was fresh and alive. Again, I thank ye, not only for the money—though the Master of the Universe knows it's needed enough—but for the mornin'. Ye've warmed a lonely woman's old heart. May yer home be warm, your children many, and your life together long and lovin'."

As the woman finished her blessing, Aradon blushed and fumbled for words as Volanna embraced her with tears, then hugged and kissed the child, who cried and pleaded to go with her. Aradon lifted her into the saddle and mounted his own horse, and the three travelers rode out of Hallifax toward Lenshaw, the last town before Corenham and a half-day away.

As they left the village, Olstan slapped his leg to get their attention. He pointed back toward Hallifax, pantomimed the gestures of the widow, pointed toward Aradon and Volanna, slowly brought his hands together, and nodded emphatically.

"What are you telling us, Olstan?" asked Volanna.

"It's pretty clear to me," said Aradon. By now he had learned to read the man's gestures fairly well. "He is affirming the words of the blacksmith's widow. He thinks we belong together."

Olstan confirmed Aradon's interpretation with vigorous nods and a huge grin, but Volanna merely looked solemnly ahead without response. Both grew quiet as they rode on, their minds sifting the nuggets from the words of the old woman. Dovey thought on them with sadness growing heavy upon her. Was it possible that the woman was right? That she could see in her heart a real love for Aradon? If it was true, it was a tragic truth, for it was a love they could never fulfill. She felt again, as she had felt many times since Maldor, a wrenching in her heart for Aradon, who was having to endure like an innocent Tantalus the nearness of a love he could never taste. She blamed herself for inflicting this anguish on him, though she knew it was more the work of fate than of her own will. And how else could she have escaped from Maldor?

Aradon, for his part, wondered at the woman's words. Could she have been right? Was Dovey indeed in love with him? If so, surely they could find a way to undo the marriage contract her father had made for her. He edged his horse toward hers.

"Uh, the blacksmith's widow seemed to think we, uh, belong together," he said.

"Yes," Volanna answered simply without looking at him.

"She, uh, she seemed to think that you, uh, that you . . . are in love with—"

"Aradon, we must not speak of this. I have told you that I am vowed to wed another, and nothing can alter that. Please forgive me for putting you through these last few days. You have risked your life for me—indeed, you almost gave it. But I can give you absolutely nothing in return. I am so sorry, Aradon. Your locket was my only hope to escape Maldor Castle, and I took advantage of you in using it to call you. I know now that I should have let myself rot away in that listing tower. It would have been better than the fate I ride to now, and better for you as well, as you could have got on with your life without enduring the proximity to the fruit you are forbidden to pluck. Can you ever forgive me?"

"Of course I can, Dovey. But surely there is something we can do to—"

"No, Aradon! There is nothing we can do. Nothing at all. Soon you will understand why. As we approach Corenham, I will tell you all."

They rode on in brooding silence, all three equally muted, one by nature and the two others by the weight of their thoughts. Shortly after midday, their road merged with the highway that would take them through Lenshaw to Corenham, and the number of travelers increased greatly. Volanna pulled her hood over her head for fear of being recognized in a village so close to the city. She explained to Aradon that there was a chill in the autumn air.

By midafternoon they arrived in Lenshaw, the largest of the villages on their journey. As they came to the square, Volanna looked about nervously and pulled the hood closer about her face. She saw approaching them a man whom she recognized, though she did not know his name. He was the village constable whom she had once seen talking with Balkert in the hallway outside Lord Aldemar's room in Morningstone. The constable was looking intently at her. She put her head down and pulled the hood tighter about her cheeks.

"Halt!" she heard him call. "You three there! Halt, I say!"

Aradon, Volanna, and Olstan drew rein as the constable and his guard rode up to them. "Tell me your names," he barked.

"I am Aradon, son of Bogarth, a blacksmith in Corenham. This is Dovey, a kitchenmaid at Morningstone, and the man on the other side of her is Olstan, who is mute, and also a servant at Morningstone."

At the introduction of Olstan the mute, a knowing look came over the constable's face. Like other village officials, he had received word that the princess was missing and that she might be in the company of a slow-witted mute and the man who had abducted both of them. "And what of the woman. Is she mute as well?"

"No sir," answered Volanna, keeping her face down and her head covered.

"Woman, I must ask you to remove your hood and show your face."

By now a crowd had gathered about the group, always curious

and ready for a show. Volanna could see no way out of complying, and slowly she raised her head and slipped off the hood, allowing her full, rich hair to billow from its confinement.

"It's the Princess Volanna!" cried someone standing nearby. Others repeated the name, and soon it was spread throughout the crowd.

"Your highness," said the constable, "it is my duty and my honor to rescue you from your abductor and return you to Morningstone."

"The Princess Volanna?" Aradon muttered, utterly shocked. He sat stunned and speechless in his saddle, staring open-mouthed at Dovey until the constable pointed to him and shouted to his guard, "Seize that man!"

Aradon quickly recovered his senses, turned his horse and galloped back down the road on which they had traveled. The soldier spurred his horse in pursuit, but the press of the crowd hampered him momentarily. On the open road Aradon urged his horse to a breakneck speed, and after rounding a bend, he left the highway and rode into Braegan Wood and wound his way into its heart. The pursuing soldier followed him into the edge of the forest but was loath to enter into its depths. He gave up the chase and returned to the village.

The strutting constable formed an ostentatious military escort, and with much fanfare, paraded the short distance from Lenshaw to Corenham and delivered the Princess Volanna to Prince Lomar at Morningstone Castle.

PART III

THE KING

CHAPTER TWENTY-EIGHT

THE GOLDEN KNIGHT

hen Aradon was convinced that he had eluded his pursuer, he slowed his horse to a walk. The day had turned cold, and the woods were filled with a heavy fog that separated the trees into planes of fading gray before him. Everything about him looked as bleak and colorless as the emptiness in his own heart. Bitterness rose within him. He felt betrayed. Why didn't the Princess Volanna tell him who she was when they first met instead of letting hope linger that love might grow between them? He told himself he would never have let himself fall for her had he known who she was, though in the depths of his heart, he knew better.

Now he had nothing to hope for. He was a fugitive and an outlaw, accused of abducting the future queen of the Seven Kingdoms. If the prophecy had him woven into its pattern, his thread was in danger of coming unraveled. It appeared that he was working against the prophecy, not to fulfill it. He was sure that Dovey—Princess Volanna (he would have to start thinking of her as such)—would defend him against the charge of abduction, but he was equally sure that Prince Lomar and Sir Stundal would never believe her, or if they did, would nevertheless act as if they did not to avenge themselves for their humiliation at the welcoming procession.

He plodded on aimlessly, head down, heedless of all about him until darkness began to fall. Though he cared little, he searched for shelter for the night and found a cleft at the base of a rocky ledge large enough for himself and his horse. He tethered the horse, removed the saddle from its back, and built a fire. He rolled a log near the fire and threw the saddle beside it, then sat down and began to rummage through his saddlebags, looking for his wallet of salt beef and cheese.

He pulled out the striped kerchief that Dovey—Princess Volanna—had used to bind the healing herb to his wounded arm. He sighed bitterly and laid it aside, then took out the Crown of Eden, still wrapped in the tapestry from Maldor. In the past few happy days with Dovey, he had so forgotten the Crown that he had not even mentioned it to her. He unwrapped it and looked at it again. The unearthly colors in the stone teased his eye, but in his gray mood, the Crown had no luster and the colors lost their magic. He wondered again what he should do with it now that it was unsafe to go into Corenham and give it to Lord Aldemar. No doubt the best plan was to seek out Father Verit and turn over the Crown to him—if he could find him, he thought bitterly. He rewrapped the Crown and threw a few more logs on the fire, then huddled down into his blanket with his back to the log and fell asleep.

Deep in the night something awakened him. He looked at the fire, which was blazing high. It should have burned low by now, he thought. He raised up on his elbow, looked across the fire, and saw there the huddled figure of a man, his face hidden in the shadows of the hood that covered his head. Aradon jumped up with sword in hand, ready to strike. The figure lifted the hood from its face and smiled at him. It was Father Verit warming two generous tankards of mead on the fire.

"What are you doing here?" Aradon asked. Then with an angry edge in his voice, he added, "Where were you when I brought Dovey—uh—the Princess Volanna to you? You promised that I would always find you when I needed you."

"I said you would always find me when you *needed* me, not merely when you wanted something from me."

"But I needed you," said Aradon. "That is, Volanna needed you. She was carrying a heavy burden and sought your help to relieve it."

"Everyone who seeks me finds me, Volanna as well as you. But

no one finds me when his or her only need is to make a difficult decision. I do not give answers to questions that are already answered.
Volanna was hoping to find a softer truth than the one she faced, but
in her heart, she knew there was no softer truth, and she didn't need
me to tell her that."

"Well, she doesn't need anything from you now," said Aradon,
bitterly. "In the spring or whenever the comet meets the star, she will
marry Prince Lomar and become our queen."

"I wouldn't be too sure of that," responded Verit. "From what I
hear, the princess has refused to marry the prince until the Crown of
Eden rests on his head. As a true servant of the prophecy, she has
insisted that all its terms be fulfilled before she carries out her part.
And apparently the Crown has not yet been found."

Aradon's heart leapt at Verit's words, and his resolve to turn over
the Crown to him weakened and collapsed. He would think more
about what Verit had just told him before deciding what to do with it.

"What do you want with me now?" he asked as he looked into
the fire. Knowing that he was now hiding the Crown from Verit, he
found it difficult to meet the man's eyes. "My questions are answered,
and I have no more to ask."

"I'm not here to answer questions. I came on a simple mission,
to supply you with a mundane need. You are now a homeless fugitive,
and I can provide you a warm shelter. Follow me." Father Verit led
Aradon deeper into the rocky cleft where he had made his camp until
they came to a heavy, wooden door set within the rock of the cliff. He
reached into his robe and handed Aradon a key. "Open it."

Aradon wondered at the strangeness of the door, emblazoned
with runes he did not understand and skillfully carved with several
intricate, bas relief figures of a mounted knight, apparently performing feats of swordsmanship and rescuing men and women flee-
ing from a green snake and a black raven with yellow eyes. In each
of the images of the knight, his armor was gilded. The door was fitted perfectly into a precisely carved opening in the stone of the cliff.
After staring for a long moment, Aradon inserted the key and
opened it. Father Verit ushered him into a cozy little room, square
and plumb, hewn out of the rock and furnished with two beds, a

table, and a fireplace already glowing with an inviting fire. On one wall hung a dark, maroon curtain.

"Who lives here?" asked Aradon.

"As of tonight, you do," replied Verit.

"I don't understand. Who prepared this place and why?"

"It was prepared for you," Verit answered.

"Then why does it have two beds? And how could you have known I was coming?"

"You said you had no more questions. I will hold you to your word," said Verit. "In a moment I must leave, but first I want you to look behind that curtain."

Aradon went to the curtain and opened it. Immediately he jumped back and drew his sword. Standing in a recess in the wall facing him was the golden-armored knight he had seen in the forest.

"You're a little itchy with that sword," said Verit, "but you can put it up. The armor is empty."

Aradon calmed his pounding heart and peeked inside the visor.

"Your trust in me is most gratifying," said Verit with a twinkle in his eye. "That armor looks to be about your size. Why don't you try it on?"

Aradon looked on the armor with wonder. "This is the armor of the golden knight who led me to you. Where is he? What is his armor doing here? Is this his home?"

"No more questions, remember?" said Verit. "However, I will tell you that there is no golden knight."

"But there is! I saw him with my own eyes. He led me to you the day I first met you."

"You led yourself to me. What you saw as a golden knight was merely a reflection of your own destiny."

"You mean, what I saw was a vision?"

"You may call it that, I suppose. This armor has not been worn in generations. If you have need of it, you may as well use it. That is, if it fits you. Quickly, try it on. I must go soon."

With Verit's help Aradon got himself into the entire suit of armor, and to his amazement it fit perfectly in every detail. He took it off again and returned it to the closet, then turned to Verit with another question on his lips. But Verit was gone.

Aradon ran out of the room and through the cleft, calling Verit's name as he ran, but his voice merely echoed off the narrow walls of the chasm. As he reached the place where he had camped, he stopped short and his eyes went wide. Standing before him was a magnificent white charger, huge and sleek and heavily muscled. The horse's mane was long and full, its eyes dark and limpid. It was the most beautiful animal Aradon had ever seen. Slowly he approached the horse. It responded to him by gently nodding its elegant head, tossing its mane about its neck like white-capped waves, just as Aradon remembered the horse of the golden knight doing when he saw it in the forest. Aradon held out his hand, and the horse nuzzled it, swishing it's full tail all the while. He looked around for his chestnut stallion, but it was nowhere to be seen. Somehow Aradon knew that he need not search for it or worry about its well-being. There was no doubt in his mind that Father Verit had taken care of everything.

ℒ

Volanna often sat by the window of her room in Lord Aldemar's manor, gazing out into the bare, winter gray trees of Braegan Wood. When she was returned to Corenham after her abduction, she had begged Lord Aldemar to let her live at his estate until the wedding, and he had gladly acceded to her request. Lady Aldemar was delighted with the arrangement.

Volanna wondered if Aradon was still in the forest and how he was surviving the winter. She was glad that she had sent Olstan to him. The idea had come to her as the pompous constable had escorted them to Morningstone. She had veered her horse close to Olstan's and asked him, whispering, if he would be willing to go into Braegan Wood, find Aradon, and help him through the winter. He had readily agreed, and as the constable's parade entered the crowded streets of Corenham, Olstan had slipped away. She was sure that with his uncanny nose for direction and tracking, he had somehow found his way to Aradon. It gave her comfort to know that Aradon was not alone. She felt sure that between Olstan's forest knowledge and Aradon's strength and quick mind, they would find a way to survive. She tried not to think of Aradon more than she would any other friend, but she did not succeed. His fine image stole into her mind continually, whether waking or sleeping, and she spent more time than she would have admitted even to Kalley looking out on the gray woods, wondering what he was doing and how he was faring.

•

Ansel arose before sunup as usual to prepare her honeycakes for the day's trade. Marcie remained in bed, which was not at all usual, and when Ansel called her a third time to get up, Marcie replied, "I don't feel so good, Mother. The smell of honeycakes makes me sick to my stomach."

"What in the king's realm has been wrong with you lately?" asked Ansel. "You used to be up with the roosters every mornin', doin' your share of the work right alongside of me. But here for the past week I've had to do all the bakin' and load the cart by myself."

Marcie began to sob. "I'm with child, Mother."

Ansel stopped her work and stamped her foot in anger. She cursed Stundal and men in general for their unfair advantage over women. "Why in thunder the creator made them so they can force us for their own pleasure, then leave us to bear all the pain, I'll never know. But I tell you, he's got a lot to answer for."

"What am I goin' to do?" asked Marcie, still crying.

"You stay here today. I will think of somethin'."

Ansel left the cottage grumbling and cursing as she pushed the cart into the street alone. By the time she returned in the evening, a plan had taken shape in her mind. After she unloaded the cart, she went to Marcie's bed and sat down beside her.

"Marcie, I want you to listen to me. I've come up with the perfect way to cover up your problem. I've got a plan that's sure to push Aradon into marrying you."

Marcie looked at Ansel as if her mind had flown. "Mother, you've spent too much time down at the Thirsty Eagle. You know good and well that Aradon hasn't showed his face in Corenham since Balkert put a price on his head. Even if he was here, it wouldn't work. We tried this already, remember? That's what got me into this trouble."

"I know, I know, but you just hear me out. We know that Aradon has sneaked home at least once since he disappeared, and he's sure to do it again. We must watch his house careful-like, to know when he comes and be ready. Besides, my plan is different this time. You won't have to go bathin' in the stream again."

"Well, I'm mighty glad of that, it bein' winter and all."

Ansel explained her entire scheme to Marcie, who looked increasingly troubled as she listened. "I don't like this at all, Mother. I don't want to do it. As much as I crave to have Aradon, I'm not wantin' to trap him into it. He would be hatin' me every time he looked at me, and neither of us would ever be happy."

"Oh, he'd get over it," said Ansel. "Besides, that boy doesn't know what he wants right now. The princess has turned his head, or maybe he has turned hers, but we all know he can't have the princess. What better choice has he got than you? We'll just be doin' the boy a favor by helpin' him make up his mind."

For a while Marcie persisted in her refusal to take any part in the plan, but in the end, Ansel prevailed. They set up a system of regular evening spying on Bogarth's cottage so they would be ready to act when Aradon returned. But the months passed, and they saw no sign of him. Marcie's belly grew larger, and she became the butt of jokes and derision flung at her by the men on her route who bought her honeycakes. Ansel angrily slung the insults back at the men, but Marcie bore them quietly and patiently, waiting for Aradon's return, hoping against all reason that in spite of the trap they were setting for him, somehow his heart would turn toward her.

ℒ♥

Almost five months after Princess Volanna's return, Lord Aldemar received an envoy from Sothemer, a village in southern Meridan.

"You have no idea how fortunate we are to be here," said the spokesman. "Indeed, we owe our lives to an unnamed knight who appeared from nowhere and disappeared in the same fashion."

"I want to hear the story of it," said Aldemar with obvious interest. "Please tell me all that happened."

"Well, after we had been long on the road, a band of six highwaymen, all armed with swords and longbows, came out of the woods and attacked us. As you can see, we are only three in number, and the attack caught us by surprise. The thieves quickly got the best of us and were making off with our money and all our goods they could carry, when out of the woods galloped a large knight clad in armor that gleamed like gold in the sunlight. The knight attacked the highwaymen with a fury. He killed three of them and unhorsed the others, who scattered into the woods, one wounded grievously. The knight rounded up the thieves' horses and brought them to us so we could retrieve our money and goods, then he simply rode off into the woods with no demand for reward. And we never saw him again."

"Most interesting," said Lord Aldemar. The story was much like many others he had heard in the months since Volanna's return. The village of Rokestrand had been terrorized by a new government that had usurped the authority of the rightful mayor. Aldemar was sure the mutiny had been instigated by Balkert. After the people had endured a short reign of cruelty and overtaxation, a knight in golden armor with his squire in attendance, had run the usurpers out of town and redistributed to the poverty-stricken people the money from the village treasury. Then he had ridden away without asking for reward or identifying himself.

A shepherd near Lewenham had told Aldemar of his sheep being stolen at night by a band of raiders. The next day they were returned by this same golden knight and his squire, and again they rode away without leaving their names. At the New Year's tournament in Newfrith, a golden-armored knight had entered the contest and won the championship. He received the victor's purse without removing his helmet or uttering a word, then rode away without identifying himself.

At the planting festival in Parandor, seven maidens had been abducted by a dozen ruffians who rode out of the woods and captured them just as the evening dance ended. The women had returned the next morning on foot, escorted by a silent knight in golden armor attended by his equally silent squire. The women reported that the knight and his armored squire had routed their abductors, leaving three dead and they didn't know how many wounded. After the knight and his squire had seen the women safely to the edge of the village, they turned and without a word, rode into the forest.

There were many other such stories, all told for the truth, but growing so with each telling that the feats of heroism took on mythical proportions and the line between truth and fancy became blurred beyond recovery. The Golden Knight was fast becoming a folk hero to the people of Meridan.

Aldemar often wondered at the golden knight's identity but had no way of discovering it. Whoever he was, he wished the man well and prayed for thirty more like him: the grip of Balkert and Stundal was tightening on Meridan in spite of Aldemar's efforts to maintain justice.

Where was Aradon? Aldemar did not know. He was probably hiding in Braegan Wood, or perhaps he had perished there. Word had come to him from Sir Hardwicke over two months ago that Aradon had taken temporary leave from training but had never returned. When the constable had returned Princess Volanna to Morningstone, she had told Aldemar that Aradon had done to rescue her and conduct her safely back to Morningstone.

Aldemar had believed her affirmation of Aradon's innocence in the abduction, but Prince Lomar, Balkert, and Stundal had chosen not to do so. Without consulting Aldemar, they had declared Aradon an outlaw and posted a reward for his capture. Aldemar had been livid when he learned of it and had sent out word to rescind the posting immediately. But he knew that his influence extended little past Corenham these days, and that in the outlying villages Aradon was still posted as a fugitive from justice with a price on his head.

It was now early spring, and it was obvious even to the naked eye that the golden comet in the nighttime sky would soon converge with its mate, the silver star. The royal astronomer had calculated that the stars would meet in exactly eleven days. Lord Aldemar had preparations well underway for the three-day, kingdom-wide celebration. Each day was to feature its own major event. The annual Seven Kingdoms jousting tournament would be held on the first day, followed by a grand feast. The coronation of Prince Lomar as the new king of Meridan would be held on the second day, followed by another feast; and the wedding of the new king to the princess would occur on the third day, followed by a final grand feast. The servants of Morningstone were again bustling about getting animals and fowl made ready for slaughter and cleaning the castle and grounds. Carpenters went out to the tournament amphitheater and made repairs to the list and stands and painted them in bright blue and red.

Lord Aldemar was pleased with the general progress of the preparations, but he was greatly concerned that the Crown of Eden was still missing. The prophecy assumed the presence of the Crown when the stars met, and it made no provision for what should be done if it were not found. As a servant of the prophecy, Aldemar saw no other course of action than to proceed with all plans as if the Crown were present. If the Crown did not appear, it would mean either that the prophecy was invalid or that King Tallis had misinterpreted the meaning of it.

Aldemar was apprehensive about the next fortnight. He felt sure that Prince Lomar would claim the throne, Crown or no crown. No doubt the sly Balkert had plans already in place to enforce the coronation. And although Princess Volanna had asserted vehemently that she would not marry Lomar until the Crown rested on his head, Aldemar was equally sure that Lomar had some plan in place to force her into the wedding as well. Aldemar was committed to protecting the princess from such coercion, but he knew that his power in the kingdom was slipping each day. His failure to win approval from the Hall of Knights of his three most recent candidates for knighthood made this slippage all too clear to him.

Aldemar had received word that all the kings of the Seven Kingdoms would be attending the three days of events, including Princess Volanna's father, King Tallis of Valomar. Aldemar had taken the precaution of communicating his fears to King Tallis weeks ago. He had advised his friend to bring a large retinue of Valomar's knights to defend his daughter against a possible forced marriage if the Crown were not found.

"Would that we had a hundred Golden Knights," sighed the exhausted Aldemar as he mounted his horse, made his way across Corenham to his home, and sank wearily into his bed.

counsel in the forest

Olstan lowered the golden-colored helm over Aradon's head and fastened its connections to the breastplate. Aradon raised the visor and asked, "Are the horses ready?" Olstan nodded. "Let's go, then." Olstan picked up the pouch of money from the bed, Aradon's winnings from the tournament in Newfrith, and tied it to his belt. "You say you have identified three homes where this money is needed?" Olstan nodded again. The two men left their cave home, mounted their horses, and rode out into the gray woods, shrouded as on almost every morning in a dense fog.

Olstan had come to the cave only a few days after Father Verit had led Aradon to it. How he found the cave, Aradon did not know. The silent man had made it known by signs that he had come to serve Aradon and did not intend to leave. Aradon had been grateful to have him, and he had become more than just an extremely useful and diligent servant; he was now a loyal friend as well. In his muteness Olstan had developed an effective set of hand signs that no one had ever bothered to learn, but Aradon learned them quickly and could now understand him almost as well as if he could speak. Soon after settling in, Olstan had shaved and groomed himself, and Aradon was surprised to find that he was much younger than he had thought, perhaps no older than Aradon himself.

As the two men rode through the woods, Aradon's thoughts were occupied by the approaching convergence of the two stars and by the

Crown of Eden, which he kept hidden behind the armor in his cave. He knew the converging stars to be the prophetic sign for the coronation of Prince Lomar and his wedding to Princess Volanna, but he also knew from what Father Verit had told him that Volanna would not consent to marry Lomar until the Crown of Eden rested upon his head.

What should he do with the Crown? It was a persistent question, and he wrestled with it often. He knew he should have given it to Father Verit or should find a way to return it to Lord Aldemar. Lomar was the rightful king-to-be, the son of Alfron and heir to Perivale's empire, and the Crown belonged on his head. But in his questing about the kingdom, Aradon had seen enough of Lomar's tyranny to know that his reign would bleed the life from Meridan and leave its people drained of hope. He would be doing the country a great favor if he buried the Crown and let Meridan's officials stew over what to do when the stars converged and the Crown remained missing. Maybe the prophecy meant for the Crown to be found by a later, more benevolent monarch.

If he buried the Crown, he would also save Princess Volanna from a miserable marriage. Aradon now understood the sorrow she had never fully expressed to him about her future. In those rare, brief moments when he dared explore the depths of his heart, he knew that his true motive for withholding the Crown was not so much his concern for Meridan as his love for Volanna.

At night his conscience broke free of the chains in which he bound it during the day and prodded him unmercifully for harboring the Crown in spite of its rightful ownership and its place in the prophecy. He knew that keeping it compromised his loyalty to the kingdom, and he was appalled at himself for placing his own selfish hopes above his honor. He now understood why Morgultha was willing to let her hand be severed from her body rather than release the Crown from her grasp. He was not sure that he could let it go either. He tried to tell himself that his reasons were different, but at night as he writhed on his bed, he knew they were the same. As long as he held the Crown, he could continue to hope for the one thing he wanted most in the world. As long as he held the Crown, there would be no wedding. Volanna would remain free, and he could persist in his quest to find a way to win her as his own.

Why did he keep fooling himself? Despite his pretensions to knighthood, he was still nothing more than a simple blacksmith, and she was the daughter of a great king and about to become queen of an empire. The sooner he shut Volanna out of his thoughts, the better. In fact, he should have forgotten her long before now. He must quit thinking of her. But he knew that he might just as well ask himself to stop breathing.

Aradon often longed to speak with his father about these matters that troubled his mind, and indeed he had slipped home to Corenham once under cover of night, but there had been little time for such talk. He thought he must risk another trip soon.

Aradon and Olstan had ridden several miles in silence when Olstan put his hand on Aradon's arm and motioned him to stop. Olstan cupped a hand to his ear, and they both listened. They heard what seemed to be the sound of a child crying—or perhaps trying hard not to cry. Olstan pointed toward a clump of bushes near a knotty oak tree, and they rode toward it. Olstan dismounted and parted the branches to reveal a little girl, about seven or eight years old, clad in gray woolen rags and shivering with cold and fright. She looked up at Aradon, mounted high above her on his huge charger, his face hidden and his armor fearful and daunting. Her eyes went wide with terror, and she started to moan.

Aradon raised his visor, a thing he never did, and smiled at the girl. "Don't be afraid, my lady. We will do you no harm. Will you be so good as to tell me your name?"

The girl said nothing but remained curled beneath the bush, shivering.

"You are cold, my lady. Olstan, please get the blanket from your bag, and while you're about it, the salt beef as well. Are you hungry, little one?"

The girl did not speak, but Aradon noticed that the mention of food brightened her eyes, and the look of fear began to fade from her face. "Wrap the blanket about her and hand her to me, Olstan, then cut her a slice of the salt beef."

With a cry of fear, the girl tried to get up and start running, but Olstan wrapped her in the blanket and handed her to Aradon, who held her close and said with a playful lilt in his voice, "You needn't fear me, my lady. As you can see, I'm a golden knight on a white horse, riding out on my constant quest to rescue fair damsels in distress. You are certainly a fair damsel, and if I'm not mistaken, you seem to be in distress. Would you be so kind as to bestow your unmerited favor upon this unworthy knight and allow him the humble pleasure of serving you with his life in all honor?"

All fear left the girl's face as she looked up at Aradon's gentle smile, which she began to reflect in her own face. "Olstan, where is that salt beef?" Olstan handed the morsel to the girl, and forgetting all else, she began to chew voraciously at it.

"Now, that I have earned your favor, perhaps you will reward me with your name," said Aradon.

"Mevan," said the girl.

"A most fitting name for such a beautiful lady. Mevan, will you be so kind as to tell me what you are doing in these dark woods?"

"I . . . I got lost."

"Lost from where? No one lives in this forest. Were you separated from your parents as they traveled through?"

Mevan shook her head.

"Then did you wander into the forest?"

Again Mevan shook her head.

"Where do you live, my lady?"

The little girl huddled into the blanket and would not look at Aradon.

"You must tell me where you live, Mevan. I will take you home."

She began to cry. "I'm not supposed to tell."

"Why can't you tell me where you live?"

"My father told me not to. No one is supposed to know."

"When did you wander away from home?

"This mornin'. We hadn't any breakfast, and I was lookin' for something to eat. Yesterday I heard my father tell about deer eatin' some bark from a tree, and I thought if I could find a tree like that, I wouldn't be hungry anymore."

"I see. Well, if you left your home afoot this morning, it can't be too far from here. We will find it. My friend Olstan here can find a button in a corn bin, can't you Olstan." The silent man smiled at the girl and nodded. "Lead the way, Olstan."

Olstan looked about the earth for footprints or other signs that might show where the girl had walked. Soon he mounted his horse and headed up a narrow trail through the trees. Aradon followed him, carrying Mevan huddled deep in the blanket. After about ten minutes Olstan stopped and motioned for Aradon to do the same. They looked ahead into the fog and saw emerging from it a small group of walking men, gray silhouettes at first that took on more explicit form as they came toward the mounted pair. Aradon lowered his visor. Soon the walking men, four in number, saw the two mounted ones and stopped short. They drew their weapons, which included a sword, a hoe, and two axes, and waited tense and crouched as Olstan and Aradon rode toward them.

"Rest easy, men," called Aradon. "I mean you no harm. What brings you into the forest?"

The men were clothed in tatters. All were thin except for one, who was quite tall and somewhat stocky in build. Their hoods were pulled closely around their heads against the cold. Their breath formed clouds in front of their faces, as if their lungs were expelling the fog they had breathed as they came through the woods. One of them stepped forward from the rest. His eyes were opened wide and rimmed with red, giving his face a look of hopeless desperation. "We be lookin' for a little girl."

"What is her name?" asked Aradon.

"I can't see that her name is any business of yours," said the man.

"Is she your daughter then?"

"Aye, that she is. And if you've done her harm, I'll see you in the grave in spite of your big horse and fine armor."

"Mevan," Aradon whispered to the girl, "look at this man and tell me if he is your father."

Cautiously she peered over the edge of the blanket, and when she saw the man, she cried out with joy. "Father, it is you! I couldn't find my way back home, and the nice knight, he—"

"Let that girl go this instant!" shouted the man as he rushed toward Aradon, ax in hand.

"Dunstan, stop! This man is not an enemy," bellowed the large man behind him. But Dunstan did not hear.

Aradon handed Mevan to Olstan and leapt from his horse, sword in hand. As Dunstan swung his ax at him, Aradon caught the handle on his own blade, and with a twist of his wrist, flipped it from the man's grasp. The man behind Dunstan ran up beside him and cried, "Dunstan, you fool. Don't you know who this is?" Dunstan rubbed his numbed hand and gaped without comprehension. "Look at his armor. Can't you see that he is the Golden Knight?"

Aradon recognized the voice of the big man, but he said nothing as he took the girl from Olstan and carried her to her father. "I believe this is the treasure you've been searching for," he said as Dunstan took her and clasped her in his arms.

"Forgive me, sir," said Dunstan. "I suppose I've been made stupid by worry. I thank ye for my daughter."

"No apology is needed," said Aradon as he handed the man his ax. "It was an honor to escort the young lady back to you. May I ask what you are doing so deep in Braegan Woods?"

The men looked at each other in silence. Then the big man said, "Sir, I would like a word with you, private-like."

Aradon agreed, and the big man sent the others back into the woods from whence they came. Dunstan clutched his daughter as if he would press her inside his breast as she filled his ear with the tale of her rescue by the famous Golden Knight, a tale that she lived to tell to her grandchildren.

When the fog had absorbed his companions, the man turned to Aradon and said, "I know who you are. I knew the moment you disarmed Dunstan. Only two men in the Seven Kingdoms know that little trick, and the other is Sir Denmore. You are too large for Denmore, and your voice confirms my suspicions. You are Aradon the blacksmith."

Aradon raised his visor and grinned at Llewenthane. "And I knew you the moment you bellowed at your friend. Who could forget that bullhorn voice?"

The two men embraced. Llewenthane held Aradon at arm's length, shook his head in wonder, and laughed. "So *you* are the notorious Golden Knight. I have long wondered who he was, but I never guessed him to be you. I thought you were still wallowing in the dirt at Hardwicke's feet." Then his face took on a look of intense gravity. "I've been hoping for an opportunity to speak to you—that is, to the Golden Knight. I have much to say. We must find a place where we can talk."

Aradon introduced Llewenthane to Olstan and explained Olstan's silence. Then they found a sheltered place between two great oaks and built a fire. Aradon removed his helmet as Olstan got a skin of mead and two small tankards from his pack. He poured the tankards full, heated them on the fire, and gave one to each of the men. They rolled a stone and a log up to the fire, where they sat and began sipping the mead. Aradon shared his tankard with Olstan.

"So, tell me how you came to be the Golden Knight?" asked Llewenthane.

"It's a long story, and some of it I can't tell," replied Aradon, "but to make it short, I was outlawed by Prince Lomar and Sir Stundal, and shortly afterward an old friend gave me this armor and the horse. Since I cannot show my face in Corenham, I've been living in Braegan Wood, wandering about the country doing all I can to justify the price on my head. And how about yourself? I'm surprised to see you here. I thought you, Anffwyn, and Unther were to be knighted before now."

"Yes, we were to have been," sighed Llewenthane. "We went through the purification ritual and the all-night vigil, after which Lord Aldemar presented us to the Hall for confirmation. But to the surprise of everyone, Sir Stundal objected. When Aldemar asked for grounds, he gave none and seemed unconcerned about it. And the reason soon became apparent. He already had enough knights lined up behind him to stop any new nominations by Lord Aldemar. Sir Benidah, Sir Fentamore, and Sir Widmont have got some kind of hold on the Hall, and most of the other knights are afraid to cross them. Except for Sir Denmore and Sir Eanor, who defended us loudly and strongly, but to no avail." Llewenthane paused and stared into the fire for a long moment before he continued.

"So I returned home and married my Eleanorre, figuring to use my warrior skills doing the sort of thing you've been doing around the countryside. But before two months were out, we had a wee one on the way, and I had to drop all such plans. I couldn't be running all over the kingdom while my wife was great with child, so I started working my late father's farm near Farandale.

"We were doing well enough. Then one day I loaded up my cart and went into Leverton to do some trading. I left Eleanorre with my mother in our cottage. When I returned, my cottage was burned, my mother dead, and my wife missing. My neighbors were gathered around the smoking ruins of my home, and when I rode up they told me that Sir Brendal, that renegade from Valomar, had been there with six mounted soldiers. They had ridden straight to my cottage, broken down the door, and taken my wife. The villagers had seen this sort of thing enough to know what they were doing. Lomar has his men over the entire kingdom seeking out beautiful women, which they bring to him for sometimes no more than a night or two before he puts them out of the castle to find their way back home on their own. And my Eleanorre is as fair as a summer sky. When my mother tried to fight them off, they threw her against the wall so hard that she died on the spot." Llewenthane's eyes grew moist, and he paused as Olstan refilled his tankard. He took a deep draught and continued in a husky voice.

"My neighbors gathered what weapons they could and went with me in pursuit. We found the murderers that night, camped in a woods toward Rallenstone. Brendal was not with them. We fell on the men, killed two, and the others escaped into the woods. Eleanorre was not harmed, though she was badly frightened. She learned from the talk of the men around the fire that none dare defile the women they bring to Prince Lomar. Apparently it was done once, and Lomar had the man eunuchized. Eleanorre and I knew we could not return home, so we parted from our friends with many heartfelt thanks for their help and escaped to Braegan Woods, where we knew no one would dare seek us out.

"We found a cave in the forest and made do for a time. But we had a few needs the forest could not supply and I had a little money, so I made a trip to Kemstead. At breakfast in the inn there, I heard what had happened to my neighbors. Brendal's interrogators had coerced someone into telling just which of them had helped me rescue my wife, and those families were all arrested and jailed, some twenty souls all told. Well, I couldn't sit by and let that happen. I'll shorten the story and spare you the details of how I did it, but I went back to Farandale under cover of night, freed my friends, and brought them into Braegan Wood. We've been here some three months now. We've built a few rude huts, and we're surviving the winter, though it's hard enough and hunger is our constant companion. We've all got a price on our heads like you, Aradon. But since no one ventures into Braegan Wood, we seem safe for the while, though we can't live this way for long."

"You needn't live this way anymore at all," said Aradon. "Brendal has been sent to prison at Morningstone. Your friends can return to their homes."

"When did this happen?" asked Llewenthane in surprise.

"Two months back—about a month after your friends came into the woods."

"That is good news," said Llewenthane, "very good news indeed! I would run back to my camp right now and tell them of it, but my main purpose in wanting to speak with you was not to tell you my own story. Ever since I first heard of your exploits among the villages, I've had a thought in my mind, and I'm bound to tell you about it if you'll sit to listen."

"Say on, friend," said Aradon. "I'm a fugitive too, and there's no one waiting for me at home."

Llewenthane started to speak but hesitated and looked hard at Olstan.

"Have no fear to speak in Olstan's presence," said Aradon. "He is as loyal and trustworthy as your own right hand. He has saved my life more than once, and at times it has almost cost him his own."

Llewenthane nodded, took a long draught from his tankard, and began to speak his heart. "I don't need to tell you that Meridan is coming under the grip of a tyrant such as this kingdom has never seen. Lomar's only interest is in what makes him feel good at the moment, and he has surrounded himself with ambitious men without human feeling whose cruelty knows no limits, men who are willing to find the right scratch for all his itches. Men like Balkert and Stundal and their hatchet man, Brendal, are feeding Lomar's lusts in exchange for power, and he isn't even king yet. Think what it will be like when he's crowned.

"The people of Meridan are desperate for help. You have come among them at just the right time to give many of them just the kind of help they needed, and as a result you are now the people's hero. They adore you. The very mention of the Golden Knight lifts the people's spirits and gives them hope. You are already a legend in Meridan and a tower of strength even to those who have never seen you or benefited directly from your bold actions. Now, what I'm about to say may seem outlandish to you, Aradon, but I beg you to hear me out. Lomar must not become king. He must be prevented. And you can do it. We can do it. All it takes is—"

"There is no way we can—"

"No, hear me out, Aradon. Just listen for a moment. It can be done. You can be the next king yourself. The people will—"

"Llewenthane, this is preposterous! I'm a blacksmith, remember? I know nothing of kingcraft, of the circles kings move in, or even of battles and strategies and treaties. I am not the kind of stuff kings are made of. The crown would not fit my hard blacksmith's head. And I don't want to be a king. Forget this, Llewenthane. You're talking to the wrong man. Go find another."

"There is no other. We can depose Lomar only if we present a new king the people will love and rally behind. You are that man. You have no idea how much the people love you, Aradon. It's not a matter of knowing statecraft, or battles, or treaties, or even of being a good warrior—though you sell yourself short there. It's a matter of your heart. You have given yourself to the people. You love them and they know it. The people of Meridan will follow you like sheep follow a shepherd. We can make this happen, and it won't be that hard to do."

Aradon shook his head. "You're forgetting the prophecy. The prophecy has named the son of Alfron as heir to the throne, and that is Prince Lomar. We mere mortals cannot pit ourselves against a hundred-twenty-year-old prophecy."

"Aradon, do you know the words of this prophecy?"

"Of course. Or, at least, I have known them. I probably couldn't recite them quite accurately."

"Then you know how it's all vague and cryptic and veiled, hidden in obscure words with uncertain meanings. How anyone could know exactly what it means is beyond me. King Alfron, Lord Aldemar, and just about everyone else jumped onto the cart when King Tallis first interpreted the prophecy twenty years ago, but Tallis could have been wrong. The philosopher king may be a genius, but he's not infallible. For all we know he looked at those stars and missed the meaning of them by half the sky. The true meaning of the prophecy may be waiting to be revealed not in words but by actions. Maybe your actions are just what the prophecy is waiting for, Aradon."

Aradon felt a flutter in his belly as he thought of Father Verit's words that he would play a part in fulfilling the prophecy and of the Crown of Eden itself, hidden in his cave. But still, the idea was preposterous. "Llewenthane, think how presumptuous it would be for me, a blacksmith's apprentice, to jump up and claim the throne of the Seven Kingdoms. It would be beyond silly for me to think that I should be king."

"Maybe that would be true if it were your own idea. But you're not the one thinking it; the people are. We in our little camp hear it all the time when we go into the villages for bartering. In every inn, every tavern, every shop, every street corner, in one way or another we hear people saying, 'We would that we had a king like the Golden Knight.' If you craved the crown, I would be uneasy about you having it. The kind of people who want crowns are least fit to wear them. You are what the people want and what they need."

Aradon got up from the stone and began to pace about the fire. "You don't realize the gravity of the thing you're suggesting. For someone to move against the throne of Meridan would be rebellion and treason."

"Rebellion against what? Treason against whom?"

"Rebellion and treason against Meridan and her rightly appointed and ordained government."

"This would not be a rebellion against Meridan; it would be a rescue of Meridan from a tyrant who will strangle her. You would not be committing treason against your kingdom; you would be liberating her from what is sure to be—has already begun to be—an oppressive reign. Does one have to accept oppression forever? Are existing governments ordained to remain in place perpetually simply because they exist? Surely not. Besides, you've already violated your own argument. You have taken up your sword against the kingdom with your exploits about the villages, undoing 'rightly appointed governments' right and left."

"That is not so," said Aradon. "The men I've deposed were not rightly appointed. They had usurped men rightly appointed by Lord Aldemar. Brendal and his men were the usurpers. But Lomar is the rightful heir to the throne, and it would be wrong to usurp his crown."

"Surely it is wrong to let evil go unchecked when you have the power to stop it. You know that Lomar is an evil man, and when he comes to the throne, the evil we now see will grow into an unthinkable tyranny. You know that is true, Aradon. How can you think it is wrong to stop this evil before it is born?"

"It's not just my own thinking that stops me. If patriots of high honor like Lord Aldemar, King Tallis, and Sir Denmore support the succession of Lomar, who am I to think I know better?"

"These are indeed men of honor. Their faith is commendable. But on this issue, they are simply mistaken. Look at what is happening in the villages, at the wrongs you have righted yourself. The dogged faith of these fine and honorable men is about to entrench these wrongs into the very soil of the land. They are mistaken, Aradon. They are simply mistaken. It may not matter in Corenham, but the people of the villages have a dark future ahead if Lomar is crowned. It is hard for me to understand why men such as these would keep defending Lomar."

"They are not defending Lomar as such. In a sense, they are not even defending Meridan. They are defending a principle of law based on truth, without which there could be no Meridan worth living in. And I fear they would defend that principle to the death, which is another reason I would not usurp the throne. I would not have men such as these harmed or killed."

"Oh, they would not be harmed," said Llewenthane. We could easily plan a coup that would leave them safe and unscathed."

"That may well be true," said Aradon, "but it does not justify my taking matters into my own hands as if I thought myself heaven's gift to the kingdom. The entire idea is outrageous—that a blacksmith's apprentice would decide he is the right man to depose the dynasty of Perivale. It's not right, Llewenthane."

"Aradon, you've got to quit thinking of yourself. Even your humility has in it a sort of backhanded selfishness. You have the key to prevent tyranny against the thousands of innocent souls in Meridan, and you won't use it because of what you think of yourself. Quit thinking of its effect on you, and start thinking about the needs of this kingdom, man! Remember, this idea was not born in your own mind; it grew from the collective minds of the people of Meridan. Who are you to gainsay them?"

"The crux of the matter is not whether I gainsay the people, or even King Tallis and Lord Aldemar. The question is, What is right? Surely it is not right for any citizen to take it into his own hands to upset the ordained powers that be. If every man or woman assumed that right, the result would be chaos and anarchy, with every man thinking he is a law unto himself, answerable to no one else, with rights that cannot be limited by the needs and wants of others."

"Sometimes it is right to upset the ordained powers. Think of Moses undermining the power of Egypt and Joshua overthrowing the cities in Canaan."

"Those men were acting under the hand of the Master of the Universe. I have received no such orders," said Aradon.

"How do you know? Do you think he always spoke to them in an audible voice? Are you sure he is not speaking to you right now through my voice, through the voices of the people of Meridan, and perhaps through others we don't even know about?"

Aradon's stomach fluttered once more as he thought again of Verit's prophecy about him and the fact that the Crown was in his possession. Could these things be voices he should heed? Seeing Aradon's silence, Llewenthane thought he was making headway with him and pressed on. "For the sake of argument, I'll grant that it could be considered wrong to move against the throne of the kingdom. But you know that sometimes a little wrong must be done so that a greater good may be accomplished. Sometimes you must slog through a little mud to get to the higher ground. Sometimes a rigid uprightness that insists by faith that things will ultimately just fall into place is a blind coward's way out."

"No, Llewenthane," Aradon answered firmly. "When you break the law for the sake of a greater good, you lose your grounds for doing the greater good. If good means anything at all, it must mean the same thing in the lesser instances as in the greater. You can't erect anything solid if you break the stones you must build with."

Llewenthane stood and shook his head in frustration. "You disappoint me, Aradon. You are the only hope the people have, and if you refuse to lead them, they have nowhere else to turn." He pulled his cloak about him and raised his hood over his red hair. "But I'll not give up hope yet, nor will I take your 'no' as a final answer. As Lomar's evil spreads around us, you may come to your senses and see the wisdom of my words. You think on it, Aradon, and meet me again at this same place in seven days. Will you promise me that?"

Aradon was silent for a moment. "Very well. If you wish it, I will meet you here again in seven days. But I feel sure it will be a futile meeting. I cannot see any reason to expect that I will change my mind."

"For now that is good enough. All I ask is that you think on it. We are desperate, Aradon. We have no other hope."

"Do you plan to enter the Seven Kingdoms Tournament?" asked Aradon.

"No, it would not yet be safe. Brendal may be put away, but I cannot be sure that we are not still outlawed. It little behooves me to put myself at risk for no good reason while my Eleanorre is with child. I go now, Golden Knight." The two men clasped each other's arms, then Llewenthane turned and strode swiftly away. Aradon watched as the big man faded to gray and was absorbed into the fog.

CHAPTER THIRTY

TÞE FLEECE

An hour later Aradon lay sprawled across his bed, staring at the Crown of Eden, turning it slowly in his hands. It was surprisingly simple in design, with no elaboration in its structure and little ornamentation engraved on its golden surface. At a distance one would not see anything unique about it at all, but as Aradon gazed at the stone set in the Crown's highest peak, its iridescence teased his eye with barely visible flashes of impossible colors completely outside the natural spectrum he knew.

It was Aradon's duty to give this Crown to those who would place it on the head of that tyrant, Lomar. He thought of the Crown on Lomar's head and Volanna in Lomar's arms, and he closed his eyes and gritted his teeth in anguish. How could he let such an outrage happen when he had the power to prevent it? Llewenthane's arguments immediately echoed in his mind. The big man had used the same reasoning to urge him to lead the people in rebellion against Lomar. Perhaps there was something to what he said after all. Keeping this Crown from Lomar's head would prevent a generation of evil and at the same time give Aradon the one desire of his heart. Wasn't it likely that the Crown had come to him to accomplish these very ends? How did one ever know exactly what the Master of the Universe wanted of him? Couldn't the fact that he had the Crown be the Master's way of telling him the Crown should be his? If so, what of the prophecy? Perhaps Llewenthane was right; King Tallis might have misinterpreted it.

But would he dare wear the Crown? Suppose it caused him to shrivel or shrink or go mad or lecherous as it had others who had worn it? He could not be concerned about such things now. If it was the Master's will that he have the Crown, the Master would take care of him. If not, what had he lost? The life he saw ahead of him without Volanna was barren as a winter field, and if the Crown gave him even a short time with her before it did its work on him, wasn't it worth the risk?

Why did the will of the Master always have to be so vague and hard to find? How could one go about finding exactly what his true will is? He remembered the story of the ancient warrior Gideon, who placed a fleece on the grass and prayed that if the Master of the Universe wanted him to lead his people in battle, on the next morning the fleece should be dry while the grass around it was saturated with dew. If such a test worked for Gideon, could he devise one that would work for him? How could he put out a fleece to test the will of the Master? The test should be no easy thing that could be explained by simple coincidence but something so unlikely that Aradon would know it to be the shout of a divine voice. But at the moment he could think of nothing.

He returned the Crown to its hiding place, wrapped himself in a cloak, and walked outside. Olstan should be returning soon. The sun was setting, and while the forest was still saturated with fog, the sky was clear overhead. Already he could see the bright silver star high above the trees and the brilliant comet, its golden tail streaming behind it, only a finger's breadth away from its goal. Were it not for the Crown being in his possession, when those two stars met, his world would end.

As he gazed at the stars, he heard hoofbeats deep in the forest. Soon Olstan appeared out of the gloom. The silent man dismounted, and as he removed his saddle and prepared his horse for the night, Aradon questioned him about the outcome of his mission. With his signs Olstan reported success and gratitude on the part of the destitute families to whom he had delivered Aradon's tournament purse. He went on to tell Aradon of the upcoming festive events in Corenham that had the village people talking—the Seven Kingdoms Tournament, the coronation of Prince Lomar, and the wedding to follow on the next day. Olstan could see that talk of the coronation and wedding troubled Aradon, so he went on to tell him of the tournament—who was coming, when it was to be held, and how the lists were being decorated and repaired. Aradon said little, so Olstan left him to his thoughts and went on into the cave.

Aradon thought about the tournament. It was a pity that he could not enter it, but his outlaw status made doing such a thing impossible. *That is, impossible for me,* he thought suddenly, *but surely not impossible for the Master of the Universe.* There was his fleece. He could enter the Seven Kingdoms Tournament and test the will of the Master. There was not a hare's chance in a pen full of hounds that he would win, but if the Master of the Universe wanted him to follow the urging of Llewenthane and take the throne of Meridan, he could show it by giving Aradon victory in the tournament.

Aradon walked about the forest until deep in the night, thinking on the idea, turning it this way and that in his mind until he well near wore it out from the handling. Finally he returned to the cave and once in bed, fell into a fitful sleep—tossing, turning, rolling about in the covers, and waking often with the outrageous idea pounding in his head like a fist on a locked door.

Aradon wrestled with the unthinkable options for the entire week but could never quite settle the decision firmly in his mind. At the end of seven days, he and Olstan left the cave for their meeting with Llewenthane.

ఎ•

"You can't be serious," boomed Llewenthane, glaring at Aradon across the fire in the same hollow where they had met the week before. "You will *think* about taking the throne *if* you win the Seven Kingdoms Tournament. Why not say you may think about doing it if water starts flowing uphill or stones start flying about like cottonwood seeds? You want me to rally the people of Meridan and have them ready on the chance that you—who have not even finished your training as a warrior and have fought only ruffians and outlaws—*may* accept the crown if you defeat all the champions of the Seven

Kingdoms? Aradon, what are you thinking? You're good—very good—but not *that* good. If you don't want to do this thing, why not just say so instead of making such a preposterous impossibility your condition for even thinking of it?"

"You are right," Aradon shot back. "Let's just forget the whole thing."

Llewenthane slapped his knees, and a sigh of exasperation exploded from his lips. "I suppose if there's any chance we are to have you at all, it must be on your terms. Very well then. Let's see what we can make of it. Now we're basing any plan we make on the assumption that you will win. Unlikely as that is, it's the only way we need to plan, for if you don't win, we have no plan and no need for one, right?"

"That's right," said Aradon. "And remember, even if I win, I have promised you nothing. I'm not yet sure I could accept the Crown under any conditions."

"You mean you want me to have a plan in place, all my men ready at arms, and even then you may not follow through? How can you expect that of the people, Aradon?"

"I'm not expecting anything of the people. I'm here only because I promised to meet with you again, not because I have made a firm commitment. As far as I'm concerned, we probably ought to forget the whole thing."

Llewenthane shook his head and sighed again. "If we had any better hope, we would be stupid to go through with this. But we have none, so we will make all our preparations on the basis of this slimmest of chances that you are giving us. So let's get on with it. I think our best hope is to make our play right at the end of the tournament. Let's see . . . All right, I have an idea. Prince Lomar will preside over the tournament. The custom is for the winner to offer the king—or in this case, Lomar—a gift of some sort, a token of fealty. Do you have such a gift?"

"I do," said Aradon. "I have the Crown of Eden."

Llewenthane looked at him, uncomprehending. "You have what?"

"You heard me right. I said I have the Crown of Eden. I found it months ago in Maldor Castle."

"You are not jesting with me. You really do have the Crown of Eden?"

"It's true," said Aradon. "How I found it is a long story. I'll tell it to you another time."

Llewenthane gaped at him in wonder. "You have the Crown of Eden, yet you're putting out a fleece. What more of a sign do you want, man?"

"Gideon did it twice, you know. I'm not trying to defend my reasons. You'll just have to indulge me," said Aradon.

Llewenthane sighed again and shook his head in exasperation. "Very well. Here is what we will do. Protection around Lomar will be lax because no one expects an uprising, especially not on a day of festivities. I and hundreds of men from the southern villages will arrive early at the amphitheater and will stake our places on the hill opposite the stand where Lomar will sit. We will have our weapons hidden inside our cloaks, and on the front row I will have at least twoscore archers who can split a pear at a hundred paces. Then I will have—"

"No doubt the Princess Volanna will be seated beside Lomar. And King Tallis and Lord Aldemar as well. I will not have them harmed."

"We will have no need to harm them. Indeed, we can protect them from harm if need be. I will instruct the archers and all others who engage the battle to protect them. Now let me suggest a plan of action. If you win the tournament, you will ride once around the list in victory. Then you will ascend the steps to the dais where Lomar sits. Take the Crown of Eden with you—I still find it hard to believe that you have it—and make as if to give it to Prince Lomar. But instead tell him and the others in the stands that I have archers with arrows aimed at them. Then turn to the crowd, accuse Lomar of crimes against the people, and proclaim him unfit to rule. I will then step forward and announce you as the people's choice as their new king. I will place the Crown on your head and you will take the place of Lomar. We will escort him, along with Balkert and Sir Stundal, to Morningstone's dungeon to be held for trial. How does that sound?"

"It sounds brilliant. Utterly brilliant." As Aradon listened to Llewenthane explain his plan, the prospect of his taking the Crown took on an aura of reality, and for the first time, he began to think of it as doable. "How did you think of such a strategy in such a short time?"

Llewenthane grinned. "I'll admit that I have thought of it before. This and a dozen other plans for getting the Golden Knight on the throne. Your insistence that you won't move unless you win the tournament merely made this plan the most feasible." The two men further discussed several details of the plan to be sure they had not overlooked any fatal flaw. Then they put out the fire and mounted their horses.

Before they parted, Llewenthane turned to his friend, his face grave and his voice tense with urgency. "Aradon, you must put aside all hesitation on this matter. For the sake of Meridan, if you win the tournament, you must take the Crown. Who knows but what the Master of the Universe will give you victory, and if he does, it is surely your sign. You will take the Crown. Do you hear me? You will take it." With that, Llewenthane turned and walked swiftly into the forest, and Aradon returned to his home. They did not see each other again until the day of the tournament.

CHAPTER THIRTY-ONE

ANSEL'S PLOT

After he talked with Llewenthane, Aradon's willingness to take the Crown if he won the tournament had taken on the hardness of a thing decided, but as the hours wore on, the idea began to stir the waters of his mind again. Usually all mental unrest would cease and he would get on about his business once he had made a decision. But something seemed amiss this time, and he could not put his finger on the problem. Over and over he paced back through all the points in favor of it and all against it until he wore ruts in his mind. He knew that Llewenthane was right: in his identity as the Golden Knight he certainly had the heart of the people with him. If he claimed the kingship for himself on the grounds that Lomar's rule would be disastrous, the people would surely back him. He had proved by his dedication to righting Lomar's injustices that he would be a more upright and worthy king than the prince. If he took the Crown himself, the prophecy would be proved invalid, and Volanna would be free to marry him.

Yet there were problems with such a course. Lord Aldemar would certainly not support any claim to the throne from outside the legal lineage of Alfron, especially from a twenty-one-year-old blacksmith who had not completed even a year of battle training. Other knights and noblemen—including his friend Sir Denmore—would likely resist as well and for similar reasons. King Tallis of Valomar would never approve of a king who did not fulfill his interpretation of the prophecy. But a tournament win would sweep away most of these objections like feathers before a chargirl's broom. The people held tournament winners in almost godlike esteem. If he won the tournament, and along with it the honor and respect of most of the people of Meridan, the Crown could not be refused him.

And as for the rightness of the act, he had already placed the entire decision in the hands of the Master of the Universe, had he not? With that done, he needn't think anymore about whether his decision was right or wrong. If the Master wanted him to sit on Lomar's throne, he would let him win the tournament. It was that simple.

If it were all so simple, so settled, so carefully thought out, why wouldn't the decision rest? Why did it rise from its bed each night and challenge him to wrestle with it again and again? He could not find the answer, and he knew that some weakness flawed the plan or some blindness obscured his view of it. He needed another mind into which he could pour the problem, stir it and watch it boil, letting the impurities come to the top so he could scoop them away.

He thought again of his father. What would Bogarth think of such a move? As Aradon considered the question, he feared that his father would never approve, and Bogarth's disapproval would crush him. But maybe he could convince his father. He could show him how it would solve so many problems: it would prevent Lomar's inevitable tyranny, save Princess Volanna from a forced marriage, and fill his own forlorn and empty future. On the other hand, perhaps it would be best not to tell Bogarth of these thoughts. Perhaps a time comes in every man's life when he must choose his own path, even if it veers from the course his father has set him on.

Throughout the day Aradon pursued his dilemma, but the course was always circular with no further insights and no rest. He was getting nowhere. Finally he decided he could not hide a matter of such magnitude from his father. He needed Bogarth's counsel. Indeed, given the far-reaching positive effects that would flow from his plan, Bogarth might not oppose it and might even give him sound advice on how to proceed. Thus heartened, he decided to risk a night-time visit to his parents' cottage.

He explained to Olstan what he was about to do, disguised him-self in beggar's clothing, and as dusk approached, the two men rode toward Corenham. "I'm not sure when I'll return," Aradon told him, "but I will get back in time to enter the Seven Kingdoms Tournament four days from now." At the edge of the woods, Aradon dismounted to continue on foot into Corenham as Olstan returned to the cave, leading Aradon's horse behind him.

It was two hours past dark when Aradon approached the cottage. He rapped on the door, and his surprised but overjoyed parents admitted him with warm embraces and tears. They shuttered the few windows still opened to the warming spring air, and although Faeren and Bogarth had already dined, she began preparing a meal for Aradon as he and his father sat at the table to talk.

Aradon listened to the crackle of the fire and savored the aroma of his mother's stew and found himself in no hurry to broach the sub-ject that had brought him home. He looked around the cottage, his lifetime home and a place where he had experienced nothing but unbounded love and happiness, and his old dream of a life of domes-tic simplicity washed over him in a wave of warmth and longing.

After telling his parents of much that had happened to him since they last talked, Aradon began to explain the terrible options that were drawing and quartering his soul. He told his father how he had found the lost Crown of Eden. What should he do with it? Should he hide it and save the kingdom of Meridan from Lomar, or should he turn it over to Lord Aldemar for the coronation?

As Aradon faced his father, he found that the rest of his inten-tions looked altogether different from the way they had appeared when he pondered them in his cave, staring at the Crown in his hands. He found that he could not bring himself to tell his father the whole of his thoughts—that he was considering claiming the Crown for himself. Somehow such schemes did not fit well in this kitchen, with his father sitting at the table and his mother busying herself about the hearth. He knew that Bogarth would not see the matter as he did, and for the first time in his life, he locked up the deepest place in his heart and hid the key from his father. Waves of guilt swept over him, which he thought sprang from the fact that he was not forthcoming with Bogarth. But in fact, the guilt was not caused by his reticence; his reticence was caused by his guilt for harboring thoughts his father might find unworthy of honor.

Bogarth could not see that there was any real dilemma facing Aradon. "Your course is clear, son. You have sworn fealty to the regent of Meridan, and you must abide by your oath."

"Not yet," Aradon replied. "I have sworn no oath. One does not take the oath of fealty until knighthood is granted."

"That is a legalistic way of evadin' your obligation," said Bogarth. "When you accepted trainin' at the regent's hand, you took on fealty to him. Even if you had not done so, you are a subject of the regent, and as a citizen of his kingdom, you owe him the same loyalty an oath would express. The oath itself is merely the formal expression of a loyalty that should exist already in the heart of every subject. Your loyalty as a citizen demands that you turn over the Crown to Lord Aldemar."

"But Lomar will be a tyrannous king," said Aradon. "I have seen ample evidence of the kind of oppression the people of Meridan will endure under the rule of his counselors. It will be an act of mercy to keep the Crown from such men."

"That has nothin' to do with the point," replied Bogarth. "It is not your place to judge kings. You are not the Master of the Universe or even a king's elector. Who are you, a mere blacksmith's son, to decide who should or should not be emperor of the Seven Kingdoms."

"But sometimes we little men are chosen to do great things. Remember Father Verit's prophecy that I would perform some act that would shake kingdoms and move armies? My decision about the Crown is almost certainly what he meant," said Aradon.

"Some of your reasonin' sounds very good except for one thing. It's all leadin' you to ignore a solid and certain truth. Your reasonin' says you can use the Crown to prevent a great evil. But truth says the Crown is not yours to deal with. It belongs to the kingdom, to the line of Perivale, to history, to the prophecy. When reasonin' goes against truth, and you come to count on the reasonin' instead of the truth, it's time to go lookin' into your own heart. You may be hidin' somethin' there that you want so badly you're usin' reasonin' to convince yourself that truth is not as true as your own thinkin'. And you can mark my words, Son, when you get to thinkin' this way, trouble is sure to follow like a stinger follows a scorpion."

Aradon's face burned red, and he turned quiet. Bogarth had veered close to the bolted chamber of his heart, and he halfway suspected that his father sensed something of what he was hiding there.

At that moment Faeren set before Aradon a huge bowl of steaming stew, and the talk turned to news of Corenham and the upcoming events surrounding the converging of the stars.

After eating Aradon went outside and strolled behind the cottage, considering the things his father had said. As he walked down the path that led to the shop, two eyes hidden behind a hedge near the path saw his face clearly, and the moment he returned to the house, Ansel left her hiding place and made her way home to give Marcie the good news.

ℒ❧

The next morning Ansel found Sir Stundal at the Thirsty Eagle. She ignored the barmaid sitting beside him and pulled a chair up to his table.

"Send her away," said Ansel. "We must talk."

Stundal looked at her and laughed. "Very well. The last time you had something to say to me, I should have listened. You seem to know things nobody else would even suspect. Leave me, wench." The girl got up in a huff. Stundal swatted her sharply on the rump and watched her walk away. Then he turned to Ansel. "What now, cakeseller?"

"Marcie is with child."

"That's not surprising. I wonder that it hasn't happened long before now. Why are you telling me?"

"You are the father. What are you goin' to do about it?"

"Nothing. Absolutely nothing. Even if the child is mine—and that's open to question—I can't assume responsibility for every bastard that some wench claims I fathered. There's not enough money in the kingdom to run such an orphanage. Besides, Marcie enticed me to do what I did."

"Make no mistake about it; the child is yours, Stundal. But I didn't think for a moment that you would do anything about it. I know you too well. Bearin' the burden of men's pleasure seems to be the lot of us women. But there's somethin' could be done to cover all this that might be good for both of us."

"What do I need to cover? I'm not hurting from this in any way, and I'm not interested in hearing any more about it. Get out of here."

Ansel made no move to go but looked Stundal steadily in the eye. "Hear me out, Stundal. You may find yourself more interested than you're athinkin'. I know where Aradon is hidin', and you can have him in chains before another day dawns."

"All right. Where is he?"

"If I tell you, you got to promise me two things: first, half the reward money posted for Aradon's capture, and second, that he be released and pardoned on condition that he wed my Marcie to cover what you done to her. Well, what do you think?"

Stundal thought for a moment. Then he began to laugh. "I like it," he said. "What better revenge could I get than to force that lunk of a blacksmith into a marriage that will have him raising my brat?" He agreed to the plan, and Ansel told him that Aradon was hiding in his parents' cottage and would likely return to the forest after sundown.

Just before sundown Stundal and four of his guards hid in a grove of trees where they knew Aradon must pass to enter the forest. An hour past dark they made out his form walking down the starlit path near the place where they hid. They captured him easily by dropping a net from the overhanging trees. He fought viciously at the net but could not escape it. Stundal's men bound him, threw him roughly across a horse, and rode around the edge of the sleeping Corenham and northeastward out of the city, picking up one of the old, abandoned highways.

They taunted Aradon all along the way, saying that he was about to pay for his humiliation of the prince and the abduction of the princess by suffering a fate worse than death. At last they came to an isolated guardhouse. There they shoved him into the dungeon, chained one ankle to the wall, and locked the rusted iron door of the cell.

Sir Stundal stood at the door grinning broadly. "Well, blacksmith, I hope you find your quarters to your liking. Being the fair man that I am, I have a way that you can get out of this place and become a free man. I will return on the morrow to tell you all about it." Stundal posted one of his guards in the anteroom and rode with the others back to Corenham.

Aradon looked about his cell. By the dim torchlight coming from the anteroom he could see that it had not been occupied in years. There was no roof but the starlit sky, which he could see through the black ribs of bare, sagging beams, hanging with traces of dry thatch. He could not clearly see all the walls of the cell for the shadows, but those he could see appeared solid. He tested his chain and found it firmly bolted into the stone. He felt as much of the wall as the chain would allow him to reach but found no hint of loose stones.

"Get still in there," called the guard.

Aradon thought his best course was to rest all he could until Stundal returned. He sat with his back to the corner of the cell and fell asleep. Between the coolness of the spring night and the hardness of the stone, he did not sleep well, but he managed to doze off and on until morning came and he could see the sky bright and blue above him. The guard brought him a dried piece of bread and a mug of water, taunting him all the while. Aradon took the food and ate in silence.

In the middle of the afternoon Aradon was awakened from a brief nap by a rapping on his cell door. He looked up to see Sir Stundal standing outside it, with Ansel at his side. What Aradon could not see was Marcie, who stood by the prison wall just around the door, kept from his view so he would not see her swollen belly. Aradon stood as Stundal began to speak, not knowing what to expect.

"Listen well, blacksmith. I have come with a very generous offer. No one but four of my guards and the two of us knows you are here. You can rot away in this prison forever, and no one will know of it. But I have a way you can get out, be pardoned for your crimes against the kingdom, and live a normal life." He paused to let his words sink into Aradon's mind, but Aradon said nothing.

"Aren't you even curious? It doesn't matter; I'm going to tell you anyway. You've been something of a wild young buck, blacksmith—

wrecking parades, wounding servants of the kingdom, running off with princesses—none of which is really serious, of course, but when you add it all up, it does begin to get the attention of a few people here and there. We've all grieved over your waywardness, and we all want to help you overcome these destructive tendencies, but we've been in something of a quandary as to how to go about it. And lo, now we have the perfect solution. Ansel's Marcie has agreed to take you off our hands and tame you down. If you will simply wed this fine young woman, known over Corenham as a paragon of virtue, you will be pardoned for your crimes and walk out of here a free man—if you call marriage freedom."

"Why are you offering me this?" asked Aradon.

"Ansel and I made a little bargain of our own. She told me how to find you. I get the glory for bringing you in, and she gets you as her son-in-law. Oh yes, and we both get the reward money for your capture." He turned to Ansel and muttered into her ear, "And there are other reasons, which the poor man will discover soon enough."

Aradon quickly ran the offer through his mind. He could see little reason not to accept it. If he refused, they would leave him chained in this isolated prison. He would miss the tournament and lose forever any possibility of wedding Volanna. And he knew that Volanna was as good as out of reach anyway. The odds of his winning the tournament were about the same as a grubworm surviving in an anthill. Marriage to Marcie—even if he had doubts about her ability to be faithful—would be infinitely better than slow death in prison.

But there was an obstacle: he did not love her. On the other hand, how much did love matter? Half the matches in the Seven Kingdoms were arranged, and if love was ever a part of these marriages, it wove itself into them over time. But this marriage to Marcie would begin with two obstacles they might never overcome. First, both of them would know that he married her only to save his own skin. What kind of marriage could grow from a beginning like that? Second, he knew that he was hopelessly in love with the Princess Volanna, and he was not sure that time would ever cause that love to fade. He would do Marcie a great injustice to marry her while loving another. The marriage itself would be an act of unfaithfulness.

"No, I cannot marry Marcie," he sighed.

When poor Marcie heard Aradon's answer, hot tears welled up in her eyes. She had cherished a hope that he would find the idea attractive in spite of the fact that he was being coerced. Ansel glared at Aradon, her eyes flashing fire. "I can't believe you're so stupid. Why in the devil's name would you choose this cold cell over a warm bed with my daughter in it? You can just rot away here in this prison, for all I care. I wouldn't want anyone with no more sense than you to marry my baby anyway. Why she cares for a lunkhead like you, I'll never understand. But care she does, and no doubt she'll be soakin' her pillow with tears while you sit here in the cold and rain. Can't you see that you're throwin' both your happiness and hers to the wind? Oh, how stupid! Stupid! Stupid! Let's go, Stundal. Let this imbecile wallow in his fate. My Marcie deserves better."

The visitors departed, leaving Aradon brooding in his chains. More than once he wondered if Ansel were not exactly right. Perhaps he was foolish not to have taken their offer. The life he had dreamed of was gone. He may as well have accepted this new life they wanted to drop into his hands, which was much like the life he had once wanted anyway. But he could not imagine how he would pretend to love one woman while the shadow of another haunted his heart. How could he live with himself each night as he took Marcie in his arms and thought only of his Dovey?

An hour before sunset, a replacement guard arrived at the guard-house, bringing food for himself and the prisoner, and the guard who had been on duty rode back to Corenham on the horse that brought his replacement.

ℒ

As Ansel had known she would, Marcie cried herself to sleep that night and the night after. But Aradon's rejection was not the only thing that troubled her rest. The thought of him sitting chained in the open cell through no fault of his own kept her awake at least as much. And she knew that his imprisonment was her doing. At least, it was caused by her complicity with her mother's scheming. She knew that she would never rest until she found some way to free him.

The next morning Marcie again claimed sickness and stayed in her bed until Ansel left to run their route without her. After she heard the door close and the wheels of the cart creak down the street, Marcie got out of bed to dress. She chose a loose skirt that she thought would diminish the effect of her rounded belly and a bodice with a neckline that swept dangerously low. She packed a large bag with two flasks of ale, a wedge of cheese, a half-loaf of bread, a large honeycake, and her mother's rolling pin.

Before midmorning she was ready. She left the cottage and walked to the shop of Darcel the wineseller, who employed a young but slow-witted man named Torval to deliver the shop's product in a sturdy old cart. Marcie had noticed how Torval gaped at her when she came into the shop to sell honeycakes, and she easily struck a bargain with him to take her out near the abandoned guardhouse where Aradon was held.

As they approached the area near the guardhouse, she had Torval let her down just out of sight of it, and after seeing him headed back toward Corenham, she walked the half-mile to the prison.

Marcie was thankful that the guard on duty was half-drunk already when she arrived, for it would make her task much easier. And he would be less likely to notice or care that she was with child. The man leered at her as she approached, his judgment so impaired that he did not even raise the question as to why she had come. She sat beside him full of smiles, laughter, and sidelong glances. With the enticement of implied promise and a flask of ale, she soon got him so tipsy he could hardly stand. Then as he lunged clumsily for her, she dealt him a forceful blow on the head with Ansel's rolling pin, and he dropped to the floor unconscious. Marcie took the keys from his belt and ran to Aradon's cell.

"Marcie, what are you doing here?" he asked.

"No time to answer that now. We got to hurry." She unlocked the door, then went to him and unlocked the bonds that held his ankle. Aradon noticed her obvious pregnancy and began to understand something of the nature of Ansel and Stundal's offer. When his ankle was free, Marcie handed him the contents of the bag.

"Eat quickly," she urged him.

"But Marcie, I've told Sir Stundal and your mother that I cannot—"

She put her finger to his lips to hush him. "I know. It doesn't matter. Just hurry. I'll be back in a moment."

Aradon wolfed down the food and half the flask of ale. Marcie went to the anteroom and returned with a longbow, a quiver half-filled with arrows, and a rusty short sword.

"I got these from the guard outside. Put them on quick-like so we can be gone."

Aradon strapped on the sword and quiver, slipped the bow over his shoulder, and with Marcie beside him, left the guardhouse and made his way into the nearby wood.

"I'll go with you through the wood until I can get back on the road to Corenham," she said, "but you must stay in the wood. You mustn't show your face in the city."

"Why are you doing this? How can I repay you?" asked Aradon.

"Don't ask why. I could never make you understand. And as for payment, I will take this." She stopped and turned him toward her. She took his face in her hands and tiptoed, ready to kiss him full upon the lips. But in the corner of her eye, she saw a movement in the woods toward the guardhouse. She looked and saw that it was a man with an arrow nocked in his bow, pointed straight at Aradon.

"Aradon!" she screamed as the man let the arrow fly.

Aradon turned too late to grasp the danger, but Marcie had already lunged in front of him, and he watched helplessly as she took the arrow in her breast. As she dropped to the ground, Aradon quickly nocked an arrow in his bow and let it fly, watching it as it pierced the guard's throat and emerged from the back of his neck. He knelt and cradled Marcie in his arms.

"Marcie, why . . . ?" he asked in anguish.

But again she placed a trembling finger on his lips. "Please, my payment," she gasped.

Aradon held her close and placed his lips on hers, and the deep sigh that slipped from her throat was her last breath. Tears welled in his eyes. He had spurned her, yet she had given her life for him. Indeed, she had given two lives. He lifted her gently and carried her back to the guardhouse. As he passed the body of the man he had just killed, he recognized him as the guard who had come to replace the one Marcie had disabled. He laid Marcie's body in the anteroom on the straw mat used by the guards at night. The wounded guard was now moaning with the pain of his throbbing head. Aradon slapped him several times across the face to bring him back to full consciousness. At the sight of Aradon and the girl's body, he came surprisingly alert.

"Listen to me very carefully," said Aradon. "Your replacement killed this girl in his attempt to stop my escape. She was the daughter of Ansel the cakeseller. When you go back to Corenham, inform Ansel so the girl can get a proper burial."

The guard, his eyes round with fear both at the escaping Aradon and the dead body of the girl, promised with an oath to carry out Aradon's instructions.

Aradon took the garrison horse and rode hard into the forest. The tournament would begin in the morning. He hoped he could get to his cave in Braegan Wood in time to don his armor and get back to the amphitheater just outside Corenham. He knew he would not make the beginning of the tournament, but he hoped he would be allowed to enter late.

CHAPTER THIRTY-TWO

The Tournament

As the day of the tournament drew near, the city of Corenham was again festively adorned. Bunting and streamers of brilliant blues and greens, strung from posts, windows, roofs, and awnings, waved and billowed in the spring breeze, charging the air itself with the excitement felt by everyone in the city.

In the days before the tournament began, citizens did only essential work in their pastures and fields, then donned their most festive clothing and hurried into town. Merchants and street sellers filled Cheaping Square and the broadest streets of the city with tables and booths. They were laden with food, drink, produce, clothing, weapons, jewelry, and any other wares that might draw coins from the purses of the throngs flocking into the city from throughout the Seven Kingdoms. All inns were full two days before the tournament, and many couples found that they could earn a week's pay in two nights by renting nothing more than a place on their cottage floors for guests to spread their sleeping mats. By noon each day inns and alehouses teemed with noise and laughter.

One by one the kings and nobles of the Seven Kingdoms arrived, attended by their retinues of knights, ladies, squires, and servants, all lavishly attired in regal colors. Freelance knights, hoping to achieve glory in the tournament, pranced into the city astride mighty chargers. Some came alone, but many were attended by squires carrying bright banners blazoned with their masters' coats of arms.

On the day before the tournament, a grim-faced King Tallis of Valomar entered Corenham in his royal carriage. He was accompanied by Queen Ravella and a company of twenty-four armed and mounted knights. Sir Stundal, affronted by Tallis's large military entourage, reported his arrival to Balkert, who immediately perceived the meaning of it. Obviously, Lord Aldemar had sent news to Tallis of Lomar's indifference to the prophecy and perhaps of his maltreatment of Volanna as well. This show of power was meant to intimidate the prince into following the letter of the prophecy. Balkert reported the king's arrival and his reading of it to Lomar.

The jousting arena where the tournament would be held was a large, natural amphitheater just east of Corenham. It consisted of a level, grassy area of about forty by one hundred yards and was surrounded on three sides by grass-covered slopes, mostly open but shaded here and there by a few great oaks. On the flat north side, a grandstand had been constructed. It had a dais in the middle, which was covered with a red-and-blue striped canopy to shade the prince and princess and their invited guests as they watched the games. Dozens of pavilions, also brightly striped, filled the plain immediately behind the grandstand like miniature castle towers topped with serpentine banners undulating in the light breeze. They were available to knights competing in the tournament for preparation or equipment repair.

Spectators began to assemble on the hillsides of the great arena early on the morning of the tournament. But even those who arrived before dawn found a large crowd of perhaps two or three hundred already assembled on the slope directly across from the royal grandstand. Along the wooden rail that surrounded the jousting arena, over forty men sat, each with a long narrow pack on the ground beside him. Llewenthane had placed himself in the center of these men, directly across from where Prince Lomar would be sitting, ready to give the signal to his archers and the citizen warriors behind him should Aradon win the tournament.

Llewenthane had almost abandoned the entire plan and spared his rustic army the trouble. Aradon could not win the tournament. Even if he did win, he had not promised explicitly to take the Crown.

Llewenthane feared this exercise would be one of futility, bound to end in disappointment. He shook his head as he sat back and watched the people begin to throng onto the hillside.

The firstcomers got the shade trees; those who arrived later settled on the grassiest areas. Most families made an outing of the day, bringing baked chicken, bread, mead, and water enough to last through the tournament. By the time the sun was an hour above the horizon, hundreds had already claimed their places and more were crowding in. Knights and their squires were arriving at the pavilions to prepare themselves and their steeds for battle. Half an hour before the tournament was to begin, spectators covered the hillside like a patchwork blanket, and the noblemen and ladies of the kingdoms filled the grandstand.

Minutes before tournament time, the royal carriage, drawn by Lomar's four black stallions and accompanied by six mounted guards, drew up before the grandstand and stopped. The herald sounded his trumpet to quiet the crowd and all eyes turned toward the grandstand as Prince Lomar, with Princess Volanna on his arm, made his way to the dais and the two took their seats. At a second signal from the herald, the participating knights, clad in a rich array of colors, lined up facing the royal pair and dipped their lances in salute.

Then Lord Aldemar stepped to the podium. "Citizens of Meridan, our brothers in the Seven Kingdoms, and guests from afar, we extend a sincere and hearty welcome to all of you. As you know, Lomar, son of Alfron, crown prince of Meridan, is to be made king of Meridan on the morrow. It is my privilege as regent of Meridan to honor the heir to Meridan's throne by requesting that he preside over today's tournament. I now present to you the Crown Prince Lomar of Meridan and his betrothed, the Princess Volanna of Valomar."

Aldemar stepped aside and bowed to the prince, expecting him to come to the podium and address the crowd. But Lomar gave no acknowledgment to the introduction. He remained seated and with a wave of his hand, signaled to the herald, who took the cue and shouted, "Let the games begin!"

By longstanding rules of the annual tournament, the participating knights were ranked by reputation. Knights of lesser ability and those who were relatively untried or unknown were required to tilt in

the first round of jousting, called the first tier. Knights of higher ranking had the advantage of bypassing the lower tiers and were added to
the lists as the competition moved into the higher tiers.

The top tiers consisted of the champions of each of the Seven
Kingdoms. They were not required to enter the lists until their chal-
lengers emerged from the competition. Knights of sufficient reputation could enter the tournament late but only at the suffrage of the
tournament president, who would evaluate the entrant's reputation
and set whatever terms he deemed fit and fair to the other knights.
Ultimately a single champion would emerge, earning the right to
challenge the defending Champion of the Seven Kingdoms, who for
the past three tournaments had been Sir Stundal of Meridan.

Llewenthane looked about the arena. Knights were milling about
as they awaited their call to the lists, but he saw nothing of the
Golden Knight. *Where could he be?* he wondered.

At the crier's call, the first two opponents, Sir Appleton of
Vensaur and Sir Danmead of Valomar, took their places at opposite
ends of the list. They waited with lances poised, their armor brilliant
in the morning sunlight, their horses, draped in richly colored skirts,
dancing with eagerness to charge. The trumpet sounded and the
crowd cheered as the two galloped toward each other. Attaining
almost full speed as they approached the center of the list, each
knight pointed his long, decorated wooden lance at the other's breast.
They met with a resounding clash of wood and metal. Sir Appleton
tumbled backward over the rear of his horse and landed on the turf
with a crash as his victorious opponent rode to the far end of the list.
Tournament pages assisted the dazed Appleton to his feet and led his
horse from the field as Sir Danmead's name was entered for the next
level of challenges and the next contestants entered the lists to reap
either glory or humiliation.

By midday the lower tiers of the competition were finished.
Llewenthane was growing concerned because Aradon had not
arrived. He knew that Aradon's decision to enter the tournament was
tentative at best. Perhaps he had decided not to compete at all.
Llewenthane continued to look all around the arena in the hope of
seeing the Golden Knight arrive before it was too late.

Most of the knights now entering the lists had earned renown for their skill, and their names were well known to the spectators. Thus the enthusiasm, the rivalry, the wagers, and the noise elevated noticeably. By early afternoon the tiered competition was completed and six knights had emerged as winners. Tournament rules called for each of these six to challenge individually one knight from among the six champions of the other Perivalian kingdoms. The champion of Meridan was Sir Stundal, who was also last year's tournament champion and thus exempt from this level of competition. The winners would be matched against one another until a single victor emerged. He would have the right to challenge Sir Stundal for the tournament prize.

Among the finalists was a crowd favorite, Sir Denmore of Meridan, who by reaching this level had improved his ranking by two tiers. He chose to challenge Sir Evermont, champion of Oranth. Evermont had defeated Denmore in last year's tournament, and Denmore was seeking redress. As he cantered past Evermont on his way to the list, his rival shouted to him, "Ah, Sir Denmore, you are about to see that lightning can indeed strike twice in the same place."

"The only lightning I'm going to see is a considerable lightening of your horse's burden," replied Denmore.

The two took their places at the ends of the list, the trumpet sounded, and they galloped headlong toward each other. Denmore's lance lodged firmly on Evermont's breastplate and lifted the surprised Oranthian from his saddle and landed him on the turf with a clattering thud. He arose, unhurt but dazed, and his squire helped him to his tent.

One by one the challenges to the other kingdom champions were made and met, and two other current champions were defeated: Sir Prentamon of Lochlaund, who was unhorsed by Sir Montaver, an unknown knight who rose from the second tier, and Sir Crandon, who defeated the champion of Vensaur.

The final round was always the highlight of the annual tournament because more was at stake. The six remaining knights had reached this top tier by being the strongest and most skilled of the entire field, thus the battles at this level were usually titanic and memorable. Sir Montaver and Sir Denmore drew the first match and took their places at the end of the list.

But before the herald could sound the charge, the drumming of hoofbeats sounded from the east. All heads turned to see an unknown knight approaching, mounted on a magnificent white charger and wearing a brightly polished breastplate and helm of golden hue. His arms were sleeved in chain mail wrought of the same metal. A full cape the color of red wine billowed behind him. Attending him was a lightly armored squire, whose face was also hidden in a visored helmet. After a momentary silence, the crowd found its collective voice and roared with delight as they recognized the unexpected visitor: the new hero of the countryfolk of Meridan, the already legendary Golden Knight.

The knight trotted to the center of the field, turned to face Prince Lomar, and dipped his lance in salute. The crowd grew silent with anticipation as he began to speak. "Sire, I humbly request permission to enter the tournament." His squire tossed at the feet of the prince a small bag of coins, the price of tournament entry.

Llewenthane and his men breathed a sigh of relief and listened carefully for Prince Lomar's response.

Lomar knew that the Golden Knight was no friend of the throne. "You are too late," he said. "The tournament began this morning; you should have entered then."

"Longstanding tournament rules do not require timely entry," replied the knight. "According to the rules, you must allow me to enter."

Princess Volanna listened closely to the knight's voice. It sounded familiar, but muffled and distorted as it was by the helmet, she could not place it. She looked hard at the man, searching for some clue to his identity. Suddenly she gasped. The blue-striped kerchief tied about his wrist was her own. Could this be Aradon? Her heart pounded at the possibility. Or was it some knight who had defeated Aradon and taken the kerchief—or found him dead and claimed his belongings? She was beside herself with apprehension. She leaned toward Lomar and whispered, "Ask him to lift his visor and identify himself."

Lomar made the request, but the knight declined, begging the prince's pardon. In spite of the vocal distortion, Volanna was almost sure the voice was Aradon's. She also noted that the Golden Knight was a very tall man, about the size of Aradon, and his squire's build resembled that of Olstan. Virtually convinced that this was Aradon, she feared for his life. It was one thing to fight undisciplined outlaws and ruffians, but surely he was no match for the best warriors in their world.

"Tell him he cannot participate unless he identifies himself," she whispered to Lomar.

But the crowd, though they could not hear all of the exchange, sensed Lomar's reluctance to admit the Golden Knight into the tournament, and two or three began to chant, "Let him fight! Let him fight! Let him fight!" Others quickly took up the chant, and soon the entire crowd joined in and raised such a roar that Lomar finally lifted his hands to quiet them.

"Very well, you may enter," he said, "but according to the tournament rules—which you are so diligent to note—you must abide by my stipulations. I say that you must challenge each of the six remaining champions, one after the other, until you either defeat them all or fall yourself. Only if you defeat each of them in succession may you challenge the Champion of the Seven Kingdoms."

Lord Aldemar was appalled at Lomar's terms. "Your Highness," he said, "no knight today, working his way up through the tiers, has had to fight more than six times. It is not right to ask this man to fight successively against the six best warriors in the empire with no rest between. The terms are unfair. I urge you to continue the tier system, with winners matching winners, and let the newcomer be entered into the rotation."

"Please, Aldemar," Lomar replied, "I am being more than fair to let this wandering vagabond enter at all. He is unproven and unranked, and he should have entered in the early tiers. And I do have the right to set the terms for late entrants."

"Surely your highness knows that the Golden Knight is not unproven," said Aldemar. "His reputation precedes him and bears witness to his battle prowess. Listen to the crowd. Everyone here knows the man is worthy."

"Yes, his reputation does precede him," replied Lomar. "He is a rebel and an outlaw who has pitted himself against duly appointed county officials and magistrates, and now he rides in here to the people's welcome as if he were a national hero. My rules will expose him for what he is and ensure that he does not ride out a hero."

Lord Aldemar rose from his seat, pale with rage. "Your 'duly appointed county officials and magistrates' are nothing more than—"

The strong voice of the Golden Knight interrupted Aldemar. "I accept your terms, your highness." He immediately wheeled his charger and loped to his place at the end of the lists.

Lomar settled in his chair, his face sporting a look of utter satisfaction with himself. Without turning he announced to the lords and officials around him, "I am taking on all wagers against this so-called Golden Knight." Because he was the prince, Lomar's wager had many takers, and a page circulated among them to record the amounts. Volanna hardly noticed Lomar's smug insult. She was virtually paralyzed with apprehension that the Golden Knight was indeed Aradon and that he was in far over his head.

The first joust pitted the Golden Knight against Sir Montaver, who had unseated the champion of Lochlaund in the previous round. The two knights took their places, the trumpet sounded, and they spurred their chargers toward each other. The horses built speed until they were galloping, and the two knights aimed their lances. They met with a resounding clash. Both lances caught solidly on the other's breastplate, but Montaver's bent in a great arc then shattered with a snap, splinters showering the air as the Golden Knight's lance lifted Montaver from his saddle and flipped him over the back of his horse. He hit the turf hard on his back and had to be carried from the field. The Golden Knight returned to his end of the list as the crowd screamed their approval. Lomar glowered darkly as Volanna breathed again in temporary relief.

The Golden Knight next faced Sir Crandon, another who had worked himself up though the tiers and had in the last round defeated the champion of Vensaur. On the first pass, both knights merely grazed each other as the points of their lances failed to find purchase on the other's armor. On the next pass, Crandon again merely grazed the Golden Knight, whose own lance broke through Crandon's shoulder plate and spun him to the earth. Crandon quickly got to his feet and drew his sword, but the Golden Knight drew his own and rode in on him. With a sweeping stroke from his superior mounted position, he knocked the weapon from Crandon's hand, ending the battle.

The Golden Knight won the next match without even deploying his weapon. Sir Renstar, the champion of Sorendale, had been wounded in his previous battle and was weakened from loss of blood. Renstar's squire tried to persuade his injured master to forfeit, but he would hear none of it. "Whether I live or die, my children for generations to come can say that their forebear once tilted against the Golden Knight of Meridan."

The injured knight's condition was obvious to the crowd and to his opponent as well, as he took his position in the list. He swayed unsteadily in the saddle and his breastplate was streaked red with blood seeping through a broken plate over his collarbone. The two knights charged. Renstar's horse wove erratically as the knight aimed his wobbly lance. The Golden Knight, unwilling to inflict further damage on the brave man, lifted his own lance as they passed. Poor Renstar, leaning sharply forward to anticipate impact, lost his balance and fell from the saddle as the Golden Knight galloped by untouched. The fallen knight lay sprawled on the turf, unable to rise until his squire and a page assisted him from the field and attended to his wounds.

The Golden Knight's next match, Sir Magralon of Valomar, gave him more of a challenge, but after two charges, Magralon picked himself up from the turf and joined the ranks of the defeated.

Lomar scowled and sank low in his chair, smarting from his wagering losses and the wild enthusiasm of the crowd at the success of their new hero. "Fortune has been with him so far," he growled, "but he will need more than fortune to win the next match. Sir Denmore is one of Meridan's two or three top knights, and he's getting better all the time. This so-called Golden Knight cannot survive much longer."

Volanna feared that Lomar was speaking the truth and had to force her hand to relax its grip on the arm of the chair as the Golden Knight and Sir Denmore stood ready in the lists, waiting for the trumpet. Sir Denmore was a favorite in Corenham, and the cheers of the crowd were almost evenly divided between the two as the trumpet sounded and their chargers thundered toward each other. The two knights crashed mightily in the center of the list as both lances splintered on impact. Each knight reeled in his saddle, but both maintained their balance and rode back to the ends of the list. They took new lances and returned to their starting positions. Once more they charged, and once more there was a titanic collision and a splintering of lances as the horses themselves were jarred sideways by the impact. The blow spun Sir Denmore sideways and tore his foot from the stirrup, but he clung to the saddle and pulled himself back into place.

Again the warriors took up new lances and again they charged. This time the Golden Knight aimed his lance at an indention in Sir Denmore's breastplate caused by the impact of their previous encounter. The knights clashed again. Denmore's lance hit the Golden Knight's shoulder, knocking him sideways, ripping through his leather helmstrap, and twisting his neck hard to the left. But the Golden Knight's lance caught solidly on Denmore's breastplate, driving him from the saddle and sprawling him to the earth, tumbling and rolling as pieces of armor flew about. Almost half the crowd moaned in disappointment as the rest found their voices again and roared with delight. Lomar stamped his foot and cursed vehemently. Volanna closed her eyes and breathed a prayer of thanks.

The Golden Knight turned and approached the dazed Denmore, who was slowly trying to lift himself from the ground. The mounted knight removed his gauntlet and reached downward, his hand open in an offer of assistance. Denmore removed his own gauntlet, grasped the extended hand, and allowed his victor to pull him to his feet. "Well done, my friend," said the Golden Knight as he turned and rode back to his place in the list. The surprised Denmore stood for a moment looking after his gallant opponent as he tried hard to identify the voice, then he walked from the field as the crowd cheered and applauded.

The next opponent was the great Sir Garafond, five-time champion of Rhondilar. A rousing cheer went up from the citizens of that country as the renowned knight rode toward the list. But the Golden

Knight raised his hand to signal a pause. He loped toward the dais and addressed the prince. "Your highness, the strap that secures my helmet is broken. I request a pause in the games to make the repair."

The angry prince responded, "You are merely looking for an excuse to rest. I have no intention of—"

"Your highness," interrupted Balkert, "could I have a word with you." He leaned toward Lomar and whispered something in his ear.

"Very well," sighed Lomar. "You have seven minutes."

As both Sir Garafond and the Golden Knight rode toward the pavilions behind the grandstand, Balkert left his seat and followed the Golden Knight to the tent secured by his squire. He crouched behind the tent and put his eye to a small tear in a seam. He watched as the squire removed the knight's helmet. "Aradon!" Balkert whispered to himself. He quietly withdrew and stepped lightly to Aradon's steed. He looked around twice, drew his knife, reached beneath the saddle, and cut halfway through the girth. Then he found Sir Stundal and reported to him the identity of the Golden Knight.

Sir Garafond rode to his tent and demanded of his squire, "Strap me to my saddle." The squire objected; the tactic was unfair if it worked and dangerous if it did not. But Garafond angrily insisted and the squire complied.

Aradon was back at his place in the list well within the allotted time. His opponent returned minutes later but received no recrimination from Lomar for the delay. The two warriors faced each other from their respective ends of the list and readied their steeds for the signal. The trumpet sounded and they charged, gathering speed as they aimed their lances. Just as Aradon's lance was about to make contact with Garafond's breastplate, Garafond deftly turned, causing Aradon's lance to deflect to the side. At the same moment Garafond's lance caught Aradon solidly on the right shoulder in the indention made by Denmore's lance. The impact twisted him to the right, dislodging his left foot from the stirrup and reeling him backward. He dropped his lance and clutched the saddle, barely maintaining his seating. The crowd gasped at the near disaster and Volanna covered her eyes.

Olstan recovered Aradon's lance, and the two knights returned to their starting places. Again they charged. This time Aradon anticipated Garafond's dodge and adjusted his aim accordingly, causing the surprised knight to move into the path of the Golden Knight's lance. Both horses reared with the strain of impact. The thrust of Aradon's lance knocked Garafond hard to the right, but as he was tied to his saddle, he did not fall. Instead his weight twisted the saddle to the side and threw his horse off balance, causing it to veer away from the list, stumble to the ground, and roll over on Garafond. Garafond's squire ran to the field, but before he could reach his master, the frightened horse struggled to his feet and tried to run. Garafond, either unconscious or dead, was still tied to the saddle and now hung nearly upside down at the horse's right flank. The horse dragged the knight a quarter of the way around the field before the girth ripped loose, leaving Garafond and his saddle in a motionless heap. The squire called for a stretcher, and pages carried Sir Garafond to his tent.

Llewenthane and his men began to feel that they had reason for hope that their man could win the tournament. They began to check the state of their weapons to be sure they were ready and accessible should they be needed.

Aradon sat in his saddle, panting and sweating from the strain of the successive jousts. Olstan took advantage of the pause to bring him a skin of water. As Aradon reached down to take the drink, he felt his saddle slip a little to the side. Apparently it had been loosened by the impact of the last joust. He rode up to Prince Lomar to request another pause to make the repair.

"How many times do you intend to disrupt this tournament?" Lomar shouted.

But Volanna urged him to grant the pause. "No knight on the field today has had to fight against such odds—six consecutive battles against the greatest warriors in the empire, and all without a break for rest. Be fair, your highness."

"And just what is your interest in this wanderer who won't show his face or give his name?" Lomar retorted. "I've watched you die your own little death each time this outlaw rides toward an opponent. I have seen your obvious relief each time he fells one. Is this the kind of loyalty I am to expect from my queen—hoping her own husband's champions are humiliated by any glory-seeking vagabond that comes along? I think you know this man. Who is he?"

Volanna could not answer. She was almost sure the knight was Aradon, but she was unwilling to confide her suspicion to Lomar, who still had Aradon posted as an outlaw in outer Meridan.

Lomar glared long at the reddening Volanna. Then he turned angrily to the Golden Knight. "I will grant you no more pauses. Either get on with the joust or get off the field!"

The Golden Knight dipped his lance in silent salute and returned to the list. Facing him at the other end was Sir Stundal, Champion of the Seven Kingdoms. The noise of the crowd ceased as if a sluice gate had suddenly stopped a rushing stream. Every spectator gazed toward the list, tense with anticipation. This was to be the battle for the Championship of the Seven Kingdoms.

Aradon and Stundal sat astride their mounts in their starting positions, Stundal's blood bay stallion prancing and pawing, eager to make the charge, Aradon's white charger standing with nostrils flared, his great sides heaving from the exertion of his previous charges. At the sound of the trumpet, the knights spurred their mounts. They gathered speed until both were galloping hard as they approached the center. Both lances connected solidly, and both snapped in two with a reverberating crack. Aradon felt his saddle slip dangerously. But he had no opportunity to attend to the problem for Sir Stundal wasted no time returning to his starting position. Aradon took another lance and prepared to charge again. At the trumpet, he spurred his horse forward. The exhausted stallion was slow in building speed, and Aradon feared his loosened saddle would not withstand the impact of Stundal's greater momentum. The knights met hard before Aradon reached the center, and again both lances shattered. The impact twisted Aradon's saddle six inches to the side, forcing him to drop his broken lance and clutch his horse's mane to keep from falling. The crowd groaned as if with one voice, and Volanna put her hand to her mouth to stifle a scream.

Aradon's saddle was now so loose it was useless. He cantered back to the end of the list, dismounted, unbuckled the saddle strap, dropped the saddle to the ground, and with Olstan's help, remounted his steed bareback. The crowd was stunned into silence. Volanna was horrified. Lomar laughed with delight and tried to increase his wagers against the Golden Knight. He got no takers. Olstan, with carefully hidden signs, begged Aradon to concede the battle and live to fight another day. But Aradon waved him away. Volanna hid her face in her hands in trembling despair.

The crowd saw no hope for their hero now and sat in heavy silence as the trumpet sounded and the great steeds surged forward. Aradon gripped the sides of his mount with his knees as best he could, and instead of holding his shield squarely in front, passed his arm completely through both its loops, thus freeing his left hand to grip the horse's mane. The great horses galloped toward each other with hooves thundering.

At the last moment before impact, Aradon leaned suddenly forward to make as small a target as possible. It worked. The point of Stundal's lance glanced off his shoulder and slipped past him. At the same time, his own lance made solid contact with Stundal's breastplate and bent in a high arc from the pressure of Stundal's greater momentum. Aradon leaned hard against the lance, but without a saddle he could get no solid purchase and felt himself slipping backward on his horse. Suddenly his lance snapped, and the release of pressure pitched Aradon forward from his mount. As he fell, he dropped his broken lance and clutched his horse's mane as the animal dragged him along the list. He tried to vault onto the horse's back, but the frightened animal, thrown off balance by his efforts, veered against the inner rail and raked him to the earth.

A moan of despair rose from the crowd. Volanna stood involuntarily and clapped her hand over her mouth to keep from crying out. She held her breath until Aradon got up from the earth and hurried toward his broken lance as Stundal turned and charged. Aradon saw that he could not reach the lance before Stundal arrived, so he stood to face the big knight's charge. To the great surprise of everyone watching, he removed his shield and slung it away.

Stundal bore down on him, his lance aimed directly at Aradon's breast. At the last moment, Aradon dodged deftly to the side, grabbed the end of the lance with both hands, and plunged it into the turf, breaking it in half and wrenching it from Stundal's hand. As Stundal turned to take another lance, Aradon picked up the broken one and gripped the small end with both hands like a club. Again Stundal charged. He anticipated Aradon's sideways dodge and aimed accordingly. But this time Aradon spun around causing Stundal's lance to deflect to the side. As Stundal passed, Aradon's spin became a mighty, full-circle swing that landed the large end of the broken lance hard on the champion's breastplate, knocking him cleanly from the saddle. The crowd roared mightily. Volanna stood and screamed, jumping up and down and clapping her hands with abandon. Lomar pounded the arm of his chair and emitted a string of emphatic curses.

As Stundal got to his feet, Aradon retrieved his shield, and both men drew their swords and faced each other, panting heavily. Stundal glared at Aradon and growled, "I know who you are, blacksmith. I should have killed you when I had the chance instead of playing games with those women. But I'm playing games no more. You have lived your last hour on earth."

Stundal attacked with a vengeance, and the duel began. Aradon retreated from the onslaught, doing little but warding off the champion's heavy strokes and managing few offensive blows of his own. The young man's assets were a quick mind, great strength, and uncanny quickness. But his liability was inexperience, and he knew it. To compensate for this lack, his tactic against experienced warriors was always to take up a defensive posture at the beginning of the duel while he studied his opponent's style and tendencies, looking for a weakness to exploit. The crowd, of course, did not understand the reason for his continued retreating and grew silent once again, thinking their champion was wearing down and getting the worst of it. Volanna clenched her hands until her knuckles were white, and tears begin to brim as hope drained from her heart.

The clanging of swords and the battering of shields went on for a quarter-hour, always with Stundal advancing and Aradon retreating. The crowd watched, breathless and intent, fearful that the Golden Knight had more than met his match. Volanna wrung her hands and breathed a desperate prayer.

Aradon was holding his own, but he was beginning to tire. He knew he must find a way inside Stundal's defense, or the sheer power of the man would soon wear him down. The only weakness Aradon had seen in Stundal's form was an occasional tendency to swing a little wide when he stroked to the left, turning his shield just enough to expose his side for a fraction of a moment too long. Aradon felt sure that a quick, well-aimed thrust could penetrate the seam between the front and back armor plates, but to lunge far enough to reach the seam and with enough power to drive a sword through it would leave him stretched out and defenseless against Stundal's for-midable backstroke. It would take a sure thrust and a lightning-quick one if it worked at all. It was a desperate chance, but he knew that if he didn't take it, he would soon be exhausted. He watched and waited. But Stundal seemed to have realized his lapse and began to tame his strokes and keep his side covered.

As Aradon began to tire, his strokes began to lose their crispness. Stundal, sensing he could now close in for the kill, feinted a stroke to the right, bringing Aradon's shield up, then swung quickly and mightily to the left. Aradon barely got his sword up to ward off the blow, and then not enough to stop it completely. Stundal's sword gashed the chain mail on Aradon's upper arm and blood came seep-ing through.

Aradon knew the battle would end soon if he did not act quickly. He would have to offer Stundal bait to tempt the too-wide stroke out of him again. He deliberately lowered his shield for a moment, and Stundal took the lure. He swung mightily as Aradon feinted, causing the stroke to go wide and exposing the seam in his armor. Aradon lunged, putting the whole of his weight into a forward thrust. But his sword deflected and missed the seam. He could not pull back quickly enough, and Stundal's backstroke fell hard upon his shield, ripping out the straps and sending it cartwheeling across the grass. Lomar leapt from his chair and shouted for joy. Volanna, with hot tears streaming from her eyes, bit her hand until it bled.

"Your little 'Golden Knight' charade is over, Blacksmith. You're worm food now, and that armor is about to be mine."

Stundal charged in for the kill, swinging his sword in great, broad strokes, knowing Aradon could now do nothing but use his own sword as a defensive weapon.

Aradon was desperate. He was near exhaustion, and it was all he could do to keep his sword between himself and Stundal's jarring blows. But despite his growing peril, his keen eye saw that Stundal's great sword strokes had become entirely too broad. The wider sweep of Stundal's swing might give him the extra split second he needed to thrust again at the seam and pull away before the backstroke came. He stopped retreating and held his ground, awaiting the opening. It came. He lunged and thrust with abandon, stretching himself beyond any possibility of pulling back. He felt his sword plunge deep into Stundal's side. He let go of the hilt and ducked low to escape the backstroke.

But the backstroke never came, for Stundal's sword flew from his hand and went spinning across the turf. He stood frozen for a terrible moment, eyes wide with horror as he stared at the hilt of Aradon's sword protruding from his side. He staggered with uneven steps in a useless attempt to remain standing, then crashed to the ground, mortally wounded. The crowd rose to their feet and roared with elation. Lomar sank deeply into his seat, scowling. Volanna collapsed into her chair and wept in relief.

Aradon stood panting as the roar of the adoring spectators filled his ears. Llewenthane's men slipped their bows from their wraps and hid them behind their backs. Olstan brought Aradon's horse and helped him to mount, and the new Champion of the Seven Kingdoms made the traditional victory circuit to acknowledge the ringing homage of the crowd.

As he trotted around the field, he tried to shut out the noise and clear his head to focus on what he was about to do. He had won the tournament: the sign he had asked for. Apparently the Master of the Universe intended him to take as his own the Crown of Eden. He rehearsed the steps Llewenthane had planned for denouncing Lomar and asserting Aradon's own claim to the throne. The ecstatic adulation of the people told him the plan would work. He had just won title as the most formidable warrior in the Seven Kingdoms, and he had their support. Olstan was waiting at the edge of the field with the Crown hidden in his saddlebag. Everything was working out perfectly. As he neared the grandstand where Prince Lomar sat, he grew more and more confident that the plan would succeed.

Aradon stopped before Prince Lomar and dipped his lance in formal salute. Lomar, badly shaken by his champion's defeat and devastated by his wagering losses, made no move to acknowledge Aradon's salute but sat slumped in his chair, scowling darkly at the new champion. After a moment of awkward silence, Lord Aldemar rose and made the obligatory speech of congratulation.

By the end of the short speech, Lomar had regained enough composure to address Aradon with a sneer. "Does not the victorious knight have the traditional gift tournament winners offer their king as a token of fealty?"

Llewenthane's archers stood tense and ready, their bows at their backs and arrows already in their hands.

Aradon cued Olstan to approach, and the squire came to his master's side and handed him a small parcel wrapped in a piece of faded tapestry. Aradon's heart beat like a hammer on an anvil as he took the parcel. But as he faced Prince Lomar, his father's voice spoke uninvited in his mind: *You have sworn fealty to your king. You must honor that oath and maintain that loyalty at any cost.* With a great effort, Aradon shut out the voice. Bogarth could not have known how high that cost would be. Aradon had never disobeyed his father, but surely he was justified in doing so now—or at least he would be forgiven for it. To give up his beloved Volanna forever to a man she despised when he had the power to prevent it was more than anyone could ask of any man.

Aradon dismounted and climbed the steps to the dais where Lomar sat. He stood before the prince with the parcel in his hand, sweating not merely from the exertion of the tournament but with the magnitude of the awful thing he was about to do. Again his father's voice invaded his mind. *Your reasonin' says you can use the Crown to prevent a great evil, but truth says the Crown is not yours to deal with. It belongs to the Kingdom, to the line of Perivale, to history, to the prophecy. When reasonin' goes against truth, and you come to count on the reasonin' instead of the truth, it's time to go lookin' into your own heart.*

Again Aradon shut out the voice and lifted his hand to unfold the tapestry, but as his fingers fumbled with the edges, he hesitated. An enormous inner struggle gripped him, and he paused until everyone around him wondered at his silence. At last, something between a groan and a sigh tore from his throat, as if his soul were being wrenched from his heart. He sagged visibly and with trembling hands, extended the parcel to Lomar.

Lomar made no move to take it but glared at Aradon and said, "I will accept no gift from a man who will not tell his name or show his face."

Aradon paused, then holding the parcel in one hand, removed his helmet with the other. Tears welled up in Volanna's eyes as she gazed at the beloved face, beaded with sweat and framed with tousled golden hair. She longed to throw herself on his breast and cling to him for life, but instead her lips silently formed his name. *Aradon, oh, Aradon.*

"I am Aradon, son of Bogarth the blacksmith," the champion said, "and this is my gift of fealty to my lord and king."

Lomar took the folded tapestry and set it on his lap. He peeled back the folds slowly, as if expecting a viper to spring from it. With the cloth fully unfolded, he gazed for the first time on the unearthly colors emanating from the stone in the Crown of Eden. His scowl dissipated, and a broad grin spread across his face. "This is indeed a most worthy gift, my champion," he said as he lifted the treasure from his lap.

When Volanna saw the Crown of Eden in Lomar's hands, all the blood drained from her face. She looked at Aradon, her eyes wide and sad and her mouth open in disbelief as she shook her head slowly in pale despair. Aradon returned the forlorn gaze but for a moment, his own heart broken and his victory empty. Without another word, he turned and descended the steps into the abyss of the rest of his life. Neither knowing nor caring where he would go, he mounted and rode from the field with Olstan following close behind.

Llewenthane and his army stood stunned as they saw their one hope of deposing Lomar die at the moment of birth. Victory was in Aradon's hands, but he had thrown it aside. What had happened to him? For a moment it had looked as though he would call them to the rebellion they so desperately desired. With bitter disappointment, they hid their weapons again and trudged from the arena, bereft of any hope that the gloom of their future would ever be dispelled.

Before Aradon rode out of sight, Prince Lomar turned to Balkert and whispered, "Take Stundal's guards and follow that man. Do nothing to him in view of the people; they would not stand to see their hero harmed. But as soon as he is out of sight, arrest Aradon the blacksmith for the abduction of the Princess Volanna and high crimes against the Kingdom of Meridan."

CHAPTER THIRTY-THREE

LOMAR'S PROPHECY

For most of the people in Corenham, the day following the tournament was another holiday. It was the day of Lomar's coronation as king of Meridan, and though this fact gave most citizens little cause for celebration, the day was made festive by the events they had witnessed in the tournament. Alehouses and the dining halls of inns filled early with breakfasting tourists eager to recount the prodigious feats of the Golden Knight, now known to be the son of Bogarth the blacksmith.

Bogarth awoke still astounded by yesterday's events. He and Faeren had attended the tournament and were amazed at the warrior their son had become. But their pride in him stemmed not so much from his jousting prowess as from his last act before leaving the podium. Although Aradon had not told his parents of his love for Princess Volanna, his mother, with a woman's inner eye for such things, had sensed it. Thus they knew something of the sacrifice their son had made in handing over the Crown and with it his hope for the future. But they wondered why Aradon had disappeared again. His delivery of the Crown to Lomar should have erased all suspicion that he was a traitor and lifted the bounty from his head. But Aradon had not been seen since the moment he rode away from the tournament.

Preparations for the coronation had begun well before dawn. The ceremony was set for late afternoon and would be followed by a grand banquet attended by the most prominent nobles of Meridan and the monarchs of the six kingdoms of the old federation.

Volanna would have been happy to sleep late, but she awoke early with a leaden feeling of dread—the residue of her horror at seeing Aradon hand the Crown of Eden to Prince Lomar—that settled into her mind like silt in a basin of water. She tried to return to the oblivion of sleep but found that door closed. She knew that the only way to drive the terrible truth from her mind was to get up and get busy. After breakfast with Kalley, she called for a coach to take them to her parents' rooms at Morningstone. She took with her all the clothing and toiletries she would need to prepare for the coronation and banquet.

For the rest of the morning, Volanna filled the ears of Tallis and Ravella with news of her year in Meridan. To spare her father anguish, she did not tell them of the worst of her encounters with Prince Lomar. But what she did tell, coupled with the message Tallis had received from Lord Aldemar, gave the king cause to ponder whether the prophecy could have gone awry. Volanna also told them of her adventures with the blacksmith Aradon in the outer provinces of Meridan—how he had rescued her from Maldor Castle, defended her from Brendal's pursuit, and escorted her safely to Morningstone. She admitted to some affection for the man, but her dogged commitment to her vow prevented her from admitting to them the whole truth—that she loved Aradon deeply—though she now knew it herself. But Queen Ravella, with a woman's sense for such things much like Aradon's mother Faeren, noticed the warming of her daughter's face and the softening of her voice when she spoke of Aradon. She strongly suspected the truth.

Shortly after the noonday meal, a courier brought a message to Volanna that Prince Lomar requested an audience with her in his chambers. She left her parents to comply, taking Kalley with her. They knocked on Lomar's door and entered to see him slouched in his chair, caressing the constrictor draped around his shoulders. The prince made no move to rise nor uttered any word of greeting.

He glowered at Kalley. "Is that girl a leech so stuck to you that she must go everywhere you go?"

"I will not be in a room alone with you," replied Volanna.

"Do you expect to have her in our bedchamber after we are wed?" asked Lomar.

"And do you expect to have that snake?" Volanna retorted.

Lomar laughed dryly. "Well spoken, my princess. But we will talk of such things at another time. For now I wish you to come with me. I have something to show you that I think you will find of great interest." Lomar returned the snake to its cage and opened his chamber door to usher the women into the hallway. He allowed Volanna to pass through the doorway but stopped Kalley. "She stays," he said.

"No, she goes with us. I've told you that I will not be alone with you until we are wed, and had I any say in the matter, I would not be alone with you even then."

Lomar said nothing, but gazed inscrutably at Volanna as he pulled from his tunic her blue and white scarf, which he held before her face. Volanna stared dumbfounded. "Where did you get that?"

"You will never know unless you send that girl away," Lomar replied. Without a word, Volanna motioned for Kalley to leave them. Then with cold dread gripping her heart, she followed Lomar as he strode down the hallway. Soon he turned aside from the known passages of the castle and led her through corridors and down stairways she had never imagined existed. The route took them ever downward, and the passageways became ever darker as they descended beneath the level of windows, beneath the castle itself, and into the bowels of the mountain. The torches on the walls became fewer and the space between them darker until Lomar took a torch from its sconce and held it aloft as they continued.

The corridors narrowed, and the rough-cut stone walls, mottled with black mildew and traces of velvety, green moss, seemed to close in on them. Volanna grew chilled by the dampness in the air and drew her cloak tighter. She kept her eyes downward to avoid tripping on the uneven stone floors, which were coated with enough moisture to reflect the gray form of Lomar walking ahead of her, seeming to writhe and jerk in the flickering torchlight. The only sound was the muted roar of the torch and the uneven staccato of their footsteps echoing like tightly wound coils in the narrow space.

Volanna stifled a scream as a dark shadow crossed the floor at Lomar's heels—a mottled gray rat was dragging the half-eaten carcass of some small creature. The rat was the harbinger of many more to come. Soon they scurried about her feet three or four at a time. Before long the foul odor of decay, urine, and excrement assailed them.

Lomar spoke for the first time. "We are almost there."

From the moment Lomar showed her the scarf, Volanna had felt a rising sense of dread. Her mind refused to examine it, but her heart sensed that she was descending into a pit where she would confront a horror that would drain her of all possibility of happiness. Now that dread loomed large and pushed hard at the door of her imagination, but she pushed back just as hard, fearful that if that door broke, so would she.

In moments they came to the end of the corridor. Before them was a gate, the metal bars of its grate as thick as Volanna's arm and flaked with brownish orange corrosion. Moist globules of green slime hung from the crossbars. In front of the gate was an armed sentry. The light of the torch on the wall filled the pockmarks and scars on his face with black shadows, making him look as hard and stonelike as the walls of the dungeon.

At Lomar's command the guard unlocked the gate and pushed hard against it. It opened with a creaking groan much like the wail of a mortally wounded calf Volanna had once heard in her father's barn. She shuddered but followed as Lomar stepped beyond the gate and entered the blackness of the foul corridor. The gate shut behind them with a groan and a dull clang, and her heart stopped in momentary panic. But she remembered the scarf in Lomar's hand and forced herself forward.

Each step now required her full attention for the floor was covered and puddled with a slippery scum. Ahead Volanna could hear the rustling and scraping of rats, running from Lomar's approaching torch and disappearing between the corroded grates of the cells that lined the passageway. The cells were mostly silent, but low moans and curses emitted from some as they passed. Volanna recoiled in horror as a skeletal hand reached toward her from one of the cells and a wizened face peered out from beneath long mats and tangles of gray hair and beard. A toothless maw opened in the face and a voice dry and papery muttered, "Water . . . water . . ." Her horror quickly melted into pity, but she could do nothing other than follow Lomar.

"I can't believe that Lord Aldemar would allow such a dungeon in Meridan," she said.

"Aldemar knows nothing of this," replied Lomar. "This is not the castle's official prison, which is in the guardhouse at the gate, but a secret dungeon that Perivale dug late in his reign to imprison those who offended him beyond what the law would punish. Indeed, it's good that Aldemar knows nothing of it, for if he did, he would surely have it filled. What a loss that would be."

After several more paces, Lomar stopped. Volanna looked up and started. Another armed guard stood directly in front of the prince. Lomar muttered something to him, and the guard silently pointed to a cell on their left. Here Lomar stopped and held the torch toward the grated door of the cell, motioning for Volanna to peer through the bars. Almost overwhelmed with dread, she shielded her eyes from the torch's glare and looked into the cell.

At first she could see nothing in the darkness. Then she barely made out what she had feared she would see—the standing form of a tall, muscular man, stripped to the waist and chained at the wrist to the far wall of the cell. The man's hands covered his eyes, shielding them from the glare, but Volanna had no doubt of his identity. When the man's eyes grew accustomed to the light, he lifted his hands to peer from under them, and she could make out his features.

"Aradon!" she said.

"Yes, Aradon," Lomar sneered. "Aradon the blacksmith, your one, true love, the great, legendary Golden Knight, the new Champion of the Seven Kingdoms, and the new hero of the countrypeople of Meridan."

"Why do you have him in this foul hole? What has he done but make you king—though that may turn out to be crime enough?" Volanna said.

Lomar grinned. "This man's crime is that he is the one person who could be a threat to my throne and come between me and my queen. But instead he will be my assurance of a compliant wife. As a servant of the prophecy, you understand prophecies, don't you, my dear one? Let me make a prophecy of my own, and you tell me whether you think it will come to pass. I, Prince Lomar of Meridan, do hereby prophesy that in all things, you, Princess Volanna of Valomar, soon to be queen of Meridan, will do exactly as I say. You will comply with my every wish, cater to my every whim, adjust to my every taste, and gratify my every desire. And as you know, my dear, my wishes, whims, tastes, and desires are, uh, often quite different from yours. Perhaps my pet Belze, whom you unfairly despise so much, will indeed share our bedchamber, and who knows what else. But I prophesy that you will not resist any whim I choose to indulge."

"I have vowed to be your wife, not your slave," replied Volanna.

Lomar stroked and twisted the blue scarf in his hand and said, "I prophesy that you will be whatever I want you to be. Now let me tell you why I have such confidence in my prophecy. Should you take it upon yourself to resist me in anything, you will receive on a silver platter one finger from the beloved hand you see chained to yonder wall. Should you make the same mistake again, you will receive another finger. And when there are no more fingers or toes, we will find other appendages and body parts to offer until nothing is left in this cell but a limbless torso. But if you become a faithful servant of my prophecy, this man will be left intact, reasonably fed, and kept fairly comfortable for a prisoner. And don't be so stupid as to think I will keep him here. Tomorrow, as you and I are pledging our troth, he will be removed to a remote prison at a location known only to Balkert and me."

"Do not listen to him, Volanna," said Aradon. "Do you think I wouldn't sacrifice my fingers and toes to keep you from falling into the pit of this creature's lusts?"

"But Aradon—"

"No, Volanna! Listen to what I say. All is not lost for me if I can know that you are living above the humiliation this man would inflict on you. That is worth more to me than a whole body."

With anguish in her voice, Volanna replied, "Aradon, I cannot—"

"Volanna, you must!" said Aradon. "I will not even feel the blade that slices away my limbs because each cut will be a message that you have not been caught in this spider's web. You must give me that. It is all I have left."

Lomar leaned against the bars of the cell, arms folded, a smirk on his face, and the scarf crushed in his fist. "Honor is such a noble thing," he said. "Noble but futile and not worth the wasting of further time. After all, we have a coronation to attend, don't we, my dear Volanna? And after that, a wedding. Do you hear, blacksmith? A wedding. My wedding. Our wedding—the beautiful, lovely, and luscious Volanna and I together forever, day after day, night after night. As you sit here in your cell, that will give you something to think about." He turned again to Volanna. "Bid a fond but final farewell to your champion, my pet."

Volanna could only gaze at Aradon as tears streamed down her cheeks. Aradon looked at her as if his eyes were cups to be filled with a draught that must last him forever.

"Enough of this maudlin sentiment," said Lomar. He pitched the blue scarf into Aradon's cell as he took Volanna's arm and led her pale and trembling back toward the gate of the dungeon. The sentry unlocked the gate as they approached, and after they had passed through it, Lomar said, "Please take note of the guards posted here, my dear one. Lest it enter your mind to tell Lord Aldemar or your father of this or to attempt a rescue between now and the wedding, I should tell you that the guard at the gate has orders to shout a word to the guard inside the moment he is threatened. That will signal the guard inside to kill the blacksmith before the gate can be opened. And if I even suspect that you have told anyone of this, it means your hero will immediately lose a finger."

In silence they ascended back into the region of sunlit rooms and fresh air, but the stifling darkness remained in Volanna's heart. She dared not return to her parents' chambers for fear that in her shaken state she might all-too-easily reveal her terrible secret. Instead she took Kalley to her old rooms, where they dressed for the coronation in near silence.

CHAPTER THIRTY-FOUR

TOE CORONATION

All the knights and nobles were gathered in the great throne hall of Morningstone Castle to witness the coronation of Prince Lomar. With much pomp and fanfare the ceremony began, and after all the proper speeches, litanies, recitations, and prayers, Lord Aldemar placed the fabled Crown of Eden upon Lomar's head and everyone in the hall stood and hailed him king of Meridan.

After the ceremony everyone adjourned to the banquet hall. Lomar was seated at the center of a table at the end of the hall, elevated on a dais above all the others. On the wall behind him hung a ceremonial shield bearing the image of the golden falcon of Perivale, and crossed beneath the shield were two bronze swords. Framing the weapons were curtains of wine red fringed with gold. Princess Volanna sat on Lomar's right, with her parents, King Tallis and Queen Ravella of Valomar, on her right. On Lomar's left sat the new chancellor apparent, Balkert.

Lord Aldemar had not been given a place in the new government nor a seat at the banquet, which gave the noblemen in the hall fodder for much gossip. Lomar's hatred of the regent was no secret, and many feared the future to be dark for this longtime servant of the kingdom.

The noblemen also noticed that another expected guest was missing—the Champion of the Seven Kingdoms. When Sir Denmore asked Balkert about Aradon's absence, Balkert explained that the Golden Knight had already been sent on an urgent quest for the new king. Denmore was not completely satisfied with the answer, but he chose not to pursue it at the moment.

After the guests settled into their places, the king's herald rapped his staff upon the floor until the hall grew silent. Then King Tallis rose from his chair with cup in hand, turned toward King Lomar, and proposed a toast. "Ladies, gentlemen, knights, citizens of Meridan and the Seven Kingdoms, pray join me in wishing health and long life to the new king of Meridan. May the Master of the Universe endow him with the wisdom, justice, mercy, and uprightness of his father Alfron. May he rule as a servant, with his heart vested in the welfare of his subjects. May he break the proud and mend the broken. May he rule in peace but be fearless and quick when battle is needed. As long as the Seven Kingdoms stand, may his reign be remembered as the moment when Perivale's folly was brought right with truth and goodness." As King Tallis ended his toast, he held his cup high toward Lomar, and all citizens in the hall stood and emulated the gesture with a loud cheer for the new king, then drank the draught of good health to him.

Lomar sat silent throughout the toast, almost sullen, until King Tallis's call for justice and uprightness, when the hint of a smile played at the corners of his mouth. As the toast ended, the guests sat again and waited for the new king to address them. But Lomar did not even rise. He merely signaled to the chamberlain, who instructed the servants to begin serving the food.

Volanna, still haunted by the image of Aradon chained in the black caverns beneath Morningstone, spoke little and could only pick at her plate. King Tallis knew that something was amiss. "What's the matter with my Dovey?" he asked her gently.

Volanna could not look at him but shook her head sadly and cast her eyes downward. "Please do not ask, Father," she said.

Tallis looked gravely at his daughter for a long moment but decided it was not the time to inquire further.

Lomar piled his plate high with three hens and several slices of cheese. With much slurping and smacking, he ate the best parts of

the hens and washed them down with several cups of wine. Mindless
of the advanced principles of etiquette long observed in the Seven
Kingdoms, he tossed the remaining pieces of the fowl to the floor
behind him. Volanna stifled her revulsion as he drained the dregs of
his sixth cup, spilling much of it on his chin and tunic, and belched
loudly. He wiped the dripping wine from his chin with his sleeve,
then waved his empty mug in the air, bellowing at the nearest servant
to fill it immediately. He tore off half a loaf of bread, settled back in
his chair, belched again, and turned his watery eyes toward Volanna.

"Wha's the matter, my princesh? Do I dishgust you?"

Volanna said nothing but sat still and straight with eyes downcast.

"The princesh is not very sociable tonight," he said. "Thash all
right; itsh time for actions inshtead of words, ishn' it, my dear?"
Oblivious to any guests who might be watching, Lomar lunged awkwardly toward Volanna, reaching for her with his greasy hand.

Volanna clutched Lomar's approaching wrist and pushed him
away so roughly that his crowned head bounced loosely on the back
of the tall chair.

Lomar glared at Volanna with reddened eyes and a reddening
face. "You are forgettin' whatsh in the dungeon, aren't you, my dear?
Tomorrow morning you can eshpect a platter bearing your beloved
shampion's first gift of himshelf."

Lomar fell into a fit of snorting giggles as all the anger drained
from Volanna's face and she went pale as a winter sky. She turned
again toward her plate, staring stiffly ahead. She felt Lomar's drunken
breath on her ear and his hands fumbling beneath her robes, and she
bit her lip as tears welled up in her eyes.

Suddenly, with much bumping and rustling, Lomar disappeared
from her side and his overturned chair clattered to the floor. She
looked up in surprise to see her father holding him by the collar, glaring at him nose to nose, his eyes livid with rage.

King Tallis spoke low but with a voice hard as iron: "No man,
whether he be king or peasant, will publicly humiliate my daughter
while there is breath in my body. The wedding is not until tomorrow,
and this hall is not a bedchamber. You will keep your drunken hands
to yourself if you want them to remain attached to your body." Tallis

released Lomar's collar with a shove, and the new king dropped roughly into his chair, where he sat disheveled and nonplussed, the Crown resting askew on his forehead. Tallis stood over him and shook an angry finger in his face. "Remember this, Lomar, and remember it well. If I ever find that you or your people have mistreated my daughter, I will forget all my vows and alliances and come down on your neck like a headsman's ax."

Tallis returned to his seat, placing his hands gently on Volanna's shoulders as he passed her chair. The hall went dead silent as everyone present gaped at the spectacle being played out before them.

Lomar, his crown still askew, rose wobbling from his chair and turned a bleary glare upon King Tallis. He opened his mouth to speak, but Balkert quickly rose beside him and whispered in his ear, "Let things be for the moment. King Tallis is a powerful ally with many friends in the hall tonight. Until we get the other kingdoms firmly under our banner, we need his goodwill. We will have ample time in the future to avenge this humiliation, and avenge it we will. But not tonight."

Lomar nodded and sat down so heavily that the Crown slipped over his forehead and completely covered his eyes. A few stifled snickers broke out among the guests. Lomar pushed the Crown back upon his head, revealing a face as red as the wine in his cup.

But the Crown would not stay in place. A moment later it slipped downward again, this time resting on his ears and the bridge of his nose. He removed it from his head and looked hard at it, then handed it to Balkert with a few muttered instructions. Balkert took his napkin, folded it carefully inside the rim of the Crown, and placed it again on Lomar's head. For a moment it appeared that the problem was solved, but after only a few minutes, the Crown fell again, this time completely covering Lomar's eyes and ears.

Volanna looked at Lomar with wonder, thinking he somehow looked much smaller. But she dismissed the absurd thought as nonsense. It must be the way he was drunkenly slumped in the large chair. A second napkin kept the crown in place for only a few seconds before it slipped down again, this time completely covering his nose. The guests had been doing their best to stifle their mirth, and only a few smothered giggles had escaped here and there, but now all attempts at control proved futile and laughter broke out unrestrained over the entire hall like steam blowing the lids off a hundred kettles. Lomar pushed the Crown up from his eyes and held it there as he struggled to his feet and stood swaying. He glared at his guests. "Out of here, all of you!" he screamed.

The sound of nearly two hundred chairs scraping the flagstone floor filled the hall as everyone arose and made their way to the doors. Volanna, King Tallis, Queen Ravella, and the others seated on the dais departed as well, leaving only the tottering Lomar with Balkert seated beside him at the table.

Lomar turned to Balkert, "What are you doin' here?"

"Well, I thought—"

"Oh, you think too mush, Baklerk—Balklurt. I get shick of it. Go do it shomewhere else. I don' need you stuck to me all the time like a bloated leech. Get out."

"But King Lomar—"

"I shaid, get out!" Lomar screamed. He angrily shoved Balkert away, the effort almost causing the new king to fall over the back of the chair.

Lomar watched Balkert leave the hall and close the door, then he dropped heavily into his chair. "Ev'rbody laughed at me. I don' care. Let 'em laugh. I'm king, now; I can have anything I want. I want Volanna, but Volanna hates me. Doesn' matter. Can have her anyway. Balkerk hates me. Tallis hates me. Stupid Tallis! Hate him too. Ev'rbody hates me. Don' care. But they laughed at me. Can't stand that. But it doesn' matter. Nothin' matters. But I don' care."

By now the Crown covered Lomar's entire face. He lifted it and yelled repeatedly for a page until one appeared at the doorway. "Bring Belze to me," he said. The page nodded but hesitated, looking at Lomar in wonder.

"Why are you lookin' at me like that?" Lomar demanded.

"I, uh, sire, it's just that you look so—so small," said the page. "Is anything wrong?"

"Are you goin' to obey my command or shtand there askin' stupid questions?"

The page bowed and left the room. In a few minutes he returned with the snake in its cage, which he placed on the table in front of Lomar.

"Now, get out," demanded Lomar.

The servant was glad to obey. Lomar slid out of his chair and took a step toward the cage, but his clothing, now much too large and loose, twisted around his legs, and he fell hard to the floor, knocking over a chair, which clattered and echoed in the empty hall. He struggled to his feet, mumbling a stream of slobbery curses, took the constrictor from its cage, and with some difficulty draped it around his shoulders. "You're really gett'n big, Belze," he said. "And so are my clothes. Stupid tailor! Ev'rthing's too big. What's happenin' Belze? Doesn' matter. Nothin' matters. I wish somethin' mattered. No, I don't. I really don' care."

Lomar climbed back into his chair and huddled against the back of it with his snake coiled loosely beside him and the Crown of Eden engulfing his head and shoulders. Within an hour he was so small that his clothing lay across his body like blankets, and he simply crawled out of them through the collar and sat naked inside the overturned Crown.

"Come to me, Belze," he said, his shrinking vocal cords rendering his voice a high-pitched squeak.

The serpent wound slowly toward him, its massive coils following exactly the path of its triangular head. The snake's black, forked tongue flicked in and out of the grinning mouth, and the baleful yellow eyes fixed on the tiny Lomar, whose body was now little thicker than its own. Slowly, even gently, the reptile wrapped itself around Lomar, who stroked its scales with hands no larger than squirrels' paws and mumbled in his treble squeak, "At least my Belze loves me. Oh, you're squeezin' too tight, Belze! Ease up a bit." But Belze did not ease up. Lomar heard an ominous hiss above his head and looked up to see the snake's gaping jaws gliding toward him with horrible slowness. He tried to scream but got out nothing more than a succession of shrill squeaks that were choked off by the reptile's mouth closing over his head. The bones of his body began to crack and snap as the snake tightened its coils around him, compressing his body into its expanding throat.

The page waiting outside the door of the hall heard the shrieks and thought it likely that rats were fighting over scraps of food beneath the tables. He fetched a broom from the kitchen, then opened the door of the hall and peered in. The room was now only dimly lighted, as the torches had burned low and only a few flickering candles remained. He could not see Lomar and assumed the king had slumped into his chair and fallen asleep. "Sire, do you wish me to kill the rat?" he called. Getting no answer, he stepped into the hall and made his way to Lomar's table. A long shadow moved across the floor at his feet. "Mercy!" he cried and jumped onto the nearest table. He watched the serpent slither across the floor with a lump in its body the size of a large rat. "The snake has done my job for me," he murmured as he watched the creature pass by. After a few moments, he got down from the table and went to Lomar's chair. He saw only the upturned Crown laying on Lomar's rumpled robe and tunic. He looked in the surrounding chairs, then in every chair in the room, then beneath every table, thinking Lomar might have stumbled and fallen into a drunken sleep. But he found no trace of him. He went immediately to awaken Balkert and tell him of the king's disappearance.

Balkert came to the hall and saw the Crown and Lomar's clothing lying in the chair, just as the page had reported. His first thought was to search the nearby closets, pantries, and anterooms, where he would likely find Lomar wenching some kitchenmaid. But when he examined the empty suit more closely, he noticed a very strange thing: while the clothing was rumpled and twisted, nothing had been undone—all buttons were buttoned and all bows tied. And most strange, the inner garments were still within the outer—even the sleeves of the tunic were totally within the sleeves of the robe. A neck chain and a ring, which Lomar never removed, were lying within the folds of the clothing. Even one of his shoes on the floor had the stocking still in it. The serpent's empty cage was on the table with the door gaping open, and it was unlike Lomar ever to leave it so. And wenching on the night before one's wedding seemed unlikely—well, perhaps not for Lomar.

Balkert sat in the chair beside Lomar's and pondered the meaning of the strange scene. He did not know what to make of it. The empty cage suggested that Lomar had left the room suddenly and unexpectedly before he could return his serpent and latch the door. Perhaps he had been frightened away or forced to leave. Had he been abducted? If so, why would he be stripped of his clothing? And why wouldn't the abductors have taken the Crown of Eden? Perhaps he was indeed wenching. Or perhaps he had been interrupted in the act. He might have been abducted after he had undressed. But none of these possibilities explained the uncanny condition of the clothing. It made no sense whatever to think that Lomar or his abductors would take the time to retie and rebutton the elaborate, complex suit. Yet, someone had apparently done just that, perhaps for no other reason than to baffle pursuers. The thought that something occult or other-worldly might have undone Lomar entered Balkert's mind briefly but flew out just as quickly, like a bird failing to find a perch, for he put no credence at all in the supernatural.

All in all, Balkert suspected that some misfortune had befallen the new king. He knew that Lomar was not loved by the people of his court, and Balkert's village takeovers in Lomar's name had made him many overt enemies. The more he thought on it, the more certain Balkert felt that some great harm had befallen the new king, but at this point he could afford to assume nothing. He must be diligent in searching for his master to divert any suspicion from himself. He had all servants awakened and the entire castle searched room by room, closet by closet, passageway by passageway. At daylight he would have the grounds around the castle searched as well.

Daylight came soon enough, but no trace of the new king was found.

CHAPTER THIRTY-FIVE

ⲦⲎⲈ ⳙⲤⳙⲢⲠⲈⲢ

Balkert sat in his chambers, his elbows on the arms of his chair and his hands clasped beneath his angular chin. He stared long at Lomar's clothing, now laid across his bed, illuminated only by the growing light of dawn at his eastern window. Although Balkert put no credence in spirits, occult magic, unearthly powers, or necromancy, he concluded by the evidence before him that some sort of evil had overtaken Lomar. Nothing supernatural was needed to explain the evil; Lomar had no shortage of fully human enemies. He mocked and ignored the noblemen of his court. He used and discarded women of all ranks. He berated and abused his best servants. Even if such behavior did not earn him a full tally of foes, the tyranny Balkert and Stundal initiated in his name in the outer reaches of Meridan surely gave him an ample supply.

Stundal was now dead and apparently Lomar as well. Who would assume the throne? As Balkert saw it, there was no obvious answer to the question. The prophecy that had given so much hope to the people had died with Lomar as it provided no alternate contingency for succession. Balkert considered the possibilities. Most of the old guard would want Lord Aldemar to continue as regent until the succession could be resolved. The younger knights and noblemen might want one of their own crowned, chosen by lots or some feat or test. He could even see the possibility that some would want to revive

Meridan's old federation with Valomar, calling on the beloved King Tallis to rule both kingdoms.

But Balkert saw no need for any of these possibilities to come to fruition. Indeed he relished the failure of the prophecy and the confusion of options for succession. Both would create exactly the chaos he needed to make the move now that he had planned to make at some propitious time in the future. Everyone knew that he was King Lomar's choice for chancellor, a choice Lomar was to have announced this very afternoon. It was most unfortunate that Lomar's disappearance could not have come one day later. There would have been no uncertainty over succession. Balkert as chancellor would simply have assumed the reigns of government. Since Lomar's intentions to appoint him were generally known, however, Balkert felt that by acting swiftly and prudently, the throne might yet be his to claim.

The six kings who had attended Lomar's coronation were lodged in guest chambers at Morningstone. Of the six, King Bronwilde of Oranth, King Thoreson of Rhondilar, and King Morgamund of Sorendale had already formed tentative alliances with Lomar, alliances of Balkert's own crafting. And like all agreements and treaties crafted by Balkert, the twine that held them together was implied threats or withdrawal of protection if the agreements were broken. Balkert called for his servant to summon the three kings to his chambers. He seated them in chairs facing the bed, stood before them, and told them what he had concluded.

"King Lomar is apparently dead."

The kings were stunned. "What has happened?" asked King Bronwilde.

"Look at this and draw your own conclusions," replied Balkert as he swept his hand above Lomar's clothing and the Crown on his bed. "A servant found these in the king's chair in the great hall long after we were all banished from the banquet last night. His serpent's cage was nearby, opened, and neither the snake nor Lomar has been seen since. I have had the entire castle searched, as well as the courtyards and the grounds around the castle walls. We have found no trace of the king at all."

King Thoreson gingerly fingered Lomar's suit. "How is it that all the clothing is yet buttoned and tied? And why is the tunic still inside the cloak? Is this some kind of trickery?"

"More likely some kind of witchcraft," replied Balkert.

Thoreson dropped the cloth as if it hid a nest of scorpions, as Balkert knew he would. He had learned that King Thoreson was among the most superstitious of men, and neither Bronwilde nor Morgamund lacked much of being his equal.

"In spite of the vaunted wisdom of the great King Tallis," continued Balkert, "he has apparently misinterpreted the prophecy. It seems that the Master of the Universe did not intend Prince Lomar to be king, nor did he intend the monarchy of Meridan to remain in the line of Perivale, since that line has now ended."

"But how can we be certain that Lomar is really dead?" asked Morgamund. "In spite of your search, he could turn up at any moment, and we could find that all this has a perfectly reasonable explanation."

"Yes, that's all too true," sighed Thoreson, "though, if I may be frank with you men, I'll say something that I would not say to anyone outside this room. I'd be a might happier if Lomar never shows up. True, I've got alliances with the man, but they were not crafted altogether to my liking. When ruffians from the mountains of Meridan overran my town of Sunderlon, Lomar volunteered to send troops to root out the outlaws. I then had to sign an agreement with him that allowed him to levy a tax on the citizens of the village for his continued protection. He shoved me into the lake and would've let me drown if I didn't meet his terms."

The other two kings nodded in agreement and told of similar treaties that Lomar had forced on them.

Balkert shook his head and sighed. "I know exactly what you mean for I was the reluctant agent who had to negotiate many of these treaties for Lomar. And to this day I feel a heavy burden of guilt for many of the terms he forced me to impose on his allies. You men can never know how many times I pled with the late prince to treat his neighbors as friends, not as vassals, but to no avail. Nor can you ever know how many times I was able to find ways to soften terms of treaties that I found entirely too harsh."

"Are you saying that, like the three of us, you'd just as soon he never shows up?" Morgamund asked.

Balkert sat looking down for a long moment before he shook his head and said with a reluctant sigh, "As much as I hate to admit it, I fear it is true. The man was not an easy master."

"Well, I suppose all this is nothing to the point," said Bronwilde. "With no evidence of his death, Meridan has no course but to wait a reasonable time for Lomar to show up. Then they must begin the process of selecting another king."

"So it seems," replied Balkert, "though all this is most unfortunate for the Kingdom of Meridan. The people have been without a king for almost twenty years, and they have looked forward to this day with great hope. Now they will be left yet without a king and with a whirlwind of uncertainty about how to get one, since the line of Perivale has apparently been cut off. It would be infinitely better for Meridan and the Seven Kingdoms if we could find a way to cut through that uncertainty and give the people a sense of security and stability by placing a king on Meridan's throne immediately."

"But what about the prophecy?" said Thoreson. "None of us wants to butt our heads against the prophecy."

"Ah, yes, the prophecy," said Balkert. "I do not doubt that King Tallis meant well in persuading the late King Alfron to accept his reading of the prophecy as the true one, but it is now obvious that the man was wrong, isn't it? My only regret is that his dogmatism has now left Meridan in chaos—without a king and with no clear means of selecting one."

"Tallis often takes too much on himself," said King Morgamund. "He thinks he is the only king in the Seven Kingdoms with a brain."

"I can't imagine why he would think such a thing," replied Balkert with only the barest hint of sarcasm. "In fact, I called the three of you here this morning to draw on your own considerable wisdom. As you know, I was to be designated chancellor of Meridan today. King Lomar was taken before he could confer the title, yet I feel the weight of the office. And in this time of national crisis, I cannot in good conscience simply walk away and let chaos reign.

Perhaps you three can advise me as to how I can guide Meridan toward choosing a wise and capable leader."

"I would think that Lord Aldemar would simply continue as regent," said Thoreson.

"Ah, yes, so he would, so he would," replied Balkert. "Our poor, dear Aldemar, the most honorable and selfless of men. Almost twenty years ago he took a task he neither wanted nor sought and has served Meridan faithfully and wisely. But the man is exhausted. Did you notice that he was not at the banquet last night? He simply hasn't the stamina to do all that his office requires. In fact, for the last few years I have tried to ease his burden by quietly taking on the administration of some of the villages near the borders of Meridan. Lord Aldemar has been living for the day of Lomar's coronation so he could be released, and I fear it might break him to call him back into service."

"Quite right, you cannot do such a thing to Lord Aldemar. Did Alfron have any kin? A brother or sister who might have spawned an heir?" said Bronwilde.

"Not one," replied Balkert.

"Perhaps there is some noble or knight fit to serve as king," said Thoreson.

"There may be several," said Balkert, "each fiercely jealous of the other. I would be loath to spawn a civil war by choosing any one of them."

"Then I see no solution. The noblemen will just have to fight it out. Anyway, it is really none of our concern; it is Meridan's problem," said Morgamund.

"Of course, from a purely legal point of view, that is true," replied Balkert. "But the Seven Kingdoms have always been something of a brotherhood, not just independent nations separated by arbitrary borders. Has it occurred to you that it may be an omen of the gods that the six kings of the old Perivalian empire are all assembled in Meridan's capital on this day of Meridan's crisis?"

"Ummm, I hadn't thought of it," said Thoreson. "An omen meaning what?"

"Meaning that you have been brought here at this time for a purpose: to guide Meridan toward choosing its next king. When you think about it, the gods knew what they were doing when they brought you here. Since the new king will of necessity be outside the line of Perivale, his succession is sure to be challenged unless he has strong backing. What stronger backing could he have than the kings of the six neighboring countries? Without such backing any choice is sure to result in civil war. Only you, sires, can save Meridan from bloody chaos."

"Well, it would be most unusual . . ." said Bronwilde.

"Unusual, yes, but I think the man must be right," said Thoreson. "The omen is clear, when you think on it, and who are we to gainsay it. What do you propose we do, Balkert?"

"I propose we call in the other three kings for an immediate council," Balkert replied. "But before they join us, I suggest that we four do a bit of planning as to how the meeting should go. It would save considerable time. It might even be best if we agree on a candidate for the new king."

"You know the men of Meridan's Hall. Do you have any suggestions?" asked Morgamund.

"We must look for a man who meets certain criteria. He should not be one of the landed nobles. As I said, such a choice would breed jealousy and result in war. He should be experienced in administration and government and should be one who was close to King Lomar and understood his goals and could continue his policies with fairness and equanimity. He also needs to be a man with some ability at statecraft, who understands how to work well with other kingdoms, and one who is willing to serve Meridan selflessly, as Lord Aldemar did, but who is young enough to endure the stress of office. Unfortunately I'm at a loss to suggest where we can find such a man."

King Bronwilde began to chuckle. "Brothers, I believe we've got the very man right here under our noses."

"What? Who?" said Balkert, innocence and surprise dripping from every inflection.

"You yourself are the very man, Balkert. You are just too humble to see it. Don't you agree, brothers?"

Thoreson and Morgamund agreed, and Balkert protested right up to the edge of refusal, just enough to redouble the three kings' affirmation. In the end, with a proper show of reluctance and unworthiness, he agreed to serve his country as king if a majority of his neighboring kings truly desired it. But he warned them that the other three kings might lack their high vision for Meridan's future. King Kor of Lochlaund had seemed to lean toward Lomar but had made no commitments and signed no alliances. King Umberland of Vensaur might be harder to bring around, as he was openly distrustful of the young prince, and that distrust was likely to carry over to Balkert. There was no question about King Tallis of Valomar. In spite of the fact that his interpretation of the prophecy had been discredited, he would undoubtedly cling to Lord Aldemar's regency and the old ways and be openly hostile to Balkert's succession. Therefore the four of them would be wise to plan the course of the council before they called in the other three kings.

"But we still have one obstacle to overcome before they will listen to us," Balkert said. "They will never agree to any alternative to the prophecy unless they are convinced that Lomar is dead, especially not King Tallis. And the condition of Lomar's clothing here is certainly too ambiguous to convince them."

"Quite right," Bronwilde said. "What do you propose, Balkert?"

"I propose a thing I would never consider were Meridan not at the point of national crisis. We must convince the other kings that Lomar is, indeed, dead. Since the present condition of Lomar's clothing will not convince them, we must alter that condition. If the clothing were torn and bloody . . ."

"I don't know about this," Morgamund shook his head. "I'm reluctant to deceive our brother kings."

"So am I," Balkert replied, "and were we not in crisis, it would never enter my mind. But we will not actually be deceiving them. We in this room are thoroughly convinced that Lomar is dead, and it behooves us to take whatever measures are needed to convince these other kings of what we know to be true. We will not be deceiving them; we will be helping them to see the truth."

"I see your point," Thoreson said, "and as a practical matter, I agree to it. Let's get it done, men. I have a couple of trusty, circumspect servants who can perform this deed quickly without anyone in the castle knowing of it."

The other kings agreed to the plan, and Thoreson called his servants, gave them Lomar's suit with explicit instructions as to how it should look when they brought it back, and sent them away with urgings to be quick.

After the servants left the room, Balkert outlined to the three conspiring kings his plan to persuade the three remaining kings and rehearsed to them their roles, giving each certain cues to follow as the meeting progressed. In half an hour Thoreson's servants returned with fragments of Lomar's suit, torn to shreds and soaked with blood. Balkert and the kings examined the cloth, expressed satisfaction with its condition, and Balkert laid it on the bed with the Crown of Eden. When he was convinced that each king had grasped his part of the strategy, he sent for Kings Kor, Umberland, and Tallis to join them in his chambers to discuss a matter of great urgency.

Balkert stood at the door and bowed low as the kings entered, inquiring about the comfort of each and of his family. "And how fare the Queen Ravella and Princess Volanna?" he asked as King Tallis walked into the room.

"They arose early and returned to Lord Aldemar's estate to prepare for the wedding," Tallis replied.

All the better, thought Balkert as he ushered Tallis to his chair. When the six monarchs were seated, each with a mug of mead in his hand, Balkert explained to them the purpose of the meeting. He told them that King Lomar had vanished and that Thoreson's servants, assisting in the search for the missing king, had found fragments of his clothing in the edge of the woods just north of Morningstone Castle, torn and bloody as they could see on the bed before them. The servants had followed a trail marked by blood on the grass and in large pools on the ground. The trail had disappeared in the depths of the woods. Surely all could agree that the new king was dead; the only question to be answered was, How did he die? In his drunkenness did he fall from his window only to be found by some animal that dragged his body into the woods? Or was he a victim of murder? Balkert did not know, but he would not rest until he got to the bottom of it.

Balkert watched with satisfaction as the kings' faces reflected the surprise and outrage he had hoped they would. Then he outlined the dilemma facing Meridan. "After waiting over a hundred years for a prophecy to be fulfilled, after long hope that stability would soon return to Meridan's government, and after three days of joyous anticipation and planning, Meridan has no king, no regent, and no legal prospect of getting either. The resulting insecurity among the people will be disastrous. Anarchy and factions will develop, which political opportunists will exploit to Meridan's detriment. Even a civil war is likely if the nobles of the country compete for the throne.

"We must unite to present a plan that shows strength and stability at once, even today. There is no rightful king. Prince Lomar was Alfron's only son, and he has disappeared, apparently the victim of an unfortunate accident or insidious foul play. We must devise a way of choosing a new king, and we must do it quickly. I would entertain suggestions from your majesties."

King Tallis immediately objected. "This is not a matter for six foreign kings to decide. We have no right to impose our will on the citizens of Meridan. Besides, evidence for Lomar's death is circumstantial. You must wait until your investigation proves that he is indeed dead."

Balkert acknowledged King Tallis's point of view and asked the other kings if they agreed.

King Bronwilde responded, "It seems clear beyond doubt to me that Lomar is dead, whatever the cause. No one could lose so much blood and survive. And Meridan's noblemen have been too long without a king to know how to choose one effectively. For the wellbeing of Meridan and the Seven Kingdoms, perhaps it would be wise for us to step in and help them through this crisis."

King Morgamund followed on cue. "My thought is that since Lomar had selected Balkert as his chancellor, he should be made regent until a permanent king can be chosen."

Just as Balkert had predicted, King Tallis objected. "Lomar had not yet announced his appointments. The only legal course for Meridan is to retain Lord Aldemar as regent until the matter of succession can be resolved by Meridan's own people. Lord Aldemar was duly appointed by the Hall of Knights at the death of King Alfron, and he certainly has the confidence of the people."

"Tallis is right," said King Umberland. "And I think we sell the people of Meridan short to claim they cannot select a new king without internal strife. None of this is our business at all."

King Kor sided with Tallis and Umberland. "I care about Meridan's leadership for one reason only. I want my stolen village back. Indeed, the only reason I came to that thief Lomar's coronation at all was to get an audience with Lord Aldemar. I know Aldemar to be a just man, and I hoped he could talk sense into the new king's thick head."

"Ah, yes, you speak of Lomar's takeover of Ridgedale," said Balkert. "That incident was most unfortunate. I personally spent a week's store of words trying to dissuade the prince from that action, but to no avail. Were I indeed chancellor today, I would have Meridan's troops withdrawn immediately."

"Would you now?" said King Kor. "Are you willing to swear to that?"

"Of course I would swear to it, but to what purpose? As you, King Umberland, and King Tallis have so pointedly noted, I am not the chancellor nor does this council have the right to make me regent," replied Balkert.

"I think I have just developed a little more interest in the internal affairs of Meridan." King Kor stood and stepped toward Balkert. Balkert tensed against the back of his chair, and his eyes grew wide as the king reached into his robe. "I have no interest in making you regent or chancellor, but if you will sign this treaty right now, I will make you king." Kor drew from his robe a scroll, which he unrolled inches from Balkert's face—an agreement promising to withdraw all Meridan troops and grant to Lochlaund sovereignty over Ridgedale forever.

"No, Kor!" Tallis almost shouted. "As you said, Aldemar is a just man. He will certainly sign your treaty."

"Maybe so, maybe not. Who knows in these times who will turn on you tomorrow. Indeed, I have wondered more than once why Aldemar allowed the thing to happen at all," said Kor.

"I can assure you that he knew nothing of it," Tallis replied. "I've had word of many crimes committed in the villages of Meridan that were carefully hidden from the ears of the regent."

"Which merely proves the rumor we've all heard of late," said Bronwilde. "Lord Aldemar is getting old and tired. He's no longer able to manage the affairs of Meridan effectively. I think Kor's proposal has merit."

"You do me great honor," said Balkert, "but surely there are many men in Meridan more suitable for kingship than I."

King Thoreson picked up his cue as he had been rehearsed. "You sell yourself short, Balkert. In fact, as I think on it, you alone possess all the right qualifications." He counted on his fingers as he spoke. "You are a citizen of Meridan; you are an appointee of the man who was king; as Lomar's counselor, you are experienced in governmental matters; you are old enough not to be a novice yet young enough to bear the stress of the office."

"I agree," Morgamund chimed in. "And I say, why dally with short measures? Meridan has been too long without a king. They do not need another regent. We've got the right man, so let's get the thing done."

King Tallis objected strenuously, and Umberland backed him vigorously as the discussion elevated into a debate and the debate into a heated exchange. But Kor refused to budge. It was not until Umberland and Kor stood nose to nose, glaring and shouting into each other's beet red faces that Balkert made his final move. "My dear kings! Please, we must stop this quarreling before a war breaks out. I will accede to your wishes if you truly believe that my kingship will be in the best interests of Meridan. I suggest that rational debate has ended and it's time to put the matter to a vote."

The two angry kings took their seats as all but Tallis and Umberland mumbled their assent. "I will not be a part of this illegal travesty," said Tallis.

"Very well, do as you like. But I cannot gainsay the collective wisdom of a majority of the monarchs of the Seven Kingdoms." Balkert then polled the kings, who voted as they had debated: Bronwilde, Thoreson, Morgamund, and Kor voted to place Balkert on the throne of Meridan. Umberland dissented, and Tallis refused to vote at all. After the polling Balkert urged the two dissenting kings to be magnanimous and give him their support as a show of unity. King

Umberland sighed and held up his hands in a gesture of defeat. "For the sake of unity in the Seven Kingdoms, I agree," he said. Tallis said nothing but sat with hands clasped against his bearded lips, deep in thought.

Balkert interpreted Tallis's silence as indecision and decided to press his advantage. "King Tallis, you have pledged your daughter in marriage to the new king of Meridan. I presume that your famed sense of honor will hold you to that promise."

"Absolutely not!" boomed King Tallis. "I pledged my daughter in marriage to King Alfron's son. You are neither Alfron's son nor the rightful king of Meridan. Not only would I not force my daughter into marriage with you, I would not allow it. And she most certainly would not consent."

A cryptic smile spread across Balkert's face. "I wouldn't be too sure of that. I will put the question to her myself, and we will see just what her response is."

Tallis stood and put his finger in Balkert's face. "I don't know what is behind the threat you just implied, but know this, Balkert, if I find that you have used any of your conniving, underhanded ways to coerce my daughter against her will, I will use every means available to me as king of Valomar to see that you go to an early grave."

Balkert reddened and glared at Tallis. "I have tried to be fair and tolerant with you, Tallis, but you have just crossed the line of my patience. Get out of my sight. Get out of my land."

"Meridan is not your land," said King Tallis as he turned and walked out of the room.

While the five remaining kings were still assembled, Balkert called Lomar's staff of aides into the room and asked Thoreson to explain to them the kings' decision and the plans that were afoot. Then Balkert dismissed the kings and instructed the aides concerning his plan for the coronation. He wanted it to take place immediately—even today, before Tallis had time to rally Meridan's nobility against him. He also wanted the coronation to be public. The people were already in a celebratory mood, and they were expecting a king to be crowned. He felt sure that the spectacle of the event and the presence of the five kings affirming his throne would have a strong visceral impact on all witnesses, which would do much to secure his position.

He chose the park at the base of Perivale's monument as the place and set midafternoon as the time. He sent criers throughout the city calling the people to Cheaping Square to witness the event. The criers were instructed to bypass Lord Aldemar's manor, however. Balkert knew that Volanna was there, and unaware of the events of the night, was preparing herself for her wedding. He set guards at the base of Aldemar's hill with instructions to let no one enter the road to the manor, not even King Tallis. If the high-minded king resisted, he just might find himself in a cell next to Aradon's.

Aradon! Balkert had almost forgotten. Lomar had instructed him to transfer the blacksmith to a prison cell in the abandoned Maldor Castle. Although Lomar was gone, Balkert still intended to make the transfer for his own purposes. But at the moment he had more falcons than he could fly. He would order it done tomorrow. Today, after all his plans were solidly in place, he would ride to Aldemar's manor and convince Princess Volanna that she should become his queen, further solidifying his grip on Meridan's throne. Securing her compliance would be simple. He would explain to her that things had not changed for Aradon. He would remain in prison according to Lomar's plan but as Balkert's hostage instead of the late prince's. He thought the princess might even be relieved at the change in bridegrooms. He knew how fervently she detested Lomar.

CHAPTER THIRTY-SIX

a king in check

King Tallis left Balkert's rooms determined that the decision of the council of the kings would not stand. He summoned a palace page as he walked briskly down the hallway, "Where can I find Sir Denmore?" he asked.

"Denmore is here in the castle even now, your majesty. He and Sir Eanor are playing chess in the west tower."

Tallis strode swiftly to the tower and found the two knights staring hard at a half-empty chessboard. "Sir Denmore, your king is missing," he said.

Denmore leaned forward and studied the pieces. "Not so. It would take Eanor ten moves to put my king in check even if I made no moves at all."

"You have lost your king, and a usurper claims his throne. Lomar disappeared in the night, and Balkert has positioned himself to receive the Crown of Eden this very afternoon."

Denmore and Eanor both stood abruptly, upsetting the chess table and sending the pieces across the floor.

"What in thunder are you saying?" demanded Denmore.

Tallis explained to them the discovery of Lomar's clothing and recounted the decision of the council of the five kings. "We must call an assembly of the Hall of Knights within the hour. Time is short. Do you know of a secret place where they can assemble?"

Eanor thought a moment. "All of Meridan's knights are in the city for the coronation, but locating them may not be easy. They will be at the archery lists, the falcon fields, in rooms at inns, with their ladies or families. Yet I think between Denmore and me, along with a few hired messengers, we can get most of them together. As to where we could meet, I hardly know—"

"I know of a place," said Denmore. "The Musty Tankard has a large back room where Aldemar often met when he needed privacy. I will secure the room."

"Good. And see that Lord Aldemar is invited as well," said Tallis. "Give me directions and I will call on some of the knights who live here in Corenham."

An hour later only eighteen of the forty-two knights of the Hall were located. Lord Aldemar was not among them, and when Tallis asked of his absence, Denmore told him of the armed guards posted at the road to Aldemar's estate allowing no one to enter. Tallis felt his heart grow numb. Apparently Ravella and Volanna were already prisoners of Balkert, and a peaceful exit from Meridan might no longer be possible.

He closed his eyes and shuddered. War: the maker of legends and heroes. The glory of Priam, Hector, Alexander, David, and Cyrus. Tallis shook his head. He knew the truth about war. War was the image and stench of hell itself—death, destruction, chaos, oblivion, grief, agony—the ultimate expression of man's independent self. Yet war had always been an ever-present necessity for selfless men as well, men who must use war as fire is used to fight fire if hell was to be contained in its quest to devour the earth.

Tallis quickly assessed his strength. The twenty-four knights he had brought from Valomar added to the eighteen knights of Meridan presently assembled plus Eanor and Denmore gave him a total of forty-four. How many could Kings Bronwilde, Thoreson, Morgamund, and Kor muster? He wondered about King Umberland. His support of Balkert was reluctant at best. When forced to choose, wouldn't he side with Tallis in the cause of Meridan? Even with Umberland's help, it was not clear to Tallis that he could muster strength superior to that of Balkert and his allies. But with or without sufficient strength, Tallis knew he would do what he must do.

He turned to the assembled knights, some sitting at the rude tables, some sitting on benches, others standing against the walls. "Knights of Meridan's Hall, by now most of you know of King Lomar's unexplained disappearance and Balkert's intention to usurp your throne. In a council held this morning, Kings Thoreson, Morgamund, Bronwilde, Kor, and Umberland threw their support behind Balkert, though Umberland's support was less than enthusiastic. I believe that Balkert's move is unlawful. The monarchs of the Seven Kingdoms have no legal say in the internal matters of Meridan. If Alfron's line is indeed cut off—and we do not yet really know that to be true, for Lomar's body has not been found—Lord Aldemar must remain as regent until Meridan can devise a way to choose its own king. Balkert will be crowned not two hours from now unless we in this room unite and act quickly. I open the floor for discussion, but it must be to the point. We haven't much time."

Sir Denmore was quick to respond. "I see no need to waste any more words. Our course is clear. Let's get on with a plan to drive that weasel Balkert back into his hole." Sir Eanor was quick to affirm Denmore's call to action, as were Sir Prestamont, Sir Karamore, and Sir Halliston.

Sir Fentamore stepped forward and said, "I agree that Balkert's move is illegal and deplorable. But remember, he has the backing of five kings. All we can count on are the score of knights presently in this room."

"You also have myself and the twenty-four knights of Valomar's hall," said Tallis.

"And we are grateful for your selfless support of our cause," continued Fentamore. "But that gives us little over forty mounted warriors, and we all know that the five kings opposing us can mount well over a hundred."

"I doubt that Umberland will support Balkert if it comes to war," said Tallis.

"I can appreciate your doubt, King Tallis," said Fentamore, "but I'm not willing to risk the odds of forty men against a hundred on the uncertainty of a doubt. My own doubt is of the possibility of victory."

"When did certainty of victory become a factor?" Denmore

retorted with heat in his voice. "We fight when our cause is certain, whether or not the outcome is."

Sir Benidah arose from his chair and said, "Sir Denmore, I hope you are not questioning the courage of those of us who believe in prudence. Fentamore's point is simply that we must weigh the cost against the probable result. The cost is clear. With forty or maybe less—we have not yet ascertained that all in this room would join your cause—against a hundred, the probable outcome is defeat and the loss of our lives or our freedom. Weigh that price against our present well-being, and the balance is questionable, at least."

"Are you saying that some in this room would actually support Balkert as your king?" asked Tallis.

"Some of us have long lost confidence in Meridan's government," said Benidah, "and no longer depend on the throne for protection. After all, the throne of Meridan has been empty for almost twenty years. Aldemar never exerted the authority of a monarch, and of late he has been growing tired. Some of the reins of government have slipped from his fingers. I, for one, appreciate the fact that Balkert has stepped in and provided order and stability in areas where it was desperately needed." Over half the knights in the room grunted with assent or nodded their heads in affirmation.

"Are you men blind or stupid or something worse?" thundered Denmore. "The reins have not slipped from Aldemar's fingers; they have been twisted from his grip by this cheat and liar who threatens our throne. Balkert has generated the chaos he has corrected, and his correction has been the imposition of tyranny on the outer edges of Meridan. This man must not be crowned—unless it is with my mace!"

"And just who will take the throne if not Balkert?" Benidah asked. "I wonder if Tallis here does not hanker for it himself? Since Alfron's death he has assumed for himself the role of unofficial leader of the Seven Kingdoms. Perhaps he craves to make it official. And what better opportunity than to goad Meridan into destroying itself with civil war, then step in and anoint himself emperor of the Seven Kingdoms."

Denmore pointed toward Sir Benidah with fire in his eyes. "I will not stand by and listen to such slander. King Tallis has assumed nothing. The role of leader has been thrust on him because of his great wisdom and valor."

"Ah, yes. The wisdom of the great Tallis is what gave us the interpretation of the prophecy that has misled Meridan for twenty years. And to what purpose? The son of Alfron is dead and so is the prophecy. So much for the fabled wisdom of the great King Tallis."

Sir Denmore stepped toward Sir Benidah as he drew his sword from its sheath. Tallis quickly stepped between them and held Denmore back. "Put up your sword, Denmore. We are not here to defend my honor but to preserve Meridan from certain tyranny."

Denmore glared for a long moment at Benidah, then sheathed his sword, and King Tallis turned toward the knights in the room. "I called you here on the assumption that you would be united in your opposition to Balkert. I came ready to join you in ousting him from your land. But I see that I may have assumed wrongly. You, the peers of Meridan, have become so fat and contented that you no longer care for justice and truth. You don't care whether your king is a lion or a jackal; you just want a king who will leave you alone. You don't care whether he taxes small farmers and villagers out of field and home as long as your barn is full, your bed soft, and your fences strong.

"I don't know what Balkert has promised you for your complicity, but do you really think you are immune to his villainy? Today it's only the tradesman and the shepherd he impoverishes, but mark my words, tomorrow it will be the knight and the nobleman. Balkert's treachery will be like a leak in a dike; it will begin as a small, insignificant trickle and will grow into a torrent that will soon break through all restraints and engulf all of you. That is the future you are choosing if you do not prevent Balkert from sitting on your throne today. And this moment is the time for decision. I want to see each man here declare himself either for or against this usurper so that all colors will be shown. Those who stand in opposition to Balkert as king, show your hands now."

Sir Denmore and Sir Eanor quickly lifted their hands high. Sir Prestamont followed soon after. After a long pause, two other knights slowly, hesitantly raised their hands to shoulder height.

"Those who stand in support of Balkert as king, show your hands now," called Tallis. Sir Benidah and Sir Fentamore lifted their hands. For a moment no one else moved. Then Benidah glared around the room. Three others raised their hands, and then one by one, five others followed. The three remaining knights made no move at all but watched in silence with impassive faces and folded arms.

"It is clear to me that Meridan has no heart to oppose this evil man. Therefore I cannot lift my arm against him either. I will not be guilty of the crime I have accused the five other kings of committing. I will not force my will on the unwilling citizens of Meridan. If you will not oppose Balkert for Meridan's sake, then I as an alien in your land must not assume that task for myself in violation of the will the Hall has just expressed. But I give you a warning. Do not believe for one moment that the prophecy will fail. Fulfillment may seem impossible at the present, but I suggest that you make no moves against what the prophecy predicts. If you do, you will be the ones who break, not the prophecy."

Sir Benidah looked at Tallis and began to laugh. "My dear King Tallis, the prophecy is already broken." Fentamore joined in the laughter, and others followed one by one. Soon the room was resounding with the derisive mirth of the dozen men facing King Tallis, who stood alone near the door. Denmore, Eanor, and Prestamont sat nearby, glaring at the floor as Tallis turned and walked out of the room.

Tallis hardly heard the laughter of the knights behind him. He stepped through the door and looked for his aide, Sir Grenston, who had been instructed to wait for him outside. But Grenston was nowhere to be seen.

Sir Denmore came outside right behind him. "What will you do now, King Tallis?"

"I must assemble my knights and lead them to Aldemar's estate. I strongly suspect that Balkert is holding my wife and daughter prisoner there, though why I cannot fathom. But my aide has disappeared, which is most strange. He is the most loyal of my knights, and he was to wait for me at this door."

"Where are your knights?" asked Denmore.

"Still camped in their pavilions behind the arena," said Tallis. "I must get to them at once." Tallis hurried to the rear of the building. His steed was gone as well.

"Sire, I smell a rotten egg in this nest. Take my horse—the roan yonder—and get to your men. I will find another and join you at Aldemar's road. Apparently I'm already branded a rebel; I may as well be a horse thief as well. They can't hang me twice."

Tallis mounted Denmore's stallion, turned to the knight with a salute and said, "Thank you, friend of Meridan." Then he wheeled the horse and spurred it toward the eastern gate of Corenham. When he left the city and reached the open road, which was lined on both sides with thick pines and oaks, he urged the horse into a gallop.

As he rounded the bend that led to the amphitheater, he suddenly pulled up short. Fifty paces ahead a felled pine lay across the road. As he stopped, six mounted warriors trotted out of the woods and surrounded him. Tallis drew his sword and prepared to charge the nearest one.

"Wait, your majesty." A seventh man, unarmed and unarmored, rode from the woods, holding up his open palm, "Rest your sword and hear me out."

"Who are you?" demanded Tallis.

"I am the new Earl of Widmont, a fair county in Meridan's far south. My lord Balkert wishes you no harm, King Tallis. But he suspects that you wish him harm. My orders are twofold: to prevent you from rallying your knights against my master and detain you until the time of the coronation."

"Balkert no longer has anything to fear from me. If Meridan will not move against your master, neither will I. But I do intend to free my wife and daughter, whom your Balkert is holding at the estate of Lord Aldemar."

"I see that we have a misunderstanding," said Widmont. "Balkert is not holding your family prisoner."

"Then the armed guards at Aldemar's road are merely decorations?"

"The guards are for their protection, not their detainment."

"That is a lie. They have no need of protection at Aldemar's estate."

"Very well, your majesty, I will tell you the truth," sighed Widmont. "The guards are to prevent anyone from entering Aldemar's estate and informing the Princess Volanna of the death of King Lomar. Balkert does not wish to prevent the princess from preparing for her wedding. She is not being held prisoner; when her preparations are completed, she will be allowed to leave the estate and proceed to the coronation."

"You are speaking nonsense. Thanks to Balkert's criminal conniving, there may be a coronation this afternoon, but without Lomar there will be no wedding."

"My lord Balkert thinks otherwise, your majesty."

"The man is mad! My daughter will never consent to marry him."

"That we shall wait to see. She will find Balkert a very persuasive man. May I suggest that you dismount and make yourself comfortable, your majesty? We have no intent to harm you. Indeed, I'm sure your own knights will travel this very road in less than an hour on their way to Balkert's coronation. At that time we shall release you to return with them."

"Why would Balkert allow me in the audience?" asked Tallis. "Wouldn't he fear that I would try to disrupt the proceedings?"

"Not at all, your majesty. Indeed, I think he half hopes you would do that very thing. You have already lost all credibility with the citizens of Meridan. Your reputation for wisdom fell hard with the failure of the prophecy. All they need now is more babbling about the prophecy or Balkert's legitimacy to prove that you are truly mad." Widmont smiled broadly.

King Tallis could do nothing to escape the trap into which he had fallen, and he knew it. The six warriors maintained their circle around him and ushered him off the road some hundred paces into the forest. He refused to dismount but sat straight and silent on Denmore's charger—which forced his captors to remain mounted in a circle around him. After the passing of an hour, the sound of hoofbeats was heard in the distance, and one of Widmont's warriors trotted to the road, looked in the direction of the amphitheater, and returned. "The knights of Valomar are coming," he said.

The circle of warriors surrounding the king parted, opening up the way for Tallis to join his knights. "You are free to go," said Widmont.

CHAPTER THIRTY-SEVEN

The Rescue

By early afternoon, the people began to assemble at Cheaping Square. Though all had heard the criers announcing Lomar's disappearance and the coronation of Balkert, they were utterly baffled by the news and hungry for more information. Many of them did not even know who Balkert was, but to those who had not had dealings with him, it did not matter. Meridan had not had a king in almost twenty years, and while Lord Aldemar's regency had been just—and until the last two or three years, efficient—the people had longed to have a king again. They looked forward to the coronation with a hope that had little to do with the name of the man to be crowned. A monarch at the helm of a nation gave its people a sense of identity, of pride in country, of security. A king gave them a focal point and a sense of completeness. A country without a king was like southbound geese with no bird at the point. Or like a choir without a choirmaster, each singer knowing the music and singing it well enough, but without passion or a sense of its significance.

Rumors and wondering about the coronation filled the inns and spilled over into the streets. Opinions flowed generously, like ale from the kegs of the taverns, and divided generally along two lines: Many thought it almost certain that Lomar had been abducted and murdered. A few who had had dealings with Balkert wondered if Lomar's blood might be found on his dagger. Others were equally sure that

Lomar was the victim of witchcraft. One chambermaid, who stopped at the Blue Heron inn after her night's work at Morningstone, reported strange sights and sounds coming from Lomar's chambers in the deep of the night.

"What sort of sights and sounds?" asked a grizzled farmer sitting nearby.

"Strange flickerin' lights showin' under his door, an' icky green smoke creepin' from it. Cold, moanin' voices wailin' from inside and blackbirds with yellow devil eyes perchin' on his window sills. It was the weirdest thing I ever saw, I tell you."

There was less opinion and less curiosity about the king-apparent, Balkert. Few people knew anything about him, for most of his dealings had been done in the name of Lomar. Most victims of his manipulations did not know that he was the manipulator. The few who did know took the news of his imminent coronation with a heavy sense of foreboding.

As Tallis and his twenty-four knights arrived at Cheaping Square, it was filled with a vast sea of humanity that overflowed like rivers into the adjoining streets. Scarcely an inch of space was left for onlookers on foot, much less mounted riders, so Tallis made no attempt to lead his knights through the crowd. He had no intention of interfering with the coronation, but if Balkert had devised some scheme to force Volanna into wedding him, that was another matter. He stopped at the edge of the assembly and looked everywhere for Volanna's carriage, but she had not yet arrived. He remained on his horse as he waited with his still-mounted knights grouped behind him. Tallis looked around the square. A portable but elaborate throne—the "summer throne" of Perivale, which had often accompanied the king on official journeys out of Corenham—had been set up on the elevated base of the monument. A draped, wine red canopy fringed with gold was hung above it.

Within minutes after Tallis arrived, trumpet fanfares blared forth from the lower gates of Morningstone Castle, and distant drummers began a steady beat. All heads turned in anticipation. Soon the crowd could see the banners of a mounted procession advancing from the castle, and soon after that, the procession itself. Leading the procession

was the king's herald, followed by the drummers. Following them were
Sir Benidah and Sir Fentamore, fully armored except for helms and
richly caped. Behind them came Balkert, riding in Lomar's open carriage drawn by the four handsome Albustian stallions. Following the
carriage were the five consenting kings mounted on their chargers, each
with two of his own knights in escort. As the procession drew near the
waiting spectators, armed guards parted the crowd, and Balkert and his
entourage made their way slowly toward the Perivale monument.

At that moment Tallis saw the carriage bearing Ravella and
Volanna approach on the far side of the crowd, escorted by four
mounted palace guards. Tallis, not wanting to make any move that
could be interpreted as a threat, dismounted from Denmore's horse
and instructed two of his knights to do the same and follow him on
foot. The rest he commanded to begin working their way slowly
around the edge of the crowd and meet him at Volanna's carriage.
With his two escorts, he made his way through the crowd toward his
wife and daughter.

Volanna and her mother were seated side by side in the carriage,
Volanna a celestial vision of feminine glory in her white gown
trimmed with silver. It was not her dress, however, but her eyes that
told the story. Round and solemn, often staring without seeing, they
looked heavy and distant, as if weighted with infinite grief. As Tallis
drew near her carriage, she looked at him not with reproach—as he
might have expected and even wished, for it would have told him that
her spirit was yet alive—but with utter despair. Ravella, her own eyes
red-rimmed and moist, clutched and stroked her daughter's hand,
which lay limp and listless in her own.

"Volanna, why are you dressed for a wedding?" Tallis asked.

Volanna cast her eyes down and said nothing. Her mother
responded, "Balkert has told her of Lomar's disappearance and of his
own coronation, and he has somehow persuaded her to become his
queen, as if her vow were yet in force."

"Volanna, what are you doing?" asked Tallis, utterly perplexed.
"You know that Lomar's disappearance releases you from your vow.
You have no obligation at all to this usurper. You can put all this
behind you and return with us to Valomar."

"No, I cannot," said Volanna quietly without lifting her eyes.

"Why, Volanna, why?" demanded Tallis. "What has this conniver said to coerce you into this wedding of doom?" Volanna still would not look up but remained silent as a single tear traced an erratic path down her cheek. "Tell me, Volanna, tell me!" said Tallis.

"I cannot, Father."

Tallis took Volanna's listless hand and cupped it within both of his. "Volanna, I know that Balkert is holding over you some doom from which you can see no escape. Behind me are twenty-four of Valomar's most valiant warriors. As you can see, they are even now making their way toward us. At my command, they will rescue you from this dark fate Balkert has imposed on you or die in the attempt. When they are within fifty paces, I will give that command."

Volanna looked up at Tallis, her eyes wide with unspeakable sadness, tears now streaming down her cheeks. "No, please, you must not do that. Trust me, Father, you must not!"

"Volanna, please tell me why!" Tallis's face was contorted in anguish.

"I cannot, Father. A year ago I made a vow to you that I did not fully understand, but I did not waver from keeping it. Now you must make a vow to me that you cannot understand. Please promise that you will not stop me from doing what I must do."

For a long moment Tallis looked hard into his daughter's anguished eyes, his heart rebelling at her outrageous request but his mind knowing that his attempt at rescue might unwittingly trigger some great tragedy. "I will take the length of the coronation ceremony to think on it."

At that moment the procession reached the steps to the platform where the throne awaited. The kings and knights dismounted. Balkert stood and waved to the crowd before descending from his carriage to stand at the base of the steps, facing the throne. Squires and attendants led away the horses and carriage. King Thoreson stepped up to the platform to make a speech eulogizing Lomar and lamenting his untimely loss while justifying the coronation of Balkert as Lomar's highest-ranking appointee. One by one, the five other kings affirmed the choice with brief speeches of their own, promising the support of their armies to maintain Balkert on Meridan's throne.

Then the herald sounded a fanfare and the drums beat again as Balkert, regally robed, ascended the steps and sat upon the throne. King Morgamund bore in his hands a tasseled cushion, on which sat the Crown of Eden. He extended the Crown toward King Thoreson, who took it and held it above the head of Balkert as he uttered the ritual words of coronation, which had been uttered over every king of Meridan since long before Perivale.

"May you serve as a ruler and rule as a servant, ordained and empowered by the Master of the Universe to render justice with mercy, peace with strength, and largess with liberality. May you succor the needy and restrain the mighty. May the land be fruitful and your reign be long. Amen." King Thoreson slowly lowered the Crown of Eden toward Balkert's head.

"Stop!" The shout split the air like a thunderclap.

Thoreson paused, the Crown hovering inches above Balkert's head, as all eyes turned toward the sound to see a tall, powerful looking old man, robed in greens and browns, standing at the far edge of the crowd with his hand raised. The man walked with purposeful strides toward the dais, and the crowd parted like the Red Sea to make way for him. Those who were near enough to see the man's face as he passed revised their first impression of him. He was not old at all, but by all appearances a very young man with hair and beard prematurely white.

"It's Father Lucidis!" exclaimed Volanna, lifted from her lethargy by the unexpected interruption.

"Actually, I believe his name is Agapes," Tallis said.

"Then you know him?" she asked.

"Yes," said Tallis, "we've met more than once."

All eyes were on the mysterious man as he mounted the steps and stood facing Balkert. King Thoreson stood behind the usurper, the Crown of Eden still poised in his hands.

"Who are you?" Balkert demanded, "and what do you mean interrupting my coronation?"

"To those whom I know, I have many names, but you have never known me at all, Balkert. As to what my being here means, it is simply this: you cannot go on with this coronation because the son of Alfron lives."

"Lomar is alive?" Balkert asked, a shadow crossing his face. "I hardly think so. He has been missing since last night, and there is strong evidence of foul play. Were he alive, he would have been found by now."

"I did not say that Lomar lives; indeed, he does not. I said the son of Alfron lives," replied Lucidis.

"You talk in riddles, old man. Explain yourself before I have you escorted to the dungeon," retorted Balkert.

"Lomar was not the son of Alfron," Lucidis replied. "The true son of Alfron and the rightful king of Meridan lives."

"The man is raving. Seize him and take him away," commanded Balkert.

The twelve guards standing at attention behind the kings moved toward Lucidis with spears thrust forward. Lucidis neither looked at the guards nor flinched. But when they were within three paces of him, they found that they could not approach nearer. When questioned later about the incident, the guards could not explain why they had stopped short of the strange man. They felt no invisible barrier, no fear or intimidation. It was simply that they could not approach him.

Lucidis turned to the assembly and spoke in a strong, clear voice. "There are three witnesses here today who will confirm to you, the people of Meridan and the Seven Kingdoms, that the son of Alfron lives. First, I call before you Gensel, wife of Rolstag."

Gensel's heart sank and her knees began to tremble when she heard her name called. But leaning on the strong arm of her husband, she made her way to the platform. Lucidis looked at her, but she could not bear his gaze. His deep, clear voice, low and gentle, reached into her heart.

"You have a burden that you have carried alone for more than a score of years. Wouldn't you like to relieve it now by sharing it with the people?"

Gensel's trembling ceased. She found her courage, dried her tears, and answered, "Yes, Father." Gensel turned to the crowd and began to tell the secret that had paced relentlessly in her mind like a caged animal for over twenty years. Her voice was tremulous at first but grew stronger and clearer as she spoke. She told of how on a cold, windy night twenty-one years ago she had been coerced by an evil, black-clad woman, one whom she took to be a witch, into exchanging the woman's baby for that of Alfron's queen.

"And what did you do with the child you took from the queen's chambers?" Lucidis asked.

Gensel explained that under threat of harm to her own child, she had done as she was instructed and left the queen's newborn son in the split of an oak tree near her cottage to be carried away by the black creature's minions.

Lucidis turned to the crowd. "I can tell you that the creature Gensel encountered that night was none other than the ancient Morgultha, preserved against death all these years by a pact with unspeakable beings of darkness. Her minions did, indeed, bear away the child left in the split oak tree. But I have servants of my own who overcame Morgultha's that night and brought the child unharmed to me."

He turned back to Gensel and in lowered tones said, "For many years you have needed to tell this tale, dear Gensel. In the telling of it you have done a great good, not only for the Kingdom of Meridan but for yourself as well. You will find that your heart is clean now and your nighttime sleep will be peaceful. Go, and be of greater courage."

Gensel looked at Lucidis, gratitude flowing from her eyes in the form of tears. She returned to the strong embrace of Rolstag, who led her down the steps.

"Now I call before you Bogarth the blacksmith," Lucidis said. Bogarth left Faeren and made his way to the platform. "Bogarth, we have met before, have we not?" Lucidis asked.

"We have, Father," replied Bogarth.

"Please recount that meeting to the people," said Lucidis.

"It was about twenty-one years ago—almost exactly twenty-one years ago," Bogarth began. "My wife and I did not live in Corenham at the time but in a village far to the south. You knocked on our door late one night and had in your arms a newborn man-child, whom you said needed parents. Faeren and I were childless and despairin' of havin' children. We were delighted to take this child and raise him as our own son."

Lucidis addressed the people. "I attest to you that the child left in the split oak is the child I brought that same night to Bogarth and Faeren. Now, Bogarth, please tell the people the name you gave to this child."

With great pride and dignity, Bogarth faced the crowd and said, "We named him Aradon."

At the name of Aradon, exclamations of surprise and wonder rippled through the crowd. Again Lucidis raised his hand for silence. Volanna looked on with wonder, not yet comprehending the implications of the mystery Lucidis was revealing. King Tallis, however, breathed a long sigh of relief and gratitude. He knew that the fulfillment of the prophecy was at hand.

"Yes," cried Lucidis, "Aradon the blacksmith, Aradon the Champion of the Seven Kingdoms, Aradon wearer of the golden armor of Perivale, Aradon the son of Alfron is your king."

The people stood for a moment in stunned silence as the words of the strange man began to sink into their minds. Then a great, welling noise arose from every tongue, blending into one, sustained shout of exultation. What hands that were not held high in sheer joy were applauding with unbounded vigor. Lucidis allowed the crowd several minutes to vent their excitement as Bogarth returned to the softly weeping Faeren.

He put his arm about her shoulder and, in a voice tremulous with mixed feelings of disbelief and pride, said to her, "Well, my dear, it seems that we have raised a king."

Volanna was in shock, wide-eyed, open-mouthed, and incredulous. Slowly she sank back into the carriage seat. "Aradon is Alfron's son?" she whispered. "I cannot believe it. I must be dreaming." Then as the news sank in, her heart leapt in wild elation. "Mother!" she cried, tears flowing from springs of joy, "Aradon is Alfron's son! Do you know what this means?"

Queen Ravella assured her daughter that she did and tried to settle her down as Lucidis again raised a hand to quiet the crowd.

"I now call your attention to my third witness," he said as he turned toward the quivering figure now sunk deep in the cushions of the throne. "Balkert, you know the whereabouts of young Aradon, son of Alfron. Please inform the citizens of Meridan."

Balkert rose angrily from the throne. "I know nothing of this Aradon, and I have no intentions of surrendering the throne of Meridan to a common blacksmith." He turned to the five kings standing behind him. "Thoreson, Morgamund, Kor, Umberland, Bronwilde—in the name of your pledge, I call on you to seize this man."

King Umberland replied, "I will hear the man out. We all want the rightful king on the throne of Meridan." The other four kings, cowed by Lucidis and the enthusiasm of the people, merely nodded in assent.

"Again I ask you, Balkert, where is Aradon, son of Alfron?"

"I told you, I do not know where—"

"I know where he is." Volanna stood and shouted from the carriage. "Even as we speak, your champion and rightful king lies chained in a filthy dungeon deep in the bowels of Morningstone, placed there by Lomar and this usurper, Balkert."

A second ripple of wonder spread throughout the crowd. Balkert's knees began to quake and buckle. He sank down to the platform and slumped against the foot of the throne, trembling uncontrollably. At once King Tallis understood why his daughter had endured Lomar's obscenity at the banquet and why she had agreed to marry Balkert.

Again Lucidis raised his hand to quiet the crowd. "Who will bring our new king to his throne?"

The voice of King Tallis rang above the crowd, "If Bogarth the blacksmith will accompany me, we will bring you your king."

Suddenly a look of fear crossed Volanna's face. "Father, someone must go with you who can find the dungeon. It is not the regular prison of Morningstone but a secret dungeon that only Lomar, Balkert, and one or two of Lomar's guards knew of. And, Father, Aradon will be in great danger as you approach his prison. If the guard at the gate suspects any attempt at rescue, he will call to the guard inside, who has instructions to kill Aradon on the spot."

"Then we must take Balkert with us," said Tallis.

"Let me go with you, Father. Please," the excited Volanna begged. "How can I wait here not knowing whether or not your rescue will be successful?"

Tallis smiled at her. "No, my daughter, you must have faith. You are about to become a bride. Stay and await your husband."

He walked up the steps and spoke briefly with Father Lucidis, who nodded and commanded two of the guards to bind Balkert's hands and set him upon a horse. King Tallis again mounted Denmore's horse, and a horse for Bogarth was temporarily commandeered from a nobleman in the crowd. Then, led by the two guards who had bound Balkert, they spurred their mounts toward Morningstone Castle. They had ridden little more than three hundred paces when Tallis heard galloping hoofbeats coming up hard behind them. He halted the guards, drew his sword, and turned to face a lone horseman mounted on a steed that he recognized as his own gray charger.

"Hold, your majesty," cried the rider. "I admit I am a horse thief, and though only a novice, I find I have a knack for it. But surely my crime is not worthy of death. Spare me and I pledge to bury my new-found talent and reform."

"Denmore!" Tallis grinned as he sheathed his sword. "It is well that you do not deny the charge since that is my horse your rump is bouncing on. How did you find him?"

"That is a long story and one that I'm not sure I want you to hear. Believe me, that rump of mine feels every bounce, thanks to the man you are about to rescue. I pray you, let me come with you. If we let Aradon rot away in prison, I will never get redress for the tumble he gave me in the tournament."

Both King Tallis and Bogarth welcomed Sir Denmore into their company, and once again they made haste for Morningstone Castle. They entered the gate and after dismounting were admitted into the guardhouse. Once inside Tallis stopped and had the guards untie the hands of Balkert, who stood before them with eyes wide and knees trembling.

"Balkert," said King Tallis, "you need not fear that we will harm you without due cause. According to the law we must place you in prison and hold you for trial, and we will uphold the law. But first you have a task to perform. You must show us the way to Aradon's cell, and you must undo the trap you have set to prevent his rescue."

"Of course," said Balkert with a tremor in his voice. "Just tell me what you want me to do."

"You will lead us into the secret dungeon where Aradon is chained. As we approach the guard at the outer gate, you will order him to admit us. Once inside you will instruct the inner guard to open Aradon's cell and release the man. And do not think of trying any trickery. If harm comes to Aradon, I will hold you responsible for his murder and with my own sword, I will kill you on the spot."

"Oh, let me do it, your majesty," said Denmore. "The blood of this traitor must not soil the sword of a king. Besides, I will enjoy it more than you would."

"Very well, Denmore. The task is yours."

King Tallis, holding a torch before him, walked by the side of Balkert as he led them downward into the secret dungeon. Bogarth walked behind Tallis, and Sir Denmore, with sword drawn, behind Balkert. As the four silent men descended deeper into the dark, chill corridors rank with mildew, dripping with rivulets of slime, and infested with sickly rats, Tallis's anger welled up within him. "What kind of creature are you, Balkert, to hold any man in this foul pit?"

"It—it wasn't my doing, noble Tallis. It was all Lomar's idea. I was planning to move him to a gentleman's prison even today."

"Save your excuses for the trial. Just remember to play your part as I have instructed when we approach the guard."

"Of course, your majesty, you can count on me to do the right thing."

When they had walked another fifty paces, they heard the voice of the guard emerge from the darkness ahead. "Stop and state your name and business."

Tallis held the torch high, and he could see the glint of light on the man's armor as he arose from his chair and the flash of his sword as he drew it from its sheath. "Speak your lines, Balkert," Tallis said, under his breath.

"I will, your majesty," replied Balkert. He took a deep, tremulous breath and suddenly shouted, "Kill Aradon now! These men are holding me prisoner."

"Kill the blacksmith!" the guard shouted into the corridor behind the closed gate. Denmore raised his sword to strike Balkert.

"No!" cried Bogarth. "Get the guard!" Bogarth took Balkert's neck in his huge hand, jerked him around, and knocked him senseless against the corridor wall.

Denmore bounded toward the guard, but Tallis was already there. Tallis could not wield his sword because of the torch in his hand, which he held toward the guard as a weapon.

"Let me have him, your majesty," shouted Denmore. With a few deft strokes and a quick feint, Denmore felled the guard with a thrust into his belly. Tallis held the torch as Denmore took the keys from the dead guard's belt and tried them one by one in the corroded lock.

As Denmore worked, they heard the creak of a rusty door sound from within the dim corridor beyond the gate.

"Hurry, Denmore! By the Son of our Master, hurry!" said Bogarth.

Denmore did his best, but the rusty keys resisted the lock, and none of them turned the tumblers.

Scuffling footsteps sounded from the darkness inside, then a chain rattled, followed suddenly by a flurry of more intense rattling and scraping sounds. A cry of agony split the air and slowly died into silence. For a moment the three men at the gate froze.

"We are too late," said Bogarth in a voice constricted by the tightness in his throat.

Denmore tried the next key, and the next, and the next, which finally turned the lock with a grind and a click. Bogarth shoved the gate open, and the three men rushed inside and down the corridor. They found the opened cell and followed King Tallis as he held the torch inside the door. On the floor sprawled the body of a naked man, a pool of blood forming in the rancid straw around his head. Standing above the body with sword in hand was another man wearing the helmet and blue tunic of a palace guard, shielding his eyes from the glare of the torch. Denmore approached him with his sword drawn. The man slowly moved his hand from his eyes and squinted at the three visitors.

"Aradon!" Bogarth cried.

Aradon grinned broadly and gestured to the man on the floor. "He ran into my manacle. I took his clothes hoping they would help me find a way to escape, though I had to tear the sleeve a bit to get it over this chain."

With eager strides and outstretched arms, Bogarth went to his son. King Tallis stood aside and held the light, a tender smile warming his face as the two men wrapped each other in a long embrace. Denmore searched the guard's ring for the key that would unlock the manacle on Aradon's wrist.

Bogarth released his son and wiped his eyes. "Aradon," he said, "it is my great honor to introduce to you his majesty, King Tallis of Valomar."

Aradon's jaw dropped like a bucket into a well and, after staring nonplussed at the renowned king, sank to his knees in obeisance.

But King Tallis would have none of it. He reached down and raised the young man to his feet. "Stand, Aradon. For you to kneel to me is inappropriate."

Aradon stood, thoroughly baffled by the king's behavior.

"Great things are afoot that we will explain to you soon," said Tallis, "but right now we need to move quickly. We are keeping important people waiting." The king began to usher Aradon toward the door, but the chain on his wrist restrained him.

"We can't let you out in public wearing that," said Denmore. "Hold out your hand." He worked the key he had chosen into the rusted keyhole, and the manacle fell open and clanked to the floor. "Perhaps I should consider locksmithing instead of horse thievery."

"Now we must hurry," said Tallis as he led them out of the cell.

"Not yet, your majesty," said Aradon. "We must release my companion, Olstan, who was imprisoned here with me. His cell is somewhere on down the corridor. I have spoken to him often, and he has responded by tapping on the bars of his cell." As he spoke, a staccato rhythm of wood on metal rang out of the darkness in the corridor. The four men followed the sound and found Olstan chained, as Aradon had been, to the wall of a filthy cell. Denmore found the key to the door, and Aradon entered the cell and embraced his silent friend. Again Denmore found the right key and sprang the manacle from his wrist, and the five men walked back to the gate of the prison.

Balkert was sprawled outside the gate where Bogarth had left him. The blacksmith bent down and shook him until he moaned and put his hand to his head. Bogarth pulled him to his feet and held him against the wall as Tallis stood before him.

"Why did you defy us?" Tallis asked.

"I knew I could do it safely because I know your kind," Balkert replied. "You have this blind allegiance to law that rules your passions like a tyrant, and I knew you would not violate that law by killing me in vengeance."

"But why did you want Aradon killed?" asked Bogarth. "His death wouldn't have done you any good now."

"I know a jury will hang me anyway. As I walk to the gallows, it would have given me great pleasure to know I had thwarted your precious prophecy and destroyed the man who would fulfill it."

"Throw this man into Aradon's cell," said King Tallis, his voice like ice. He led the way and Bogarth half carried, half dragged the stumbling man back into the dungeon and dropped him to the floor against the wall where Aradon had been chained. He held Balkert's arm as Denmore clamped the manacle on his wrist and locked it.

"Let's get out of this place," said Bogarth. Denmore locked the cell door behind them, hung the key ring on his belt, and the five men made for the exit.

CHAPTER THIRTY-EIGHT

The Son of Alfron

Questions burned into Aradon's mind as he followed Denmore, Bogarth, and Tallis through the dark tunnels that led out of Perivale's dungeon. But he held his peace until they emerged into the sunlit halls of Morningstone. The daylight surprised him greatly. Lying in the blackness of the mountain's core, it had been impossible for him to think it was anything but night. He drew in a deep, satisfying breath, as if taking light into his lungs to purge himself of the darkness that had begun to seep into his soul.

Denmore closed the door to the secret tunnels as King Tallis placed the torch in a sconce on the wall and turned to the company.

"Sir Denmore, if you will take Olstan to Balkert's chambers and have him bathed and clothed in Balkert's finest, Bogarth and I will see to Aradon's grooming. Meet us at the entrance in half an hour."

"Gladly, your majesty," said Denmore. "Come, Olstan. We'll have you looking like a peacock when they see you again." Olstan was wary at first, but Denmore's breezy manner and gentle courtesy soon put him at ease, and he followed as the knight led him toward Balkert's quarters.

Tallis hailed a page standing at the entrance of the great hall. The young man recognized the king of Valomar and without hesitation placed himself at Tallis's disposal.

"Please enlist the service of two additional pages and at least ten palace servants. Send one page to unlock the door to Balkert's chambers and the other to Lomar's chambers. Instruct five servants to draw water for a bath in Balkert's rooms and the five others to prepare a bath in Lomar's rooms. And quickly. Don't walk, run."

"But your majesty, Balkert is at the coronation, and Lomar is—"

"I know, I know," Tallis interrupted. "The baths are needed for other purposes. Please ask no more questions; just be quick."

"As you wish, your majesty." The page bowed and trotted away.

"Will someone please tell me what is going on?" pled Aradon.

"We haven't the time now," said Tallis as he took Aradon by the arm and ushered him toward the wide stairway in Morningstone's great hall.

"Where are you taking me?" asked Aradon as they climbed the stairway.

"To Lomar's chambers, which were formerly the rooms of King Alfron," said Tallis.

"Where is Lomar? Why hasn't he been crowned, yet? What is this coronation the page spoke of?"

"Your questions are too complex for simple answers."

"Please tell me something, your majesty, I beg of you. I can make no sense of this at all."

"Here we are at Lomar's rooms," Tallis replied. At that moment a page trotted up behind them with a key in his hand. He opened the door, and the three men entered. "Aradon, please rest assured that your father and I will tell you everything, but for the moment you must be patient. Bogarth, clean up the boy while I go find him something to wear." Tallis disappeared through the door to the other rooms of Lomar's lodgings.

"We must hurry and get you bathed and dressed," said Bogarth. "People are waitin' for us at Cheaping Square."

The five servants entered, each carrying two large buckets of water hanging from the ends of poles laid across their shoulders. They were followed by a serving girl carrying a large towel and a washing cloth. The men set the buckets on the floor and moved Lomar's bathing tub from a closet. After they had poured the water into the tub, the servants bowed and left the rooms, and Aradon undressed and slipped into the cool water. Bogarth searched Lomar's cabinets until he found a razor for Aradon to use on the stubble on his face.

"Father," Aradon said as he splashed and scrubbed, "I can make no sense of this at all. Please tell me what is happening. Why are you dressing me up? Why is King Tallis making over me so much? Where are you taking me? Who is waiting? Why are they waiting? Are Lomar and Volanna wed?" With this question he stopped bathing and waited for the answer, utterly still, not even breathing.

"No, son. Lomar and Volanna did not marry, and Lomar is dead."

Aradon's heart leapt with sudden elation. "What strange news! How did Lomar die? And—and where is Princess Volanna?"

"The princess is well and safe. As to how Lomar died, I do not know."

Aradon continued to ask more questions as he bathed, but Bogarth would answer only the simplest ones, awaiting the return of King Tallis to address the others.

Aradon stepped from the tub and toweled himself dry. He was using the razor on his face when Tallis entered the room carrying across his arms an ivory-colored silk shirt, a handsome tunic, breeches, and a robe of deep burgundy trimmed with gold.

"That's a suit fit for a king," said Aradon.

"It is a king's suit; it belonged to King Alfron." Tallis opened the shirt and held it toward Aradon. "Come on, put your arms in the sleeves."

The confounded Aradon shook his head in amazement, "Please, your majesty, can the servants find me something else? It is not fit for me to wear the king's robes."

"Aradon, I assure you that what we are doing is right and proper. Now put your arms in this shirt," Tallis instructed.

Aradon bowed to the king and reached to take the shirt from his hands. "Very well, I will obey your command, but I will dress myself, your majesty. It is not fit that a king such as you should dress a blacksmith such as me as if you were my valet."

Tallis pulled the shirt from him and replied firmly, "Aradon, put your arms in this shirt." With wonder showing in his eyes, Aradon did as he was commanded and allowed the king to dress him head to foot in Alfron's finery. King Tallis performed the task with great care, smoothing wrinkles, knotting ties, brushing dust and lint from the fabric, and kneeling before the son of his old friend to lace the leather boots on his feet, much to Aradon's consternation. But the young man held his peace and allowed the king to proceed.

"Bogarth, send the page for the serving girl," ordered Tallis as he brushed Aradon's leather boots with the towel. "Tell her to bring a comb and a brush."

Bogarth complied, and within minutes the girl entered with the comb and brush in her hand. She curtsied low to King Tallis while stealing wide-eyed, sidelong glances at the finely dressed young man standing before her. Tallis sat Aradon in a chair and put the girl to work on his hair. She gladly complied, smoothing out the tangles with deep strokes of the comb and patting down the most unruly of the golden waves with her caressing hand. When her task was done, the girl stepped back. Tallis had Aradon stand as he took Alfron's royal robe and shook out the heavy folds, which billowed and flapped and shimmered with muted highlights of crimson iridescence. He draped the robe across Aradon's wide shoulders, fastened the gold clasp at his throat, and stepped back beside Bogarth to survey the results.

King Tallis's heart stood still for a moment as he looked at Aradon. The young man was almost the exact image of Tallis's old friend, the late King Alfron, as Tallis remembered him the first time they had met. Even the suit was the one that Alfron had worn at the time, and every item of Alfron's clothing fit Aradon perfectly, as if tailored expressly for him. If there had been room in Tallis's mind for any doubt about Aradon's parentage, the sight of the young man now standing before him would have dispelled it. He swallowed hard and turned to the big blacksmith beside him.

"Well, Bogarth, what do you think?"

"Your majesty, it's not right easy to say what I'm thinkin' now." Bogarth's eyes were blinking with the mist gathering in them. "I'm havin' some mighty strange feelin's. I know this is the babe I held in my arms twenty-one years ago, but as I see him standin' there now, he looks like he's never been anything but a king."

The serving girl, looking for an excuse to linger, had busied her-self gathering the bath cloth and towels. She now stood transfixed, clutching them to her heart as she gazed in unabashed awe at the magnificent creature standing before her.

Tallis turned to her and said, "We thank you heartily for your help. You may go now."

Tallis had to repeat the command to shake the girl from her reverie. Then with a face flushed pink, she curtsied deeply and left the room.

"Now will someone please tell me just what is going on?" Aradon pled.

"Yes, we shall do that now, Aradon," said Tallis. He bade the thoroughly baffled young man to take the chair again as he and Bogarth drew up seats for themselves and sat down facing him.

Bogarth cleared his throat, rubbed his hands on his knees, drew a deep breath, and said, "Aradon, brace yourself. We are about to tell you some things you've never thought of, some things that may shock you to the core. I, uh, that is, we—your mother and I—uh, we—"

"Please speak plainly, Father. I must know what you need to tell."

Bogarth looked straight into Aradon's eyes and spoke directly but gently. "You are not really the son of my own body. You were brought to your mother—that is, to Faeren and me—as an infant to raise as our own son. And that is how we raised you. You have been the joy of our lives, and I'm sure I have loved you better than if you had sprung from my own loins."

Aradon stared long at Bogarth. "Then, who—?"

King Tallis answered, "You are the son of Alfron and rightful king of Meridan. Even as we speak, the people await your coronation at Cheaping Square."

Aradon sat stunned, staring at Tallis and Bogarth, playing their words over and over in his mind but finding them emptied of all meaning. After a long moment, he put his hands to his head and closed his eyes to steady the whirling inside as waves upon waves of questions rushed into his mind too rapidly to be articulated. The two men waited with patience and respect, knowing he must have at least a little time to cope with what he had heard.

Aradon's life had suddenly taken on a shape he did not recognize. It was as if the wrong foundation had been laid for the house that was to be built upon it. He opened his eyes and saw the shimmering robe flowing across his lap and onto the floor. It was as if he had become someone else. But he was not someone else, he was Aradon the blacksmith, shoved onstage without lines to act the lead role in the middle of the play. But it was not a play. It was real. He had thought he wanted to be king to win the hand of his beloved, but now he saw the silliness of that dream. He knew nothing of ruling, and the prospect of making the right decisions for an entire country was utterly terrifying. How could he get out of this? If he was truly Alfron's son, he could not get out of it, could he? Panic welled up inside; he could not handle the weight of the responsibility. But he had no choice, did he? If he was to be king, he would have to be king, and there was nothing more to be said.

Finally Aradon raised his head and spoke. "You tell me I am the son of King Alfron. At the moment I can make the words mean nothing to me. But I know this—" He looked steadily at Bogarth, "King Alfron may have begotten me, but you are my true father, and I will never own another."

"Oh, but I think you may," replied Bogarth, his eyes twinkling and a smile playing at his lips. "You see, King Tallis here is about to become your father-in-law. Surely you can make for him a fatherly place in your heart."

"You will marry my daughter, will you not?" asked King Tallis.

With eyes brimming and voice choking, Aradon could not answer. For the first time he realized that the desire of his heart, which he had given up, was about to be granted him. The two wise men sitting before him understood completely. But Tallis turned to Bogarth with a twinkle in his own eye and said, "Well, apparently your son has reservations about marrying my daughter, but as the new king of Meridan I fear the poor man has no choice. It is his royal duty. The marriage pact was signed before he was christened. The wedding will follow the coronation immediately. Come, Aradon, we are keeping the people waiting."

Aradon rose with knees trembling slightly and a tight churning in the pit of his stomach and walked with Tallis and Bogarth into the hallway. Suddenly Tallis stopped and turned to him. "I almost forgot, you need to make a couple of decisions concerning the upcoming ceremonies. It is customary for the king-elect to choose his own crown-bearer for the coronation and one or more groomsmen for the wedding. Have you anyone in mind?"

Aradon laughed softly, shaking his head with wonder as he answered. "Now I think I can see the hand of the Master of the Universe in this thing. Even if I had to call them here from the far side of the earth, I would choose my father Bogarth as crown-bearer and my two friends Olstan and Sir Denmore as groomsmen. And all three are right here with me."

"Very good," said Tallis with a nod of approval.

Denmore was waiting with Olstan at the gate of the castle. Olstan was handsomely outfitted in a dark green suit and matching robe from Balkert's wardrobe. He had been reluctant to take the man's clothes, but Denmore had explained, "It's not as if you're stealing; you're merely trading. Remember, he is now wearing the chain you wore this morning." As Bogarth and King Tallis approached with Aradon in tow, Denmore stared at the young king-to-be and said, "I suppose this means you won't be shoeing my horse anymore."

"Nothing is certain," replied Aradon. "Right now I can think of nowhere I would rather be than at my anvil. Have you told Olstan what is about to happen?"

"I have," said Denmore.

"Then you both will understand the personal request I wish to make of each of you. Will you consent to be my groomsmen in the wedding?"

Olstan grinned broadly and nodded in affirmation as he clapped Aradon on the shoulder. Denmore, perhaps for the first time in his life, was speechless. After a moment he knelt before Aradon and said with grave sincerity, "My king, I am greatly humbled that you would choose me for this honor. I will gladly serve you in this way and in any other from this day forward, even to the giving of my life."

Horses had been brought to the gate for Aradon and Olstan. The five men mounted, this time with King Tallis and Sir Denmore on their own steeds, and the guards escorted them toward Cheaping Square and the waiting crowd. As they approached the square, trumpets blared, the drums began their beat, and the throng of people raised a ringing cheer that did not die as the guards made a path through the crowd for them to pass through. The company stopped at the steps of the monument, the five men dismounted, and the guards led their horses away.

King Tallis and Bogarth, one on each side of Aradon, escorted him up the steps to the dais where Father Lucidis waited, the Crown of Eden in his hands. Sir Denmore and Olstan stood at the base of the platform. Tallis spoke briefly to Father Lucidis, who handed to Bogarth the cushion bearing the Crown. Then King Tallis took his place just behind the throne to the left as Bogarth stood to the right.

Lucidis led Aradon to the throne and had him sit upon it. Then Lucidis raised his hands to quiet the crowd and took his place directly behind the throne. With both hands he took the Crown from the cushion Bogarth held and raised it high above Aradon's head. In a voice that without effort reached every ear in the vast assembly, Lucidis recited the ancient charge:

"May you serve as a ruler and rule as a servant, ordained and empowered by the Master of the Universe to render justice with mercy, peace with strength, and largess with liberality. May you succor the needy and restrain the mighty. May the land be fruitful and your reign be long. Amen." He solemnly lowered the Crown until it rested on Aradon's head. Then he raised his hands high and addressed all the people. "Citizens, friends, and guests, I present to you his majesty, Aradon, king of Meridan."

Thousands of voices burst forth with great cries of unrestrained joy. Young women screamed and clapped and bounced up and down as if they had springs in their toes. Older women lifted their open palms and prayed their joyful thanks to the cloudless heavens. Men raised their arms in the air and bellowed until their voices went dry and husky. The exultant sound continued for several minutes before it began to form itself into a steady rhythm as men and women began to clap their hands to the beat of an accompanying drum. Somewhere half a dozen people began to chant with the rhythm, "Long live King

Aradon," and in moments the entire crowd took up the chant, louder and louder until the streets rang with the noise.

Aradon sat unmoving, absorbing the tribute as if in a dream. He did not notice when King Tallis stepped over to Bogarth, whispered something into his ear, and the two of them left the platform, leaving only Father Lucidis and the new king to face the jubilant celebration. Aradon began to wonder whether the chant would continue forever when the drummers ceased and the musicians began to play a stately march. It took two or three minutes more for the chanting to dwindle away as the music grew in volume.

Sir Denmore and Olstan ascended the steps and took their places on each side of the throne. As if by magic, the crowd parted, creating an arrow-straight aisle directly in front of the throne, revealing Princess Volanna standing at the far end, her hand on the arm of King Tallis and her white gown shimmering in the sunlight like an angelic apparition. Every eye was on her as she and her father began to march slowly toward the throne.

Aradon stared entranced, afraid to believe the truth of what his eyes were showing him. He did not feel the two subtle nudges against his right shoulder, but the sharp pinch that followed shook him from his daze. He looked up to see Olstan making furtive signals for him to stand. Aradon was not certain his legs would bear him, but he managed to rise from the throne and stand unsupported, though his knees began to tremble as he watched the glory of Volanna approach. He now understood the wisdom in the tradition of having a grooms-man on each side of the bridegroom, especially as she ascended the steps and smiled with a radiance that melted him like a cake of butter in the sun. He felt the steadying hands of Denmore and Olstan on his back, hidden from the crowd by his voluminous robe, and righted himself as Volanna took her place at his side.

Aradon gazed enraptured at the incomparable face he had abandoned hope of ever seeing again, now looking up at him in utter adoration. The voice of Father Lucidis reciting the marriage liturgy reached his ears as a distant sound devoid of meaning. He tried to focus his mind on the words, fearing that afterward when he tried to recall this moment of ecstasy, he would be able to remember absolutely nothing. But it was futile. The perfection of the face before him absorbed his whole being. Thus he stood gazing, suspended in time until Volanna began to smile broadly, tilting her face upward toward his with eager expectation. Aradon became aware that Lucidis's voice had ceased and that all eyes were on him. After a moment of expectant silence, Denmore leaned toward Aradon's ear and whispered, "Kiss her, you big lug—I mean, your majesty—or I shall do it for you." Aradon reddened. Apparently he had already recited his vows, though he could not recall uttering a single word. He swallowed hard, drew in a long breath, then took Volanna in his arms and performed his duty admirably, much to the delight of the people.

Again the crowd took up the fervent chant, "Long live King Aradon and Queen Volanna!" as the new royal couple descended the steps and guards led them through the adoring multitude to the waiting carriage. They took their seats, and Volanna snuggled tightly against Aradon, clasping his hand dearly in both of hers and beaming her ecstatic smile to the people waving and shouting about them. Mounted guards escorted the carriage up the cobbled street toward Morningstone Castle as scores of youths and maidens came out of the crowd to give happy chase before falling away in exhaustion.

CHAPTER THIRTY-NINE

The Blending Stars

How would you like your guests to be seated, your majesty?"
Aradon had not even known that a grand banquet
would follow his coronation and wedding. He much
would have preferred to be left alone with his new bride, but the lord
chamberlain had met him in the great hall of Morningstone and was
now asking him to make decisions about seating at the king's table.
Aradon bent toward Volanna and whispered, "Is there a proper protocol for this sort of thing?"

"You are the king," she answered. "Your wish is his command."

Aradon had King Tallis seated on his right hand and Bogarth
next to Tallis. Volanna was seated on Aradon's left, with Faeren and
Queen Ravella to the left of her. Aradon asked the lord chamberlain
to seat the knights, guests, and noblemen of the kingdoms according
to normal protocol, which meant the highest-ranking personages
were seated nearest the king and those of lesser importance further
away. Aradon commanded only one change in the normal order. He
had Sir Denmore and Olstan seated at the highest-ranking table in
the hall, next to Lord and Lady Aldemar.

With the seating decisions made, Aradon moved toward his seat
at the high table. Again the lord chamberlain stopped him. "Your
majesty, though coronations are few in Meridan, it has always been
the custom for the new king and his kin to receive his guests as they
enter the hall." Aradon sighed and allowed himself to be led to a

place near the door, where he stood at the head of a line that included Queen Volanna, Queen Ravella, Bogarth, and Faeren. King Tallis stood with King Aradon to help with the introduction of the guests as they filed by.

First in line were Lord and Lady Aldemar, who needed no introduction to the new king. Aldemar bowed low to Aradon, and he bowed low in return. Aldemar smiled with amusement as King Tallis placed his hand on Aradon's shoulder and said, "As the king, it is not proper for you to bow to your subjects. It is not that we royal ones are in any way innately superior, but the duty of our office demands that we act the part of king, which means that we exude confidence and act assured at all times."

"You can be assured that any confidence I exude at this moment is indeed an act," replied Aradon.

"No, not an act, but an enactment," Tallis corrected him. "As kings we are symbolic embodiments of our kingdoms and all that makes them function. In our office resides the concept of law, authority, unity, and security. You must hold these treasures with an air of assurance that gives your subjects confidence in them. They want you to be strong. They want you to be worthy of honor. It is your duty to accept it as your due so they can sleep in peace at night."

"King Tallis is quite right," Lord Aldemar interjected. "Kingship is nine parts symbol and one part reality. In the best kings, the two are an indistinguishable blend."

"If you wish to indicate favor toward a subject, a slight nod of the head is sufficient," said Tallis, demonstrating the gesture as he spoke.

"Thank you, sire," said the new king as he turned toward Lord Aldemar and nodded his head emphatically.

Aldemar laughed and said, "King Aradon, son of my old friend King Alfron. You are so like your father. I should have known who you were the day you turned away from the cakeseller's daughter, may her soul rest in peace. The mark of Alfron is written in every feature of your face and every movement of your body. I knew I was getting old, but I didn't realize I was going blind."

"You are not blind, Lord Aldemar. You have been Meridan's eyes, mind, and heart for almost twenty years, and your sight has led the kingdom well and held the throne intact for the son of your old friend. In King Alfron's name, I thank you for all you have done for Meridan. I only hope I can rule half as well."

"I thank you, King Aradon," Aldemar replied. "For the past five years, misgivings about the future of Meridan have shortened my nights. But tonight my sleep will be peaceful and easy, knowing you are on the throne. I believe you will be the sort of king that minstrels will sing of and legends will embellish for generations to come. May your reign be long."

"Thank you, Lord Aldemar," replied Aradon. "I know you want to rest, and you've certainly earned it. But I beg of you to sit with me for a while on the carriage of government until I can handle the reins alone."

"Of course, your majesty. I will serve you gladly for as long as I am needed." With that, Lord Aldemar bowed again as his lady curtsied and they moved on. But not before Queen Volanna gave her a warm embrace.

"Well spoken, my son," said Tallis before the next guest stepped up. "With words like that you will have your kingdom in the palm of your hand before the night is out."

After the last nobleman had passed through the line, Aradon and his newly extended family took their seats. The food was served and the banquet began. Aradon found himself strangely shy in the presence of his new bride, but he was relieved to find that it mattered little. Volanna, who had just tonight met Faeren for the first time, was getting to know her new mother-in-law. Aradon took advantage of the opportunity to quiz King Tallis on the many questions churning in his mind about his father Alfron, about Father Verit, and about the prophecy and how he had almost caused it to fail when he secretly held the Crown of Eden in his possession. Tallis was in his element; he relished discussing such things.

"You see, Aradon," he said, "there is a great paradox here. It might seem that you could have unwittingly brought about the fulfillment of the prophecy sooner if you had kept the Crown for yourself instead of giving it to Prince Lomar. But the truth is, that would have undone the prophecy. Had you not been willing to give up the

Crown, you would have been unfit to wear it. Had you stolen it for selfish reasons instead of letting it come to you according to destiny, it would in turn have been stolen from you. But I am speaking as if anything other than what occurred was possible, which is not the case. The events as they played themselves out were inevitable and unalterable. It was all according to prophecy. There is no such thing as what might have been."

"What I am saying," explained Aradon, "is that the prophecy was extremely precarious. It was not inevitable at all. I could easily have broken it, and I almost did. When I stood before Lomar with the Crown in my hands, I was torn between giving it to him or keeping it for myself. The choice was entirely mine, and I truly did not know which course I would choose until the moment I gave it up. Nothing in the prophecy constrained me to make the choice I made, and I came very near to killing the prophecy."

"All that is true," Tallis replied, "except that you came nowhere near killing the prophecy. You are speaking as if prophecy and free will are mutually exclusive opposites. That is not the case; prophecy is unalterable, but it is dependent upon and subsidiary to free will. In spite of the prophecy, you were always free to make any choice you wanted. The fact that an event has been foretold does not place a lock on free will. The future does not unfold to the constrictions of what is prophesied in advance; prophecy is merely history seen from the other end. Prophecy has looked into the future and seen the event. It merely describes the event before it happens instead of after. Prophecy is a passive observer, if you will, reporting events it has already seen. Seeing those events before they happen does not cause them to happen any more than predicting that summer will come is the cause of its coming. Certainly you were free to choose the Crown or not, but the prophecy simply 'knew' ahead of time that you would not choose it because it had looked at the event as if it had already happened."

"In all these twenty years, did you ever question the prophecy yourself, or your interpretation of it?"

"I've had enough experience with this sort of thing to keep my faith even when there seems no possible way for things to come out right." Tallis looked up at Aradon and smiled as he added, "Almost. I admit that when Lomar disappeared and the Crown was inches from Balkert's head, I saw no hope for the prophecy. There was no son of Alfron to fulfill it, and I was ready to wrench my daughter from that usurper's web and return to Valomar. Now I am ashamed of my lack of faith."

Aradon moved on to another subject. "What can you tell me about the Crown of Eden? I have heard the legends of its power since I was a small boy, and Father Verit told me somewhat of it. When I found it resting on the skull of Perivale in Maldor Castle, I strongly suspected it was his undoing. Did it destroy Lomar as well?"

"The effect of the Crown depends upon the wearer. It sometimes makes hidden characteristics of the wearer physically visible. In Lomar's case—Father Agapes told me something of it after the wedding—the Crown manifested in his body the condition of his soul. Lomar's lusts and cravings had expanded to the point that they dominated his being and left no room for his soul, which was shunted aside and starved until it shrank to the point of vanishing. He had become little more than a craving himself. The Crown acted on his body to express the condition of his soul and shrank it until it was completely swallowed by the evil in which he had wrapped himself. But to some kings the Crown has brought great good. The ancient King David is said to have worn it, and in spite of his many human failures, he lived before the Master of the Universe with a true heart that was enhanced by the presence of the Crown—not caused, mind you, but merely enhanced and amplified. So the effect of the Crown always depends upon the heart of the wearer."

"What of the imprint of Morgultha's fingers on the Crown? Isn't that some kind of evil omen?" Aradon asked.

"The earth itself bears the imprint of the grip of man's ancient adversary, the Dark One. Yet the earth retains all the good the Master of the Universe infused into it at creation. Man's duty still is to exercise benevolent dominion over creation and nourish that good within it in spite of the imprint of evil. Your duty to the Kingdom of Meridan is the same."

"Who was Lomar? Was he another son of Alfron—in fact, my brother?"

Tallis explained that Lomar was the son of Morgultha and told Aradon how she had coerced Gensel the midwife into switching him with Aradon at birth. "She thought her son would possess supernatural powers. She was under the illusion that through deep levels of unholy ritual, she had mated with the Dark One himself to conceive him. Those who practice satanic rituals often think they are making direct contact with the very lord of all evil, but because the trancelike state they achieve makes all reality appear as a hellish horror, mere human males are mistaken for the Master of Deceit."

"One other thing, sire," said Aradon. "When I was trying to decide whether to keep the Crown for myself or give it to Lord Aldemar, I followed the example of the ancient Gideon and tested the will of the Master of the Universe. If he wanted me to take the Crown, his sign should be to let me win the tournament. But even after winning the tournament, I felt a great uneasiness about taking the Crown. I've not been able to make out the meaning of it all. Why did he give me the apparent sign when it has since become obvious that for me to have taken the Crown would have brought me disaster?"

"Ah, yes. The fallacy of the fleece, I call it," replied Tallis. "People put out fleeces for the wrong reason. You were trying to get the Master of the Universe to make your decision for you, which is something he will not do. We are created with free will, and that means we are by nature decision makers. It ill behooves us to throw back at our maker the very responsibility he designed us to take on. This was not at all what Gideon was trying to do. He was not trying to determine the will of his God; he was trying to determine with certainty that it was indeed God who was speaking.

"Fleeces are never needed when we have a clear view of what is right and wrong. You knew in your heart that it was not right for you to take the Crown. That is why your conscience kept prodding you. Your desires muddied up the clarity of your mind, and you could not bring yourself to make the hard decision that would thwart those desires. Yet when you thrust those desires aside and made the decision on the basis of what you knew to be true and right, the Master freely gave you the deepest desire of your heart. That is the way of heaven. You can truly have only what you are willing to give up."

Aradon fell into a reflective mood as he pondered the things his new father-in-law had told him. Tallis left him to his thoughts and turned to speak with Bogarth. At first, the blacksmith was intimidated by the king's office and great reputation, but Tallis acted so little the king that Bogarth soon warmed to him, and the two men found that they were much alike at heart. In the hour that followed, they sowed the beginnings of what became a long and fast friendship. Tallis, a keen observer, had already detected Bogarth's commitment to honor and the strong bond that existed between him and Aradon.

"Bogarth, I think I know why the future king of Meridan was placed in your hands," he said. "Alfron and his queen were both fated to die in the boy's infancy, and the Master of the Universe arranged to have him raised by the best parents a future king could possibly have. I am convinced that Aradon will be a great king, and that is due in no small part to your influence on him."

"I thank you for your kind words, your majesty, and I do hope you are right. But he also had the makin's of a fine blacksmith, and that would've made me just as proud."

As the banquet progressed, Kalley, sitting at a table with the other ladies-in-waiting, looked about the hall until her eye was caught by Olstan, who was sitting at the table with Lord Aldemar and Sir Denmore. As she ate, she frequently cast a look in his direction. She had first noticed him as he stood in his new finery beside King Aradon at the wedding. She had thought him a fine-looking figure of a man and now found her eyes often turning toward him as if they had a will of their own. She did not notice that he was silent for he was sitting beside the gregarious, word-loving Sir Denmore, a situation that gave one little necessity or opportunity to speak. Volanna had told Kalley of the mute she had befriended months before in Morningstone's kitchen, but as she looked upon Olstan now, she did not make the connection.

After a while she noticed Olstan quietly rise from the table and carry his plate across the hall to an uncrowded servant's table not far from her own. The fact was that Olstan felt out of place dining with the great ones and had moved to a table more to his liking. Kalley's heart beat a little faster as her mind began to concoct a scheme to meet the attractive young man. She reached beneath the table and loosened the ties on her shoe, then got up from her seat and walked toward the table where Olstan was sitting. She walked behind him as if to go on past, but instead stepped out of her shoe, leaving it on the floor behind his chair.

"Oh," she squealed, hopping on one foot toward the table where Olstan sat. He looked up as Kalley pointed to her shoe. "I seem to have lost my shoe. I wonder if you would be so kind as to pick it up for me."

Olstan arose and bowed to Kalley, picked up the shoe and handed it to her.

"Thank you, sir," she said.

Olstan bowed again.

Kalley sat in the chair beside Olstan's, looked up at him, and smiled shyly before turning her back to put on her shoe. When she had turned again toward Olstan, she said, "I believe you and I have something in common. I am Kalley, Queen Volanna's friend and her lady-in-waiting. I believe you are King Aradon's squire and his friend as well."

Olstan nodded and bowed.

"Well, tell me your name," said Kalley.

Olstan shook his head and pointed to his mouth.

"Oh, well, just chew it up. I know your name anyway. It's Olstan, isn't it?"

He nodded and bowed again.

"Oh, quit being so courteous," she smiled. "Sit down, and let's talk."

Olstan sat.

"I hope you won't think me forward, but I thought since we both are in the employ of King Aradon and Queen Volanna—doesn't it sound strange to call Aradon 'King'?—we may as well get to know each other. Don't you think so?"

Olstan smiled and nodded.

"What do you think of your master becoming king?"

Olstan turn his palms up and spread them apart.

"It's all quite amazing, isn't it."

He nodded again.

"Queen Volanna can hardly believe it yet. This morning she woke up in deep despair, thinking she would be forced to marry Prince Lomar because of her vow and the prophecy, when she really loved Aradon. She didn't know he had died in the night. I mean Lomar, not Aradon—King Aradon, that is. We'll all have to get used to saying that, won't we? Then that weasel Balkert came and talked to her and she got even worse. And now I know why. Balkert forced her to agree to wed him to keep Aradon alive, or at least, from being sliced apart. And why does everyone call him a weasel? I mean Balkert, not Aradon. Isn't it just wonderful the way things worked out? She did fulfill the prophecy and she married the man she loved. She is so happy she can hardly believe she is awake. Is Aradon—I mean King Aradon—as happy as she is?"

Olstan smiled and nodded.

"Oh, I just knew it. It's so like a fairy tale. I just love happy endings, don't you?"

Olstan nodded, again, gazing at the attractive, loquacious girl with growing fascination.

"Here I am doing all the talking. Tell me something about yourself."

Olstan suddenly looked panicked, but he was saved by a page who walked up at just that moment. "The king and queen request the presence of both of you," he said. Olstan stood, bowed to Kalley, and offered his hand as she rose from her seat, and the two of them went to do the bidding of the king and queen.

After King Tallis had engaged Bogarth in conversation and Queen Ravella had turned her attention to Faeren, Aradon and Volanna were left to each other. Aradon wanted to speak with his new bride, but he still could not find his tongue in this moment of wonder. He marveled again and again at the turn of fortune that gave him not only the deepest desire of his heart, not a mere knighthood but the very kingship of Meridan. It was all too sudden. He loved Volanna deeply. He basked in the warm radiance of her presence. But now that she was really his, how could he ever dare approach her? It was different when he was a blacksmith and he thought her a kitchenmaid. But how could he, born a tradesman, untrained in the ways of nobles and kings, ever come to feel himself her equal?

He looked at the sleeve of his coat, made of the richest fabric he had ever seen, and at the gold rings Tallis had placed on his fingers. It was more gold than he had ever seen at one time. He glanced at the vaulted ceiling of the hall, the dressed stones, the tapestries, the antlers and pelts from Alfron's kills, the oaken tables, and the heavy curtains. He had never before been in this hall and had never seen such wealth and richness. And now it all belonged to him. This was Volanna's natural world but not his. He was used to a daub-and-wattle wall with a thatched roof and a planked floor. Could he even sleep on a king's feather mattress? The thought of the huge bed he had seen in Alfron's chambers led him to another: this was his wedding night. He, Aradon the blacksmith, was wed to the daughter of the great King Tallis, the princess of Valomar and now queen of Meridan, perhaps one day even empress of the Seven Kingdoms. It was all too sudden, too soon. He picked at his food as the awkward silence grew between him and his bride.

Volanna laid her hand on his arm. "Aradon, are you having regrets about your hasty wedding?"

He looked at her, entranced yet again by the perfection of her face. Her dark hair was framed with a brilliant halo of warm auburn by the light from the torches on the wall behind her, and her face glowed with the soft light of the candle on the table. Or perhaps the glow was from the look of utter adoration in her eyes. "No, no, Dovey . . . Volanna . . . I—"

"You may call me Dovey. It will be the name I reserve solely for the two men I love most in the world. But you are so quiet. Surely you are happy with your good fortune—or do you think marrying me is good fortune?"

"Marrying you is such good fortune I can hardly believe it yet. I think it will take time for me to fit the two halves of this day together. They are like the two halves of my life. This morning I was a blacksmith's son, facing a future of darkness in a cold, foul prison, forever cut off from light and love. Tonight I am master of the finest castle in our world. I am the son of kings and the king of a thriving nation. I am wed to the most beautiful woman I have ever seen, who is the one desire of my heart. I am having a bit of trouble coming to terms with just who I really am."

"You are Aradon." She spoke the name as if it were holy. "You are Aradon whether at the anvil or on the throne. The trappings don't make the man. The Crown does not increase your stature nor did bending over the hoof of a horse diminish it. Whether you wear a blacksmith's apron or a royal robe, you are Aradon. That alone is enough for me, and that alone will be enough for the Kingdom of Meridan."

"You have the wisdom of your father," he said. "Yet it was a blacksmith who fell in love with a kitchenmaid and a king who married a princess. The fact that they are the same person splits my mind apart like the halves of a melon. Though I know with my mind that I am king, I look upon this hall, these clothes, the nobles sitting about me through the eyes of a blacksmith. This castle engulfs me like a cavern of history. I am swallowed in the halls and trappings of Perivale, Rhondale, Manddwyn, and Alfron."

"I know something that might help," said Volanna, her eyes bright and her smile dazzling as she bent toward Aradon and whispered in his ear. In a moment he, too, smiled and nodded in enthusiastic affirmation. He called for a page and sent him to fetch Olstan and Kalley.

To Volanna's surprise, she saw the two servants walking together as they approached from the far side of the hall. Kalley's face was flushed, and her eyes were wide and bright.

"Do the two of you already know each other?" asked Volanna.

"Oh yes, we just met. Didn't we, Olstan?"

Olstan nodded.

"We've been talking together, and since we are both servants of royalty, it turns out that we have a lot in common, don't we?"

Again, Olstan nodded.

"Do you mean you have already learned that much of his language?" asked Aradon. "It took me weeks."

"What do you mean, 'his language,' your majesty? We spoke normally in our own tongue."

"I mean his hand signs, of course. Since Olstan cannot speak, he has developed a very effective and eloquent language of hand signs."

Kalley was confused. "What do you mean, he cannot speak?" She thought back on their conversation, and indeed, she could not remember hearing him utter a single word. She looked at Olstan. "Is it true that you cannot speak?"

Olstan nodded and bowed to the girl.

Kalley put her hands to her face, blushed deeply, and hung her head in shame. "Oh, I'm so sorry, Olstan. I didn't know. I have made a silly fool of myself chattering so like a magpie that I didn't even notice that you were saying nothing. Please forgive me, sir. Talking too much is my greatest fault."

Olstan then made a short series of hand signs, which Aradon interpreted. "He says it doesn't matter. He enjoyed your conversation immensely."

Olstan smiled at Kalley, and her heart melted as all words were banished from her mind.

Aradon and Volanna drew the two servants near and spoke low to them, giving them a series of orders and bidding them to depart quietly to carry them out. As Olstan turned to leave, Kalley leaned to Volanna's ear and whispered, "I have always admired strong, silent men."

"You two should be a perfect match," laughed Volanna. "Like the spigot and the bucket."

In less than half an hour, Olstan and Kalley returned and told Aradon that everything was arranged. By this time the guests were well into the feast and so engaged in conversation that few noticed as the young king and queen slipped out of the hall. They went to their respective chambers and changed from their finery into simpler garb. Then Olstan and Kalley led them to a door in the back of the castle, where a servant waited with Aradon's white stallion, already saddled and loaded with a roll of blankets and a large wallet of breads, cheeses, nuts, fruits, and wine.

"Tell King Tallis and Bogarth not to worry about us. We will return by noon tomorrow," said Aradon. He lifted Volanna into the saddle, then mounted behind her. With one hand holding her dearly around the waist and the other gripping the reins, he urged the horse forward and rode off into the warm, spring night on a road brightly lit by the light of the golden comet blending with the silver star.

ℒ♥

As the horse carrying the happy couple trotted down the road toward Braegan Wood, they did not see the very large, coal black raven circling the castle far above them. The raven saw them, however, and ceased its circling to get a closer look at the couple. Seeing the dark hair of the woman and the golden hair of the man, the bird hovered above them, maintaining a distance of a hundred yards. The yellow eyes of the blackbird watched intently as the horse carried its two riders into the forest, then it swooped down to follow a half-minute behind. The bird could no longer see the couple through the dense growth, but it continued to follow, flitting from tree to tree and always keeping the horse within earshot until the sound of its hooves ceased. Then the bird flew from its tree-limb perch and alit on the forest floor. A moment later, in a short burst of gray smoke, its form changed into that of a very tall woman, hooded and robed from head to foot in draping black.

The dark creature moved silently toward the place where she had last heard the sound of the horse. Soon she could see the stallion, huge and white in the light of the blending stars, tethered to a tree with a ring of chest-high bushes growing beneath its wide-stretched arms. As she approached she saw every item of male and female clothing—dress, breeches, tunic, bodice, and underthings—carelessly tossed over the bushes. From beyond the greenery she heard, above the rushing noise of the waterfall, the sound of splashing accompanied by musical laughter, from both a melodic soprano and a rich, masculine baritone.

The black-robed creature smiled, if the stretching of her lips to reveal her long, white teeth could be called a smile. With her left hand she drew two small casks from her robes, opened one of them slightly with her thumb and looked inside at the black, crawling cluster of venomous spiders. Satisfied, she closed the cask and moved silently toward the bushes where the clothing lay. She crouched behind the brush and peered over it at the naked couple laughing and splashing in the water. She spread open the male tunic, held the cask of spiders above it, and began to undo the latch.

"No, Morgultha," commanded a low, clear voice from behind her.

The black-clad woman turned in surprise to face a very tall man robed in forest colors, his long, white hair and beard shimmering in the starlight. In his raised right hand he held a sword, its blade a bright, glowing orange, as if made of fire.

"Ah, my ancient enemy, the being of a thousand names. So it was you who took the babe," she said as she stood and walked toward him. "I might have known. Very clever of you, hiding the boy right under my nose in the cottage of a simple blacksmith while for twenty-one years I searched the halls of every king and nobleman in the Seven Kingdoms and beyond. He was even my prisoner for a moment, but in my carelessness, I let him slip through my hands because it did not occur to me that he could be the one I was searching for. But now I have found him and you cannot stop me from disposing of him." She began to laugh.

"Quiet, Morgultha!" Lucidis commanded sternly. "I will not allow you to harm or even to disturb this couple."

"You are forgetting something, are you not?" hissed Morgultha. "When the primeval human couple in Eden freely chose to follow my master, the Dark Lord, your master conceded to him dominion over the earth, which also meant the right for evil to have sway over its inhabitants. Your master has honored that law ever since, which means you must turn aside and let me have my way."

"You are wrong, and you know it," Lucidis replied. "Your master's evil has always been limited and measured by the Master of the Universe. Be warned, slave of darkness, tonight no evil will pass the barrier of my sword, for tonight a child is to be conceived who will be the key to his father's quest to unite the Seven Kingdoms."

"And if I ignore your warning?" Morgultha began advancing slowly toward Lucidis.

"Your long and evil life will end on this spot. When your master deceived the first couple and drove them into the wilderness, my charge was to guard the gate of Eden. I stood at that gate with this very sword in my hand from that moment until Paradise was destroyed in the Great Flood. From that time forward, my charge has been to watch over the Stone of Eden, which now rests in the Crown you crave. I have never failed my charge, and be assured, Morgultha, I will not fail it now."

For a long moment, the black-robed creature stood and glared with baleful eyes at the defender of the Crown. "Very well then, my ancient enemy, this battle is yours. But our war is not yet over, and even you cannot thwart me forever. We will part for now, but we will meet again, at which time the outcome will surely be different."

As Morgultha spoke, her voice grew coarse and crackly. Her form slowly diminished in size until it dissolved into a mist in the shadows, from which a large, black raven emerged and flew up through the trees and disappeared into the starlit sky.

ABOUT THE AUTHOR

As an illustrator and designer of covers to many best-selling books, THOMAS WILLIAMS' artistry sits on millions of bookshelves worldwide. As an author and dramatist, his previous four books include two volumes of plays. Tom and his wife, Faye, live in Middle Tennessee.